MAGPIE MURDERS

Also by Anthony Horowitz

The House of Silk
Moriarty
Trigger Mortis

MAGPIE MURDERS

ANTHONY HOROWITZ

First published in Great Britain in 2016 by Orion Books,
an imprint of The Orion Publishing Group Ltd
Carmelite House, 50 Victoria Embankment,
London EC4Y 0DZ

An Hachette UK company

1 3 5 7 9 10 8 6 4 2

A CIP catalogue record for this book is
available from the British Library.

ISBN (Hardback) 978 1 4091 5836 3
ISBN (Export Trade Paperback) 978 1 4091 5837 0

Typeset at The Spartan Press Ltd,
Lymington, Hants

Printed in Great Britain by Clays Ltd, St Ives plc

www.orionbooks.co.uk

MAGPIE MURDERS

Crouch End, London

A bottle of wine. A family-sized packet of Nacho Cheese Flavoured Tortilla Chips and a jar of hot salsa dip. A packet of cigarettes on the side (I know, I know). The rain hammering against the windows. And a book.

What could have been lovelier?

Magpie Murders was number nine in the much-loved and world-bestselling Atticus Pünd series. When I first opened it on that wet August evening, it existed only as a typescript and it would be my job to edit it before it was published. First, I intended to enjoy it. I remember going straight into the kitchen when I came in, plucking a few things out of the fridge and putting everything on a tray. I undressed, leaving my clothes where they fell. The whole flat was a tip anyway. I showered, dried and pulled on a giant Maisie Mouse T-shirt that someone had given me at the Bologna Book Fair. It was too early to get into bed but I was going to read the book lying on top of it, the sheets still crumpled and unmade from the night before. I don't always live like this, but my boyfriend had been away for six weeks and while I was on my own I'd deliberately allowed standards to slip. There's something quite comforting about mess, especially when there's no one else there to complain.

Actually, I hate that word. Boyfriend. Especially when it's used to describe a fifty-two-year-old, twice-divorced man. The trouble is, the English language doesn't provide much in the way of an alternative. Andreas was not my partner. We didn't see each other regularly enough for that. My lover? My other half? Both made me wince for different reasons. He was from Crete. He taught Ancient Greek at Westminster School and he rented a flat in Maida Vale, not so far from me. We'd talked about moving in together but we were afraid it would kill the relationship, so although I had a full wardrobe of his clothes, there were frequently times when I didn't have *him*. This was one of them. Andreas had flown home during the school holidays to be with his family: his parents, his widowed grandmother, his two teenaged sons and his ex-wife's brother all lived in the same house in one of those complicated sorts of arrangements that the Greeks seem to enjoy. He wouldn't be back until Tuesday, the day before school began, and I wouldn't see him until the following weekend.

So there I was on my own in my Crouch End flat, which was spread over the basement and ground floor of a Victorian House in Clifton Road, about a fifteen-minute walk from Highgate tube station. It was probably the only sensible thing I ever bought. I liked living there. It was quiet and comfortable and I shared the garden with a choreographer who lived on the first floor but who was hardly ever in. I had far too many books, of course. Every inch of shelf space was taken. There were books on top of books. The shelves themselves were bending under the weight. I had converted the second bedroom into a study although I tried not to work at home. Andreas used it more than I did – when he was around.

I opened the wine. I unscrewed the salsa. I lit a cigarette. I began to read the book as you are about to. But before you do that, I have to warn you.

This book changed my life.

You may have read that before. I'm embarrassed to say that I splashed it on the cover of the first novel I ever commissioned, a very ordinary Second World War thriller. I can't even remember who said it, but the only way that book was going to change someone's life was if it fell on them. Is it ever actually true? I still remember reading the Brontë sisters as a very young girl and falling in love with their world: the melodrama, the wild landscapes, the gothic romance of it all. You might say that *Jane Eyre* steered me towards my career in publishing, which is a touch ironic in view of what happened. There are plenty of books that have touched me very deeply: Ishiguro's *Never Let Me Go,* McEwan's *Atonement*. I'm told a great many children suddenly found themselves in boarding school as a result of the Harry Potter phenomenon and throughout history there have been books that have had a profound effect on our attitudes. *Lady Chatterley's Lover* is one obvious example, *1984* another. But I'm not sure it actually matters *what* we read. Our lives continue along the straight lines that have been set out for us. Fiction merely allows us a glimpse of the alternative. Maybe that's one of the reasons we enjoy it.

But *Magpie Murders* really did change everything for me. I no longer live in Crouch End. I no longer have my job. I've managed to lose a great many friends. That evening, as I reached out and turned the first page of the typescript, I had no idea of the journey I was about to begin and, quite frankly, I wish I'd never allowed myself to get pulled on board. It was all down to that bastard Alan Conway. I hadn't liked him the day I'd met him although the strange thing is that I'd always loved his books. As far as I'm concerned, you can't beat a good whodunnit: the twists and turns, the clues and the red herrings and then, finally, the satisfaction of having everything explained to you in a way that makes you kick yourself because you hadn't seen it from the start.

That was what I was expecting when I began. But *Magpie Murders* wasn't like that. It wasn't like that at all.

I hope I don't need to spell it out any more. Unlike me, you have been warned.

MAGPIE MURDERS

An Atticus Pünd Mystery

Alan Conway

About the author

Alan Conway was born in Ipswich and educated first at Woodbridge School and then at the University of Leeds, where he gained a first in English Literature. He later enrolled as a mature student at the University of East Anglia to study creative writing. He spent the next six years as a teacher before achieving his first success with *Atticus Pünd Investigates* in 1995. The book spent twenty-eight weeks in the *Sunday Times* bestseller list and won the Gold Dagger award given by the Crime Writers' Association for the best crime novel of the year. Since then, the *Atticus Pünd* series has sold eighteen million books worldwide, translated into thirty-five languages. In 2012, Alan Conway was awarded an MBE for services to literature. He has one child from a former marriage and lives in Framlingham in Suffolk.

The Atticus Pünd series

Atticus Pünd Investigates
No Rest for the Wicked
Atticus Pünd Takes the Case
Night Comes Calling
Atticus Pünd's Christmas
Gin & Cyanide
Red Roses for Atticus
Atticus Pünd Abroad

Praise for Atticus Pünd

'Everything you could want from a British whodunnit. Stylish, clever and unpredictable.' *Independent*

'Watch out Hercule Poirot! There's a smart little foreigner in town – and he's stepping into your shoes.'

Daily Mail

'I'm a fan of Atticus Pünd. He takes us back to the golden age of crime fiction and reminds us where we all began.'

Ian Rankin

'Sherlock Holmes, Lord Peter Wimsey, Father Brown, Philip Marlowe, Poirot . . . the truly great detectives can probably be numbered on the fingers of one hand. Well, with Atticus Pünd you may need an extra finger!' *Irish Independent*

'A great detective story needs a great detective and Atticus Pünd is a worthy addition to the fold.' *Yorkshire Post*

'Germany has a new ambassador. And crime has its greatest detective.' *Der Tagesspiegel*

'Alan Conway is clearly channelling his inner Agatha Christie. And good luck to him! I loved it.' Robert Harris

'Half Greek, half German but always 100 per cent right. The name? It's Pünd – Atticus Pünd.' *Daily Express*

SOON TO BE A MAJOR BBC1 TELEVISION SERIES

ONE

Sorrow

1

23 July 1955

There was going to be a funeral.

The two gravediggers, old Jeff Weaver and his son, Adam, had been out at first light and everything was ready, a grave dug to the exact proportions, the earth neatly piled to one side. The church of St Botolph's in Saxby-on-Avon had never looked lovelier, the morning sun glinting off the stained glass windows. The church dated back to the twelfth century although of course it had been rebuilt many times. The new grave was to the east, close to the ruins of the old chancel where the grass was allowed to grow wild and daisies and dandelions sprouted around the broken arches.

The village itself was quiet, the streets empty. The milkman had already made his deliveries and disappeared, the bottles rattling on the back of his van. The newspaper boys had done their rounds. This was a Saturday, so nobody would be going to work and it was still too early for the homeowners to begin their weekend chores. At nine o'clock, the village shop would open. The smell of bread, fresh out of the oven, was already seeping out of the baker's shop next door. Their first customers would be arriving soon. Once breakfast was over, a chorus of lawnmowers would start up. It was July, the busiest time of the year for Saxby-on-Avon's keen army of gardeners and with the Harvest Fair just a month away roses were already being pruned, marrows carefully measured. At half past one there was to be a cricket match on the village green. There would be an ice-cream van, children playing, visitors having picnics in front of their cars. The tea shop would be open for business. A perfect English summer's afternoon.

But not yet. It was as if the village was holding its breath in respectful silence, waiting for the coffin that was about to begin its journey from Bath. Even now it was being loaded into the hearse, surrounded by its sombre attendants – five men and a women, all of them avoiding each other's eye as if they were unsure where to look. Four of the men were professional undertakers from the highly respected firm of Lanner & Crane. The company had existed since Victorian times when it had been principally involved in carpentry and construction. At that time, coffins and funerals had been a sideline, almost an afterthought. But, perversely, it was this part of the business that had survived. Lanner & Crane no longer built homes, but their name had become a byword for respectful death. Today's event was very much the economy package. The hearse was an older model. There were to be no black horses or extravagant wreaths. The coffin itself, though handsomely finished, had been manufactured from what was, without question, inferior wood. A simple plaque, silver-plated rather than silver, carried the name of the deceased and the two essential dates:

Mary Elizabeth Blakiston
5 April 1887 – 15 July 1955

Her life had not been as long as it seemed, crossing two centuries as it did, but then it had been cut short quite unexpectedly. There had not even been enough money in Mary's funeral plan to cover the final costs – not that it mattered as the insurers would cover the difference – and she would have been glad to see that everything was proceeding according to her wishes.

The hearse left exactly on time, setting out on the eight-mile journey as the minute hand reached half past nine. Continuing at an appropriately sedate pace, it would arrive at the church on the hour. If Lanner & Crane had had a slogan, it might well have been: 'Never late'. And although the two mourners travelling with the coffin might not have noticed it, the countryside had never looked lovelier, the fields on the other side of the low, flint walls sloping down towards the River Avon, which would follow them all the way.

In the cemetery at St Botolph's, the two gravediggers examined their handiwork. There are many things to be said about a funeral – profound, reflective, philosophical – but Jeff Weaver got it right as, leaning on his spade and rolling a cigarette in between his grubby fingers, he turned to his son. 'If you're going to die,' he said, 'you couldn't choose a better day.'

2

Sitting at the kitchen table in the vicarage, the Reverend Robin Osborne was making the final adjustments to his sermon. There were six pages spread out on the table in front of him, typed but already covered in annotations added in his spidery hand. Was it too long? There had been complaints recently from some of his congregation that his sermons had dragged on a bit and even the bishop had shown some impatience during his address on Pentecost Sunday. But this was different. Mrs Blakiston had lived her entire life in the village. Everybody knew her. Surely they could spare half an hour – or even forty minutes – of their time to say farewell.

The kitchen was a large, cheerful room with an Aga radiating a gentle warmth the whole year round. Pots and pans hung from hooks and there were jars filled with fresh herbs and dried mushrooms that the Osbornes had picked themselves. Upstairs, there were two bedrooms, both snug and homely with shag carpets, hand-embroidered pillowcases and brand-new skylights that had only been added after much consultation with the church. But the main joy of the vicarage was its position, on the edge of the village, looking out onto the woodland that everyone knew as Dingle Dell. There was a wild meadow, speckled with flowers in the spring and summer, then a stretch of woodland whose trees, mainly oaks and elms, concealed the grounds of Pye Hall on the other side – the lake, the lawns, then the house itself. Every morning, Robin Osborne awoke to a view that could not fail to delight him. He sometimes thought he was living in a fairy tale.

The vicarage hadn't always been like this. When they had inherited the house – and the diocese – from the elderly Reverend Montagu, it had been very much an old man's home, damp and unwelcoming. But Henrietta had worked her magic, throwing out all the furniture that she deemed too ugly or uncomfortable and scouring the second-hand shops of Wiltshire and Avon to find perfect replacements. Her energy never ceased to amaze him. That she had chosen to be a vicar's wife in the first place was surprising enough but she had thrown herself into her duties with an enthusiasm that had made her popular from the day they had arrived. The two of them could not be happier than they were in Saxby-on-Avon. It was true that the church needed attention. The heating system was permanently on the blink. The roof had started leaking again. But their congregation was more than large enough to satisfy the bishop and many of the worshippers they now considered as friends. They wouldn't have dreamed of being anywhere else.

'She was part of the village. Although we are here today to mourn her departure, we should remember what she left behind. Mary made Saxby-on-Avon a better place for everyone else, whether it was arranging the flowers every Sunday in this very church, visiting the elderly both here and at Ashton House, collecting for the RSPB or greeting visitors to Pye Hall. Her home-made cakes were always the star of the village fête and I can tell you there were many occasions when she would surprise me in the vestry with one of her almond bites or perhaps a slice of Victoria sponge.'

Osborne tried to picture the woman who had spent most of her life working as the housekeeper at Pye Hall. Small, dark-haired, and determined, she had always been in a rush, as if on a personal crusade. His memories of her seemed mainly to be in the mid-distance because, in truth, they had never spent that much time in the same room. They had been together at one or two social occasions perhaps, but not that many. The sort of people who lived in Saxby-on-Avon weren't outright snobs, but at the same time they were very well aware of class and although a vicar might be deemed a suitable addition to any social gathering, the same could not be said of someone who was, at the end of the day, a cleaner. Perhaps she had been aware of this. Even at church she had tended to take a pew at the very back. There was something quite deferential about the way she insisted on helping people, as if she somehow owed it to them.

Or was it simpler than that? When he thought about her and looked at what he had just written, a single word came to mind. Busybody. It wasn't fair and it certainly wasn't something he would ever have spoken out loud, but he had to admit there was some truth to it. She was the sort of woman who had a finger in every pie (apple and blackberry included), who had made it her business to connect with everyone in the village. Somehow, she was always there when you needed her. The trouble was, she was also there when you didn't.

He remembered finding her here in this very room, just over a fortnight ago. He was annoyed with himself. He should have expected it. Henrietta was always complaining about the way he left the front door open, as if the vicarage were merely an appendage to the church, rather than their private home. He should have listened to her. Mary had shown herself in and she was standing there, holding up a little bottle of green liquid as if it were some medieval talisman used to ward off demons. '*Good morning, vicar! I heard you were having trouble with wasps. I've brought you some peppermint oil. That'll get rid of them. My mother always used to swear by it!*' It was true. There had been wasps in the vicarage – but how had she known? Osborne hadn't told anyone except Henrietta and she surely wouldn't have mentioned it. Of course, that was to be expected of a community like Saxby-on-Avon. Somehow, in some unfathomable way, everyone knew everything about everyone and it had often been said that if you sneezed in the bath someone would appear with a tissue.

Seeing her there, Osborne hadn't been sure whether to be grateful or annoyed. He had muttered a word of thanks but at the same time he had glanced down at the kitchen table. And there they were, just lying there in the middle of all his papers. How long had she been in the room? Had she seen them? She wasn't saying anything and of course he didn't dare ask her. He had ushered her out as quickly as he could and that had been the last time he had seen her. He and Henrietta had been away on holiday when she had died. They had only just returned in time to bury her.

He heard footsteps and looked up as Henrietta came into the room. She was fresh out of the bath, still wrapped in a towelling dressing gown. Now in her late forties, she was still a very attractive woman with chestnut hair tumbling down and a figure that clothing catalogues would have described as 'full'. She came from a very different world, the youngest daughter of a wealthy farmer with a thousand acres in West Sussex, and yet when the two of them had met in London – at a lecture being given at the Wigmore Hall – they had discovered an immediate affinity. They had married without the approval of her parents and they were as close now as they had ever been. Their one regret was that their marriage had not been blessed with any children but of course that was God's will and they had come to accept it. They were happy simply being with each other.

'I thought you'd finished with that,' she said. She had taken butter and honey out of the pantry. She cut herself a slice of bread.

'Just adding a few last-minute thoughts.'

'Well, I wouldn't talk too long if I were you, Robin. It is a Saturday, after all, and everyone's going to want to get on.'

'We're gathering in the Queen's Arms afterwards. At eleven o'clock.'

'That's nice.' Henrietta carried a plate with her

breakfast over to the table and plumped herself down. 'Did Sir Magnus ever reply to your letter?'

'No. But I'm sure he'll be there.'

'Well, he's leaving it jolly late.' She leant over and looked at one of the pages. 'You can't say that.'

'What?'

' "The life and soul of any party".'

'Why not?'

'Because she wasn't. I always found her rather buttoned-up and secretive, if you want the truth. Not easy to talk to at all.'

'She was quite entertaining when she came here last Christmas.'

'She joined in the carols, if that's what you mean. But you never really knew what she was thinking. I can't say I liked her very much.'

'You shouldn't talk about her that way, Hen. Certainly not today.'

'I don't see why not. That's the thing about funerals. They're completely hypocritical. Everyone says how wonderful the deceased was, how kind, how generous when, deep down, they know it's not true. I didn't ever take to Mary Blakiston and I'm not going to start singing her praises just because she managed to fall down a flight of stairs and break her neck.'

'You're being a little uncharitable.'

'I'm being honest, Robby. And I know you think exactly the same – even if you're trying to convince yourself otherwise. But don't worry! I promise I won't disgrace you in front of the mourners.' She pulled a face. 'There! Is that sad enough?'

'Hadn't you better get ready?'

'I've got it all laid out upstairs. Black dress, black hat, black pearls.' She sighed. 'When I die, I don't want to wear black. It's so cheerless. Promise me. I want to be buried in pink with a big bunch of begonias in my hands.'

'You're not going to die. Not any time soon. Now, go upstairs and get dressed.'

'All right. All right. You bully!'

She leant over him and he felt her breasts, soft and warm, pressing against his neck. She kissed him on the cheek, then hurried out, leaving her breakfast on the table. Robin Osborne smiled to himself as he returned to his address. Perhaps she was right. He could cut out a page or two. Once again, he looked down at what he had written.

'Mary Blakiston did not have an easy life. She knew personal tragedy soon after she came to Saxby-on-Avon and she could so easily have allowed it to overwhelm her. But she fought back. She was the sort of woman who embraced life, who would never let it get the better of her. And as we lay her to rest, beside the son whom she loved so much and whom she lost so tragically, perhaps we can take some solace from the thought that they are, at last, together.'

Robin Osborne read the paragraph twice. Once again, he saw her standing there, in this very room, right next to the table.

'*I heard you were having trouble with wasps.*'

Had she seen them? Had she known?

The sun must have gone behind a cloud because suddenly there was a shadow across his face. He reached out, tore up the entire page and dropped the pieces into the bin.

3

Dr Emilia Redwing had woken early. She had lain in bed for an hour trying to persuade herself that she might still get back to sleep, then she had got up, put on a dressing gown and made herself a cup of tea. She had been sitting in the kitchen ever since, watching the sun rise over her garden and, beyond it, the ruins of Saxby Castle, a thirteenth-century structure which gave pleasure to the many hundreds of amateur historians who visited it but which cut out the sunlight every afternoon, casting a long shadow over the house. It was a little after half past eight. The newspaper should have been delivered by now. She had a few patient files in front of her and she busied herself going over them, partly to distract herself from the day ahead. The surgery was usually open on Saturday mornings but today, because of the funeral, it would be closed. Oh well, it was a good time to catch up with her paperwork.

There was never anything very serious to treat in a village like Saxby-on-Avon. If there was one thing that would carry off the residents, it was old age and Dr Redwing couldn't do very much about that. Going through the files, she cast a weary eye over the various ailments that had recently come her way. Miss Dotterel, who helped at the village shop, was getting over the measles after a week spent in bed. Nine-year-old Billy Weaver had had a nasty attack of whooping cough but it was already behind him. His grandfather, Jeff Weaver, had arthritis but then he'd had it for years and it wasn't getting any better or worse. Johnny Whitehead had cut his hand. Henrietta Osborne, the vicar's wife, had managed to step on a clump of deadly nightshade – *atropa belladonna* – and had somehow infected her entire foot. She had prescribed a week's bed rest and plenty of water. Other than that, the warm summer seemed to have been good for everyone's health.

Not everyone's. No. There had been a death.

Dr Redwing pushed the files to one side and went over to the stove where she busied herself making breakfast for both her and her husband. She had already heard Arthur moving about upstairs and there had been the usual grinding and rattling as he poured himself his bath. The plumbing in the house was at least fifty years old and complained loudly every time it was pressed into service, but at least it did the job. He would be down soon. She cut the bread for toast, filled a saucepan with water and placed it on the hob, took out the milk and the cornflakes, laid the table.

Arthur and Emilia Redwing had been married for thirty years; a happy and successful marriage, she thought to herself, even if things hadn't gone quite as they had hoped. For a start, there was Sebastian, their only child, now twenty-four and living with his beatnik friends in London.

How could he have become such a disappointment? And when exactly was it that he had turned against them? Neither of them had heard for him for months and they couldn't even be sure if he was alive or dead. And then there was Arthur himself. He had started life as an architect – and a good one. He had been given the Sloane Medallion by the Royal Institute of British Architects for a design he had completed at art school. He had worked on several of the new buildings that had sprung up immediately after the war. But his real love had been painting – mainly portraits in oils – and ten years ago he had given up his career to work as a full-time artist. He had done so with Emilia's full support.

One of his works hung in the kitchen, on the wall beside the Welsh dresser, and she glanced at it now. It was a portrait of herself, painted ten years ago, and she always smiled when she looked at it, remembering the extended silences as she sat for him, surrounded by wild flowers. Her husband never talked when he worked. There had been a dozen sittings during a long, hot summer and Arthur had somehow managed to capture the heat, the haze in the late afternoon, even the scent of the meadow. She was wearing a long dress with a straw hat – like a female Van Gogh, she had joked – and perhaps there was something of that artist's style in the rich colours, the jabbing brushstrokes. She was not a beautiful woman. She knew it. Her face was too severe, her broad shoulders and dark hair too masculine. There was something of the teacher or perhaps the governess in the way she held herself. People found her too formal. But he had found something beautiful in her. If the picture had hung in a London gallery, nobody would be able to pass it without looking twice.

It didn't. It hung here. No London galleries were interested in Arthur or his work. Emilia couldn't understand it. The two of them had gone together to the Summer Exhibition at the Royal Academy and had looked at work by James Gunn and Sir Alfred Munnings. There had been a controversial portrait of the Queen by Simon Elwes. But it all looked very ordinary and timid compared to his work. Why did nobody recognise Arthur Redwing for the genius that he undoubtedly was?

She took three eggs and lowered them gently into the pan – two for him, one for her. One of them cracked as it came into contact with the boiling water and at once she thought of Mary Blakiston with her skull split open after her fall. She couldn't avoid it. Even now she shuddered at the memory of what she had seen – and yet she wondered why that should be. It wasn't the first dead body she had encountered and working in London during the worst of the Blitz she had treated soldiers with terrible injuries. What had been so different about this?

Perhaps it was the fact that the two of them had been close. It was true that the doctor and the housekeeper had very little in common but they had become unlikely friends. It had started when Mrs Blakiston was a patient. She'd suffered an attack of shingles that had lasted for a month and Dr Redwing had been impressed both by her stoicism and good sense. After that, she'd come to rely on her as a sounding board. She had to be careful. She couldn't breach patient confidentiality. But if there was something that troubled her, she could always rely on Mary to be a good listener and to offer sensible advice.

And the end had been so sudden: an ordinary morning, just over a week ago, had been interrupted by Brent – the groundsman who worked at Pye Hall – on the phone.

'Can you come, Dr Redwing? It's Mrs Blakiston. She's at the bottom of the stairs in the big house. She's lying there. I think she's had a fall.'

'Is she moving?'

'I don't think so.'

'Are you with her now?'

'I can't get in. All the doors are locked.'

Brent was in his thirties, a crumpled young man with dirt beneath his fingernails and sullen indifference in his eyes. He tended the lawns and the flower beds and occasionally chased trespassers off the land just as his father had before him. The grounds of Pye Hall backed onto a lake and children liked to swim there in the summer, but not if Brent was around. He was a solitary man, unmarried, living alone in the house that had once belonged to his parents. He was not much liked in the village because he was considered shifty. The truth was that he was uneducated and possibly a little autistic but the rural community had been quick to fill in the blanks. Dr Redwing told him to meet her at the front door, threw together a few medical supplies and, leaving her nurse/receptionist – Joy – to turn away any new arrivals, hurried to her car.

Pye Hall was on the other side of Dingle Dell, fifteen minutes on foot and no more than a five-minute drive. It had always been there, as long as the village itself, and although it was a mishmash of architectural styles it was certainly the grandest house in the area. It had started life as a nunnery but had been converted into a private home in the sixteenth century then knocked around in every century since. What remained was a single, elongated wing with an octagonal tower – constructed much later – at the far end. Most of the windows were Elizabethan, narrow and mullioned, but there were also Georgian and Victorian additions with ivy spreading all around them as if to apologise for the indiscretion. At the back, there was a courtyard and the remains of what might have been cloisters. A separate stable block was now used as a garage.

But its main glory was its setting. A gate with two stone griffins marked the entrance and a gravel drive passed the Lodge House where Mary Blakiston lived, then swept round in a graceful swan's neck across the lawns to the front door with its Gothic arch. There were flower beds arranged like daubs of paint on an artist's palette and, enclosed by ornamental hedges, a rose garden with – it was said – over a hundred different varieties. The grass stretched all the way down to the lake with Dingle Dell on the other side: indeed, the whole estate was surrounded by mature woodland, filled with bluebells in the spring, separating it from the modern world.

The tyres crunched on the gravel as Dr Redwing came to a halt and saw Brent, waiting nervously for her, turning his cap over in his hands. She got out, took her medicine bag and went over to him.

'Is there any sign of life?' she asked.

'I haven't looked,' Brent muttered. Dr Redwing was startled. Hadn't he even tried to help the poor woman? Seeing the look on her face, he added, 'I told you. I can't get in.'

'The front door's locked?'

'Yes, ma'am. The kitchen door too.'

'Don't you have any keys?'

'No, ma'am. I don't go in the house.'

Dr Redwing shook her head, exasperated. In the time she had taken to get here, Brent could have done something; perhaps fetched a ladder to try a window upstairs. 'If you couldn't get in, how did you telephone me?' she asked. It didn't matter, but she just wondered.

'There's a phone in the stable.'

'Well, you'd better show me where she is.'

'You can see through the window...'

The window in question was at the edge of the house, one of the newer additions. It gave a side view of the hall with a wide staircase leading up to the first floor. And there, sure enough, was Mary Blakiston, lying sprawled out on a rug, one arm stretched in front of her, partly concealing her head. From the very first sight, Dr Redwing was fairly sure that she was dead. Somehow, she had fallen down the stairs and broken her neck. She wasn't moving, of course. But it was more than that. The way the body was lying was too unnatural. It had that broken-doll look that Redwing had observed in her medicine books.

That was her instinct. But looks could be deceptive.

'We have to get in,' she said. 'The kitchen and the front door are locked but there must be another way.'

'We could try the boot room.'

'Where is that?'

'Just along here...'

Brent led her to another door at the back. This one had glass panes and although it was also securely closed, Dr Redwing clearly saw a bunch of keys, still in the lock on the other side. 'Whose are those?' she asked.

'They must be hers.'

She came to a decision. 'We're going to have to break the glass.'

'I don't think Sir Magnus would be too happy about that,' Brent grumbled.

'Sir Magnus can take that up with me if he wants to. Now, are you going to do it or am I?'

The groundsman wasn't happy, but he found a stone and used it to knock out one of the panes. He slipped his hand inside and turned the keys. The door opened and they went in.

Waiting for the eggs to boil, Dr Redwing remembered the scene exactly as she had seen it. It really was like a photograph printed on her mind.

They had gone through the boot room, along a corridor and straight into the main hall, with the staircase leading up to the galleried landing. Dark wood panelling surrounded them. The walls were covered with oil paintings and hunting trophies: birds in glass cases, a deer's head, a huge fish. A suit of armour, complete with sword and shield, stood beside a door that led into the living room. The hallway was long and narrow with the front door, opposite the staircase, positioned exactly in the middle. On one side there was a stone fireplace, big enough to walk into. On the other, two leather chairs and an antique table with a telephone. The floor was made up of flagstones, partly covered by a Persian rug. The stairs were also stone with a wine red carpet leading up the centre. If Mary Blakiston had tripped and come tumbling down from the landing, her death would be easily explained. There was very little to cushion a fall.

While Brent waited nervously by the door, she examined the body. She was not yet cold but there was no pulse. Dr Redwing brushed some of the dark hair away from the face to reveal brown eyes, staring at the fireplace. Gently, she closed them. Mrs Blakiston had always been in a hurry. It was impossible to escape the thought. She had quite literally flung herself down the stairs, hurrying into her own death.

'We have to call the police,' she said.

'What?' Brent was surprised. 'Has someone done something to her?'

'No. Of course not. It's an accident. But we still have to report it.'

It was an accident. You didn't have to be a detective to work it out. The housekeeper had been hoovering. The Hoover was still there, a bright red thing, almost like a toy, at the top of the stairs stuck in the bannisters. Somehow she had got tangled up in the wire. She had tripped and fallen down the stairs. There was nobody else in the house. The doors were locked. What other explanation could there be?

Just over a week later, Emilia Redwing's thoughts were interrupted by a movement at the door. Her husband had come into the room. She lifted the eggs out of the pan and gently lowered them into two china egg cups. She was relieved to see that he had dressed for the funeral. She was quite sure he would have forgotten. He had put on his dark Sunday suit, though no tie – he never wore ties. There were a few specks of paint on his shirt but that was to be expected. Arthur and paint were inseparable.

'You got up early,' he said.

'I'm sorry, dear. Did I wake you?'

'No. Not really. But I heard you go downstairs. Couldn't you sleep?'

'I suppose I was thinking about the funeral.'

'Looks like a nice day for it. I hope that bloody vicar won't go on too long. It's always the same with Bible-bashers. They're too fond of the sound of their own voice.'

He picked up his teaspoon and brought it crashing down onto his first egg.

Crack!

She remembered the conversation she'd had with Mary

Blakiston just two days before Brent had called her to the house. Dr Redwing had discovered something. It was quite serious, and she'd been about to go and find Arthur to ask his advice when the housekeeper had suddenly appeared as if summoned by a malignant spirit. And so she had told her instead. Somehow, during the course of a busy day, a bottle had gone missing from the surgery. The contents, in the wrong hands, could be highly dangerous and it was clear that somebody must have taken it. What was she to do? Should she report it to the police? She was reluctant because, inevitably, it would make her look foolish and irresponsible. Why had the dispensary been left unattended? Why hadn't the cupboard been locked? Why hadn't she noticed it before now?

'Don't you worry, Dr Redwing,' Mary had said. 'You leave it with me for a day or two. As a matter of fact, I may have one or two ideas . . .'

That was what she had said. At the same time there had been a look on her face which wasn't exactly sly but which was knowing, as if she had seen something and had been waiting to be consulted on this very matter.

And now she was dead.

Of course it had been an accident. Mary Blakiston hadn't had time to talk to anyone about the missing poison and even if she had, there was no way that they could have done anything to her. She had tripped and fallen down the stairs. That was all.

But as she watched her husband dipping a finger of toast into his egg, Emilia Redwing had to admit it to herself. She was really quite concerned.

4

'Why are we going to the funeral? We hardly even knew the woman.'

Johnny Whitehead was struggling with the top button of his shirt, no matter how hard he tried, he couldn't slot it into the hole. The truth was that the collar simply wouldn't stretch all the way round his neck. It seemed to him that recently all his clothes had begun to shrink. Jackets that he had worn for years were suddenly tight across the shoulders and as for trousers! He gave up and plopped himself down at the breakfast table. His wife, Gemma, slid a plate in front of him. She had cooked a complete English breakfast with two eggs, bacon, sausage, tomato and fried slice – just how he liked.

'Everyone will be there,' Gemma said.

'That doesn't mean *we* have to be.'

'People will talk if we aren't. And anyway, it's good for business. Her son, Robert, will probably clear out the house now that she's gone and you never know what you might find.'

'Probably a lot of junk.' Johnny picked up his knife and fork and began to eat. 'But you're right, love. I suppose it can't hurt to show our faces.'

Saxby-on-Avon had very few shops. Of course, there was the general store, which sold just about everything anyone could possibly need – from mops and buckets to custard powder and six different sorts of jam. It was quite a miracle really how so many different products could fit in such a tiny space. Mr Turnstone still ran the butcher's shop round the back – it had a separate entrance and plastic strips hanging down to keep away the flies – and the fish van came every Tuesday. But if you wanted anything exotic, olive oil or any of the Mediterranean ingredients that Elizabeth David put in her books, you would have to go into Bath. The so-called General Electrics Store stood on the other side of the village square but very few people went in there unless it was for spare light bulbs or fuses. Most of the products in the window looked dusty and out-of-date. There was a bookshop and a tea room that only opened during the summer months. Just off the square and before the fire station stood the garage, which sold a range of motor accessories but not anything that anyone would actually want. That was about it and it had been that way for as long as anyone could remember.

And then Johnny and Gemma Whitehead had arrived from London. They had bought the old post office, which had long been empty, and turned it into an antique shop with their names, written in old-fashioned lettering, above the window. There were many in the village who remarked that bric-a-brac rather than antiques might be a more accurate description of the contents but from the very start the shop had proved popular with visitors who seemed happy to browse amongst the old clocks, Toby jugs, canteens of cutlery, coins, medals, oil paintings, dolls, fountain pens and whatever else happened to be on display. Whether anyone ever actually bought anything was another matter. But the shop had now been there for six years, with the Whiteheads living in the flat above.

Johnny was a short, broad-shouldered man, bald-headed and, even if he hadn't noticed it, running to fat. He liked to dress loudly, rather shabby three-piece suits, usually with a brightly coloured tie. For the funeral, he had reluctantly pulled out a more sombre jacket and trousers in grey worsted although, like the shirt, it fitted him badly. His wife, so thin and small that there could have been three of her to one of him, was wearing black. She was not eating a cooked breakfast. She had poured herself a cup of tea and was nibbling a triangle of toast.

'Sir Magnus and Lady Pye won't be there,' Johnny muttered as an afterthought.

'Where?'

'At the funeral. They won't be back until the weekend.'

'Who told you that?'

'I don't know. They were talking about it in the pub. They've gone to the south of France or somewhere. All right for some, isn't it! Anyway, people have been trying to reach them but so far no luck.' Johnny paused, holding up a piece of sausage. To listen to him speaking now, it would have been obvious that he had lived most of his life in the East End of London. He had a quite different accent when he was dealing with customers. 'Sir Magnus isn't going to be too happy about it,' he went on. 'He was very fond of Mrs Blakiston. They were as thick as thieves, them two!'

'What do you mean? Are you saying he had a thing with her?' Gemma wrinkled her nose as she considered the 'thing'.

'No. It's not like that. He wouldn't dare – not with his missus on the scene, and anyway, Mary Blakiston was nothing to write home about. But she used to worship him. She thought the sun shone out of his you know where! And she'd been his housekeeper for years and years. Keeper of the keys! She cooked for him, cleaned for him, gave half her life to him. I'm sure he'd have wanted to be there for the send-off.'

'They could have waited for him to get back.'

'Her son wanted to get it over with. Can't blame him, really. The whole thing's been a bit of a shock.'

The two of them sat in silence while Johnny finished his breakfast. Gemma watched him intently. She often did this. It was as if she were trying to look behind his generally placid exterior, as if she might find something he was trying to conceal. 'What was she doing here?' she asked suddenly. 'Mary Blakiston?'

'When?'

'The Monday before she died. She was here.'

'No, she wasn't.' Johnny laid down his knife and fork. He had eaten quickly and wiped the plate clean.

'Don't lie to me, Johnny. I saw her coming out of the shop.'

'Oh! The shop!' Johnny smiled uncomfortably. 'I thought you meant I'd had her up here in the flat. That would have been a right old thing, wouldn't it.' He paused, hoping his wife would change the subject but as she showed no sign of doing so, he went on, choosing his words carefully. 'Yes... she did look in the shop. And I suppose that would have been the same week it happened. I can't really remember what she wanted, if you want the truth, love. I think she may have said something about a present for someone but she didn't buy nothing. Anyway, she was only in for a minute or two.'

Gemma Whitehead always knew when her husband was lying.

She had actually seen Mrs Blakiston emerging from the shop and she had made a note of it, somehow divining that something was wrong. But she hadn't mentioned it then and decided not to pursue the matter now. She didn't want to have an argument, certainly not when the two of them were about to set off for a funeral.

As for Johnny Whitehead, despite what he had said he remembered very well his last encounter with Mrs Blakiston. She had indeed come into the shop, making those accusations of hers. And the worst of it was that she had the evidence to back them up. How had she found it? What had put her on to him in the first place? Of course, she hadn't told him that but she had made herself very clear. The bitch.

He would never have said as much to his wife, of course, but he couldn't be more pleased that she was dead.

5

Clarissa Pye, dressed in black from head to toe, stood examining herself in the full-length mirror at the end of the hallway. Not for the first time, she wondered if the hat, with its three feathers and crumpled veil, wasn't a little excessive. *De trop*, as they said in French. She had bought it on impulse from a second-hand shop in Bath and had regretted it a moment later. She wanted to look her best for the funeral. The whole village would be there and she had been invited to coffee and soft drinks afterwards at the Queen's Arms. With or without? Carefully, she removed it and laid it on the hall table.

Her hair was too dark. She'd had it cut specially and although René had done his usual, excellent work, that new colourist of his had definitely let the place down. She looked ridiculous, like something off the cover of *Home Chat*. Well, that decided it, then. She would just have to wear the hat. She took out a tube of lipstick and carefully applied it to her lips. That looked better already. It was important to make an effort.

The funeral wouldn't begin for another forty minutes and she didn't want to be the first to arrive. How was she going to fill in the time? She went into the kitchen where the washing up from breakfast was waiting but she didn't want to do it while she was wearing her best clothes. A book lay, face down, on the table. She was reading Jane Austen – dear Jane – for the umpteenth time but she didn't feel like that either right now. She would catch up with Emma Woodhouse and her machinations in the afternoon. The radio perhaps? Or another cup of tea and a quick stab at the *Telegraph* crossword? Yes. That was what she would do.

Clarissa lived in a modern house. So many of the buildings in Saxby-on-Avon were solid, Georgian constructions made of Bath stone with handsome porticos and gardens rising up in terraces. You didn't need to read Jane Austen. If you stepped outside, you would find yourself actually in her world. She would have much rather lived beside the main square or in Rectory Lane, which ran behind the church. There were some lovely cottages there; elegant and well kept. 4 Winsley Terrace had been built in a hurry. It was a perfectly ordinary two-up-two-down with a pebble-dash front and a square of garden that was hardly worth the trouble. It was identical to its neighbours apart from a little pond which the previous owners had added and which was home to a pair of elderly goldfish. Upper Saxby-on-Avon and Lower Saxby-on-Avon. The difference could not have been more striking. She was in the wrong half.

The house was all she had been able to afford. Briefly, she examined the small, square kitchen with its net curtains, the magenta walls, the aspidistra on the window sill and the little wooden crucifix hanging from the Welsh dresser where she could see it at the start of every day. She glanced at the breakfast things, still laid out on the table: a single plate, one knife, one spoon, one half-empty jar of Golden Shred marmalade. All at once, she felt the onrush of emotions that she had grown used to over the years but which she still had to fight with all her strength.

She was lonely. She should never have come here. Her whole life was a travesty.

And all because of twelve minutes.

Twelve minutes!

She picked up the kettle and slammed it down on the hob, turning on the gas with a savage twist of her hand. It really wasn't fair. How could a person's whole life be decided for them simply because of the timing of their birth? She had never really understood it when she was a child at Pye Hall. She and Magnus were twins. They were equals, happily protected by all the wealth and privilege which surrounded them and which the two of them would enjoy for the rest of their lives. That was what she had always thought. How could this have happened to her?

She knew the answer now. Magnus himself had been the first to tell her, something about an entail which was centuries old and which meant that the house, the entire estate, would go to him simply because he was the firstborn, and the title, of course, because he was male, and there was nothing anyone could do about it. She had thought he was making it up just to spite her. But she had found out soon enough. It had been a process of attrition, starting with the death of her parents in a car accident when she was in her mid-twenties. The house had passed formally to Magnus and from that moment, her status had changed. She had become a guest in her own home and an unwanted one at that. She had been moved to a smaller room. And when Magnus had met and married Frances – this was two years after the war – she had been gently persuaded to move out altogether.

She had spent a miserable year in London, renting a tiny flat in Bayswater and watching her savings run out. In the end, she had become a governess. What choice was there for a single woman who spoke passable French, who played the piano and who could recite works of all the major poets but who had no other discernible skills? In a spirit of adventure she had gone to America; first to Boston, then to Washington. Both the families she had worked for had been quite ghastly and of course they had treated her like dirt even though she was in every respect more experienced and (although she would never have said it herself), more refined. And the children! It was clear to her that American children were the worst in the world with no manners, no breeding and very little intelligence. She had, however, been well paid and she had saved every penny – every cent – that she had earned and when she could stand it no more, after ten long years she had returned home.

Home was Saxby-on-Avon. In a way it was the last place she wanted to be but it was where she had been born and where she had been brought up. Where else could she go? Did she want to spend the rest of her life in a bedsit in Bayswater? Fortunately, a job had come up at the local school and with all the money she had saved, she had just about been able to afford a mortgage. Magnus hadn't helped her, of course. Not that she would have dreamed of asking. At first it had galled her, seeing him driving in and out of the big house where the two of them had once played. She still had a key – her own key – to the front door! She had never returned it and never would. The key was a symbol of everything she had lost but at the same time it reminded her that she had every right to stay. Her presence here was almost certainly a source of embarrassment for her brother. There was some solace in that.

Bitterness and anger swept through Clarissa Pye as she stood on her own in her kitchen, the kettle already hissing at her with a rising pitch. She had always been the clever one, her not Magnus. He had come bottom of the class and received dreadful reports while the teachers had been all over her. He had been lazy because he knew he could be. He had nothing to worry about. She was the one who'd had to go out and find work, any work, to support herself from day to day. He had everything and – worse – she was nothing to him. Why was she even going to this funeral? It suddenly struck her that her brother had been closer to Mary Blakiston than he had ever been to her. A common housekeeper, for heaven's sake!

She turned and gazed at the cross, contemplating the little figure nailed into the wood. The Bible made it perfectly clear: 'Thou shalt not covet thy neighbour's house, thou shalt not covet thy neighbour's wife, nor his manservant, nor his maidservant, nor his ox, nor his ass, nor anything that is thy neighbour's.' She tried so hard to apply the words of Exodus, Chapter 20, Verse 17 to her life and, in many ways, she had almost succeeded. Of course she would like to be richer. She would like to have the heating on in the winter and not worry about the bills. That was only human. When she went to church, she often tried to remind herself that what had happened was not Magnus's fault and even if he was not the kindest or the gentlest of brothers – not, actually by a long way – she must still try to forgive him. 'For if ye forgive men their trespasses, your heavenly Father will also forgive you.'

It wasn't working.

He'd invited her up for dinner now and then. The last time had been just a month ago, and sitting down to dinner in the grand hall with its family portraits and minstrel gallery, one of a dozen guests being served food and wine on fine plates and in crystal glasses, that was when the thought had first wormed itself into her head. It had remained there ever since. It was there now. She had tried to ignore it. She had prayed for it to go away. But in the end she'd had to accept that she was seriously contemplating a sin much more terrible than covetousness and, worse, she had taken the first step towards putting it into action. It was madness. Despite herself, she glanced upwards, thinking about what she had taken and what was hiding in her bathroom cabinet.

Thou shalt not kill.

She whispered the words but no sound came out. Behind her, the kettle began to scream. She snatched it up, forgetting that the handle would be hot, then slammed it down again with a little cry of pain. Tearfully, she washed her hand under the cold tap. It was nothing more than she deserved.

A few minutes later, forgetting her tea, she swept the hat off the table and left for the funeral.

6

The hearse had reached the outskirts of Saxby-on-Avon and, inevitably, its route took it past the entrance to Pye Hall with its stone griffins and now silent Lodge House. There was only one main road from Bath and to have approached the village any other way would have involved too much of a detour. Was there something unfortunate about carrying the dead woman past the very home where she had once lived? Had anyone asked them, the undertakers, Geoffrey Lanner and Martin Crane (both descended from the original founders) would have said quite the opposite. On the contrary, they would have insisted, is there not a certain symbolism in the coincidence, a sense even of closure? It was as if Mary Blakiston had come full circle.

Sitting in the back seat, and feeling sick and empty with the coffin lying behind him, Robert Blakiston glanced at his old house as if he had never seen it before. He did not turn his head to keep it in sight as they drove past. He did not even think about it. His mother had lived there. His mother was now dead, stretched out behind him. Robert was twenty-eight years old, pale and slender, with black hair cut short in a straight line that tracked across his forehead and continued in two perfect curves around each ear. He looked uncomfortable in the suit he was wearing, which was hardly surprising as it wasn't his. It had been lent to him for the funeral. Robert did have a suit but his fiancée, Joy, had insisted that it wasn't smart enough. She had managed to borrow a new suit from her father, which had been the cause of one argument, and had then persuaded him to wear it, which had led to another.

Joy was sitting next to him in the hearse. The two of them had barely spoken since they'd left Bath. Both of them were lost in their thoughts. Both of them were worried.

It sometimes seemed to Robert that he had been trying to escape from his mother almost from the day he had been born. He had actually grown up in the Lodge House, just the two of them living on top of each other, each of them dependent on the other but in different ways. He had nothing without her. She was nothing without him. Robert had gone to the local school where he had been considered a bright child, one that would do well if he could only set his mind to his studies a little more. He had few friends. It often worried the teachers to see him, standing on his own in the noisy playground, ignored by the other children. At the same time, it was completely understandable. There had been a tragedy when he was very young. His younger brother had died – a terrible accident – and his father had left the family soon afterwards, blaming himself. The sadness of it still clung to him and the other children avoided it as if they were afraid of becoming contaminated.

Robert never did very well in class. His teachers tried to make allowances for his poor behaviour and lack of progress, taking account of his circumstances, but even so they were secretly relieved when he reached sixteen and left. This, incidentally, had been in 1945, at the end of a war in which he had been too young to fight but which had taken his father away for long stretches of time. There were many children whose education had suffered and in that sense he was just another casualty. There was no question of his going to university. Even so, the year that followed was a disappointing one. He continued living with his mother, doing occasional odd jobs around the village. Everyone who knew him agreed that he was underselling himself. Despite everything, he was much too intelligent for that sort of life.

In the end it was Sir Magnus Pye – who employed Mary Blakiston and who had stood in loco parentis for the last seven years, who had persuaded Robert to get a proper job. On his return from National Service, Sir Magnus had helped him find an apprenticeship as a mechanic in the service department of the main Ford motorcar supplier in

Bristol. Perhaps surprisingly, his mother had been far from grateful. It was the only time she ever argued with Sir Magnus. She was worried about Robert. She didn't want him living alone in a distant city. She felt that Sir Magnus had acted without consulting her, even going behind her back.

It didn't actually matter very much because the apprenticeship did not last long. Robert had been away for just three months when he went out drinking at a public house, the Blue Boar, in Brislington. He became involved in a fight, which turned nasty, and the police were called in. Robert was arrested and although he wasn't charged, his employers took a dim view and ended the apprenticeship. Reluctantly, Robert came home again. His mother behaved as if she had somehow been vindicated. She had never wanted him to leave and if he had only listened to her, he would have saved them both a lot of trouble. It seemed to everyone who knew them that they never really got on well again from that day.

At least he had found his vocation. Robert liked cars and he was good at fixing them. As it happened, there was a vacancy for a full-time mechanic at the local garage and although Robert didn't have quite enough experience, the owner had decided to give him a chance. The job didn't pay much but it did offer accommodation in a small flat above the workshop as part of the package. That suited Robert very well. He had made it quite clear that he no longer wanted to live with his mother, that he found the Lodge House oppressive. He had moved into the flat and had been there ever since.

Robert Blakiston wasn't ambitious. Nor was he particularly inquisitive. He might have continued with an existence that was adequate – nothing more, nothing less. But everything had changed when he had mangled his right hand in an accident that could have taken it off altogether. What had happened was quite commonplace and wholly avoidable: a car he'd been working on had come tumbling off the jack stand, missing him by inches. It was the falling jack that had smashed into him and he had staggered into Dr Redwing's surgery with his hand cradled and blood streaming down his overalls. That was when he'd met Joy Sanderling who had just started as the new nurse and receptionist. Despite his pain, he had noticed her at once: very pretty, with sand-coloured hair framing her face and freckles. He thought about her in the ambulance, after Dr Redwing had dressed his broken bones and sent him to Royal United Hospital in Bath. His hand had long since healed but he always remembered the accident and he was glad it had happened because it had introduced him to Joy.

Joy lived with her parents at their home in Lower Westwood. Her father was a fireman who had once been on active service, based at the station in Saxby-on-Avon, but who now worked in administration. Her mother stayed at home looking after her older son who was in need of full-time care. Like Robert, Joy had left school at sixteen and had seen very little of the world outside the county of Somerset. Unlike him, however, she had always had ambitions to travel. She had read books about France and Italy and had even learned a few words of French from Clarissa Pye, who had given her private lessons. She had been working with Dr Redwing for eighteen months, coming into the village every morning on the bright pink motor scooter that she had bought on the never-never.

Robert had proposed to Joy in the churchyard and she had accepted. The two of them were planning to get married at St Botolph's the following spring. They would use the time until then to save up enough money for a honeymoon in Venice. Robert had promised that, on the first day they were there, he would take her for a ride in a gondola. They would drink champagne as they floated beneath the Bridge of Sighs. They had it all planned.

It was so strange to be sitting next to her now – with his mother in the back, still coming between them but in a very different way. He remembered the first time he had taken Joy to the Lodge House, for tea. His mother had been utterly unwelcoming in that way he knew so well, putting a steel lid on all her emotions so that only a cold veneer of politeness showed through. How very nice to meet you. Lower Westwood? Yes, I know it well. And your father a fireman? How interesting. She had behaved like a robot – or perhaps an actor in a very bad play and although Joy hadn't complained, hadn't been anything but her sweet self, Robert had sworn he would never put her through that again. That evening he had argued with his mother and in truth the two of them had never really been civil to each other from that time.

But the worst argument had happened just a few days ago, when the vicar and his wife were away on holiday and Mary Blakiston was looking after the church. They had met outside the village pub. The Queen's Arms was right next to St Botolph's and Robert had been sitting in the sunshine, enjoying a pint after work. He had seen his mother walking through the cemetery: she'd probably been arranging the flowers ready for the weekend services, which were being conducted by a vicar from a neighbouring parish. She had seen him and come straight over.

'You said you'd mend the kitchen light.'

Yes. Yes. Yes. The light above the cooker. It was just the bulb but it was difficult to reach. And he'd said he'd do it a week ago. He often looked into the Lodge House when there was a problem. But how could something so trivial have developed into such a stupid row, the two of them not exactly shouting at each other but talking loudly enough for everyone sitting outside the pub to hear.

'Why don't you leave me alone? I just wish you'd drop dead and give me a bit of peace.'

'Oh yes. You'd like that, wouldn't you!'

'You're right! I would.'

Had he really spoken those words to her – and in public? Robert twisted round and stared at the blank surface of the wood, the coffin lid with its wreath of white lilies. And just a few days, not even a week later, his mother had been found at the bottom of the stairs at Pye Hall. It was the groundsman, Brent, who had come to the garage and told him the news and even as he'd spoken there had been a strange look in his eyes. Had he been at the pub that evening? Had he heard?

'We're there,' Joy said.

Robert turned back. Sure enough, the church was in front of them, the cemetery already full of mourners. There must have been at least fifty of them. Robert was surprised. He had never thought his mother had so many friends.

The car slowed down and stopped. Somebody opened the door for him.

'I don't want to do this,' Robert said. He reached out and took hold of her, almost like a child.

'It's all right, Rob. I'll be with you. It'll be over soon.'

She smiled at him and at once he felt better. What would he do without Joy? She had changed his life. She was everything to him.

The two of them got out and began to walk towards the church.

7

The bedroom was on the third floor of the Hotel Genevieve, Cap Ferrat, with views over the gardens and terraces. The sun was already blazing in a clear, blue sky. It had been an excellent week: perfect food, superb wine, rubbing shoulders with the usual Mediterranean crowd. Even so, Sir Magnus Pye was in a bad mood as he finished his packing. The letter that had arrived three days ago had quite spoiled his holiday. He wished the bloody vicar had never sent it. Absolutely typical of the church, always meddling, trying to spoil everyone's fun.

His wife watched him languidly from the balcony. She was smoking a cigarette. 'We're going to miss the train,' she said.

'The train doesn't leave for three hours. We've got plenty of time.'

Frances Pye ground out her cigarette and came into the

room. She was a dark, imperious woman, a little taller than her husband and certainly more imposing. He was short and round with florid cheeks and a dark beard that had spread hesitantly across his cheeks, not quite managing to lay claim to his face. Now fifty-three, he liked to wear suits that accentuated his age and his status in life. They were tailor-made for him, expensive, complete with waistcoat. The two of them made an unlikely pair: the country squire and the Hollywood actress, perhaps. Sancho Panza and Dulcinea del Toboso. Although he was the one with the title, it actually rested more easily on her. 'You should have left at once,' she said.

'Absolutely not,' Magnus grunted, trying to force down the lid of his suitcase. 'She was only a bloody housekeeper.'

'She lived with us.'

'She lived in the Lodge House. Not the same thing at all.'

'The police want to talk to you.'

'The police can talk to me once I get back. Not that I've got anything to tell them. The vicar says she tripped over an electric wire. Damn shame, but it's not my fault. They're not going to suggest I murdered her or something?'

'I wouldn't put it past you, Magnus.'

'Well, I couldn't have. I was here the whole time with you.'

Frances Pye watched her husband struggling with the suitcase. She didn't offer to help. 'I thought you were fond of her,' she said.

'She was a good cook and she did a good job cleaning. But if you want the truth, I couldn't really stand the sight of her – her and that son of hers. I always thought there was something a bit difficult about her, the way she scuttled around the place with that look in her eyes . . . like she knew something you didn't.'

'You should still have gone to the funeral.'

'Why?'

'Because the village will notice you aren't there. They won't like you for it.'

'They don't like me anyway. And they'll like me even less when they hear about Dingle Dell. What do I care? I never set out to win any popularity contests and anyway, that's the trouble with living in the country. All people do is gossip. Well, they can think what they like of me. In fact, the whole lot of them can go to Hell.' He clicked the locks shut with his thumbs and sat back, panting slightly from the exertion.

Frances looked at him curiously and for a moment there was something in her eyes that hovered between disdain and disgust. There was no longer any love in their marriage. They both knew that. They stayed together because it was convenient. Even in the heat of the Côte D'Azur, the atmosphere in the room was cold. 'I'll call down for a porter,' she said. 'The taxi should be here by now.' As she moved to the telephone, she noticed a postcard lying on a table. It was addressed to Frederick Pye at an address in Hastings. 'For heaven's sake, Magnus,' she chided him. 'You never sent that card to Freddy. You promised you would and it's been sitting here all week.' She sighed. 'He'll have got back home before it arrives.'

'Well, the family he's staying with can send it on. It's not the end of the world. It's not as if we had anything interesting to say.'

'Postcards are never interesting. That's not the point.'

Frances Pye picked up the telephone and called down to the front desk. As she spoke, Magnus was reminded of something. It was the mention of the postcard that had done it, something she had said. What was it? In some way, it was connected with the funeral that he would be missing today. Oh yes! How very strange. Magnus Pye made a mental note for himself, one that he would not forget. There was something he had to do and he would do it as soon as he got home.

8

'Mary Blakiston made Saxby-on-Avon a better place for everyone else, whether it was arranging the flowers every Sunday in this very church, looking after the elderly, collecting for the RSPB or greeting visitors to Pye Hall. Her home-made cakes were always the star of the village fête and I can tell you there were many occasions when she would surprise me in the vestry with one of her almond bites or perhaps a slice of Victoria sponge.'

The funeral was proceeding in the way that funerals do: slowly, gently, with a sense of quiet inevitability. Jeffrey Weaver had been to a great many of them, standing on the sidelines, and took a keen interest in the people who came and went and, indeed, those who came and stayed. It never occurred to him that one day, in the not too far-off future, he would be the one being buried. He was only seventy-three and his father had lived to be a hundred. He still had plenty of time.

Jeffrey considered himself a good judge of character and cast an almost painterly eye over the crowd gathered around the grave that he had himself dug. He had his opinions about every one of them. And what better place than a funeral for a study in human nature?

First there was the vicar himself with his tombstone face and long, slightly unkempt hair. Jeffrey remembered when he had first come to Saxby-on-Avon, replacing the Reverend Montagu who had become increasingly eccentric in old age, repeating himself in his sermons and falling asleep during evensong. The Osbornes had been more than welcome when they arrived even if they were a slightly odd couple, she so much shorter than him, quite plump and pugnacious. She certainly never held back with her opinions, which Jeffrey rather admired – although it probably wasn't a good idea for a vicar's wife. He could see her now, standing behind her husband, nodding when she agreed with what he was saying, scowling when she didn't. They were definitely close. That was for sure. But they were odd in more ways than one. What, for example, was their interest in Pye Hall? Oh yes, he had seen them a couple of times, slipping into the woodland that reached the bottom of their garden and which separated their property from Sir Magnus Pye. Quite a few people used Dingle Dell as a short cut to the manor house. It saved having to go all the way down to the Bath Road and then coming in through the main entrance. But normally, they didn't do it in the middle of the night. What, he wondered, were they up to?

Jeffrey had no time for Mr and Mrs Whitehead and never really spoke to them. As far as he was concerned, they were Londoners and had no place in Saxby-on-Avon. The village didn't need an antique shop anyway. It was a waste of space. You could take an old mirror, an old clock or whatever, put a stupid price on it and call it an antique but it was still only junk and more fool those that thought otherwise. The fact was, he didn't trust either of them. It seemed to him that they were pretending to be something they weren't – just like the stuff they were selling. And why had they come to the funeral? They'd hardly known Mary Blakiston and certainly she'd never have had anything good to say about them.

Dr Redwing and her husband had every right to be here, on the other hand. She was the one who had found the body – along with Brent, the groundsman, who had also turned up and who was standing with his cap in hand, his curly hair tumbling over his forehead. Emilia Redwing had always lived in the village. Her father, Dr Rennard, had worked in the surgery before her. He hadn't come today but that wasn't surprising. He was in a residential home in Trowbridge and the word was that he himself wasn't much longer for this world. Jeffrey had never had any serious illness but he had been treated by both of them. Old Doctor Rennard had actually delivered his son – a midwife as well as a doctor back in the days when it was quite common for one man to be both. And what of Arthur Redwing? He was listening to the vicar with a look that teetered on the edge of impatience and boredom. He was a handsome man. There was no doubt of that. An artist, not that he'd made any money out of it. Hadn't he done a portrait of Lady Pye a while ago, up at the hall? Anyway, the two of them were the sort of people you could rely on. Not like the Whiteheads. It was hard to imagine the village without them.

The same was true of Clarissa Pye. She had certainly dolled herself up for the funeral and looked a little ridiculous in that hat with its three feathers. What did she think this was? A cocktail party? Even so, Jeffrey couldn't help feeling sorry for her. It must be hard enough living here with her brother lording it over her. It was all right for him, swanning around in his Jag while his sister taught at the village school, and she hadn't been a bad teacher by all accounts, even if the children had never much liked her. It was probably because they sensed her unhappiness. Clarissa was all on her own. She had never married. She seemed to spend half her life in the church. He was always seeing her coming in and out. To be fair to her, she often stopped to have a chat with him but then of course she didn't really have anyone to talk to unless she was on her knees. She looked a bit like her brother, Sir Magnus, although not in a way that did her any favours. At least she'd had the decency to turn up.

Somebody sneezed. It was Brent. Jeffrey watched him as he wiped his nose with the back of his sleeve then glanced from side to side. He had no idea how to behave himself in a crowd but that was hardly surprising. Brent spent most of his life in his own company and, unlike Clarissa, he preferred it that way. He worked long hours up at the hall and sometimes, after he finished, he might be found having a drink or supper at the Ferryman, where he had his own table and his own chair, looking out over the main road. But he never socialised. He had no conversation. Sometimes Jeffrey wondered what went on in his head.

He ignored the other mourners and settled on the boy who had arrived with the hearse, Robert Blakiston. Jeffrey felt sorry for him too: it was his mother they were burying, even if the two of them had been at it hammer and tongs. It was well known in the village how the two of them didn't get on and he'd actually heard with his own ears what Robert had said to her outside the Queen's Arms, just the evening before the accident had happened. '*I wish you'd drop dead. Give me a bit of peace!*' Well, he wasn't to be blamed for that. People often say things they regret and nobody could have known what was going to happen. The boy was certainly looking miserable enough as he stood there, next to the neat, pretty girl who worked at the doctor's surgery. Everyone in the village knew that they were courting and the two of them were very well suited. She was obviously worried about him. Jeffrey could see it in her face and the way she hung on to his arm.

'She was part of the village. Although we are here today to mourn her departure, we should remember what she left behind . . .'

The vicar was coming to the end of his address. He was on the last page. Jeffrey looked round and saw Adam entering the cemetery from the footpath at the far end. He was a good boy. You could always rely on him to turn up at exactly the right moment.

And here was something rather strange. One of the mourners was already leaving even though the vicar was still speaking. Jeffrey hadn't noticed him standing at the very back of the crowd, separate from them. He was a middle-aged man dressed in a dark coat with a black hat. A Fedora. Jeffrey had only glimpsed his face but thought it familiar. He had sunken cheeks and a beak-like nose. Where had he seen him before? Well, it was too late. He was already out of the main gate, making his way towards the village square.

Something made Jeffrey look up. The stranger had passed beneath a large elm tree that grew on the edge of the cemetery and something had moved, sitting on one of the branches. It was a magpie. And it wasn't alone. Looking a second time, Jeffrey saw that the tree was full of them. How many were there? It was difficult to see with the thick leaves obscuring them but in the end he counted seven and that put him in mind of the old nursery rhyme he had learned as a child.

One for sorrow,
Two for joy,
Three for a girl,
Four for a boy,
Five for silver,
Six for gold,
Seven for a secret,
Never to be told.

Well, wasn't that the strangest thing? A whole crowd of magpies in one tree, as if they had gathered here for the funeral. But then Adam arrived, the vicar finished his address, the mourners began to leave and the next time Jeffrey looked up, they had gone.

TWO

Joy

1

The doctor did not need to speak. His face, the silence in the room, the X-rays and test results spread across his desk said it all. The two men sat facing each other in the smartly furnished office at the bottom end of Harley Street and knew that they had reached the final act of a drama that had been played out many times before. Six weeks ago, they hadn't even known each other. Now they were united in the most intimate way of all. One had given the news. The other had received it. Neither of them allowed very much emotion to show in their face. It was part of the procedure, a gentlemen's agreement, that they should do their best to conceal it.

'May I ask, Dr Benson, how long would you say I have remaining?' Atticus Pünd asked.

'It's not easy to be precise,' the doctor replied. 'I'm afraid the tumour is very advanced. Had we been able to spot it earlier, there's a small chance that we might have operated. As it is . . .' He shook his head. 'I'm sorry.'

'There is no need to be.' Pünd spoke the perfect, studied English of the cultivated foreigner, enunciating every syllable as if to apologise for his German accent. 'I am sixty-five years old. I have had a long life and I will say that in many respects it has been a good one. I had expected to die on many occasions before now. You might even say that death has been a companion of mine, always walking two steps behind. Well, now he has caught up.' He spread his hands and managed to smile. 'We are old acquaintances, he and I, and he gives me no reason to be afraid. However, it will be necessary for me to arrange my affairs, to put them in order. It would help me to know, therefore, in general terms . . . are we speaking weeks or months?'

'Well, there will be a decline, I'm afraid. These headaches of yours will get worse. You may experience seizures. I can send you some literature, which will give you the general picture, and I'll prescribe some strong painkillers. You might like to consider some sort of residential care. There's a very good place in Hampstead I can recommend, run by the Marie Curie Memorial Foundation. In the later stages, you will require constant attention.'

The words faded into the distance. Dr Benson examined his patient with a certain amount of puzzlement. The name Atticus Pünd was familiar to him, of course. He was often mentioned in the newspapers – a German refugee who had managed to survive the war after spending a year in one of Hitler's concentration camps. At the time of his arrest he had been a policeman working in Berlin – or perhaps it was Vienna – and after arriving in England, he had set himself up as a private detective, helping the police on numerous occasions. He did not look like a detective. He was a small man, very neat, his hands folded in front of him. He was wearing a dark suit, a white shirt and a narrow, black tie. His shoes were polished. If he had not known otherwise, the doctor might have mistaken him for an accountant, the sort who would work for a family firm and who would be utterly reliable. And yet there was something else. Even before he had heard the news, the first time he had entered the surgery, Pünd had exhibited a strange sense of nervousness. His eyes, behind the round, wire-framed glasses, were endlessly watchful and he seemed to hesitate, every time, before he spoke. The strange thing was that he was more relaxed, now, after being told the news. It was as if he had always been expecting it and was merely grateful that, at last, it had been delivered.

'Two or three months,' Dr Benson concluded. 'It could be longer, but after that I'm afraid you will find that your faculties will begin to worsen.'

'Thank you very much, doctor. The treatment I have

received from you has been exemplary. May I ask that any further correspondence should be addressed to me personally and marked "Private & Confidential"? I have a personal assistant and would not wish him to know of this quite yet.'

'Of course.'

'The business between us is concluded?'

'I would like to see you again in a couple of weeks. We will have to make arrangements. I really think you should go and look at Hampstead.'

'I will do that.' Pünd got to his feet. Curiously, the action did not add a great deal to his overall height. Standing up, he seemed to be overpowered by the room with its dark wooden panels and high ceiling. 'Thank you again, Dr Benson.'

He picked up his walking stick, which was made of rosewood with a solid, bronze handle, eighteenth century. It came from Salzburg and had been a gift from the German ambassador in London. On more than one occasion, it had proved to be a useful weapon. He walked past the receptionist and the doorman, nodding politely at each of them, and went out into the street. Once there, he stood in the bright sunlight, taking in the scene around him. He was not surprised to discover that his every sense had been heightened. The edges of the buildings seemed almost mathematically precise. He could differentiate the sound of every car as it merged into the general noise of the traffic. He felt the warmth of the sun against his skin. It occurred to him that he might well be in shock. Sixty-five years old and it was unlikely that he was going to be sixty-six. It would take some getting used to.

And yet, as he walked up Harley Street towards Regents Park, he was already putting it all into context. It was just another throw of the dice and, after all, his entire life had been lived against the odds. He knew well, for example, that he owed his very existence to an accident of history. When Otto 1, a Bavarian prince, had become King of Greece in 1832, a number of Greek students had chosen to emigrate to Germany. His great-grandfather had been one of them and fifty-eight years later, Atticus himself had been born to a German mother, a secretary working at the *Landespolizei* where his father was a uniformed officer. Half Greek, half German? It was a minority if ever there was one. And then, of course, there had been the rise of Nazism. The Pünds were not only Greek. They were Jewish. As the great game had continued, their chances of survival had diminished until only the most reckless gambler would have taken a punt on their coming through. Sure enough he had lost: his mother, his father, his brothers, his friends. Finally he had found himself in Belsen and his own life had been spared only by a very rare administrative error, a chance in a thousand. After the liberation, it had given him another full decade of life so could he really complain that a final throw had now gone against him? Atticus Pünd was nothing if not generous of spirit and by the time he had reached the Euston Road he was at peace with himself. All was as it should be. He would not complain.

He took a taxi home. He never used the tube train, disliking the presence of so many people in close proximity; so many dreams, fears, resentments jumbled together in the darkness. He found it overpowering. Black cabs were so much more stolid, cocooning him from the real world. There was little traffic in the middle of the day and he soon found himself in Charterhouse Square in Farringdon. The taxi pulled up outside Tanner Court, the very elegant block of flats where he lived. He paid the driver, added a generous tip, and went in.

He had bought the flat with the profits he had made from the Ludendorff Diamond affair[1]: two bedrooms, a light and spacious living room looking out onto the square and, most importantly, a hallway and an office where he was able to meet clients. As he took the lift to the seventh floor, he reflected that he had no cases to investigate at the moment. All in all, that was just as well.

'Hello, there!' The voice came from the office before

---

1 See *Atticus Pünd Takes the Case*

Pünd had even closed the front door and a moment later, James Fraser came bouncing out of the office, a bundle of letters in his hand. Blond-haired and in his late twenties, this was the assistant and private secretary that Pünd had mentioned to Dr Benson. A graduate out of Oxford University, a would-be actor, broke, and perennially unemployed, he had answered an advertisement in the *Spectator* thinking that he would stay in the job for a few months. Six years later, he was still there. 'How did it go?' he asked.

'How did *what* go?' Pünd asked in turn. Fraser of course had no idea where he'd been.

'I don't know. Whatever it was you went for.' James smiled that school-boyish smile of his. 'Anyway, Inspector Spence called from Scotland Yard. He wants you to give him a call. Someone from *The Times* wants you to do an interview. And don't forget, you've got a client arriving here at half past twelve.'

'A client?'

'Yes.' Fraser sifted through the letters he was holding. 'Her name is Joy Sanderling. She rang yesterday.'

'I do not recall speaking to a Joy Sanderling.'

'You didn't speak to her. I did. She was calling from Bath or somewhere. She sounded in a bit of a bad way.'

'Why did you not ask me?'

'Should I have?' Fraser's face fell. 'I'm terribly sorry. We haven't got anything on at the moment and I thought you'd appreciate a new case.'

Pünd sighed. He always looked a little pained and put upon – it was part of his general demeanour – but on this occasion, the timing could not have been worse. Even so, he did not raise his voice. As always, he was reasonable. 'I'm sorry, James,' he said. 'I cannot see her right now.'

'But she's already on her way.'

'Then you'll have to tell her that she has wasted her time.'

Pünd walked past his secretary and into his private rooms. He closed the door behind him.

2

'You said he would see me.'

'I know. I'm awfully sorry. But he's too busy today.'

'But I took a day off work. I came on the train all the way from Bath. You can't treat people this way.'

'You're absolutely right. But it wasn't Mr Pünd's fault. I didn't look at his diary. If you like, I can pay back your train fare out of petty cash.'

'It's not just the train fare. It's my whole life. I have to see him. I don't know anyone else who can help.'

Pünd heard the voices from behind the double door that led into his sitting room. He was resting in an armchair, smoking the Sobranie cigarette – black with a gold tip – that he favoured. He had been thinking about his book, the work of a lifetime, already four hundred pages long and nowhere near complete. It had a title: *The Landscape of Criminal Investigation*. Fraser had typed up the most recent chapter and he drew it towards him. *Chapter Twenty-six: Interrogation and Interpretation*. He could not read it now. Pünd had thought it would take another year to complete the book. He no longer had that year.

The girl had a nice voice. She was young. He could also tell, even on the other side of a wooden barrier, that she was on the edge of tears. Pünd thought briefly about his illness. Intracranial neoplasm. The doctor had given him three months. Was he really going to spend that time sitting on his own like this, thinking about all the things he couldn't do? Annoyed with himself, he neatly ground out the cigarette, got up and opened the door.

Joy Sanderling was standing in the corridor, talking to Fraser. She was a small girl, petite in every sense, with fair hair framing a very pretty face and childlike blue eyes. She had dressed smartly to come and see him. The pale raincoat with the sash tying it at the waist was unnecessary in this weather but it looked good on her and he suspected that she had chosen it because it made her seem businesslike. She looked past Fraser and saw him. 'Mr Pünd?'

'Yes.' He nodded slowly.

'I'm sorry to disturb you. I know how busy you are. But – please – if you could just give me five minutes of your time? It would mean so much.'

Five minutes. Although she could not know it, it meant so much to both of them.

'Very well,' he said. Behind her, James Fraser looked annoyed, as if he had somehow let the side down. But Pünd had made up his mind the moment he had heard her voice. She had sounded so lost. There had been enough sadness today.

He took her into the office, which was comfortable if a little austere. There was a desk and three chairs, an antique mirror, engravings in gold frames, all in the Biedermeier style of nineteenth-century Vienna. Fraser followed them in and took his place at the side of the room, sitting with his legs crossed and a notepad balanced on his knee. He didn't really have to write anything down. Pünd, who never lost sight of a single detail, would remember every word that was said.

'Please continue, Miss Sanderling.'

'Oh, please, call me Joy,' the girl replied. 'Actually, my first name is Josie. But everyone calls me Joy.'

'And you have come all this way from the city of Bath.'

'I would have come a lot further to see you, Mr Pünd. I've read about you in the newspapers. They say you're the best detective who ever lived, that there's nothing you can't do.'

Atticus Pünd blinked. Such flattery always made him a little uncomfortable. With a slightly twitchy movement, he adjusted his glasses and half-smiled. 'That is very kind of you but, perhaps we are getting ahead of ourselves, Miss Sanderling. You must forgive me. We have been very rude. We have not offered you a coffee.'

'I don't want a coffee, thank you very much, and I don't want to waste too much of your time. But I desperately need your help.'

'Then why don't you begin by telling us what it is that brings you here?'

'Yes. Of course.' She straightened herself in her chair. James Fraser waited with his pen poised. 'I've already told you my name,' she began. 'I live in a place called Lower Westwood with my parents and my brother, Paul. Unfortunately, he was born with Down's syndrome and he can't look after himself but we're very close. Actually, I love him to bits.' She paused. 'Our house is just outside Bath but I work in a village called Saxby-on-Avon. I have a job in the local surgery, helping Dr Redwing. She's terribly nice, by the way. I've been with her for almost two years now and I've been very happy.'

Pünd nodded. He had already taken to this girl. He liked her confidence, the clarity with which she expressed herself.

'A year ago, I met a boy,' she went on. 'He came in because he'd hurt himself quite badly in a car accident. He was mending the car and it almost fell on him. The jack hit his hand and broke a couple of bones. His name is Robert Blakiston. We hit it off pretty much straight away and I started going out with him. I'm very much in love with him. And now the two of us are engaged to be married.'

'You have my congratulations.'

'I wish it was as easy as that. Now I'm not sure that the wedding is going ahead at all.' She produced a tissue and used it to dab at her eye but in a way that was more business-like than overly emotional. 'Two weeks ago, his mother died. She was buried last weekend. Robert and I went to the funeral together and of course it was horrible. But what made it even worse was the way people looked at him... and since then, all the things they have been saying. The thing is, Mr Pünd, they all think he did it!'

'You mean... that he killed her?'

'Yes.' It took her a few moments to compose herself. Then she continued. 'Robert never had a very happy relationship with his mother. Her name was Mary and she worked as a housekeeper. There's this big place – I suppose you'd say it was a manor house – called Pye Hall. It's owned by a man called Sir Magnus Pye, and it's been in his family for centuries. Anyway, she did the cooking, the cleaning, the shopping – all that sort of thing – and she lived in the Lodge House down at the gates. That was where Robert grew up.'

'You do not mention a father.'

'There is no father. He left them, during the war. It's all very complicated and Robert never talks about it. You see, there was a family tragedy. There's a big lake at Pye Hall and it's said to be very deep. Robert had a younger brother called Tom and the two of them were swimming together in the lake. Robert was fourteen. Tom was twelve. Anyway, Tom got out of his depth and he drowned. Robert tried to save him but he couldn't.'

'Where was the father at this time?'

'He was a mechanic at Boscombe Downs, working for the RAF. It's not that far away and he was at home quite a lot but he wasn't there when it happened. And when he found out – well, you'd have to ask Robert, not that he remembers very much of it, I'm sure. The point is that his parents just tore each other apart. He blamed her for not looking after the boys properly. She blamed him for being away. I can't tell you very much because Robert never speaks about it and the rest is just village gossip. Anyway, the upshot was that he moved out leaving the two of them living alone in the Lodge. They got divorced later on and I've never even met him. He wasn't at the funeral – or if he was, I didn't see him. His name is Matthew Blakiston but that's about all I know.

'Robert grew up with his mother but the two of them were never happy together. Really, they should have moved. They should never have stayed near that horrible place. I don't know how she did it, walking past the lake where her own son had died, seeing it every day. I think it poisoned her . . . It reminded her of the boy she'd lost. And maybe part of her blamed Robert even though he was nowhere near when it happened. People do behave like that, don't they, Mr Pünd. It's a sort of madness...'

Pünd nodded. 'It is true that we have many ways of coping with loss,' he said. 'And grief is never rational.'

'I only met Mary Blakiston a few times, although of course I saw her in the village quite a bit. She often used to come to the surgery. Not because she was ill. She and Dr Redwing were good friends. After Robert and I got engaged, she invited us round to the Lodge for tea – but it was horrible. She wasn't exactly unfriendly but she was so cold, asking me questions as if I was applying for a job or something. We had tea in the front room and I can still see her with her cup and saucer, sitting in her chair in the corner. She was like a spider in a web. I know I shouldn't say things like that, but that was what I thought. And poor Robert was completely in her shadow. He was so different when he was with her, quiet and shy. I don't think he said a word. He just stared at the carpet as if he had done something wrong and was about to be told off. You should have seen how she treated him! She didn't have a single good word to say about him. She was dead set against our marriage. She made that much clear. And all the time the clock was ticking away. There was this huge grandfather clock in the room and I couldn't wait for it to strike the hour so we could be on our way.'

'Your fiancé no longer lived with his mother? At the time of her death?'

'No. He was still in the same village but he'd moved into a flat above the garage where he works. I think it was one of the reasons he took the job, to get away from her.' Joy folded the tissue and slipped it into her sleeve. 'Robert and I love each other. Mary Blakiston made it clear that she didn't think I was good enough for him but even if she hadn't died, it wouldn't have made any difference. We're going to get married. We're going to be happy together.'

'If it does not distress you, Miss Sanderling, I would be interested to know more about her death.'

'Well, as I say, it happened on a Friday, two weeks ago.

She'd gone up to Pye Hall to do the cleaning – Sir Magnus and Lady Pye were away – and somehow she tripped when she was doing the hoovering and fell down the stairs. Brent, who works in the grounds, saw her lying there and called the doctor but there was nothing anyone could do. She'd broken her neck.'

'Were the police informed?'

'Yes. A detective inspector came round from the Bath constabulary. I didn't actually talk to him but apparently he was very thorough. The wire of the Hoover was in a loop at the top of the stairs. There was nobody else in the house. All the doors were locked. It was obviously just an accident.'

'And yet you say that Robert Blakiston is accused of her murder.'

'That's just the village talking and it's why you've got to help us, Mr Pünd.' She drew a breath. 'Robert argued with his mother. The two of them often argued. I think they had never really escaped from the unhappiness of what had happened all those years before and in a way it was hurting both of them. Well, they had a nasty row outside the pub. Lots of people heard them. It started because she wanted him to mend something in the Lodge. She was always asking him to do odd jobs for her and he never refused. But this time he wasn't happy about it and there was a lot of name-calling and then he said something which I know he didn't mean but everyone heard him so it doesn't matter if he meant it or not. "I wish you'd drop dead".' The tissue came out again. 'That's what he said. And three days later she was.'

She fell silent. Atticus Pünd sat behind his desk, his hands neatly folded, his face solemn. James Fraser had been taking notes. He came to the end of a sentence and underlined a single word several times. Sunlight was streaming in through the window. Outside, in Charterhouse Square, office workers were beginning to appear, carrying their lunchtime sandwiches into the fresh air.

'It is possible,' Pünd muttered, 'that your fiancé did

have good reason to kill his mother. I have not met him and I don't wish to be unkind but we must at least entertain the possibility. The two of you wished to marry. She stood in the way.'

'But she didn't!' Joy Sanderling was defiant. 'We didn't need her permission to get married and it wasn't as if she had money or anything like that. Anyway, I know Robert had nothing to do with it.'

'How can you be so sure?'

Joy took a deep breath. This was clearly something she hadn't wanted to explain but she knew she had no choice. 'The police say that Mrs Blakiston died around nine o'clock in the morning. Brent called Dr Redwing just before ten and when she got to the house, the body was still warm.' She paused. 'The garage opens at nine o'clock – the same time as the surgery – and I was with Robert until then. We left his flat together. My parents would die if they found out, Mr Pünd, even though we're engaged. My father was a fireman and now he works for the union. He's a very serious sort of person and terribly old-fashioned. And having to look after Paul all the time, it's made both my parents very protective. I told them I was going to the theatre in Bath and that I was staying overnight with a girlfriend. But the fact is that I was with Robert all night and I left him at nine o'clock in the morning, which means he couldn't have had anything to do with it.'

'How far, may I ask, is the garage from Pye Hall?'

'It's about three or four minutes on my motor scooter. I suppose you could walk there in about a quarter of an hour, if you cut across Dingle Dell. That's what we call the meadow on the edge of the village.' She scowled. 'I know what you're thinking, Mr Pünd. But I saw Robert that morning. He brought me breakfast in bed. He couldn't do that, could he, if he was thinking of murdering somebody?'

Atticus Pünd did not reply but he knew from his experience that murderers could, indeed, smile and make pleasant conversation one minute and strike violently the next. His experiences during the war had also taught him much about what he called the institutionalisation of murder; how, if you surrounded murder with enough forms and procedures, if you could convince yourself that it was an absolute necessity, then ultimately it would not be murder at all.

'What is it you wish me to do?' he asked.

'I don't have a great deal of money. I can't even really pay you. I know it's wrong of me and I probably shouldn't have come here. But it's not right. It's just so unfair. I was hoping you could come to Saxby-on-Avon – just for one day. I'm sure that would be enough. If you were to look into it and tell people that it was an accident and that there was nothing sinister going in, I'm sure that would put an end to it. Everyone knows who you are. They'd listen to you.'

There was a brief silence. Pünd took off his glasses and wiped them with a handkerchief. Fraser knew what was coming. He had been with the detective long enough to recognise his mannerisms. He always polished his glasses before he delivered bad news.

'I am sorry, Miss Sanderling,' he said. 'There is nothing I can do.' He held up a hand, stopping her before she could interrupt. 'I am a private detective,' he continued. 'It is true that the police have often asked me to help them with their enquiries but in this country I have no official status. That is the problem here. It is much more difficult for me to impose myself, particularly in a case like this where, to all intents and purposes, no crime has been committed. I have to ask myself on what pretext I would be able to enter Pye Hall.

'I also must take issue with your basic proposition. You tell me that Mrs Blakiston was killed as the result of an accident. The police evidently believe so. Let us assume that it was an accident. All I can do then is to confront the gossip of certain villagers in Saxby-on-Avon who have overheard an unfortunate conversation and have made of it what they will. But such gossip cannot be confronted. Rumours and malicious gossip are like bindweed. They cannot be cut back, even with the sword of truth. I can, however, offer you this comfort. Given time, they will wither and die of their own volition. That is my opinion. Why do you and your fiancé even wish to remain in this part of the world if it is so disagreeable to you?'

'Why should we have to move?'

'I agree. If you would take my advice, it would be to stay where you are, to get married, to enjoy your lives together. Above all, ignore this . . . I believe the word is "tittle-tattle". To confront it is to feed it. Left alone, it will go away.'

There was nothing more to be said. As if to emphasise the point, Fraser closed his notebook. Joy Sanderling got to her feet. 'Thank you very much, Mr Pünd,' she said. 'Thank you for seeing me.'

'I wish you the very best, Miss Sanderling,' Pünd replied – and he meant it. He wanted this girl to be happy. During the entire time he had been talking to her, he had forgotten his own circumstances, the news he had heard that day.

Fraser showed her out. Pünd heard a few brief mutters, then the front door opened and closed. A moment later, he came back into the room.

'I say, I'm terribly sorry about that,' he muttered. 'I was trying to tell her that you didn't want to be disturbed.'

'I am glad I saw her,' Pünd replied. 'But tell me, James. What was the word that I saw you underscoring several times as we spoke?'

'What?' Fraser flushed. 'Oh. Actually, it wasn't anything important. It wasn't even relevant. I was just trying to look busy.'

'It struck me that might be the case.'

'Oh. How?'

'Because at that moment, Miss Sanderling was not saying anything of particular interest. The motor scooter, though. Had it been any colour but pink, it might have been significant.' He smiled. 'Could you bring me a cup of coffee, James? But after that, I think, I do not want to be disturbed.'

He turned and went back into his room.

3

Joy Sanderling made her way back to Farringdon tube station, her path taking her round the side of Smithfield meat market. There was a lorry parked outside one of the many entrances and as she went past, two men in white coats were bundling out an entire sheep's carcass, raw and bloody. The sight of it made her shudder. She didn't like London. She found it oppressive. She couldn't wait to be on the train home.

She had been disappointed by her meeting with Atticus Pünd, even though (she admitted it now) she had never really expected anything from it. Why should the most famous detective in the country be interested in her? It wasn't even as if she would have been able to pay him. And what he had said had been true. There was no case to solve. Joy knew that Robert hadn't killed his mother. She had been with him that morning and would certainly have heard him if he had left the house. Robert could be moody. He often snapped out, saying things that he regretted. But she had been with him long enough to know that he would never hurt anyone. What had happened at Pye Hall had been an accident, nothing more. All the detectives in the world would have been no match for the wagging tongues of Saxby-on-Avon.

Still, she had been right to come. The two of them deserved their happiness together, Robert in particular. He had been so lost until he had met her and she wasn't going to allow anyone to drive them apart. They weren't going to move. They weren't going to take any notice of what people thought of them. They were going to fight back.

She reached the station and bought a ticket from the man in the kiosk. Already a thought was taking shape in her mind. Joy was a modest girl. She had been brought up in a very close and (despite her father's politics) conservative family. The step that she was now considering shocked her but she could see no other way. She had to protect Robert.

She had to protect their life together. Nothing was more important than that.

Before the tube train had arrived she knew exactly what she was going to do.

4

In a restaurant on the other side of London, Frances Pye cast a careless eye over the menu and ordered grilled sardines, a salad, a glass of white wine. Carlotta's was one of those Italian family restaurants behind Harrods: the manager was married to the chef and the waiters included a son and a nephew. The order was taken, the menus removed. She lit a cigarette and leant back in her chair.

'You should leave him,' her lunch companion said.

Jack Dartford, five years her junior, was a darkly handsome man with a moustache and an easy smile, dressed in a double-fronted blazer and cravat. He was looking at her with concern. From the moment they had met, he had noticed something strained about her. Even the way she was sitting now seemed nervous, defensive, one hand stroking the other arm. She had not taken off her sunglasses. He wondered if she had a black eye.

'He'd kill me,' she replied. She smiled curiously. 'Actually, he *did* try to kill me in a way – after our last row.'

'You're not serious!'

'Don't worry, Jack. He didn't hurt me. It was all bluster. He knows something's up. All those telephone calls, days off in London, the letters . . . I told you not to write to me.'

'Does he read them?'

'No. But he's not stupid. And he talks to the postman. Every time I've received a handwritten letter from London, he's probably heard about it. Anyway, it all came to the fore over dinner last night. He more or less accused me of seeing someone else.'

'You didn't tell him about me!'

'Afraid he'll come after you with a horsewhip? I wouldn't put it past him. But no, Jack, I didn't tell him about you.'

'Did he hurt you?'

'No.' She took off her sunglasses. She looked tired but there were no bruises around her eyes. 'It was just unpleasant. It's always unpleasant where Magnus is concerned.'

'Why won't you leave him?'

'Because I have no money. You have to understand that Magnus has a vindictive streak the size of the Panama Canal. If I tried to walk out on him, he'd surround himself with lawyers. He'd make sure that I left Pye Hall with nothing more than the clothes I was wearing.'

'I have money.'

'I don't think so, darling. Certainly not enough.'

It was true. Dartford worked in the money market, which in the true sense wasn't really work at all. He dabbled. He made investments. But recently he'd had an unlucky streak and he very much hoped that Frances Pye had no idea how close he was to rock bottom. He couldn't afford to marry her. He couldn't afford to run away with her. The way things were going, he could barely afford lunch.

'How was the South of France?' he asked, changing the subject. That was where they had met, playing tennis together.

'It was boring. I'd have much preferred it if you'd been there.'

'I'm sure. Did you get in any tennis?'

'Not really. To be honest, I was quite glad to leave. We got a letter in the middle of the week. A woman at Pye Hall had tripped on a wire, fallen down the stairs and broken her neck.'

'My God! Was Freddy there?'

'No. He was staying with friends down in Hastings. He's still there, as a matter of fact. He doesn't seem to want to come home.'

'I don't blame him. So who was she?'

'The housekeeper. A woman called Mary Blakiston. She'd been with us for years and she's going to be almost impossible to replace. And that wasn't the end of it. When we finally got back last Saturday we discovered we'd been burgled.'

'No!'

'I'm telling you. It was the groundsman's fault – at least, that's what the police think. He'd smashed a pane of glass at the back of the house. He had to do it, to let the doctor in.'

'Why did you need a doctor?'

'Pay attention, Jack. It was for the dead woman. Brent, the groundsman, had seen her through the window, just lying there. He called the doctor and the two of them broke into the house to see if they could help. Well, obviously there wasn't anything they could do. But after that, he just left the door with its broken pane. He didn't even bother to get it boarded up. It was an open invitation to burglars and the burglars accepted it, thank you very much.'

'Did you lose very much?'

'Not personally, no. Magnus keeps most of his valuables in a safe and they couldn't open that. But they marauded through the place. Did quite a bit of damage. Pulled open drawers and scattered the contents – that sort of thing. It took all of Sunday and yesterday to clear it up.' She reached out with the cigarette and Dartford slid an ashtray in front of her. 'I'd left some jewellery beside the bed and I lost that. It makes you feel uneasy, thinking you've had strangers in the bedroom.'

'I'll say.'

'And Magnus lost his precious treasure trove. He wasn't at all happy about that.'

'What treasure was that?'

'It's Roman, mainly silver. It's been in the family for generations, ever since they dug it up on their land. It came from some sort of burial site. There were rings, armlets, some decorative boxes, coins. We had it in a display case in the dining room. Of course, he'd never had it insured even though it was meant to be worth a fortune. Well, it's a bit late now...'

'Were the police helpful?'

'Of course not. We had some chap come over from Bath. He sniffed around, wasted a lot of fingerprint powder, asked impertinent questions and then disappeared. Completely useless.'

The waiter arrived with the glass of wine. Dartford had been drinking Campari and soda. He ordered another. 'It's a shame it wasn't Magnus,' he remarked, once the waiter had gone.

'What do you mean?'

'The lady who fell down the stairs. It's a shame it wasn't him.'

'That's a dreadful thing to say.'

'I'm only saying what you're thinking, darling. I know you well enough. I assume you'd inherit the whole caboodle if Magnus popped his clogs.'

Frances blew out cigarette smoke and looked curiously at her companion. 'As a matter of fact, the house and the grounds would all go to Freddy. There's some sort of entail on the estate. It's been that way for generations.'

'But you'd be all right.'

'Oh yes. And of course, I'd get a lifetime interest in Pye Hall. The only thing I couldn't do is sell the place. But it's not going to happen. Magnus is in perfect health, certainly for his age.'

'Yes, Frances. But a big house like that. A wire stretched out across the stairs. You never know what might happen. Maybe those burglars of yours could return and finish him off.'

'You're not serious!'

'It's just a thought.'

Frances Pye fell silent. This wasn't the sort of conversation to be having, particularly in a crowded restaurant. But she had to admit that Jack was right. Life without Magnus would be considerably simpler and a great deal more enjoyable. It was just a shame that lightning didn't have the habit of striking twice.

On the other hand, though, why not?

5

Dr Emilia Redwing tried to see her father once a week although it wasn't always possible. If the surgery were busy, if she had home or hospital calls to make, if there was too much paperwork on her desk, then she would be forced to put it off. Somehow, it was always easy to make an excuse. There was always a good reason not to go.

She derived very little pleasure from the visits. Dr Edgar Rennard had been eighty years old when his wife had died and although he had continued living in his home in nearby King's Abbott, he had never really been the same. Emilia had soon got used to the telephone calls from the neighbours. He had been found wandering in the street. He wasn't feeding himself properly. He was confused. At first, she had tried to persuade herself that he was simply suffering from chronic grief and loneliness but as the symptoms had presented themselves, she had been forced to make the obvious diagnosis. Her father had senile dementia. He wasn't going to get any better. In fact the prognosis was a great deal worse. She had briefly considered taking him in with her at Saxby-on-Avon but that wouldn't have been fair to Arthur and anyway she couldn't possibly become an old man's full-time carer. She still remembered the guilt, the sense of failure, that she had felt the first time she had taken him to Ashton House, a residential home converted from a hospital in the Bath valley just after the war. Curiously though, it had been easier to persuade her father than it had been to persuade herself.

This wasn't a good day to have made the fifteen-minute drive to Bath. Joy Sanderling was in London, seeing someone on what she had described as a personal matter. Mary Blakiston's funeral had taken place just five days ago and there was a sense of disquiet in the village that was hard to define but which, she knew from experience, might well lead to further calls on her time. Unhappiness had a way of affecting people in just the same way as the flu and even the burglary at Pye Hall struck her as being part of that general infection. But she couldn't put off the visit any longer. On Tuesday, Edgar Rennard had taken a tumble. He had been seen by a local doctor and she had been assured that there was no serious damage. Even so, he was asking for her. He was off his food. The matron at Ashton House had telephoned her and asked her to come.

She was with him now. They had got him out of bed but only as far as the chair beside the window and he was sitting there in his dressing gown, so thin and crumpled that Emilia almost wanted to cry. He had always been strong, robust. As a little girl, she had thought the entire world rested on his shoulders. Today it had taken him five minutes before he had even recognised her. She had seen this creeping up on them. It wasn't so much that her father was dying. It was more that he had lost the desire to live.

'I have to tell her...' he said. His voice was husky. His lips had difficulty shaping the words. He had said this twice before but he still hadn't made himself understood.

'Who are you talking about, Papa? What is it you have to tell?'

'She has to know what happened... what I did.'

'What do you mean? What are you talking about? Is this something to do with Mama?'

'Where is she? Where is your mother?'

'She's not here.' Emilia was annoyed with herself. She should never have mentioned her mother. It would only confuse the old man. 'What do you want to tell me, Daddy?' she said, more gently.

'It's important. I don't have very long.'

'That's nonsense. You're going to be fine. You just have to try and eat something. I could ask the matron for a sandwich, if you like. I can stay here with you while you have it.'

'Magnus Pye . . .'

How extraordinary that he should have spoken that name. Of course he would have known Sir Magnus when he worked at Saxby-on-Avon. He would have treated the whole family. But why mention him now? Was Sir Magnus in some way connected with what had happened, whatever it was that her father wanted to explain? The trouble with dementia was that, as well as leaving huge gaps in the memory, it also jumbled things together. He might be thinking of something that had happened five years ago or five days ago. To him, they were the same.

'What about Sir Magnus?' she asked.

'Who?'

'Sir Magnus Pye. You mentioned him. There was something you wanted to tell me.'

But the vacant stare was back in his eyes. He had retreated into whatever world it was that he inhabited. Dr Emilia Redwing stayed with him for another twenty minutes but he barely noticed she was there. After that, she exchanged a few words with the matron and left.

She drove home with a nagging sense of worry but by the time she had parked the car, she had put her father out of her mind. Arthur had said that he would cook the supper that night. The two of them would probably watch *Life With the Lyons* on television and go to bed early. Dr Redwing had already seen the surgery appointments list for the following day and knew that she was going to be busy.

She opened the door and smelled burning. For a moment she was concerned but there was no smoke and the smell was somehow distant, more a memory of a fire than an actual one. She went into the kitchen and found Arthur sitting at the table – slumped there, actually – drinking whisky. He hadn't even begun to cook the dinner and she knew at once that something was wrong. Arthur did not deal well with disappointment. Without meaning to, he somehow celebrated it. So what had happened? Dr Redwing looked past him and saw a painting, leaning against the wall, the wooden frame charred, the canvas largely eaten away. It was a portrait of a woman. He had clearly painted it – she recognised his style immediately – but it took her a moment or two longer to realise who it was.

'Lady Pye,' he muttered, answering her question before she had time to ask it.

'What's happened? Where did you find it?'

'It was on a bonfire near the rose garden . . . at Pye Hall.'

'What were you doing there?'

'I was just walking. I cut through Dingle Dell and there was no one around so I thought I'd stroll through the gardens down to the main road. I don't know what drew me to it. Maybe it was meant to be.' He drank some more. He wasn't drunk. He was using the whisky as a sort of prop. 'Brent wasn't around. There was no sign of anyone. Just the bloody painting thrown out with the rest of the trash.'

'Arthur . . .'

'Well, it's their property. They paid for it. I suppose they can do with it as they want.'

Dr Redwing remembered. Sir Magnus had commissioned the portrait for his wife's fortieth birthday and she had been grateful at the time, even when she discovered how little Sir Magnus intended to pay. It was a commission. It meant so much to Arthur's self-esteem and he had set about the work with enthusiasm. He had painted Frances Pye over three sittings in the garden – with Dingle Dell in the background. He hadn't been given nearly enough time and to begin with Lady Pye had been a reluctant sitter. But even she had been impressed by the result; a portrait that brought out everything that was good in her and which showed her relaxed, half-smiling, in command. Arthur had been quietly satisfied with the result and at the time so had Sir Magnus, hanging it prominently in his great hall.

'It must be a mistake,' she said. 'Why would they want to throw it out?'

'They were burning it,' Arthur replied, heavily. He gestured vaguely at the canvas. 'He seems to have cut it to pieces first.'

'Can you save it? Is there anything you can do with it?'

She knew the answer. The woman's imperious eyes had survived; the dark, sweeping hair, part of one shoulder. But most of the painting was blackened. The canvas had been slashed and burned. She didn't even want it in the house.

'I'm sorry,' Arthur said. 'I haven't done the supper.'

He emptied his glass and walked out of the room.

6

'Have you seen this?'

Robin Osborne was reading a copy of the *Bath Weekly Chronicle* and Henrietta had never seen him look so angry. There really was something quite Old Testament about him, she thought, with his black hair falling to the collar, his white face, his bright, angry eyes. Moses would have looked much the same with the golden calf. Or Joshua storming the walls of Jericho. 'They're going to cut down Dingle Dell!'

'What are you talking about?' Henrietta had made two cups of tea. She put them down and moved further into the room.

'Sir Magnus Pye has sold it for development. They're going to build a new road and eight new houses.'

'Where?'

'Right here!' The vicar gestured at the window. 'Right at the bottom of our garden! That's going to be our view from now on – a row of modern houses! *He* won't see them, of course. He'll be on the other side of the lake and I'm sure he'll leave enough trees to form a screen. But you and me . . .'

'He can't do it, can he?' Henrietta went round so that she could read the headline. NEW HOMES FOR SAXBY-ON-AVON. It seemed to be a remarkably up-beat interpretation of such an act of vandalism. Her husband's hands were visibly shaking as he held the paper. 'The land's protected!' she went on.

'It doesn't matter if it's protected or not. It seems he's got permission. The same thing's been going on all over the country. It says here that work will begin before the end of the summer. That means next month or the month after. And there's nothing we can do.'

'We can write to the bishop.'

'The bishop won't help. Nobody will.'

'We can try.'

'No, Henrietta. It's too late.'

Later that evening, as they stood together preparing the supper, he was still upset.

'This dreadful, dreadful man. He sits there, in that big house of his, looking down at the rest of us – and it wasn't even as if he did anything to deserve it. He just inherited it from his father and his father before him. This is 1955, for heaven's sake. Not the Middle Ages! Of course, it doesn't help having the bloody Tories still in power but you'd have thought we'd have moved away from the days when people were given wealth and power simply because of an accident of birth.

'When did Sir Magnus do anything to help anyone else? Look at the church! We've got the leaking roof, the new heating system that we can't afford and he's never put his hand in his pocket to stump up so much as a shilling. He hardly ever comes to services in this, the very church he was christened in. Oh! And he's got a plot reserved in the cemetery. The sooner he inhabits it, the better – if you ask me.'

'I'm sure you don't mean that, Robin.'

'You're right, Hen. It was a wicked thing to say and it was quite wrong of me.' Osborne paused and took a breath. 'I'm not opposed to new housing in Saxby-on-Avon. On the contrary, it's important if the village is going to keep hold of its young people. But this development has got nothing to do with that. I very much doubt that anyone around here will be able to afford the new houses. And you mark my words. They'll be nasty modern things, quite out of keeping with the village.'

'You can't stand in the way of progress.'

'Is this progress? Wiping out a beautiful meadow and

a wood that's been there for a thousand years? Frankly, I'm surprised he can get away with it. All the time we've been living here, we've loved Dingle Dell. You know what it means to us. Well, a year from now, if this goes ahead, we're going to be stuck here next to a suburban street.' He put down the vegetable peeler and took off the apron he had been wearing. 'I'm going to the church,' he announced, suddenly.

'What about dinner?'

'I'm not hungry.'

'Would you like me to come with you?'

'No. Thank you, my dear. But I need time to reflect.' He put on his jacket. 'I need to ask for forgiveness.'

'You haven't done anything.'

'I've said things that I shouldn't have said. And I have thoughts in my head, also, that shouldn't be there. To feel hatred for your fellow man . . . it's a terrible thing.'

'Some men deserve it.'

'That is certainly true. But Sir Magnus is a human like the rest of us. I shall pray that he has a change of heart.'

He left the room. Henrietta heard the front door open and close, then set about clearing the kitchen. She was deeply concerned about her husband and knew only too well what the loss of Dingle Dell would mean to the two of them. Was there something she could do about it? Perhaps if she went to see Sir Magnus Pye herself . . .

Meanwhile, Robin Osborne was cycling up the High Street, on his way to the church. His bicycle was something of a joke in the village, a terrible old bone-rattler with wheels that wobbled and a metal frame that weighed a ton. There was a basket suspended from the handlebars and it was usually filled with prayer books or fresh vegetables which he had grown himself and which he liked to distribute as gifts to poorer members of his congregation. This evening it was empty.

As he pedalled into the village square, he passed Johnny Whitehead and his wife who were walking, arm in arm, heading for the Queen's Arms. The Whiteheads did not often go to church, certainly not more than they had to. For them, as in so much of their life, it was a question of keeping up appearances and with that in mind they both called out a greeting to the vicar. He ignored them. Leaving his bicycle at the entrance to the cemetery, he hurried on and disappeared through the main door.

'What's wrong with him?' Johnny wondered out loud. 'He didn't look at all happy.'

'Maybe it was the funeral,' Gemma Whitehead suggested. 'It can't be very nice having to bury someone.'

'No. Vicars are used to it. In fact, they enjoy it. Funerals give them a reason to feel important.' He looked up the road. Next to St Botolph's, the garage lights had flickered out. Johnny saw Robert Blakiston crossing the forecourt. He was closing for the night. He glanced at his watch. It was six o'clock exactly. 'Pub's open,' he said. 'Let's get in there.'

He was in a good mood. Gemma had let him go to London that day – even she couldn't force him to spend his whole life in Saxby-on-Avon – and it had been nice to return to a few haunts and to see a few old friends. More than that, he'd actually enjoyed being in the city with the traffic all around him and dust and dirt in the air. He liked the noise. He liked people in a hurry. He'd done his best to get used to the countryside but he still felt that he had about as much life here as a stuffed marrow. Catching up with Derek and Colin, having a few beers together, wandering down Brick Lane had been like rediscovering himself and he had come away with fifty pounds in his pocket too. He'd been quite surprised but Colin hadn't thought twice.

'Very nice, Johnny. Solid silver and a bit of age to it too. Get it from a museum, did you? You should visit us more often!'

Well, drinks were on him tonight even if the Queen's Arms was about as cheerful as the cemetery it stood next to. There were a few locals inside. Tony Bennett was on the jukebox. He held the door open for his wife and the two of them went in.

7

Joy Sanderling was on her own in the dispensary that also served as the main office at Dr Redwing's surgery.

She had let herself in with her own keys. She had keys to every part of the building except for the cupboard containing the dangerous medicines and even this she could open, as she knew where Dr Redwing kept her spare. She had decided what she was going to do. The very thought of it made her heart beat faster but she going ahead anyway.

She pulled a sheet of paper out of a drawer and fed it into the typewriter, the Olympia SM2 De Luxe model that she had been supplied with when she began the job. It was a portable. She would have preferred something a little heavier for all the typing she had to do but it wasn't in her nature to complain. She looked down at the white page as it curved round towards her and for a moment she thought of her arrival at Tanner Court and her meeting with Atticus Pünd. The famous detective had disappointed her but she felt no ill will towards him. It had been kind of him to see her particularly as he hadn't been looking at all well. She was used to seeing sick people. Her time at the surgery had given her a sort of premonition. She could sense at once when something was seriously wrong, even before the patient had been in to see the doctor, and she had known at once that Pünd was in need of help. Well, that wasn't any concern of hers. The fact was that he had been right. Now that she thought about it, she could see that it would have been impossible to stem the tide of vicious gossip within the village. There was nothing he would have been able to do.

But there was something she could.

Choosing her words carefully, she began to type. It didn't take her very long. The entire thing could be contained in three or four lines. When she had finished, she examined what she had written and now that it was there, in black and white, in front of her, she wondered if she could really go through with this. She couldn't see any alternative.

There was a movement in front of her. She looked up and saw Robert Blakiston standing on the other side of the counter, in the waiting area. He was wearing his overalls, covered in oil and grime. She had been so focused on what she had been doing that he had entered without her hearing. Guiltily, she pulled the page out of the typewriter and laid it face down on the desk.

'What are you doing?' she asked.

'I came in to see you,' he said. Of course, he would have only just shut down the garage and he must have come straight here. She hadn't told him she was going to London. He would assume she had been here all day.

'What sort of day have you had?' she asked, brightly.

'Not too bad.' He glanced at the face-down letter. 'What's that?' His tone was suspicious and she realised she had turned it over a little too quickly.

'Just something for Dr Redwing,' she said. 'It's a private letter. Medical stuff.' She hated lying to him but there was no way she was going to tell him what she had written.

'Do you want to go for a drink?'

'No. I ought to get back to Mum and Dad.' She saw a look pass across his face and for a moment she was worried. 'Is something wrong?' she asked.

'Not really. I just wanted to be with you.'

'When we're married, we'll be together all the time and nobody will be able to do anything about it.'

'Yeah.'

She considered changing her mind. She could have gone out with him. But her mother had cooked a special dinner and Paul, her brother, became agitated when she was late. She had promised she would read to him tonight, before bed. He always enjoyed that. Taking the letter with her, she got up and went through the door that connected the two areas. She smiled and kissed him on the cheek. 'We're going to be Mr and Mrs Robert Blakiston and we're going to live together and we're never going to be apart again.'

Suddenly, he took hold of her. Both hands were around her and the grip was so strong that he almost hurt her. He kissed her and she saw that there were tears in his eyes. 'I couldn't bear to lose you,' he said. 'You're everything to me. I mean it, Joy. Meeting you was the best thing that ever happened to me and I'm not going to let anyone stop us being together.'

She knew what he meant. The village. The rumours.

'I don't care what people say,' she told him. 'And anyway, we don't have to stay in Saxby. We can go anywhere we want.' She realised that this was exactly what Pünd had said. 'But we will stay here,' she went on. 'You'll see. Everything will be all right.'

They parted company soon after that. He went back to his little flat to shower and change out of his work overalls. But she did not return to her parents. Not yet. She still had the note she had written. It had to be delivered.

8

At exactly that moment, and a little further up the road, Clarissa Pye heard someone ringing at her front door. She had been preparing her dinner, something quite new that had suddenly turned up in the village shop; frozen fish cut into neat fingers and covered in breadcrumbs. She had poured out some cooking oil but, fortunately, she hadn't yet popped them into the pan. The doorbell rang a second time. She laid the cardboard packet on the kitchen counter and went to see who it was.

A shadowy, distorted figure could be seen on the other side of the granite glass windows set into the front door. Could it be a travelling salesman at this time of the night? The village had recently had a veritable plague of them, as bad as the locusts that had descended on Egypt. Uneasily, she opened the door, glad that the security chain was still in place, and peered through the crack. Her brother, Magnus

Pye, stood in front of her. She could see his car, a pale blue Jaguar, parked in Winsley Terrace behind him.

'Magnus?' She was so surprised she didn't quite know what to say. He had only ever visited her here on two occasions, once when she was ill. He hadn't been at the funeral and she hadn't seen him since he got back from France.

'Hello, Clara. Can I come in?'

Clara was the name he had always called her, from the time they were children. The name reminded her of the boy he had once been and the man he had become. Why had he chosen to grow that awful beard? Hadn't anyone told him that it didn't suit him? That it made him look like some sort of mad aristocrat out of a cartoon? His eyes were slightly grey and she could see the veins in his cheeks. It was obvious he drank too much. And the way he was dressed! It was as if he had been playing golf. He was wearing baggy trousers tucked into his socks and a bright yellow cardigan. It was almost impossible to imagine that they were brother and sister – and more than that. Twins. Perhaps it was the different paths that life had taken them in their fifty-three years but they were nothing like each other any more, if they ever had been.

She closed the door, released the security chain, then opened it again. Magnus smiled – although the twitch of his lips could have signified anything – and stepped into the hallway. Clarissa was going to take him into the kitchen but then she remembered the box of frozen fish lying next to the hob and led him the other way instead. Left turn or right turn. Number 4, Winsley Terrace was not like Pye Hall. In this house there were very few choices.

The two of them went into the living room, a clean, comfortable space with a swirly carpet, a three-piece suite and a bay window. There was an electric fire and a television. For a moment, they stood there uncomfortably.

'How are you?' Magnus asked.

Why did he want to know? What did he care? 'I'm very well, thank you,' Clarissa said. 'How are you? How is Frances?'

'Oh. She's all right. She's up in London . . . shopping.'

There was another awkward pause. 'Can I get you something to drink?' Clarissa asked. Perhaps this was a social visit. She couldn't think of any other reason for her brother to be here.

'That would be nice. Yes. What have you got?'

'I have some sherry.'

'Thank you.'

Magnus sat down. Clarissa went over to the corner cupboard and took out a bottle. It had been there since Christmas. Did sherry go off? She poured two glasses, sniffed them, then carried them over. 'I was sorry to hear about the burglary,' she said.

Magnus shrugged. 'Yes. It wasn't a nice thing to come home to.'

'When did you get back from France?'

'Saturday evening. We walked in and found the whole place ransacked. It was that damn fool Brent, not fixing up the back door. I'm glad I've got rid of him. He'd been getting on my nerves for a while now. Not a bad gardener but I never did like his attitude.'

'Have you fired him?'

'I think it's time he moved on.'

Clarissa sipped her sherry. It clung to her lip as if reluctant to enter her mouth. 'I heard you lost some of the silver.'

'Most of it, actually. To tell you the truth, it's been a bit of a trying time – what with everything else.'

'You mean, Mary Blakiston.'

'Yes.'

'I was sorry not to see you at the funeral.'

'I know. It's a shame. I didn't know...'

'I thought the vicar wrote to you.'

'He did – but I didn't get his note until it was too late. Bloody French post office. Actually, that was what I wanted to talk to you about.' He hadn't touched his sherry. He looked around the room as if seeing it for the first time. 'Do you like it here?'

The question took her by surprise. 'It's all right,'

she said, and then more determinedly, 'Actually, I'm very happy here.'

'Are you?' He made it sound as if he didn't believe her.

'Well, yes.'

'Because, the thing is, you see, the Lodge House is empty now...'

'You mean the Lodge House at Pye Hall?'

'Yes.'

'And you want me to move in?'

'I was thinking about it on the plane home. It's a damn shame about Mary Blakiston. I was very fond of her, you know. She was a good cook, a good housekeeper but above all she was discreet. When I heard about this bloody accident, I knew she was going to be very hard to replace. And then I thought about you...'

Clarissa felt a cold shudder run the length of her body. 'Magnus, are you offering me her job?'

'Why not? You've hardly worked since you got back from America. I'm sure the school doesn't pay you very much and you could probably use the cash. If you moved into the Lodge House, you could sell this place and you might enjoy being back in the hall. You remember, you and me chasing around the lake? Croquet on the lawn! Of course, I'd have to talk about it with Frances. I haven't mentioned it to her yet. I thought I'd sound you out first. What do you say?'

'Can I think about it?'

'Absolutely. It was just a thought but it might actually work out very well.' He lifted his glass, had second thoughts and put it down again. 'Always good to see you, Clara. It would be marvellous if you moved back in.'

Somehow she managed to show him to the door and stood there watching as he climbed into his Jaguar and drove away. Clarissa's breath was not coming easily. Even speaking to him had taken a gigantic effort. She felt wave after wave of nausea spreading through her. There was no feeling in her hands. She had heard the expression 'numb with anger' but she had never realised it could be a reality.

He had offered her a job, working as his skivvy. Mopping floors and doing the washing up – dear God! She was his sister. She had been born in that house. She had lived there until she was in her twenties, eating the same food as him. She had only moved out after the death of their parents and Magnus's wedding, the two events following, shamefully fast, one upon the other. Ever since that day, she had been nothing to him. And now this!

There was a reproduction of Leonardo da Vinci's *The Virgin of the Rocks* in the hallway. The Virgin Mary might have turned her head from John the Baptist and looked in alarm as Clarissa Pye stomped up to the first floor with vengeance in her eyes.

Certainly, she wasn't going there to pray.

9

By half past eight, darkness had fallen on Saxby-on-Avon.

Brent had decided to work late. Quite apart from the lawns and all the weeding, there were fifty varieties of rose to be deadheaded and the yew trees to be trimmed. When he had docked the wheelbarrow and his various tools in the stable, he walked round the lake and out through Dingle Dell, following a path that would take him close to the vicarage and on to the Ferryman, the village's second pub, which stood at the lower crossroads.

It was just as he reached the edge of the wood that something made him turn back. He had heard something. He quickly ran his eyes over the house itself, squinting through the darkness. There were a couple of lights burning on the ground floor but no sign of any movement. As far as he knew, Sir Magnus Pye was in alone. He'd driven back from the village an hour ago but his wife was away for the day, in London. Her car was still out of the garage.

He saw a figure, walking up the pathway from the main gate. It was a man, on his own. Brent had good eyesight and the moon was out but he couldn't be sure if it was anyone from the village. It was hard to tell as the visitor was wearing a hat that concealed most of his face. There was something about the way he was walking that was a little odd. He was half-stooping, keeping to the shadows, almost as if he didn't want to be seen. It was a late hour to be visiting Sir Magnus. Brent considered turning back. There'd been that burglary, the same day as the funeral, and everyone was on the alert. It wouldn't take him a minute to go back across the lawn and check that everything was all right.

He decided against it. After all, it wasn't any business of his who visited Pye Hall and following the discussion he'd had with Sir Magnus that same afternoon, after what Sir Magnus had said to him, he certainly felt no loyalty towards his employer, or his wife. It wasn't as if they'd ever looked after him. They'd taken him for granted. Brent had been working from eight in the morning until the middle of the night for years now with never a word of thanks and at a salary that was frankly laughable. He wouldn't normally go drinking in the middle of the week but as it happened, he had ten bob in his pocket which he was going to spend on fish and chips and a couple of pints. The Ferryman stood at the bottom end of the village. It was a shabby, ramshackle place, much less genteel than the Queen's Arms. They knew him there. He always sat at the same seat near the window. Over the next couple of hours he might exchange half a dozen words with the barman but for Brent that amounted to a conversation. He put the visitor out of his mind and continued on his way.

He had another strange encounter before he reached the pub twenty-five minutes later. As he emerged from the woods, he came upon a single, slightly dishevelled woman walking towards him and recognised Henrietta Osborne, the vicar's wife. She must have come from her house, which was just up the road, and she had left in a hurry. She had thrown on a pale blue parka, a man's, presumably her husband's. Her hair was untidy. She looked distracted.

She saw him. 'Oh, good evening, Brent,' she said. 'You're out late.'

'I'm going to the pub.'

'Are you? I was just wondering . . . I was looking for the vicar. I don't suppose you've seen him?'

'No.' Brent shook his head, wondering why the vicar would be out at this time of the night. Had the two of them had a row? Then he remembered. 'There was someone up at Pye Hall, Mrs Osborne. I suppose it might have been him.'

'Pye Hall?'

'They were just going in.'

'I can't imagine why he'd want to go up there.' She sounded nervous.

'I don't know who it was.' Brent shrugged.

'Well, good night.' Henrietta turned and went back the way she had come, heading towards her home.

An hour later, Brent was sitting with his fish and chips, sipping his second pint. The room was thick with cigarette smoke. Music had been playing loudly on the jukebox but there was a pause between discs and he heard the bicycle as it went past, heading up towards the crossroads. He glanced out and saw it as it went past. The sound it made was unmistakeable. So he had been right. The vicar had been down at Pye Hall and now he was on his way home. He had been there for quite a while. Brent thought briefly about his meeting with Henrietta Osborne. She'd been worried about something. What was going on? Well, it was nothing to do with him. He turned away and put it all out of his head.

But he would be reminded of it soon enough.

10

Atticus Pünd read the story in *The Times* the following morning.

BARONET MURDERED

Police were called to the Wiltshire village of Saxby-on-Avon following the death of Sir Magnus Pye, a wealthy local landowner. Detective Inspector Raymond Chubb, speaking on behalf of the Bath constabulary, confirmed that the death is being treated as murder. Sir Magnus is survived by his wife, Frances, Lady Pye, and his son, Frederick.

He was in the sitting room at Tanner Court, smoking a cigarette. James Fraser had brought him the newspaper and a cup of tea. Now he returned, carrying an ashtray.

'Have you seen the front page?' Pünd asked.

'Absolutely! It's terrible. Poor Lady Mountbatten...'

'I'm sorry?'

'Her car was stolen! And in the middle of Hyde Park!'

Pünd smiled, a little sadly. 'That was not the story to which I referred.' He turned it round to show to his assistant.

Fraser read the paragraphs. 'Pye!' he exclaimed. 'Wasn't that—'

'It was indeed. Yes. He was the employer of Mary Blakiston. His name was mentioned in this room just a few days ago.'

'Quite a coincidence!'

'It is possible, yes. Coincidences do occur. But in this instance, I am not so sure. We are talking here of death, of two unexpected deaths in the same house. Do you not find that intriguing?'

'You're not going to go down, are you?'

Atticus Pünd considered.

It had certainly not been in his mind to take on any more work. The time remaining to him simply would not allow it. According to Dr Benson, he had at best three months of reasonable health, which might not even be enough to catch a killer. Anyway, he had already made certain decisions. He intended to use that time to put his affairs in order. There was the question of his will, the disbursement of his home and property. He had left Germany with almost nothing of his own but there was the collection of eighteenth-century Meissen figurines which had belonged to his father and which had, miraculously, survived the war. He would like to see them in a museum and had already written to the

Victoria and Albert in Kensington. It would comfort him to know that the musician, the preacher, the soldier, the seamstress and all the other members of his little family would still be together after he had gone. They were, after all, the only family that he had.

He would make a bequest for James Fraser who had been with him during his last five cases and whose loyalty and good humour had never failed him, even if he had never helped very much when it came to the investigation of crime. There were various charities that he wished to benefit, in particular the Metropolitan and City Police Orphans Fund. Above all, there were the papers relating to his masterwork, *The Landscape of Criminal Investigation*. It would have taken him another year to finish it. There was no possibility of presenting it to a publisher in its present state. But he had thought that he might be able to collate all his notes, along with the newspaper clippings, letters and police reports, so that some student of criminology might be able to assemble the whole thing at a future date. It would be sad to have done so much work for nothing.

These had been his plans. But if there was one thing that life had taught him, it was the futility of making plans. Life had its own agenda.

Now he turned to Fraser. 'I told Miss Sanderling that I was unable to help her because I had no official reason to present myself at Pye Hall,' he said. 'But now a reason has presented itself and I see that our old friend Detective Inspector Chubb is involved.' Pünd smiled. The old light had come into his eyes. 'Pack the bags, James, and bring round the car. We are leaving at once.'

THREE

A Girl

1

Atticus Pünd had never learned to drive. He was not wilfully old-fashioned. He kept himself informed of all the latest scientific developments and would not hesitate to use them – in the treatment of his illness, for example. But there was something about the pace of change that concerned him, the sudden onrush of machines in every shape and size. As televisions, typewriters, fridges and washing machines became more ubiquitous, as even the fields became crowded with electric pylons, he sometimes wondered if there might not be hidden costs for a humanity that had already been sorely tested in his lifetime. Nazism, after all, had been a machine in itself. He was in no rush to join the new technological age.

And so, when he had bowed to the inevitable and agreed that he needed a private car, he had left the whole business to James Fraser who had gone out and returned with a Vauxhall Velox four-door saloon, a good choice Pünd had to admit; sturdy and reliable with plenty of space. Fraser of course was boyishly excited. It had a six-cylinder engine. It would go from zero to sixty in just twenty-two seconds. The heater could be set to de-ice the windscreen in the winter. Pünd was just happy that it would get him where he wanted to go and – a sober, unremarkable grey – it would not scream out that he had arrived.

The Vauxhall, with James Fraser at the wheel, pulled in outside Pye Hall after the three-hour drive from London, which they had taken without stopping. There were two police cars parked on the gravel. Pünd got out and stretched his legs, grateful to be released from the confined space. His eyes travelled across the front of the building, taking in its grandeur, its elegance, its very Englishness. He could tell at once that it had belonged to the same family for many generations. It had an unchanging quality, a sense of permanence.

'Here's Chubb,' Fraser muttered.

The familiar face of the detective inspector appeared at the front door. Fraser had telephoned him before they left and Chubb had evidently been awaiting their arrival. Plump and cheerful, with his Oliver Hardy moustache, he was dressed in an ill-fitting suit with one of his wife's latest knitting creations below, this one a particularly unfortunate mauve cardigan. He had put on weight. That was the impression he always gave. Pünd had once remarked that he had the look of a man who has just finished a particularly good meal. He came bounding down the front steps, evidently pleased to see them.

'Herr Pünd!' he exclaimed. It was always 'herr' and somehow Chubb implied that that there was some failing in Pünd's character being born in Germany. After all, he might have been saying, let's not forget who won the war. 'I was very surprised to hear from you. Don't tell me you've had dealings with the late Sir Magnus.'

'Not at all, Detective Inspector,' Pünd replied. 'I had never met him and only knew of his death from the newspapers this morning.'

'So what brings you here?' His eyes travelled over to James Fraser and seemed to notice him for the first time.

'It is a strange coincidence.' In fact, Fraser had often heard the detective remark that there was no such thing as a coincidence. There was a chapter in *The Landscape of Criminal Investigation* where he had expressed the belief that everything in life had a pattern and that a coincidence was simply the moment when that pattern became briefly visible. 'A young lady from this village came to see me yesterday. She told me of a death that had taken place in this very house two weeks ago—'

'Would that be the housekeeper, Mary Blakiston?'

'Yes. She was concerned that certain people were making false accusations about what had occurred.'

'You mean, they thought the old girl had been deliberately killed?' Chubb took out a packet of Players, the same brand he always smoked, and lit one. The index and third fingers of his right hand were permanently stained – like old piano keys. 'Well, I can put your mind at rest on that one, Herr Pünd. I looked into it myself and I can tell you it was an accident pure and simple. She was doing the hoovering at the top of the stairs. She got tangled up in the wire and tumbled down the full length. Solid flagstone at the bottom, unlucky for her! Nobody had any reason to kill her and anyway she was locked in the house, on her own.'

'And what of the death of Sir Magnus?'

'Well, that's quite a different kettle of fish. You can come in and take a butcher's if you like – and that's the right word for it. I'm going to finish this first, if you don't mind. It's pretty nasty in there.' He deliberately screwed the cigarette into his lips and inhaled. 'At the moment, we're treating it as a burglary that went wrong. That seems the most obvious conclusion.'

'The most obvious conclusions are the ones I try to avoid.'

'Well, you have your own methods, Herr Pünd, and I won't say they haven't been helpful in the past. What we've got here is a local land owner, been in the village all his life. It's early days but I can't see that anyone would have a grudge against him. Now, someone came up here around half past eight last night. He was actually spotted by Brent, the groundsman, as he was finishing work. He hasn't been able to give us a description but his first impression was that it wasn't anyone from the village.'

'How could he know that?' Fraser asked. He had been ignored up until this moment and felt a need to remind the others he was still there.

'Well, you know how it is. It's easier to recognise someone if you've seen them before. Even if you can't see their face, there's something about the shape of their body or the way they walk. Brent was fairly sure this was a stranger. And anyway, there was something about the way this man went up to the house. It was as if he didn't want to be seen.'

'You believe this man was a burglar,' Pünd said.

'The house had already been burgled once just a few days before.' Chubb sighed as if it irritated him having to explain it all again. 'After the death of the housekeeper, they had to smash a back window to get in. They should have got it reglazed but they didn't and a few days after that someone broke in. They got away with a nice little haul of antique coins and jewellery – Roman, would you believe it. Maybe they had a look around while they were there. There's a safe in Sir Magnus's study which they might have been unable to open but now they knew it was there, they could come back and have a second crack at it. They thought the house was still empty. Sir Magnus surprised them – and there you have it.'

'You say he was killed violently.'

'That's an understatement.' Chubb needed to fortify himself with another lungful of smoke. 'There's a suit of armour in the main hall. You'll see it in a minute. Complete with sword.' He swallowed. 'That's what they used. They took his head clean off.'

Pünd considered this for a moment. 'Who found him?'

'His wife. She'd been on a shopping trip to London and she got home at around nine fifteen.'

'The shops closed late.' Pünd half-smiled.

'Well, maybe she had dinner too. Anyway, as she arrived, she saw a car driving off. She's not sure of the make but it was green and she saw a couple of letters off the registration plate. FP. As luck would have it, they're her own initials. She came in and found him lying at the foot of the stairs almost exactly where the body of his housekeeper had been the week before. But not all of him. His head had rolled across the floor and landed next to the fireplace. I'm not sure you'll be able to talk to her for a while. She's in hospital in Bath, still under sedation. She's the one who called the police and I've heard a recording of the conversation. Poor woman, she can hardly get the words out, screaming and sobbing. If this was a murder, you can certainly strike her off the list of suspects unless she's the world's greatest actress.'

'The body, I take it, has gone.'

'Yes. We removed it last night. Needed a strong stomach, I can tell you.'

'Was anything removed from this house on this second occasion, Detective Inspector?'

'It's hard to be sure. We'll need to interview Lady Pye when she's up to it. But on first appearance, it doesn't seem so. You can come in, if you like, Herr Pünd. You're not here in any official capacity, of course, and maybe I should have a quick word with the Assistant Commissioner, but I'm sure no harm can come of it. And if anything does spring to mind, I can rely on you to let me know.'

'Of course, Detective Inspector,' Pünd said although Fraser knew that he would do no such thing. He had accompanied Pünd on five separate enquiries and knew that the detective had a maddening habit of keeping everything under his hat until it suited him to reveal the truth.

They climbed three steps but Pünd stopped before he entered the front door. He crouched down. 'Now that is strange,' he said.

Chubb gazed at him in disbelief. 'Are you going to tell me that I've missed something?' he demanded. 'And we haven't even gone inside!'

'It may have no relevance at all, Detective Inspector,' he replied, soothingly. 'But you see the flower bed beside the door...'

Fraser glanced down. There were flower beds running all the way along the front of the house, divided by the steps that led up from the driveway.

'Petunias, if I'm not mistaken,' Chubb remarked.

'Of that I am unsure. But do you not see the handprint?'

Both Chubb and Fraser looked more closely. It was true. Somebody had stuck their hand in the soft earth just to the left of the door. From the size of it, Fraser would have said that it belonged to a man. The fingers were outstretched. It was very odd, Fraser thought. A footprint would have been more conventional.

'It probably belongs to the gardener,' Chubb said. 'I can't think of any other explanation.'

'And you are probably right.' Pünd sprang back to his feet and continued forward.

The door led directly into a large, rectangular room with a staircase in front of them and two more doors, left and right. Fraser saw at once where the body of Sir Magnus had lain and he felt the usual stirring in the pit of his stomach. There was a Persian rug, gleaming darkly, still soaked with blood. The blood had spread onto the flagstones, stretching towards the fireplace, encircling the legs of one of the leather chairs that stood there. The whole room stank of it. A sword lay diagonally, with its hilt close to the stairs, its blade pointing towards the head of a deer that looked down with glass eyes, perhaps the only witness to what had occurred. The rest of the armour, an empty knight, stood beside one of the doors with a living room beyond. Fraser had been to many crime scenes with his employer. Often he had seen the bodies lying there – stabbed, shot, drowned, whatever. But it struck him that there was something particularly macabre about this one, almost Jacobean with the dark wooden panelling and the minstrel gallery.

'Sir Magnus knew the person who killed him,' Pünd muttered.

'How can you possibly know?' Fraser asked.

'The position of the suit of armour and the layout of the room.' Pünd gestured. 'See for yourself, James. The entrance is behind us. The armour and the sword are further inside the room. If the killer had come to the front door and wished to attack Sir Magnus, it would have been necessary to go round him to reach the weapon and at that moment, if the door was open, Sir Magnus could have made good his escape. However, it seems more likely that Sir Magnus was showing someone out. They come in from the living room. Sir Magnus is first. His killer is behind him. As he opens the front door, he does not see that his guest has drawn out the sword. He turns, sees the guest moving towards him, perhaps pleads with him. The killer strikes. And all is as we see it.'

'It still might have been a stranger.'

'You would invite a stranger into the house, late in the evening? I do not think so.' Pünd looked around him. 'There is a painting missing,' he remarked.

Fraser followed his eyes and saw that it was true. There was a bare hook on the wall next to the door and a section of the woodwork had faded slightly, a telltale rectangle that clearly delineated the missing work of art.

'Do you think it could be relevant?' Fraser asked.

'Everything is relevant,' Pünd replied. He took one last look around him. 'There is nothing more for me to see here. It would be interesting to learn exactly how the housekeeper was discovered when she died two weeks ago but we will come to that in due course. Can we proceed into the living room?'

'Of course,' Chubb said. 'The door leads into the living room and Sir Magnus had his study on the other side. There's a letter we found there that may interest you.'

The living room had a much more feminine feel than the entrance hall with an oyster pink carpet, plush curtains with a floral pattern, comfortable sofas and occasional tables. There were photographs everywhere. Fraser picked one up and examined the three people standing together in front of the house. A round-faced man with a beard, wearing an old-fashioned suit. Next to him, a few inches taller than him, a woman staring into the camera lens with a look of impatience. And a boy, in school uniform, scowling. It was obviously a family photograph if not a particularly happy one: Sir Magnus, Lady Pye, and their son.

A uniformed policeman stood, guarding the door on the far side. They went straight through into a room dominated by an antique desk set square between two bookshelves with windows opposite giving views across the front lawn and down to the lake. The floor was polished, wooden boards partly covered by another rug. Two armchairs faced into the room with an antique globe between them. The far wall was dominated by a fireplace, and it was evident from the ashes and charred wood that someone had recently lit a fire. Everything smelled faintly of cigar smoke. Fraser noticed a humidor and a heavy glass ashtray on a side table. The wooden panelling from the entrance hall was picked up again with several more oil paintings which might have hung here as long as the house itself. Pünd went over to one of them – a picture of a horse in front of a stable, very much in the style of Stubbs. He had noticed it because it was slightly perpendicular to the wall, like a half-open door.

'It was like that when we came in,' Chubb remarked.

Pünd took a pen out of his pocket and used it to hook the painting, pulling it towards him. It was hinged along one side and concealed a very solid-looking safe set in the wall.

'We don't know the combination,' Chubb continued. 'I'm sure Lady Pye will tell us when she's up to it.'

Pünd nodded and transferred his attention to the desk. It was quite likely that Sir Magnus had been sitting here in the hours before he died and that, therefore, the papers strewn across the surface might have something to say about what had actually happened.

'There's a gun in the top drawer,' Chubb said. 'An old service revolver. It hasn't been fired – but it's loaded. According to Lady Pye, he usually kept it in the safe. He might have brought it out because of the burglary.'

'Or it could be that Sir Magnus had reason to be nervous.' Pünd opened the drawer and glanced at the gun. It was indeed a .38 Webley Revolver. And Chubb was right. It had not been used.

He closed the drawer and turned his attention to the surface of the desk, beginning with a series of drawings, architectural blueprints from a company called Larkin Gadwall based in Bath. They showed a cluster of houses, twelve in total, stretching out in two lines of six. A number of letters were piled up next to it, correspondence with the local council, a paper trail that must ultimately lead to the granting of planning permission. And here was the proof of it, a smart brochure with the heading: Dingle Drive, Saxby-on-Avon. All of these occupied one corner of the desk. A telephone stood at the other, with a notepad next to it. Someone, presumably Sir Magnus, had written in pencil – the pencil itself lay nearby.

ASHTON H
Mw
A GIRL

The words were written neatly at the top of the page but after that, Sir Magnus must have become agitated. There were several lines crossing each other, an angry scrawl. Pünd handed the page to Fraser.

'A girl?' Fraser asked.

'These would seem to be notes taken down from a telephone conversation,' Pünd suggested. 'Mw may stand for something. Note that the w is in lower case. And the girl? Perhaps it is the subject of which they spoke.'

'Well, he doesn't seem to have been too pleased about it.'

'Indeed not.' Finally, Pünd turned to an empty envelope and next to it the letter that Chubb must have been referring to and which lay at the very centre of the desk. There was no address, just a name – Sir Magnus Pye – handwritten in black ink. It had been roughly torn open. Pünd took out a handkerchief and used it to pick up the envelope. He examined the paper carefully, then replaced it and, with equal care, picked up the letter beside it. This was typewritten and addressed to Sir Magnus Pye with a date – 28 July 1955 – the actual day that the murder had taken place. He read:

You think you can get away with it? This village was here before you and it will be here after you and if you think you can ruin it with your bilding and your money-making

> you are so, so wrong. You think again, you bastard, if you want to live here. If you want to live.

The letter was not signed. He laid it back on the desk so that Fraser could read it.

'Whoever wrote this can't spell "building",' Fraser remarked.

'He may also be a homicidal maniac,' Pünd added, gently. 'This letter would seem to have been delivered yesterday. Sir Magnus was killed a matter of hours after it arrived – which is what was promised.' He turned to the Detective Inspector. 'I would imagine this relates in some way to the diagrams,' he said.

'That's right,' Chubb agreed. 'I've put a call in to these people, Larkin Gadwall. They're developers in Bath and it seems they had some sort of deal with Sir Magnus. I'll be heading their way this afternoon and you can join me if you like.'

'You're most generous.' Pünd nodded. His attention was still focused on the letter. 'There is something about this that I find a little peculiar,' he said.

'I think I'm ahead of you there, Pünd.' The detective beamed, pleased with himself. 'The envelope is handwritten even though the letter is typed. You'd have thought that would be a dead giveaway if the sender wanted to hide his or her identity. My guess is they sealed the letter first, then realised they needed to put the name on the front but it wouldn't fit into the typewriter. I've done the same myself often enough.'

'You may well be right, Detective Inspector. But that was not the peculiarity that had occurred to me.'

Chubb waited for him to continue but, standing on the other side of the desk, James Fraser knew that he would do no such thing. He was right. Pünd had already turned his attention to the fireplace. He took the pen back out of his jacket pocket and rummaged around in the ashes, found something, carefully separated it from the rest. Fraser went over and looked down at a scrap of paper, barely larger than a cigarette card, blackened at the edges. This was the sort of moment he loved, working with Pünd. It would never have occurred to Chubb to examine the fireplace. The policeman would have taken a cursory look at the room, called for forensics and then been on his way. But here was a clue and one that might crack the case wide open. The fragment might have a name written on it. Even a few letters would provide a handwriting sample which might indicate who had been in the room. Sadly, however, in this case, the paper was blank although Pünd did not seem dispirited. Far from it.

'You see, Fraser,' he exclaimed. 'There is a slight discolouration, a stain. And, I think, it will be possible to discern at least part of a fingerprint.'

'A fingerprint?' Chubb had heard the word and came over.

Fraser looked more closely and saw that Pünd was right. The stain was dark brown in colour and his immediate thought was spilled coffee. But at the same time, he could see no obvious relevance. Anyone could have torn up a sheet of paper and thrown it in the fire. Sir Magnus might well have done it himself.

'I'll get the lab to have a look at it,' Chubb said. 'And they can run their eye over that letter too. It's just possible I may have jumped to conclusions, thinking about that burglar.'

Pünd nodded. He straightened up. 'We must find accommodation,' he announced, suddenly.

'You're planning to stay?'

'With your permission, Detective Inspector.'

'Absolutely. I believe they have rooms at the Queen's Arms. It's a pub next to the church but they do B & B too. If you want a hotel, you'd be better off in Bath.'

'It will be more convenient to remain in the village,' Pünd replied.

Fraser sighed inwardly, imagining the lumpy beds, ugly furniture and spluttering bath taps that always seemed to accompany local hospitality. He had no money himself apart from what Pünd paid him and that was little enough. But that didn't prevent him from having expensive tastes. 'Do you want me to check it out?' he asked.

'We can go there together.' He turned to Chubb. 'What time will you be travelling to Bath?'

'I have an appointment at Larkin Gadwall at two o'clock and we can go straight from there to the hospital and see Lady Pye, if you like.'

'That is excellent, Detective Inspector. I must say that it is a great pleasure to be working with you again.'

'Likewise. I'm very glad to see you, Herr Pünd. Headless bodies and all that! The moment I got the call, I knew this was right up your street.'

Lighting another cigarette, he made his way back to his car.

2

To Fraser's chagrin, the Queen's Arms had two rooms vacant and without even going upstairs to examine them, Pünd took them both. They were as bad as he had imagined, too, with sloping floors and windows too small for the walls in which they were set. He had a view of the village square. Pünd looked out over the cemetery but made no complaint. On the contrary, there was something about the view that seemed to amuse him. Nor did he complain about the lack of comfort. When he had first started working at Tanner Court, Fraser had been surprised to discover that the detective slept in a single bed, more a cot really, with a metal frame, the blankets neatly folded back. Although Pünd had once been married, he never spoke of his wife and showed no further interest in the opposite sex. But even so, such austerity in a smart London flat seemed more than a little eccentric.

The two of them had lunch together downstairs, then stepped outside. There was a small crowd of people gathered around the bus shelter in the village square but Fraser got the impression that they were not waiting for a bus. Something had clearly interested them. They were talking in an animated sort of way. He was sure that Pünd would want to go over and see what the fuss was about but at that moment a figure appeared in the cemetery, walking towards them. It was the vicar. That much was obvious from his clerical shirt and dog collar. He was tall and lanky with unkempt, black hair. Fraser watched as he picked up a bicycle that had been resting against the gate and guided it out onto the road, the wheels creaking noisily with every turn.

'The vicar!' Pünd exclaimed. 'In an English village, he is the one man who knows everyone.'

'Not everyone goes to church,' Fraser returned.

'They do not need to. He makes it his business to know even the atheists and the agnostics.'

They went over to him and intercepted him before he could make his getaway. Pünd introduced himself.

'Oh yes,' the vicar exclaimed, blinking in the sunlight. He frowned. 'I know the name, I'm sure. The detective? You're here, of course, because of Sir Magnus Pye. What a terrible, terrible business. A small community like Saxby-on-Avon cannot be prepared, in any way, for such an event and it is going to be very hard for us to come to terms with it. But forgive me. I haven't told you my name. Robin Osborne. I'm the vicar here at St Botolph's. Well, you had probably worked that out for yourself, given your line of work!'

He laughed and it occurred to Pünd – it had even occurred to Fraser – that this was an exceptionally nervous man, that he was almost unable to stop talking and that the words were pouring out of him in an attempt to cover up whatever was actually passing through his mind.

'I would imagine that you knew Sir Magnus quite well,' Pünd said.

'Passably well. Yes. Sadly, I saw him less than I would have liked. Not a very religious man. He came to services all too seldom.' Osborne drew himself in. 'Are you here to investigate the crime, Mr Pünd?'

Pünd replied that this was the case.

'I'm a little surprised that our own police force should

need any extra assistance – not of course, that it is in any way unwelcome. I already spoke to Detective Inspector Chubb this morning. He suggested to me that it may have been an intruder. Burglars. You are aware, I'm sure, that Pye Hall was targeted very recently.'

'Pye Hall appears to have had more than it's fair share of misfortune.'

'The death of Mary Blakiston, you mean?' Osborne pointed. 'She is resting just over there. I officiated myself.'

'Was Sir Magnus popular in the village?'

The question took the vicar by surprise and he struggled to find the right answer. 'There may have been those who envied him. He had considerable wealth. And then, of course, there was the matter of Dingle Dell. It would be true to say that it aroused strong feelings.'

'Dingle Dell?'

'It's a strip of woodland. He had sold it.'

'To Larkin Gadwall,' Fraser interceded.

'Yes. Those are the developers, I believe.'

'Would you be surprised to learn, Mr Osborne, that Sir Magnus had received a death threat as a direct result of his intentions?'

'A death threat?' The vicar was more flustered than ever. 'I would be very surprised. I'm sure nobody around here would send such a thing. This is a very peaceful village. The people who live here aren't like that at all.'

'And yet you spoke of strong feelings.'

'People were upset. But that's not the same thing.'

'When did you last see Sir Magnus?'

Robin Osborne was keen to be on his way. He was holding his bicycle as if it were an animal, straining at the leash. And this last question offended him. It was clear, in his eyes. Was he being suspected of something? 'I haven't seen him for a while,' he replied. 'He was unable to attend Mary Blakiston's burial which was a pity but he was in the south of France. And before that, I was away myself.'

'Where?'

'On holiday. With my wife.' Pünd waited for more and

Osborne obligingly filled in the silence. 'We had a week together in Devonshire. Actually, she'll be waiting for me right now, so if you don't mind . . .' With a half-smile, he pushed his way between them, the gears of his bicycle grinding.

'I'd say that he was nervous about something,' Fraser muttered.

'Yes, James. He was certainly a man with something to hide.'

As the detective and his assistant made their way towards their car, Robin Osborne was cycling as quickly as he could down to the vicarage. He knew he had not been entirely honest: not lying but omitting certain aspects of the truth. It was true, however, that Henrietta was waiting for him and would have expected him some time ago.

'Where have you been?' she asked as he took his place in the kitchen. She served a home-made quiche with a bean salad and sat down next to him.

'Oh. I was just in the village.' Osborne mouthed a silent grace. 'I met that detective,' he went on, barely leaving time for the amen. 'Atticus Pünd.'

'Who?'

'You must have heard of him. He's quite famous. A private detective. You remember that school in Marlborough? There was a teacher who was killed during a play. He worked on that.'

'But why do we need a private detective? I thought it was a burglar.'

'It seems the police may have been wrong.' Osborne hesitated. 'He thinks it has something to do with the Dell.'

'The Dell!'

'That's what he thinks.'

They ate in silence. Neither of them seemed to be enjoying the food. Then Henrietta spoke, quite suddenly. 'Where did you go last night, Robin?' she asked.

'What?'

'You know what I'm talking about. Sir Magnus being killed.'

'Why on earth would you ask me such a thing?' Osborne put down his knife and fork. He took a sip of water. 'I felt anger,' he explained. 'It's one of the mortal sins. And there were things in my heart that were . . . that should not have been there. I was upset because of the news but that's no excuse. I needed to spend time alone so I went up to the church.'

'But you were gone such a long time.'

'It wasn't easy for me, Henrietta. I needed the time.'

She wasn't going to speak, then thought again. 'Robin, I was so worried about you. I came out looking for you. As a matter of fact, I bumped into Brent and he said he'd seen someone going up to the hall—'

'What are you suggesting, Hen? Do you think I went up to Pye Hall and killed him? Took his head off with a sword? Is that what you're saying?'

'No. Of course not. It's just that you were so angry.'

'You're being ridiculous. I didn't go anywhere near the house. I didn't see anything.'

There was something else Henrietta wanted to say. The bloodstain on her husband's sleeve. She had seen it with her own eyes. The following morning she had taken the shirt and washed it in boiling water and bleach. It was on the washing line even now, drying in the sun. She wanted to ask him whose blood it was. She wanted to know how it had got there. But she didn't dare. She couldn't accuse him. Such a thing was impossible.

The two of them finished their lunch in silence.

3

Sitting in a reproduction captain's chair with its curved back and swivelling seat, Johnny Whitehead was also thinking about the murder. Indeed, throughout the morning he had thought of little else, blundering around like a bull in his own china shop, rearranging objects for no reason and smoking incessantly. Gemma Whitehead had finally lost her temper with him when he had knocked over and broken a nice little Meissen soap dish, which, though chipped, had still been priced at nine shillings and sixpence.

'What is the matter with you?' she demanded. 'You're like a bear with a sore head today. And that's your fourth cigarette. Why don't you go out and get some fresh air?'

'I don't want to go out,' Johnny said, moodily.

'What's wrong?'

Johnny stubbed out his cigarette in a Royal Doulton ashtray shaped like a cow and priced at six shillings. 'What do you think?' he snapped.

'I don't know. That's why I'm asking you.'

'Sir Magnus Pye! That's what's wrong.' He stared at the smoke still rising from the twisted cigarette butt. 'Why did someone have to go and murder him? Now we've got the police in the village, knocking on doors, asking questions. They'll be here soon enough.'

'What does it matter? They can ask us anything they want.' There was a fractional pause, long enough to make itself felt. 'Can't they?'

'Of course they can.'

She examined him, a sharp look in her eye. 'You haven't been up to anything, have you, Johnny?'

'What are you talking about?' There was a wounded tone in his voice. 'Why do you even ask that? Of course I haven't been up to anything. What could I possibly get up to, stuck out here in the sticks?' It was the old argument: city versus countryside, Saxby versus almost anywhere else in the world. They'd had it often enough. But even as he spoke the words, he was remembering how Mary Blakiston had confronted him all too recently in this very building, how much she had known about him. She had died suddenly and so had Sir Magnus, both of them within two weeks of each other. That wasn't a coincidence and the police certainly wouldn't think so. Johnny knew how they worked. They would already be drawing up files, looking at everyone who lived in the neighbourhood. It wouldn't be too long before they came after him.

Gemma walked over and sat down next to him, laying a hand on his arm. Although she was so much smaller than him, so much frailer, she was the one with the strength and they both knew it. She had stood by him when they'd had their troubles in London. She had written to him every week, long letters full of optimism and good cheer, when he was 'away'. And when he had finally come home, it had been her decision that had brought them to Saxby-on-Avon. She had seen the antique shop advertised in a magazine and had thought it would allow Johnny to maintain some of the practices of his old life whilst providing a stable, honest basis for the new.

Leaving London had not been easy, especially for a boy who had lived his whole life within earshot of the Bow Bells, but Johnny had seen the sense of it and had reluctantly gone along with it. But she knew that he had been diminished by it. Loud, cheerful, trusting, irascible Johnny Whitehead could never be completely at home in a community where everyone was being endlessly judged and where disapproval could mean total ostracism. Had it been wrong of her to bring him here? She still allowed him trips back to the city although they always made her nervous. She didn't ask him what he got up to and he didn't tell her. But this time it was different. He had been there only a few days earlier. Could that visit possibly be connected with what had happened?

'What did you do in London?' she asked.

'Why do you want to know?'

'I was just wondering.'

'I saw some of the blokes – Derek and Colin. We had lunch, a few drinks. You should have come.'

'You wouldn't want me there.'

'They asked after you. I went past the old house. It's flats now. It made me think. We had a lot of happy times there, you and me.' Johnny patted the back of his wife's hand, noticing how thin it had become. The older she got, the less of her there seemed to be.

'I've had enough of London for one lifetime, Johnny.' She withdrew her hand. 'And as for Derek and Colin, they were never your friends. They didn't stand by you when things went belly-up. I did.'

Johnny scowled. 'You're right,' he said. 'I'm going out for a walk. Half an hour. That'll blow away the cobwebs.'

'I'll come with you, if you like.'

'No. You'd better mind the shop.' Nobody had come in since they had opened that morning. That was another thing about murder. It discouraged the tourists.

She watched him leave, heard the bell on the door make its familiar jangle. Gemma had thought they would be all right coming here, leaving their former lives behind them. No matter what Johnny had said at the time, it had been the right decision. But two deaths, one following hard upon the other, had changed everything. It was as if those old shadows had somehow stretched out and found them.

Mary Blakiston had been here. For the first time in a very, very long time the housekeeper had come to the shop and, when challenged, Johnny had lied about it. He had claimed she was buying someone a present but Gemma knew that wasn't true. If Mary had wanted a present she would have gone into Bath, to Woolworth or Boots the Chemist. And less than a week later she had died. Was there some link between the two events and, if so, was there a further link that led to the death of Sir Magnus Pye?

Gemma Whitehead had come to Saxby-on-Avon because she thought it would be safe. Sitting alone, in the dingy shop surrounded by hundreds of unnecessary items, trinkets and knick-knacks which nobody seemed to want and which, today anyway, nobody had come in to buy, she wished with all her heart that she and Johnny could be anywhere else.

4

Everyone in the village thought they knew who had killed Sir Magnus Pye. Unfortunately, no two theories were the same.

It was well known that Sir Magnus and Lady Pye were at loggerheads. They were seldom seen together. If they turned up at church, they kept a distance between them. According to Gareth Kite, the landlord of the Ferryman, Sir Magnus had been having an affair with his housekeeper, Mary Blakiston. Lady Pye had killed both of them – although how she had managed the first death when she was on holiday in France, he hadn't explained.

No, no. It was Robert Blakiston who was the killer. Hadn't he threatened his mother just days before she died? He had killed her because he was angry with her and had gone on to kill Sir Magnus when he had somehow discovered the truth. And then there was Brent. The groundsman lived alone. He was definitely peculiar. There were rumours that Sir Magnus had fired him the very day that he had died. Or what about the stranger who had come to the funeral? Nobody wore a hat like that unless it was to conceal their identity. Even Joy Sanderling, that nice girl who worked for Dr Redwing, was suspected. The strange announcement that had gone up on the notice board next to the bus shelter definitely showed that there was more to her than met the eye. Mary Blakiston had taken against her. So she had died. Sir Magnus Pye had found out. He had died too.

And then there was the destruction of Dingle Dell. Although the police had not released details of the threatening message that had been found on Sir Magnus's desk, it was well known how much anger the proposed development had provoked. The longer you had lived in the village, the more angry you were likely to be and by this logic, old Jeff Weaver, who was eighty-three and who had tended the churchyard for as long as anyone could remember, became the number one suspect. The vicar, too, had plenty to lose. The vicarage backed directly onto the proposed development site and it had often been remarked how he and Mrs Osborne liked to lose themselves in the wood.

Curiously, one resident who had every reason to kill Sir Magnus but whose name had been left out of the loop, was Clarissa Pye. The impoverished sister had been by turns ignored and humiliated but it had not occurred to any of the villagers that this might make her a murderess. Perhaps it was the fact that she was a single woman – and a religious one at that. Perhaps it was her eccentric appearance. The dyed hair was absurd, visible at fifty yards. She tried too hard with her hats, her imitation jewellery, her wardrobe of once-fashionable cast-offs when really simpler, more modern clothes would have suited her better. Her physique was against her too: not fat, not masculine, not dumpy, but perilously close to all three. In short, she was something of a joke in Saxby-on-Avon and jokes do not commit murder.

Sitting in her home in Winsley Terrace, Clarissa was trying not to think about what had happened. For the last hour, she'd been absorbed by the *Daily Telegraph* crossword – though normally she'd finish it in half that time. One clue in particular had confounded her:

16. Complained endlessly about Bobby

The answer was a nine-letter word, the second letter O, the fourth letter I. She knew that it was staring her in the face but for some reason it wouldn't come to her. Was the solution a synonym of 'complained' or was it somebody famous, first name Bobby? It seemed very unlikely. The *Telegraph* crossword didn't usually involve celebrities unless they were classical writers or artists. In which case, could 'Bobby' have some other meaning that had eluded her? She chewed briefly on the Parker Jotter that was her special crossword pen. And then, quite suddenly it hit her. The answer was so obvious! It had been in front of her all the time. 'Complained endlessly'. So drop the D at the end of the word. 'About' indicating an anagram. And a Bobby?

Perhaps the capital B was a little unfair. She entered the missing letters . . . **Policeman** and of course that made her think of Magnus, of the police cars she had seen driving through the village, the uniformed officers who would be up at Pye Hall even now. What would happen to the house now that her brother was dead? Presumably, Frances would continue living there. She wasn't allowed to sell it. That was all part of the entail, the complicated document that had defined the ownership of Pye Hall over the centuries. It would now pass to her nephew, Freddy, the next in line. He was only fifteen years old and the last time Clarissa had seen him he had struck her as shallow and arrogant, a little like his father. And now he was a millionaire!

Of course, if he and his mother died, if – for example – there was a terrible car accident, then the property, but not the title, would have to move sideways. That was an interesting thought. Unlikely, but interesting. Really, there was no reason why it couldn't happen. First Mary Blakiston, then Sir Magnus. Finally . . .

Clarissa heard a key turning in the front door and quickly folded the newspaper and set it aside. She wouldn't want anyone to think that she had been wasting time; that she had nothing to do. She was already on her feet and moving towards the kitchen as the door opened and Diana Weaver came in. The wife of Adam Weaver who did odd jobs around the village and helped out at the church, she was a comfortably middle-aged woman with a no-nonsense attitude and a friendly smile. She worked as a cleaner: two hours a day at the doctor's surgery and the rest of the week divided between various houses in Saxby-on-Avon with just one afternoon once a week here. Seeing her as she bustled in with the oversized plastic bag she always carried, already buttoning the coat which surely wasn't needed on such a warm day, it occurred to Clarissa that this was a real cleaning lady, which is to say a lady for whom such work was entirely appropriate and indeed necessary. How could Magnus have possibly placed her in the same category? Had he really been serious or had he come here simply to insult her? She wasn't sorry he was dead. Quite the opposite.

'Good afternoon, Mrs Weaver,' she said.

'Hello there, Miss Pye.'

Clarissa could tell at once that something was wrong. The cleaner was downcast. She seemed nervous. 'There's some ironing to do in the spare bedroom. And I've bought a new bottle of Ajax.' Clarissa had got straight to the point. It wasn't her habit to engage in conversation: it wasn't just a question of propriety. She could barely afford to pay for the two hours each week and she wasn't going to eat into them with small talk. But although Mrs Weaver had divested herself of her coat, she hadn't moved and didn't seem in any hurry to start work. 'Is something the matter?' she asked.

'Well . . . it's this business at the big house.'

'My brother.'

'Yes, Miss Pye.' The cleaner seemed more upset that she had any right to be. It wasn't as if she had worked there. She had probably only spoken to Magnus once or twice in her life. 'It's a horrible thing to happen,' she went on. 'In a village like this. I mean, people have their ups and their downs. But I've lived here forty years and I've never known anything like it. First poor Mary. And now this.'

'I was just thinking about it myself,' Clarissa agreed. 'I am mortified. My brother and I weren't close but even so he was still blood.'

Blood.

She shuddered. Had he known he was about to die?

'And now we've got the police here,' Diana Weaver continued. 'Asking questions and disturbing everyone.' Was that what she was worried about? The police? 'Do you think they have any idea who did it?'

'I doubt it. It only happened last night.'

'I'm sure they'll have searched the house. According to my Adam . . .' She paused, unsure whether to spell it out. '. . . someone took his head clean off his shoulders.'

'Yes. That's what I heard.'

'That's horrible.'

‘It certainly was very shocking. Are you going to be able to work today or would you like to go home?’

‘No, no. I prefer to keep myself busy.’

The cleaner went into the kitchen. Clarissa glanced at the clock. Mrs Weaver had actually started work two minutes late. She would make sure she made up the time before she left.

5

The meeting at Larkin Gadwall had not been particularly illuminating. Atticus Pünd had been shown the brochure for the new development – everything in watercolour with smiling families, sketched in almost like ghosts, drifting through their new paradise. Planning permission had been approved. Construction was due to start the following spring. Philip Gadwall, the senior partner, insisted that Dingle Dell was an unremarkable piece of woodland and that the new homes would benefit the neighbourhood. ‘It’s very much in the council’s mind that we regenerate our villages. We need new homes for local families if we’re going to keep the villages alive.’

Chubb had listened to all this in silence. It struck him that the families in the brochure, with their smart clothes and brand-new cars, didn’t look local at all. He was quite glad when Pünd announced that he had no further questions and they were able to get back out into the street.

It turned out that Frances Pye had already left hospital and had insisted on returning home, so that was where the three men – Pünd, Fraser and Chubb – went next. The police cars had already left Pye Hall by the time they arrived. Driving past the Lodge and up the gravel driveway, Pünd was struck by how normal everything looked with the afternoon sun already dipping behind the trees.

‘That must have been where Mary Blakiston lived,’ Fraser said, pointing to the silent Lodge House as they passed.

‘At one time with her two sons, Robert and Tom,’ Pünd

said. 'Let us not forget that the younger of the two children also died.' He gazed out of the window, his face suddenly grim. 'This place has seen a lot of death.'

They pulled in. Chubb had driven ahead of them and was waiting for them at the front door. A square of police tape hung limply around the handprint in the soil and Fraser wondered if it had been linked to the gardener, Brent, or to anyone else. They went straight into the house. Someone had been busy. The Persian rug had been removed, the flagstones washed down. The suit of armour had gone too. The police would have held on to the sword – it was, after all, the murder weapon. But the rest of the armour would have been too grim a reminder of what had occurred. The whole house was silent. There was no sign of Lady Pye. Chubb hesitated, unsure how to proceed.

And then a door opened and a man appeared, coming out of the living room. He was in his late thirties, with dark hair and a moustache, wearing a blue blazer with a crest on the front pocket. He had a lazy walk, one hand in his pocket and a cigarette in the other. Fraser had the immediate thought that this was a man whom it would be easy to dislike. He did not just arouse antipathy; he almost seemed to cultivate it.

The new arrival was surprised to find three visitors in the hall and he didn't try to conceal it. 'Who are you?' he demanded.

'I was about to ask you the same,' Chubb replied, already bristling. 'I'm with the police.'

'Oh.' The man's face fell. 'Well, I'm a friend of Frances's – Lady Pye. I've come down from London to look after her – hour of need and all that. The name's Dartford, Jack Dartford.' He held a hand out vaguely, then withdrew it. 'She's very upset, you know.'

'I'm sure.' Pünd stepped forward. 'I would be interested to know how you heard the news, Mr Dartford.'

'About Magnus? She rang me.'

'Today?'

'No. Last night. Immediately after she'd called the

police. She was actually quite hysterical. I'd have come down straight away but it was a bit late to hit the road and I had meetings this morning so I said I'd arrive around lunchtime, which is what I did. Picked her up at the hospital and brought her here. Her son, Freddy, is with her, by the way. He'd been staying with friends on the south coast.'

'You will forgive me for asking, but I wonder why she selected you out of all of her friends in what you term her hour of need?'

'Well, that's easy enough to explain, Mr . . . ?'

'Pünd.'

'Pünd? That's a German name. And you've got the accent to go with it. What are you doing here?'

'Mr Pünd is helping us,' Chubb cut in, shortly.

'Oh – all right. What was the question? Why did she ask me?' For all his bluster, it was evident that Jack Dartford was casting around for a safe answer. 'Well, I suppose it was because we'd just had lunch together. I actually went with her to the station and put her on the train back to Bath. I'd have been uppermost in her mind.'

'Lady Pye was with you in London on the day of the murder?' Pünd asked.

'Yes.' Dartford half-sighed, as if he had given away more than he had intended. 'We had a business lunch. I advise her about stocks and shares, investments . . . that sort of thing.'

'And what did you do after lunch, Mr Dartford?'

'I just told you—'

'You told us that you accompanied Lady Pye to the station. But we know that she came to Bath on a late evening train. She reached the house around half past nine. I take it, therefore, that you spent the afternoon together.'

'Yes. We did.' Dartford was looking increasingly uncomfortable. 'We killed a bit of time.' He thought for a moment. 'We went to a gallery. The Royal Academy.'

'What did you see?'

'Just some paintings. Dreary stuff.'

'Lady Pye has said that she went shopping.'

'We did a bit of shopping too. She didn't buy anything though . . . not that I can remember. She wasn't really in the mood.'

'I have one last question for you, if you will forgive me, Mr Dartford. You say that you are a friend of Lady Pye. Would you have described yourself as a friend of the late Sir Magnus, too?'

'No. Not really. I mean, I knew him of course. I quite liked him. Decent enough sort of chap. But Frances and I used to play tennis together. That's how we met. So I saw rather more of her than of him. Not that he minded! But he wasn't particularly sporty. That's all.'

'Where is Lady Pye?' Chubb asked.

'She's in her room, upstairs. She's in bed.'

'Asleep?'

'I don't think so. She wasn't when I looked in a few minutes ago.'

'Then we would like to see her.'

'Now?' Dartford saw the answer in the detective's implacable face. 'All right, I'll take you up.'

6

Frances Pye was lying on her bed, wrapped in a dressing gown and half-submerged in a wave of crumpled sheets. She had been drinking champagne. There was a half-empty glass on the table beside her, along with a bottle, slanting out of an ice bucket. Sedative or celebration? To Fraser's eye, it could have been either and the look on her face as they came in was just as hard to decipher. She was annoyed to be interrupted but at the same time she had been expecting it. She was reluctant to talk but had already geared herself up to answer the questions that must come her way.

She was not alone. A teenaged boy, dressed in whites as if for cricket, lounged in a chair, one leg crossed over the other. He was obviously her son. He had the same dark hair, swept back across his forehead, the same haughty eyes. He was eating an apple. Neither mother nor son looked particularly grieved by what had happened. She could have been in bed with a touch of flu. He could have been visiting her.

'Frances . . .' Jack Dartford introduced them. 'This is Detective Inspector Chubb. He's from the Bath police.'

'We saw each other briefly the night it happened,' Chubb reminded her. 'I was there when you were taken off in the ambulance.'

'Oh yes.' The voice was husky, uninterested.

'And this is Mr Pond.'

'Pünd.' Pünd nodded his head. 'I am assisting the police. My assistant, James Fraser.'

'They want to ask you a few questions.' Dartford was deliberately attempting to insinuate himself into the room. 'I'll hang around, if you like.'

'That's all right, thank you, Mr Dartford.' Chubb answered the question for her. 'We'll call you if we need you.'

'I really don't think I ought to leave Frances on her own.'

'We won't keep her very long.'

'It's all right, Jack.' Frances Pye settled back onto the pile of cushions that had been heaped up behind her. She turned to the three unwanted visitors. 'I suppose we ought to get this over with.'

There was a brief moment of awkwardness as Dartford tried to work out what to do next and even Fraser could see what was going through his mind. He wanted to tell her what he had said about the London visit. He wanted to make sure that her account tallied with his. But there was no way Pünd was going to allow that to happen. Separate the suspects. Set them against each other. That was how he worked.

Dartford left. Chubb closed the door and Fraser drew up three chairs. There was plenty of furniture in the bedroom, which was large, with tumbling curtains, thick carpets, fitted wardrobes and an antique dressing table whose bowed legs seemed barely up to the weight of all the bottles, boxes, bowls and brushes piled up on the surface. Fraser, who liked to read Charles Dickens, thought at once of Miss Havisham in *Great Expectations*. The whole room was chintzy, slightly Victorian. All that was missing was the cobwebs.

Pünd sat down. 'I'm afraid I have to ask you some questions about your husband,' he began.

'I quite understand. It's a ghastly business. Who would so such a thing? Please go ahead.'

'You might prefer to ask your son to leave.'

'But I want to stay!' Freddy protested. There was a certain arrogance in his voice, all the more inappropriate as it hadn't yet broken. 'I've never met a real detective.' He stared insolently at Pünd. 'How come you've got a foreign name? Do you work for Scotland Yard?'

'Don't be rude, Freddy,' his mother said. 'You can stay – but only if you don't interrupt.' Her eyes flickered over to Pünd. 'Do begin!'

Pünd took off his glasses, polished them, put them on again. Fraser guessed that he would be uncomfortable talking in front of the boy. Pünd was never good with children, particularly English ones who had grown up in the belief that he was still the enemy. 'Very well. May I ask, first, if you were aware of your husband having received any threats in recent weeks?'

'Threats?'

'Had he received any letters or telephone calls that might have suggested his life was in danger?'

There was a large, white telephone on the bedside table, next to the ice bucket. Frances glanced at it before answering. 'No,' she said. 'Why would he have?'

'There was, I believe, a property with which he was involved. The new development...'

'Oh! You mean Dingle Dell!' She muttered the name contemptuously. 'Well, I don't know about that. There were bound to be a few raised temperatures in the village. People around here are very narrow-minded and Magnus was expecting a few protests. But death threats? I hardly think so.'

'We found a note on your husband's desk,' Chubb cut in. 'It was unsigned, typewritten and we have every reason to believe that whoever wrote it was very angry indeed.'

'What makes you think that?'

'The letter made a very specific threat, Lady Pye. There's also the weapon that we found, the service revolver in his desk.'

'Well, I know nothing about that. The gun was usually in the safe. And Magnus didn't mention any threatening letter to me.'

'May I ask, Lady Pye . . .' Pünd sounded apologetic. 'What were your movements in London yesterday? I do not wish to intrude,' he continued, hurriedly, 'but it is necessary for us to establish the whereabouts of everyone who is involved.'

'Do you think Mummy's involved?' Freddy asked, eagerly. 'Do you think she did it?'

'Freddy, be quiet!' Frances Pye glanced at her son disdainfully, then turned her eyes back to Pünd. 'It is an intrusion,' she said. 'And I've already told the Detective Inspector exactly what I was doing, but if you must know, I had lunch at Carlotta's with Jack Dartford. It was quite a long lunch. We were talking business. I don't really understand anything about money and Jack is terribly helpful.'

'What time did you leave London?'

'I was on the seven-forty train.' She paused, perhaps realising that there was a lengthy interval to be explained. 'I went shopping after lunch. I didn't buy anything but I strolled down Bond Street and into Fortnum & Mason.'

'It is quite pleasant to kill time in London,' Pünd agreed. 'Did you perhaps look into an art gallery?'

'No. Not this time. There was something on at the Courtauld, I think, but I wasn't really in the mood.'

So Dartford had been lying. Even James Fraser picked up on the obvious discrepancy between the two accounts of the afternoon but before either of them could remark upon it, the telephone rang – not in the bedroom but downstairs. Lady Pye glanced briefly at the handset on the table beside her and frowned. 'Would you go and answer that please, Freddy?' she asked. 'Whoever it is, tell than I'm resting and don't want to be disturbed.'

'What if it's for Daddy?'

'Just tell them we're not taking any calls. There's a good boy.'

'All right.' Freddy was a little annoyed to be dismissed from the room. He slouched off the chair and out of the door. The three of them listened to the ringing as it echoed up from downstairs. After less than a minute, it stopped.

'The phone's broken up here,' Frances Pye explained. 'This is an old house and there's always something going wrong. At the moment it's the phones. Last month it was the electrics. We also have woodwork and dry rot. People may complain about Dingle Dell but at least the new houses will be modern and efficient. You have no idea what it's like living in an ancient pile.'

It occurred to Fraser that she had adroitly changed the subject, moving away from what she had – or had not – been doing in London. But Pünd did not seem too concerned. 'What time did you return to Pye Hall on the night of your husband's murder?' he asked.

'Well, let me see. The train would have got in about half past eight. It was very slow. I'd left my car at Bath station and by the time I'd driven over here, it must have been about nine twenty.' She paused. 'A car drove out just as I arrived.'

Chubb nodded. 'You did mention that to me, Lady Pye. I don't suppose you managed to see the driver.'

'I may have glimpsed him. I don't know why I say that. I'm not even certain it was a man. It was a green car. I already told you. It had the letters FP in the registration. I'm afraid I can't tell you the make.'

'Just the one person in it?'

'Yes. In the driving seat. I saw his shoulders and the back of his head. He was wearing a hat.'

'You saw the car leave,' Pünd said. 'How would you say it was being driven?'

'The driver was in a hurry. He skidded as he turned into the main road.'

'He was driving to Bath?'

'No. The other way.'

'You then proceeded to the front door. The lights were on.'

'Yes. I let myself in.' She shuddered. 'I saw my husband at once and I called the police.'

There was a long silence. Lady Pye seemed genuinely exhausted. When Pünd spoke again, his voice was gentle. 'Do you by any chance know the combination of your husband's safe?' he asked.

'Yes, I do. I keep some of my more expensive jewellery there. It hasn't been opened, has it?'

'No, not at all, Lady Pye,' Pünd assured her. 'Although it is possible that it had been opened some time recently as the picture behind which it was concealed was not quite flush with the wall.'

'That might have been Magnus. He kept money in there. And private papers.'

'And the combination?' Chubb asked.

She shrugged. 'Left to seventeen, right to nine, left to fifty-seven, then turn the dial twice.'

'Thank you.' Pünd smiled sympathetically. 'I am sure you are tired, Lady Pye, and we will not keep you much longer. There are just two more questions I wish to ask you. The first concerns a note which we also found on your husband's desk and which seems to have been written in his hand.'

Chubb had brought the notepad, now encased in a plastic evidence bag. He passed it to Lady Pye who quickly scanned the three lines written in pencil:

ASHTON H
Mw
A GIRL

'This is Magnus's handwriting,' she said. 'And there's nothing very mysterious about it. He had a habit of making notes when he took a telephone call. He was always forgetting things. I don't know who or what Ashton H is. MW? I suppose that could be somebody's initials.'

'The M is large but the w is small,' Pünd pointed out.

'Then it might be a word. He did that too. If you asked him to buy the newspaper when he went out, he'd jot down Np.'

'Could it be that this Mw angered him in some way? He takes no further notes but there are several lines. You can see that he has almost torn the sheet of paper with the pencil.'

'I have no idea.'

'And what about this girl?' Chubb cut in. 'Who might that be?'

'I can't tell you that either. Obviously, we needed a new housekeeper. I suppose someone could have recommended a girl.'

'Your former housekeeper, Mary Blakiston—' Pünd began.

'Yes. It has been a horrible time – just horrible. We were away when it happened, in the south of France. Mary had been with us for ever. Magnus was very close to her. She worshipped him! From the moment she moved into the Lodge, she was beholden to him, as if he were some sort of monarch and she'd been asked to join the royal guard. Personally, I found her rather tiresome although I shouldn't speak ill of the dead. What else do you want to know?'

'I noticed that there is a painting missing from the wall in the great hall where your husband was discovered. It hung next to the door.'

'What's that got to do with anything?'

'Every detail is of interest to me, Lady Pye.'

'It was a portrait of me.' Frances Pye seemed reluctant to answer. 'Magnus didn't like it so he threw it out.'

'Recently?'

'Yes. It can't have been more than a week ago, actually. I don't remember exactly when.' Frances Pye sank back into her pillows, signalling that she had spoken enough. Pünd nodded and, following his cue, Fraser and Chubb stood up and the three of them left.

'What did you make of that?' Chubb asked as they left the room.

'She was definitely lying about London,' Fraser said. 'If you ask me, she and that Dartford chap spent the afternoon together – and they certainly weren't shopping!'

'It is evident that Lady Pye and her husband no longer shared a bed,' Pünd agreed.

'How do you know?'

'It was obvious from the décor of the bedroom, the embroidered pillows. It was a room without any trace of a man.'

'So there are two people with a good reason to kill him,' Chubb muttered. 'The oldest motive in the book. Kill the husband and run off together with the loot.'

'You may be right, Detective Inspector. Perhaps we will find a copy of Sir Magnus Pye's will in his safe. But his family has been in this house for many years and it is likely, I would think, that it will pass directly to his only son and heir.'

'And a nasty piece of work he was too,' Chubb remarked.

The safe in fact contained little of interest. There were several pieces of jewellery, about five hundred pounds in different currencies and various documents: some recent, some dating back as much as twenty years. Chubb took them with him.

He and Pünd parted company at the door, Chubb returning to his home in Hamswell where his wife, Harriet, would be waiting for him. He would know her mood instantly. As he had once confided in Pünd, she communicated it by the speed of her knitting needles.

Pünd and Fraser shook hands with him, then returned to the questionable comforts of the Queen's Arms.

7

More people had gathered around the bus shelter on the far side of the village square, clearly exercised by something they had seen. Fraser had noticed a crowd of them that morning when they checked into the pub and clearly they had spread the word. Something had happened. The entire village needed to know.

'What do you think that's all about?' he asked as he parked the car.

'Perhaps we should find out,' Pünd replied.

They got out and walked across the square. Whitehead's Antiques and the General Electrics Store was already closed and in the still of the evening, with no traffic passing through, it was easy to hear what the small crowd was saying.

'Got a right nerve!'

'She should be ashamed.'

'Flaunting herself like that!'

The villagers did not notice Pünd and Fraser until it was too late, then parted to allow the two men access to whatever it was they had been discussing. They saw it at once. There was a glass display case mounted next to the bus shelter with various notices pinned inside: minutes of the last council meeting, church services, forthcoming events. Among these, a single sheet of paper had been added with a typewritten message.

<u>TO WHOM IT MAY CONCERN</u>

There have been many rumours about Robert Blakiston circulating in the village. Some people have suggested that he may have had something to do with the tragic death of his mother, Mary Blakiston, on Friday morning at 9.00 a.m. These stories are hurtful and ill-informed and wrong. I was with Robert at that time in his flat above the garage and had been with him all night. If necessary, I will swear to this in a court of law. Robert and I are engaged to be married. Please show us a little kindness and stop spreading these malicious rumours.

Joy Sanderling

James Fraser was shocked. There was a side to his nature, something woven in by his years in the English private school system, that was easily offended by any public display of emotion. Even two people holding hands in the street seemed to him to be unnecessary and this declamation – for it seemed to him no less – went far beyond the pale. 'What was she thinking of?' he exclaimed as they moved away.

'Was it the contents of the announcement that most struck you?' Pünd replied. 'You did not notice something else?'

'What?'

'The threat that was sent to Sir Magnus Pye and this confession of Joy Sanderling, they were produced by the same typewriter.'

'Good lord!' Fraser blinked. 'Are you sure?'

'I am certain. The tail of the e has faded and the t slants a little to the left. It is not just the same model. It is the same machine.'

'Do you think she wrote the letter to Sir Magnus?'

'It is possible.'

They took a few steps in silence, then Pünd began again. 'Miss Sanderling has been forced to take this action because I would not help her,' he said. 'She is willing to sacrifice her good reputation, knowing full well that news of this may well reach her parents who will, as she made clear to us, be upset by her behaviour. This is my responsibility.' He paused. 'There is something about the village of Saxby-on-Avon that concerns me,' he went on. 'I have spoken to you before of the nature of human wickedness, my friend. How it is the small lies and evasions which nobody sees or detects but which can come together and smother you like the fumes in a house fire.' He turned and surveyed the surrounding buildings, the shaded square. 'They are all around us. Already there have been two deaths: three, if you include the child who died in the lake all those years ago. They are all connected. We must move quickly before there is a fourth.'

He crossed the square and went into the hotel. Behind him, the villagers were still muttering quietly, shaking their heads.

FOUR

A Boy

1

Atticus Pünd awoke with a headache.

He became aware of it before he opened his eyes and the moment he did open them, it intensified as if it had been waiting for him, lying in ambush. The force of it quite took his breath away and it was as much as he could do to reach out for the pills that Dr Benson had given him and which he had left, the night before, beside the bed. Somehow his hand found them and swept them up but he was unable to find the glass of water, which he had also prepared. It didn't matter. He slid the pills into his mouth and swallowed them dry, feeling their harsh passage down his throat. Only a few minutes later, when they were safely lodged in his system, already dissolving and sending their antipyretics through his bloodstream and into his brain did he find the glass and drink, washing the bitter taste from his mouth.

For a long time he lay where he was, his shoulders pressed against the pillows, gazing at the shadows on the walls. Piece by piece, the room came back into focus: the oak wardrobe, slightly too big for the space in which it stood, the mirror with its mottled glass, the framed print – a view of the Royal Crescent in Bath – the sagging curtains which would draw back to reveal a view of the cemetery. Well, that was appropriate. Waiting for the pain to subside, Atticus Pünd reflected on his fast approaching mortality.

There would be no funeral. He had seen too much of death in his lifetime to want to adorn it with ritual, to dignify it as if it was anything more than what it was . . . a passage. Nor did he believe in God. There were those who had come out of the camps with their faith intact and he admired them for it. His own experience had led him to believe in nothing. Man was a complicated animal capable of extraordinary good and great evil – but he was definitely on his own. At the same time, he was not afraid of being proved wrong. If, after a lifetime of considered reason he found himself being called to judgment in some sort of starry chamber, he was sure he would be forgiven. From what he understood, God was the forgiving sort.

It did occur to him though that Dr Benson had been a little too optimistic. There would be more of these attacks and they would incapacitate him more seriously as the thing in his head made its irredeemable progress. How long would it be before he was no longer able to function? That was the most frightening thought – that thought itself might become no longer possible. Lying alone in his room at the Queen's Arms, Pünd made two promises to himself: the first was that he would solve the murder of Sir Magnus Pye and make good the debt that he owed to Joy Sanderling.

The second he refused to articulate.

An hour later, when he came down to the dining room dressed as ever in a neatly pressed suit, white shirt and tie, it would have been impossible to tell how his day had begun and certainly James Fraser was quite unaware that anything was wrong but then, the young man was remarkably unobservant. Pünd remembered their first case together when Fraser had failed to notice that his travelling companion, on the three-fifty train from Paddington, was actually dead. There were many who were surprised that he managed to hold down his job as a detective's assistant. In fact, Pünd found him useful precisely because he was so obtuse. Fraser was a blank page on which he could scribble his theories, a plain sheet of glass in which he might see his own thought processes reflected. And he was efficient. He had already ordered the black coffee and single boiled egg that Pünd liked for his breakfast.

They ate in silence. Fraser had ordered the full English for himself, an amount of food that Pünd always found bewildering. Only when they had finished did he lay out the day ahead. 'We must visit Miss Sanderling once again,' he announced.

'Absolutely. I thought you'd want to start with her. I still can't believe she would put up a notice like that. And writing to Sir Magnus—'

'I think it is unlikely that she made the threats herself. But it was the same machine. Of that there is no doubt.'

'Maybe someone else had access to it.'

'She works at the doctor's surgery. That is where we will find her. You must find out at what time it opens.'

'Of course. Do you want me to let her know we're coming?'

'No. I think it will be better if we turn up by surprise.' Pünd poured himself another inch of coffee. 'I am interested, also, to find out more about the death of the housekeeper, Mary Blakiston.'

'Do you think it's connected?'

'There can be no doubt of it. Her death, the burglary, the murder of Sir Magnus, these are surely three steps in the same journey.'

'I wonder what Chubb will make of that clue you found. The scrap of paper in the fireplace. There was a fingerprint on it. That might tell us something.'

'It has already told me a great deal,' Pünd said. 'It is not the fingerprint itself that is of interest. It will be of no assistance, unless it belongs to someone with a criminal record, which I doubt. But how it came to be there, and why the paper was burnt. These are indeed questions that might go to the very heart of the matter.'

'And knowing you, you already have the answers. In fact, I bet you've solved the whole thing, you old stick!'

'Not yet, my friend. But we will catch up with Detective Inspector Chubb later and we will see . . .'

Fraser wanted to ask more but he knew that Pünd would refuse to be drawn. Put a question to him and the best you would get would be a response that made little or no sense and which would, in itself, be more annoying than no answer at all. They finished their breakfast and a few minutes later, they left the hotel. Stepping out into the village square, the first thing they noticed was that the display case next to the bus shelter was empty. Joy Sanderling's confession had been removed.

2

'Actually, I took it down myself. I did it this morning. I don't regret putting it there. I made the decision when I saw you in London. I had to do something. But after what happened here – I mean, with Sir Magnus and the police asking questions and everything – it just didn't seem appropriate. Anyway, it had done the job. As soon as one person had read it, the whole village would know. That's how it is around here. People have been giving me a few strange looks, I can tell you, and I don't think the vicar was too pleased. But I don't care. Robert and I are going to be married. What we do is our business and I'm not going to put up with people telling lies about him or about me.

Joy Sanderling was sitting on her own in the modern, single-storey surgery that stood in upper Saxby-on-Avon, surrounded by houses and bungalows that had all gone up at about the same time. It was an unattractive building, cheaply constructed and utilitarian in design. Dr Redwing's father had compared it to a public toilet at the time it was built, although he, of course, had practiced from his own home. Dr Redwing herself thought it no bad thing that she was able to separate her work from her private life. There were many more people living in the village than there had been in Edgar Rennard's time.

Patients entered through a glazed door that opened directly into a waiting area with a few faux-leather sofas, a coffee table and a scattering of magazines: old copies of *Punch* and *Country Life*. There were some toys for children, donated by Lady Pye, although that had been a long time ago and they really needed to be replaced. Joy sat in an adjoining office – the dispensary – with a window that slid across so that she could speak to the patients directly. She had an appointments book in front of her, a telephone and a typewriter to one side. Behind her, there were shelves and a cupboard filled with medical supplies, filing cabinets containing patient records and a small refrigerator, which occasionally housed drugs or the various samples that needed to be sent on to the hospital. There were two doors: one each side. The one on her left led into the reception area, the one on her right to Dr Redwing's office. A light bulb, next to the telephone, would flash on when the doctor was ready to see her next patient.

Jeff Weaver, the gravedigger, was in there now, accompanying his grandson for a final check-up. Nine-year-old Billy Weaver had made a complete recovery from his whooping cough and had come bouncing into the surgery with a determination to be out of there as soon as possible. There were no other patients on the waiting list and Joy had been surprised when the door had opened and Atticus Pünd had walked in with his fair-haired assistant. She had heard they were in the village but had not expected to see them here.

'Have your parents been made aware of what you wrote?' Pünd asked.

'Not yet,' Joy said. 'Although I'm sure someone will tell them soon enough.' She shrugged. 'If they find out, what does it matter? I'll move in with Robert. That's what I want anyway.'

It seemed to Fraser that she had changed in the brief time since they had met in London. He had liked her then and had been quietly disappointed when Pünd had refused to help her. The young woman on the other side of the window was still very appealing, exactly the sort of person you'd want to talk to if you weren't feeling well. But there was a harder edge to her too. He noticed that she hadn't come round to greet them, preferring to stay in the other room.

'I didn't expect to see you, Mr Pünd,' she said. 'What do you want?'

'You may feel that I was unfair to you when you came to see me in London, Miss Sanderling, and perhaps I should apologise. I was merely honest with you. At the time, I did not think I could help you with the situation in which you found yourself. However, when I read of the death of Sir Magnus Pye, I felt I had no choice but to investigate the matter.'

'You think it has something to do with what I told you?'

'That may well be the case.'

'Well, I don't see how I can help you. Unless you think I did it.'

'Would you have a reason to wish him dead?'

'No. I hardly even knew him. I saw him occasionally but I had nothing to do with him.'

'And what of your fiancé, Robert Blakiston?'

'You don't suspect *him*, do you?' Something flared in her eyes. 'Sir Magnus was never anything but kind to him. He helped Robert get his job. They never quarrelled. They hardly ever saw each other. Is that why you're here? Because you want to turn me against him?'

'Nothing could be further from the truth.'

'Then what do you want?'

'As a matter of fact, I am here to see Dr Redwing.'

'She's with a patient at the moment but I expect she'll be finished quite soon.'

'Thank you.' Pünd had not been offended by the girl's hostility but it seemed to Fraser that he was looking at her rather sadly. 'I must warn you,' he continued, 'that it will be necessary for me to speak with Robert.'

'Why?'

'Because Mary Blakiston was his mother. It is always possible that he might hold Sir Magnus to be partly responsible for her death and that alone would provide him with a motive for the murder.'

'Revenge? I very much doubt it.'

'At any event, he once lived at Pye Hall and there is a relationship between him and Sir Magnus which I need to explore. I tell you this because it occurs to me that you might wish to be present when we speak.'

Joy nodded. 'Where do you want to see him? And when?'

‘Perhaps he might come to my hotel when it conveniences him? I am staying at the Queen’s Arms.’

‘I’ll bring him when he finishes work.’

‘Thank you.’

The door of Dr Redwing’s office opened and Jeff Weaver came out, holding the hand of a small boy who was wearing short trousers and a school jacket. Joy waited until they had gone, then moved to a door at the side of her office. ‘I’ll tell Dr Redwing you’re here,’ she said.

She disappeared from sight. It was exactly the opportunity that Pünd had been waiting for. He signalled to Fraser who quickly drew a sheet of paper out of his jacket pocket, leaned through the window and fed it upside-down into the typewriter. Leaning over the machine, he pressed several of the keys at random then pulled the sheet out and handed it to Pünd who examined the letters and nodded his satisfaction before handing it back.

‘Is it the same?’ Fraser asked.

‘It is.’

Joy Sanderling returned to the reception desk. ‘You can go in,’ she said. ‘Dr Redwing is free until eleven.’

‘Thank you,’ Pünd said, then added almost as an afterthought, ‘Do you alone have the use of this office, Miss Sanderling?’

‘Dr Redwing comes in from time to time, but nobody else,’ Joy replied.

‘You are quite sure of that? Nobody else would have access to this machine?’ He gestured at the typewriter.

‘Why do you want to know?’ Pünd said nothing so she continued. ‘Nobody comes in here except for Mrs Weaver. She’s the mother of the little boy who just left and she cleans the surgery twice a week. But I very much doubt that she would use the typewriter and certainly not without asking.’

‘While I am here, I would also be interested in your opinion of the new homes that Sir Magnus was intending to build. He was planning to cut down the woodland known as Dingle Dell—’

'You think that was why he was killed? I'm afraid you don't have much understanding of English villages, Mr Pünd. It was a stupid idea. Saxby-on-Avon doesn't need new houses and there are plenty of better places to build them. I hate seeing trees being cut down and almost everyone in the village thinks the same. But nobody would have killed him because of that. The worst they would have done is written to the local newspaper or complained about it in the pub.'

'Maybe the development will no longer go ahead now that he is not here to oversee it,' Pünd suggested.

'I suppose that's possible.'

Pünd had proved his point. He smiled and moved towards the office door. Fraser, who had folded the sheet of paper in half and slipped it into his pocket, followed.

3

The office was small and square and so exactly what anyone would expect from a doctor's surgery that it might almost have inspired a cartoon in one of the old *Punch* magazines that lay on the reception table. There was an antique desk placed centrally with two chairs facing it, a wooden filing cabinet and a shelf stacked with medical volumes. To one side, a curtain could be drawn to create a separate cubicle with another chair and a raised bed. A white coat hung on a hook. The only unexpected touch in the room was an oil painting, which showed a dark-haired boy leaning against a wall. It was clearly the work of an amateur but Fraser, who had studied art at Oxford, thought it was rather good.

Dr Redwing herself was sitting upright, making notes on a case file in front of her, a rather severe woman in her early fifties. Everything about her was angular: the straight line of her shoulders, her cheekbones, her chin. You could have drawn her portrait using a ruler. But she was polite enough as she gestured for her two guests to sit down. She finished what she was writing, screwed the top back on her pen and smiled. 'Joy tells me you're with the police.'

'We are here in a private capacity,' Pünd explained. 'But it is true that we have worked with the police on occasion and are assisting Inspector Chubb now. My name is Atticus Pünd. This is my assistant, James Fraser.'

'I've heard of you, Mr Pünd. I understand you're very clever. I hope you can get to the bottom of this. It's a dreadful thing to happen in a small village and coming so soon after the death of poor Mary . . . I really don't know what to say.'

'I understand that you and Mrs Blakiston were friends.'

'I wouldn't go as far as that – but yes, we did see quite a bit of each other. I think people underestimated her. She was a very intelligent woman. She hadn't had an easy life, losing one child and bringing the other up on her own. But she coped very well and she was helpful to many people in the village.'

'And it was you who found her after her accident.'

'It was actually Brent, the groundsman at Pye Hall.' She stopped herself. 'But I assumed you wanted to talk to me about Sir Magnus.'

'I am interested in both occurrences, Dr Redwing.'

'Well, Brent called me from the stable. He had seen her through the window, lying in the hallway, and he feared the worst.'

'He hadn't gone in?'

'He didn't have a key. In the end we had to break down the back door. Mary had left her own keys in the lock on the other side. She was at the bottom of the stairs and it looked as if she had tripped over the cable of her Hoover which was at the top. Her neck was broken. I don't think she had been dead very long. She was still warm when I found her.'

'It must have been very distressing for you, Dr Redwing.'

'It was. Of course, I'm used to death. I've seen it many times. But it's always more difficult when it's someone you know personally.' She hesitated for a moment, a series of conflicting thoughts passing across her dark, serious eyes. Then she came to a decision. 'And there was something else.'

'Yes?'

'I did think about mentioning this to the police at the time and maybe I should have done so. And maybe I'm wrong to be telling you now. The thing is, I'd persuaded myself that it wasn't relevant. After all, nobody was suggesting that Mary's death was anything but a tragic accident. However, given what's happened and since you're here . . .'

'Please, go on.'

'Well, just a few days before Mary died, we had an incident here at the surgery. We were quite busy that day – we had three patients in a row – and Joy had to pop out a couple of times. I asked her to buy me some lunch from the village store. She's a good girl and she doesn't mind doing that sort of thing. I'd also left some papers at my house and she went out and got them for me. Anyway, at the end of the day, when we were tidying up, we noticed that a bottle had gone missing from the dispensary. As you can imagine, we keep a close eye on all our medicines, especially the more dangerous ones, and I was particularly concerned by its disappearance.'

'What was the drug?'

'Physostigmine. It's actually a cure for belladonna poisoning and I'd had to get some in for Henrietta Osborne, the vicar's wife. She'd managed to step on a clump of deadly nightshade in Dingle Dell and as I'm sure you'll know, Mr Pünd, atropine is an active ingredient in that particular plant. Physostigmine is effective in small doses but a larger amount can quite easily kill you.'

'And you say it was taken.'

'I didn't say that. If I had any reason to believe that, I would have gone straight to the police. No. It could have been misplaced. We have a lot of medicines here and although we're very careful, it has happened before. Or it could be that Mrs Weaver, who cleans here, had dropped and broken it. She's not a dishonest woman but it would be just like her to clean up the mess and say nothing about it.' Dr Redwing frowned. 'I mentioned it to Mary Blakiston though. If someone in the village had made off with it for some reason, she'd have certainly been able to find out. She was a bit like you, in a way. A detective. She had a way of rooting things out of people. And in fact she did tell me she had one or two ideas.'

'And a few days after this incident, she was dead.'

'Two days, Mr Pünd. Exactly two days.' There was a sudden silence as the significance – unspoken – hung in the air. Dr Redwing was looking increasingly uncomfortable. 'I'm sure her death had nothing to do with it,' she continued. 'It was an accident. And it's not as if Sir Magnus was poisoned. He was struck down with a sword!'

'On the day that the physostigmine was removed, can you recall who came to the surgery?' Pünd asked.

'Yes. I went back to the appointment book to check. As I just said, three people came in that morning. Mrs Osborne I've already mentioned. Johnny Whitehead has an antique shop in the village square. He had quite a nasty cut on his hand, which had gone septic. And Clarissa Pye – she's Sir Magnus's sister – looked in with a stomach upset. There was nothing very much the matter with her to be honest with you. She lives on her own and she's a bit of a hypochondriac. Really she just likes to have a chat. I don't think this missing bottle had anything to do with what happened but it's been on my conscience and I suppose it's best if you're aware of all the facts.' She glanced at her watch. 'Is there anything else?' she asked. 'I don't mean to be rude but I have to be on my rounds.'

'You have been most helpful, Dr Redwing.' Pünd got to his feet and seemed to notice the oil painting for the first time. 'Who is the boy?' he asked.

'Actually, it's my son – Sebastian. That was painted just a few days before his fifteenth birthday. He's in London now. We don't see a great deal of him.'

'It's very good,' Fraser said with real enthusiasm.

The doctor was pleased. 'My husband, Arthur, painted it.

I think he's a quite exceptional artist and it's one of my greatest regrets that his talent hasn't been recognised. He's painted me a couple of times and he did a quite lovely portrait of Lady Pye—' She broke off. Fraser was surprised how agitated she had suddenly become. 'You haven't asked me anything about Sir Magnus Pye,' she said.

'Is there something you wish to tell me?'

'Yes.' She paused as if challenging herself to continue. When she spoke again, her voice was cold and controlled. 'Sir Magnus Pye was a selfish, uncaring and egotistical man. Those new houses of his would have ruined a perfectly attractive corner of the village but that's not the end of it. He never did anything kind for anyone. Did you notice the toys in the waiting room? Lady Pye gave them to us, but as a result of it she'd expect us to bow and touch our forelock every time she came near. Inherited wealth will be the ruin of this country. Mr Pünd. That's the truth of it. They were an unpleasant couple and if you ask me, you're going to have your work cut out.' She took one last look at the portrait. 'The fact is, that half the village will have been glad to see him dead and if you're looking for suspects, well, they might as well form a line.'

4

Everyone knew Brent, the groundsman at Pye Hall, but at the same time no one knew him at all. When he walked through the village or took his usual seat at the Ferryman, people might say 'There's old Brent', but they had no idea how old he was and even his name was something of a mystery. Was it his first name or his last name? There were a few who might remember his father. He had been 'Brent' too and had done the same job – in fact the two of them had worked together for a while, old Brent and young Brent, pushing out the wheelbarrow and digging the soil. His parents had died. Nobody was quite sure how or when but it had happened in another part of the country – in Devonshire, some people said. A car accident. So young Brent had become old Brent and now lived in the pocket-sized cottage where he had been born, on Daphne Road. It was part of a terrace but his neighbours had never been invited in. The curtains were always drawn.

Somewhere in the church, it might have been possible to find a record of a birth, in May 1917, of one Neville John Brent. There must have been a time when he was Neville: at school or as a Local Defence Volunteer (his status as a farm worker had excluded him from fighting in the war). But he was a man without a shadow – or perhaps a shadow without a man. He was both as prominent and as unremarkable as the weather vane on the steeple of St Botolph's. The only reason anyone would have noticed it would have been if they had woken up one day to find out it wasn't there.

Atticus Pünd and James Fraser had tracked him down in the grounds of Pye Hall where he was carrying on his work, weeding and deadheading, as if nothing unusual had occurred. Pünd had prevailed upon him to stop for half an hour and the three of them were sitting together in the rose garden, surrounded by a thousand blooms. Brent had rolled a cigarette with hands so grubby that the whole thing would surely taste of dirt once he lit it. He came across as a boy-man, sullen and uncomfortable, shifting awkwardly in clothes that were too large for him, his curly hair flopping over his forehead. Fraser felt uncomfortable sitting next to him. Brent had a strange, slightly unsavoury quality; a sense of some secret that he was refusing to share.

'How well did you know Mary Blakiston?' Pünd had begun with the first death although it occurred to Fraser that the groundsman had been a principal witness at both events. Indeed, he might have been the last person to see both the housekeeper and her employer alive.

'I didn't know her. She didn't want to know me.' Brent seemed offended by the question. 'She used to boss me about. Do this, do that. Even had me up in her place moving the furniture, fixing the damp. Not that she had any right. I worked for Sir Magnus, not her. That's what I used to tell her. I'm not surprised someone pushed her down those stairs, the way she carried on. Always meddling. I'm sure she got up quite a few peoples' noses.' He sniffed loudly. 'I won't speak ill of the dead but she was a right busybody and no mistake.'

'You assume she was pushed? The police are of the opinion that it was an accident, that she fell.'

'That's not for me to say, sir. Accident? Someone done her in? I wouldn't be surprised either way.'

'It was you who saw her, lying in the hall.'

Brent nodded. 'I was doing the borders next to the front door. I looked in the window and there she was, lying at the bottom of the stairs.'

'You heard nothing?'

'There was nothing to hear. She was dead.'

'And there was nobody else in the house.'

'I didn't see anyone. There could have been, I suppose. But I was there a few hours and I didn't see anyone come out.'

'So what did you do?'

'I tapped on the window to see if she'd wake up but she wasn't moving so in the end I went to the stable and used the outside phone to call Dr Redwing. She made me break the glass in the back door. Sir Magnus wasn't happy about that. In fact, he blamed me for the break-in that happened later on. It wasn't my fault. I didn't want to break anything. I just did what I was told.'

'You argued with Sir Magnus?'

'No, sir. I wouldn't do that. But he wasn't pleased and when he wasn't pleased you'd better keep clear, I can tell you.'

'You were here the evening that Sir Magnus died.'

'I'm here every evening. At this time of the year, I never get away much before eight o'clock and it was about eight fifteen that night – not that I get paid any extra.' It was strange but the more Brent spoke, the more eloquent he became. 'He and Lady Pye weren't keen to put their hands in their pockets. He was on his own that night.

She was up in London. I saw him working late. There was a light on in the study and he must have been expecting someone because there was a visitor who arrived just as I left.'

Brent had already mentioned this to Detective Inspector Chubb. Unfortunately, he had been unable to provide a description of the mysterious arrival. 'I understand you did not manage to see his face,' Pünd said.

'I didn't see him. I didn't recognise him. But later on, when I thought about it, I knew who he was.' The announcement came as a surprise to Pünd who waited for the groundsman to continue. 'He was at the funeral. When they buried Mrs Blakiston, he was there. I knew I'd seen him before. I noticed him standing at the back of the crowd – but at the same time I hardly noticed him, if you know what I mean. He kept himself to himself, like he didn't want to be noticed, and I never saw his face. But I know it was the same man. I'm sure it was the same man – on account of the hat.'

'He was wearing a hat?'

'That's right. It was one of those old-fashioned hats, like they had ten years ago, pulled down low over his face. The man who came to Pye Hall at eight fifteen, he was the same man. I'm sure of it.'

'Can you tell me anything more about him? His age? His height?'

'He wore a hat. That's all I can tell you. He was here. He didn't talk to anyone. And then he left.'

'What happened when he came to the house?'

'I didn't wait to see. I went down to the Ferryman for a pie and a pint. I had a bit of money in my pocket, what Mr Whitehead gave me, and I couldn't wait to be on my way.'

'Mr Whitehead. He owns the antique shop—'

'What about him?' Brent's eyes narrowed with suspicion.

'He paid you some money.'

'I never said that!' Brent realised he had spoken too freely and searched for a way out. 'He'd paid me the fiver that he owed me. That's all. So I went for a pint.'

Pünd let the matter drop. It would be all too easy to offend a man like Brent and, once offended, he wouldn't utter another word. 'So you left Pye Hall at around a quarter past eight,' he said. 'That might have been only a matter of minutes before Sir Magnus was killed. I wonder if you can explain to us a handprint that we discovered in the flower bed beside the front door?'

'That police chap asked me about that and I already told him. It wasn't my handprint. What would I be doing sticking my hand in the soil?' He gave a queer sort of smile.

Pünd tried another tack. 'Did you see anyone else?'

'As a matter of fact, I did.' Brent glanced slyly at the detective and his assistant. All this time he had been holding the cigarette he had rolled but now he stuck it between his lips and lit it. 'I went down the Ferryman like I told you. And I was on my way when I run into Mrs Osborne, the vicar's wife. God knows what she's doing out in the middle of the night – and looking like nobody's business too. Anyway, she asked if I'd seen her husband. She was upset about something. Maybe even afraid. You should have seen the look on her face! Well, I told her it might have been him I'd seen at Pye Hall and the fact is he might have been there and all . . .'

Pünd frowned. 'The person you saw at the hall, the man in the hat, you said just now that he was at the funeral.'

'I know I said that, sir. But they were both there, him and the vicar. You see, I was having my pint and I saw the vicar go past on his bicycle. That was a while later.'

'How much later?'

'Thirty minutes. Maybe an hour. I heard it go past. You can hear that bicycle from one end of the village to the other with its clacking and its grinding and it definitely went past the pub while I was in there. And where could he have come from except from the hall? He certainly hadn't cycled from Bath.' Brent eyed the detective over his cigarette, daring him to disagree.

'You have been very helpful,' Pünd said. 'I have just one more question. It relates to the Lodge where Mrs Blakiston lived. You mentioned to me that you occasionally did work for her there and I wonder if you might have a key?'

'Why do you want to know?'

'Because I would like to go in.'

'I'm not sure about that,' the groundsman muttered. He screwed the cigarette round between his lips. 'You want to go in, you'd best talk to Lady Pye.'

'This is a police investigation,' Fraser cut in. 'We can go where we like and it might mean trouble for you if you don't co-operate.'

Brent looked doubtful but he wasn't prepared to argue. 'I can take you up there now.' He nodded his head at the roses. 'But then I've got to get back to these.'

Pünd and Fraser followed Brent back to the stable from where he retrieved a key attached to a large piece of wood, then walked with him down the drive to the Lodge House that stood at the end, two storeys high with sloping roofs, a massive chimney, Georgian windows and a solid front door. This was where Mary Blakiston had lived while she was working as Sir Magnus Pye's housekeeper. To begin with there had been a husband and two boys but one by one the family had left her until she was finally alone. Perhaps it was the position of the sun or the oaks and elms that surrounded the place but it seemed to be cast in permanent shadow. It was obviously empty. It looked and felt deserted.

Brent opened the front door with the key he had retrieved. 'Do you want me to come in?' he asked.

'It would be helpful if you could remain a little longer,' Pünd replied. 'We will not take up too much more of your time.'

The three of them went into a small hallway with two doors, a corridor and a flight of stairs leading up. The wallpaper was old-fashioned, floral. The pictures were images of English birds and owls. There was an antique table, a coat stand and a full-length mirror. Everything looked as if it had been there for a long time.

'What is it you want to see?' Brent asked.

'That, I cannot tell you,' Pünd replied. 'Not yet.'

The downstairs rooms had little to offer. The kitchen was basic, the living room dowdy, dominated by an old-fashioned grandfather clock. Fraser remembered how Joy Sanderling had described it, ticking away as she tried to make an impression on Robert's mother. Everything was very clean, as if Mary's ghost had just been in. Or perhaps it had never left. Someone had picked up the mail and piled it on the kitchen table but there was very little of it and nothing of interest.

They went upstairs. Mary's bedroom was at the end of the corridor with a bathroom next door. She had slept in the same bed that she must have once shared with her husband: it was so heavy and cumbersome that it was hard to imagine anyone bringing it here after he had left. The bedroom looked out over the road. In fact none of the main rooms had a view back to Pye Hall as if the house had been purposefully designed so that the servant would never glance in the direction of her employers. Pünd passed two doors that opened into bedrooms. Nobody had slept in them for some time. The beds were stripped, the mattresses already showing signs of mould. A third door, opposite them, had been broken, the lock forced.

'The police did that,' Brent explained. He sounded unhappy about it. 'They wanted to go in but they couldn't find the key.'

'Mrs Blakiston kept it locked?'

'She never went in.'

'How do you know?'

'I already told you. I come here lots of times. I fixed the damp and laid the carpets downstairs and she was always calling me in. But not this room. She wouldn't open the door. I'm not even sure she had the key. That's why the police broke it down.'

They went inside. The room was disappointing: like the rest of the house, it was utterly stripped of life with a single bed, an empty wardrobe and a window cut into the eaves with a work table below. Pünd went over to it and looked out. There was a view through the trees and he could just glimpse the edge of the lake with the threatened woodland, Dingle Dell, beyond. He noticed a single drawer in the middle of the table and opened it. Inside, Fraser saw a strip of black leather forming a circle with a small disc attached. It was a dog collar. He reached forward and took it out.

'Bella,' he read. The name was in capital letters.

'Bella was the dog,' Brent said, unnecessarily. Fraser was a little annoyed. He might have guessed as much.

'Whose dog?' Pünd asked.

'The younger kid. The one who died. He had a dog but it didn't last long.'

'What happened to it?'

'It ran off. They lost it.'

Fraser put the collar back. It was so small – it must have belonged to a mere puppy. There was something inexpressibly sad about it, sitting in the empty drawer. 'So this was Tom's room,' Fraser muttered.

'It would seem possible, yes.'

'I suppose it would explain why she locked the door. The poor woman couldn't bear to come in here. I wonder why she didn't move.'

'She may not have had a choice.'

Both of them were speaking in low voices, as if they were afraid of disturbing ancient memories. Meanwhile, Brent was shuffling around, anxious to be on his way. But Pünd took his time leaving the house. Fraser knew that he was not so much searching for clues as sensing the atmosphere – he had often heard him talk about the memory of crime, the supernatural echoes left behind by sadness and violent death. There was even a chapter in that book of his. 'Information and Intuition' or something like that.

Only when they were outside did he speak. 'Chubb will have removed anything of interest. I am keen to know what he found.' He glanced at Brent who was already shuffling into the distance, making his way back towards the manor house. 'And that one, also, he told us a great deal.' He looked around him, at the trees pressing in. 'I would not wish to live here,' he said. 'There is no view.'

'It is rather oppressive,' Fraser agreed.

'We must find out from Mr Whitehead how much money he paid to Brent and for what reason. Also, we must speak again with the Reverend Osborne. He must have had a reason to come here on the night of the murder. And then there is the question of his wife . . .'

'He said that Mrs Osborne was afraid.'

'Yes. Afraid of what, I wonder.' He took a last look back. 'There is something about the atmosphere of this house, James. It tells me that there is a great deal to fear.'

5

Raymond Chubb did not like murder. He had become a policeman because he believed in order and he considered the county of Somerset, with its neat villages, hedgerows and ancient fields to be one of the most ordered and civilised parts of the country – if not the world. Murder changed everything. It broke the gentle rhythm of life. It turned neighbour against neighbour. Suddenly nobody was to be trusted and doors, which were usually left open at night, were locked. Murder was an act of vandalism, a brick thrown at a picture window and somehow it was his job to put together the pieces.

Sitting in his office in the Orange Grove police station in Bath, he reflected on his current investigation. This business with Sir Magnus Pye had not got off to an inauspicious start. It was one thing to be stabbed in your own home – but to be decapitated with a medieval sword in the middle of the night was quite simply outrageous. Saxby-on-Avon was such a quiet place! Yes, there had been that business with the cleaner, the woman who had tripped up and fallen down the stairs, but this was something else again. Could it really be true that one of the villagers, living in a Georgian house perhaps, going to church and playing for the local cricket team, mowing their lawn on Sunday mornings and selling home-made marmalade at the village fête was a homicidal maniac? The answer was – yes, quite possibly. And their identity might well be provided by the book sitting on the desk in front of him now.

He had found nothing in Sir Magnus's safe of any interest. And it had looked as if the Lodge House was going to be a waste of time too. And then, an eagle-eyed constable, young Winterbrook, had made his discovery amongst the cookery books in Mary Blakiston's kitchen. He was going to go far, that boy. He just needed to show a more serious attitude and a bit more ambition and he'd be an inspector in no time. Had she hidden it there deliberately? Had she been afraid of someone coming into the house – her son, perhaps, or Sir Magnus himself? Certainly, it wasn't something she'd want to leave lying around, containing as it did malicious observations on just about everyone in the village. There was Mr Turnstone (the butcher) who deliberately short-changed his customers, Jeffrey Weaver (the undertaker) who was apparently cruel to his dog, Edgar Rennard (the retired doctor) who took bribes, Miss Dotterel (the village shop) who drank. Nobody seemed to have escaped her attention.

It had already taken him two whole days to go through it all and by the end of that time he felt almost sullied. He remembered seeing Mary Blakiston, glassy-eyed at the bottom of the stairs at Pye Hall, already cold and stiff. At the time he had felt pity for her. Now he wondered what had motivated her as she shuffled round the village permanently suspicious, permanently on the look out for trouble. Couldn't she, just once, have found something good? Her handwriting managed to be cramped and spidery yet very neat – as if she were some sort of accountant of evil. Yes! Pünd would like that one. It was exactly the sort of thing he might say. Each entry was dated. This volume covered three and a half years and Chubb had already sent Winterbrook back to the house to see if he could find any earlier editions – not that he didn't have plenty enough to be getting on with.

Mrs Blakiston had two or three special favourites who turned up on page after page. Curiously, despite the acrimony between them, her son Robert wasn't one of them although Josie – or Joy – had become an object of disdain the moment she had been introduced. She really hated the groundsman, Brent. His name kept on appearing. He was rude, he was lazy, he arrived late, he pilfered, he spied on the Boy Scouts when they were camping in Dingle Dell, he drank, he told lies, he never washed. It seemed that she had shared her thoughts with Sir Magnus Pye; at least, that was what she suggested in one of her last entries.

28 July
Finally, some sense! Sir M has asked Brent to leave his employ. It happened last night up at the hall. Brent not at all happy. Scowling this morning and deliberately tramped through a bed of aquilegia. Saw him with my own eyes and mentioned it to dear Sir M who told me that it didn't matter as he was going anyway. And about time too. I've told him often enough. Sir M didn't mention reason but there could be so many. Plenty of young men looking for work in the area, I said, and a good thing too. Suggested advertisement in *The Lady* but Sir M prefers agency as more discreet. More expensive too – not that it would matter to him, I suppose.

A day later, she had been dead. And a week after that, Sir M had died too. A coincidence? Surely the two of them hadn't been killed on account of a trampled bunch of flowers.

Chubb had marked seven more entries, which, he thought, might somehow relate to the case. All but one of them were recent and so more likely to be relevant to the murder of Sir Magnus. Once again he flicked through them, reading them in the order that seemed to make most sense.

13 July
An interesting talk with Dr Redwing. How many thieves can there be in one village? This is very serious. A drug

has been stolen from her surgery. She wrote down the name for me. Physostigmine. She says a large dose could quite possibly be fatal. I told her she should go to the police but of course she doesn't want to because she thinks she'll be blamed. I like Dr R but I do sometimes question her judgment. Having that girl working there, for example. And she isn't quite as careful as she thinks. I've been into the surgery lots of times and I could have just walked in and helped myself. When did it happen? I think Dr R is wrong. Not the day she says but the day before. I saw her coming out and I knew something was wrong. I saw it in her face. And the way she was holding her handbag. The surgery was empty (absolutely no sign of the girl) when I went in. She'd definitely been there alone and the medicine cupboard was left open so could easily have taken contents. What would she want it for? Pop it in her brother's tea – maybe revenge. Can't be happy being number two! But I have to be careful. I can't make accusations. Something to think about.

9 July
Arthur Reeve too upset to talk. His medal collection gone! A horrible thing to happen. The thief broke in through the kitchen window – cut himself on glass. You'd have thought that would be a big enough clue but the police weren't interested, of course. They said it must have been children – but I don't think so. The thieves knew exactly what they wanted. The Greek Medal alone was worth a tidy sum. Typical how nobody cares any more. I went in and had a cup of tea with him. Did wonder if *our friend* might be involved but didn't say anything. I'll have a look in and see – but careful. Leopards and spots! Terrible to have someone like this living in the village. And dangerous? I really should have told Sir Magnus. Hilda Reeve not even interested. Not helping her husband – says she can't see what all the fuss is about. Stupid woman. Can't think why he married her.

11 July
Visited Whitehead in his shop while his wife was out and told him what I knew. Of course he denied everything. Well, he would, wouldn't he? I showed him the piece I'd found in the newspaper and he said that was all behind him, actually accused me of trying to make trouble for him. Oh no, I told him. You're the one making trouble here. He said he'd never been anywhere near Arthur's home. But his shop is stuffed with all manner of bits and pieces and you have to wonder where he gets it front. He dared me to go public. He said he'd sue me. We'll see!

Chubb might have ignored both these entries. Arthur Reeve and his wife were an elderly couple and had once run the Queen's Arms. It would be hard to imagine anyone less likely to be involved in Sir Magnus's death – and how could the theft of his medals have any possible relevance? The meeting with Whitehead made no sense. But tucked into the back of the diary he had found a newspaper clipping, faded and brittle and it had forced him to think again.

GANGLAND FENCE RELEASED FROM JAIL

He achieved brief notoriety as part of the Mansion Gang – a network of professional burglars who targeted mansion blocks in Kensington and Chelsea. Arrested for receiving stolen goods, John Whitehead was released from Pentonville Prison after serving just four years of a seven-year sentence. Mr Whitehead, who is married, is believed to have left London.

There was no picture but Chubb had already checked that there was indeed a Johnny Whitehead living with his wife in the village and that it was the same Johnny Whitehead who had once been arrested in London. There had been plenty of organised criminals operating in the city during and after the war and the Mansion Gang had been notorious. Whitehead had been their fence and now he ran an antique store no less! He looked again at the two words in Mary Blakiston's handwriting. *And dangerous?* The question mark was certainly apposite. If Whitehead was an ex-criminal and she had tried to expose him, could he have been responsible for her death? If she had talked about him to Sir Magnus, might he have been forced to strike again? Chubb carefully set the newspaper article aside and went back to the diary.

7 July
Shocking. I always knew there was something about Rev Osborne and his wife. But this!!!! I wish old Montagu had stayed. Really, really don't know what to say or do. Nothing, I suppose. Who would believe me? Dreadful.

6 July
Lady Pye back from London. Again. All these trips she makes, everyone knows what's going on. But nobody will say anything. I suppose these are the times we live in. I feel sorry for Sir Magnus. Such a good man. Always so kind to me. Does he know? Should I say something?

The last entry that Chubb had selected had been written almost four months earlier. Mary Blakiston had written several entries about Joy Sanderling but this one followed their first meeting. She had written it in black ink, using a much thicker nib. The letters were splattered onto the page and Chubb could almost feel the anger and disgust as her pen travelled across the paper. Mary had always been a fairly impartial observer. Which is to say, she had been equally spiteful and unpleasant about everyone she encountered. But she seemed to have a special reserve for Joy.

15 March
Tea with little Miss Sanderling. She says her name is Josie but 'call me Joy'. I will not call her that. There is no joy in this marriage. Why can't she understand?

I will not let it happen. Twelve years ago I lost my first son. I will not allow her to take Robert away from me. I gave her tea and biscuits and she just sat there with that stupid smile on her face – so young, so ignorant. She prattled on about her parents and her family. She has a brother with Down's syndrome! Why did she have to tell me that? Robert just sat there, saying nothing, and all the time I was thinking about this awful sickness infecting her family and how much I wanted her to leave. I should have told her then and there. But she's obviously the sort of girl who won't listen to the likes of me. I will talk to Robert later. I won't have it. I really won't. Why did this stupid girl have to come to Saxby?

For the first time, Chubb felt a real dislike for Mary Blakiston, almost a sense that she had deserved to die. He would never actually say that about anyone but he had to admit that the whole diary was pure poison and this entry was unforgivable. It was the reference to Down's syndrome that most upset him. Mary described it as 'an awful sickness.' It wasn't. It was a condition, not an illness. What sort of woman could see it as a threat to her own bloodline? Had she really pulled up the drawbridge on her son's marriage simply to protect future grandchildren from some sort of contamination? It beggared belief.

Part of him hoped that this would turn out to be the only volume of Mary Blakiston's memoirs. He dreaded having to wade through any more pages of misery and resentment – didn't she have anything good to say about anyone? But at the same time, he knew he had stumbled on too valuable a resource to ignore. He would have to show it all to Atticus Pünd.

He was glad that the detective had turned up in Somerset. The two of them had worked together on that case in Marlborough, a headmaster who had been killed during the performance of a play. This business had many of the same hallmarks: a tangle of suspects and different motives and not one but two deaths that might or might not be related. In the privacy of his own home, Chubb would admit the truth, which was that he couldn't make head or tail of it. Pünd had a way of seeing things differently. Maybe it was in his nature. Chubb couldn't help but smile. All his life he'd been brought up to think of the Germans as his enemy. It was strange having one on his side.

It was equally strange that Joy Sanderling had actually brought him here. It had already occurred to Chubb that she and her fiancé, Robert Blakiston, had the most compelling reason for wanting to see Mary Blakiston dead. They were young and in love and she had wanted to stop the wedding for the very worst and most hateful of reasons. For a brief moment he himself had shared their feelings. But if they had planned to kill her, why would they have tried to get Pünd involved? Could it have been an elaborate smokescreen?

Turning these thoughts over in his mind, Raymond Chubb lit a cigarette and went through the pages again.

6

In his masterwork, *The Landscape of Criminal Investigation*, Atticus Pünd had written: *'One can think of the truth as eine vertiefung – a sort of deep valley which may not be visible from a distance but which will come upon you quite suddenly. There are many ways to arrive there. A line of questioning that turns out to be irrelevant still has the power to bring you nearer to your goal. There are no wasted journeys in the detection of a crime.'* In other words, it did not matter that he had not yet seen Mary Blakiston's diary and had no idea of its contents. Although he and Inspector Chubb were taking two very different approaches, it was inevitable that eventually they would meet.

After they had left the Lodge House, he and Fraser had walked the short distance to the vicarage, following the road rather than using the short cut through Dingle Dell, enjoying the warmth of the afternoon. Fraser had rather taken to Saxby-on-Avon and was a little puzzled that the detective seemed so immune to its charms. Indeed, it struck him that Pünd hadn't been quite himself since they had left London, lapsing into long silences, lost in his thoughts. The two of them were now sitting in the living room where Henrietta had brought them tea and home-made biscuits. It was a bright, cheerful room with dried flowers in the fireplace and French windows that looked out onto a well-kept garden with woodland beyond. There was an upright piano, several shelves of books, door curtains that would be drawn in the winter. The furniture was comfortable. None of it matched.

Robin and Henrietta Osborne were sitting next to each other on a sofa and could not have looked more awkward or, frankly, more guilty. Pünd had barely started his interrogation but they were already defensive, clearly dreading what might come next. Fraser understood what they were going through. He had seen it before. You could be completely blameless and respectable but the moment you talked to the detective you became a suspect and nothing you said could be taken at face value. It was all part of the game and it seemed to him that the Osbornes weren't playing it too well.

'On the night that Sir Magnus Pye was murdered, Mrs Osborne, you left your home. This would have been about eight fifteen.' Pünd waited for her to deny this and when she didn't, added: 'Why?'

'May I ask who told you that?' Henrietta countered.

Pünd shrugged. 'Believe me, it is of no importance, Mrs Osborne. It is my task to establish where everyone was at the time of the death, to piece together the jigsaw you might say. I ask questions and I receive answers. That is all.'

'It's just that I don't like the idea of being spied on. That's the trouble with living in a village. Everyone is always looking at you.' The vicar patted her gently on the hand and she continued. 'Yes. I was out looking for my husband at about that time. The thing is . . .' She hesitated.

'We were both rather upset about some news we'd just heard and he'd gone off on his own. When it was getting dark and he hadn't come home, I began to wonder where he was.'

'And where in fact were you, Mr Osborne?'

'I went to the church. Whenever I need to sort myself out, that's where I go. I'm sure you understand.'

'Did you walk or did you go on your bicycle?'

'The way you ask that question, Mr Pünd, I suspect you already know the answer. I took the bike.'

'What time did you return home?'

'I suppose it would have been about half past nine.'

Pünd frowned. According to Brent, he had heard the vicar cycle up past the Ferryman about half an hour after he had arrived. That would have been about nine o'clock or nine fifteen. There was a discrepancy, at least fifteen minutes missing. 'You are sure of that time?' he asked.

'I'm absolutely sure,' Henrietta cut in. 'I've already told you: I was concerned. I certainly had one eye on the clock and it was exactly half past nine when my husband arrived. I had kept his dinner for him and I sat with him while he ate it.'

Pünd did not pursue the matter. There were three possibilities. The first and most obvious was that the Osbornes were lying. Certainly the woman seemed nervous, as if she were trying to protect her husband. The second was that Brent had been mistaken – although he had seemed surprisingly reliable. And the third . . . ? 'I would imagine that it was the announcement of the new housing development that had upset you,' he said.

'Exactly.' Osborne pointed at the window, at the view beyond. 'That's where it's going to be. Right there at the end of our garden. Well, of course, this house isn't ours. It belongs to the church and my wife and I won't be here for ever. But it seems such a destructive thing to do. So unnecessary.'

'It may never happen,' Fraser said. 'What with Sir Magnus being dead and all that . . .'

'Well, I'm not going to celebrate any person's death.

That would be quite wrong. But I will admit to you that when I heard the news I did entertain precisely that thought. It was wrong of me. I shouldn't allow my personal feelings to poison my judgement.

'You should take a look at Dingle Dell,' Henrietta cut in. 'If you haven't walked there, you won't understand why it means so much to us. Would you like me to show you?'

'I would like that very much,' Pünd replied.

They had finished the tea. Fraser quietly helped himself to another biscuit and they all went out through the French windows. The vicarage garden extended for about twenty yards, sloping downhill with flower beds on each side of a lawn that became wilder and more unkempt the further they went from the house. It had been deliberately landscaped that way. There was no fence or barrier between the Osbornes' property and the wood beyond making it impossible to say where one ended and the other began.

Quite suddenly they were in Dingle Dell. The trees – oak, ash and Wych Elm – closed in on them without warning, surrounding them and cutting off the world outside. It was a lovely place. The late afternoon sun, slanting through the leaves and branches, had become a soft green and there were butterflies dancing in the beams . . . 'Purple Hairstreak,' Henrietta muttered. The ground was soft underfoot: grass and patches of moss with clumps of flowers. There was something curious about the wood. It wasn't a wood at all. It was a dell, much smaller, and yet now they were in it there seemed to be no edges, no obvious way out. Everything was very hushed. Although a few birds were flitting around the trees, they did so without making any sound. Only the drone of a bumblebee disturbed the silence and it was gone as quickly as it had come.

'Some of these trees have been here for two or three hundred years,' Osborne said. He looked around him. 'You know that Sir Magnus found his treasure trove here? Roman coins and jewellery, probably buried to keep them safe. Every time we walk here, it's different. Wonderful toadstools later in the year. All sorts of different insects, if you're into that sort of thing...'

They came to a clump of wild garlic, the white flowers bursting out like stars and then beyond it another plant, this one a tangle of spikey leaves that sprawled across the path.

'Atropa Belladonna,' Pünd said. 'Deadly nightshade. I understand, Mrs Osborne, that you unfortunately stepped on a specimen and poisoned yourself.'

'Yes. It was very stupid of me. And unlucky too – it somehow cut my foot.' She laughed nervously. 'I can't imagine what possessed me to come out without my shoes. I suppose I like the feeling of the moss on the soles of my feet. Anyway, I certainly learned my lesson. I'll steer clear of it from now on.'

'Do you want to go on?' Osborne asked. 'Pye Hall is just on the other side.'

'Yes. It would be interesting to see it again,' Pünd replied.

There was no actual path. They continued through the green haze, arriving at the far edge of the wood as unexpectedly as they had entered it. Suddenly the trees parted and there, in front of them was the lake, still and black, with the lawn easing its way down towards it from Pye Hall. Freddy Pye was outside, kicking a football around and Brent was kneeling in front of a flower bed with a pair of secateurs. Neither of them had noticed the little party as they had arrived. From where they were standing, the Lodge House was completely out of sight, hidden by its own woodland screen.

'Well, here we are,' Osborne said. He put his arm around his wife, then thought better of it and let it drop. 'Pye Hall is quite splendid, really. It was a nunnery at one stage. It's been in the same family for centuries. At least that's one thing they can't do – knock it down!'

'It is a house that has seen a great deal of death,' Pünd remarked.

'Yes. I suppose that's true of many country houses...'

'But not quite so recently. You were away when Mary Blakiston died.'

'I already told you that, when we met outside the church.'

'You said you were in Devonshire.'

'That's right.'

'Where exactly?'

The vicar seemed nonplussed. He turned his head away and his wife broke in angrily. 'Why are you asking us these questions, Mr Pünd? Do you really think that Robin and I made it up about being away? Do you think we sneaked back and pushed poor Mrs Blakiston down the stairs? What possible reason could we have? And I suppose we lopped off Sir Magnus's head to save Dingle Dell even though it may not make a jot of difference. His beastly son might go ahead with it anyway.'

Atticus Pünd spread his hands and sighed. 'Mrs Osborne, you do not understand the demands of police and detective work. Of course I do not believe the things that you suggest and it gives me no pleasure to ask you these questions. But everything must be in its place. Every statement must be verified, every movement examined. It may be that you do not wish to tell me where you were. Eventually, you will have to tell the Inspector. I am sorry if you consider it an intrusion.'

Robin Osborne glanced at his wife who replied. 'Of course we don't mind telling you. It's just not very nice being treated as suspects. If you talk to the manager of the Sheplegh Court Hotel, he'll tell you we were there all week. It's near Dartmouth.'

'Thank you.

They turned and walked back through Dingle Dell; Pünd and Robin Osborne in front, Henrietta and James Fraser behind. 'It was of course you who officiated at the funeral of Mrs Blakiston,' Pünd said.

'That's right. It was lucky we were back in time, although I suppose I could always have cut my holiday short.'

'I wonder if you remarked upon a person who was unknown to the village. He was standing on his own, I believe, separate from the other mourners. I have been told that he was wearing an old-fashioned hat.'

Robin Osborne considered. 'There was someone there wearing a Fedora, I think,' he said. 'They left quite abruptly as I recall. But I'm afraid I can't tell you very much more than that. As you can imagine, I had my mind on other things. He certainly didn't come for drinks at the Queen's Arms.'

'Did you happen to notice Robert Blakiston during the service? I would be interested to know your impressions of how he behaved.'

'Robert Blakiston?' They had reached the clump of belladonna and Osborne was careful to avoid it. 'I wonder why you're asking about him,' he went on. 'If you must know, I feel rather sorry for him. I heard about the argument he had with his mother. The village was full of gossip after she died. I wasn't having any of it. I think people can be quite cruel – or thoughtless, anyway. Often it's the same thing. I can't say I know Robert very well. He hasn't had an easy life but he's found himself a young lady now and I couldn't be more pleased for him. Miss Sanderling works at the doctor's surgery and I'm sure she'll help him settle down. The two of them have asked me to marry them at St Botolph's. I'm very much looking forward to it.'

He paused, then went on.

'He and his mother quarrelled. That's common knowledge. But I was observing him throughout the service – he and Josie were standing quite close to me – and I would have said he was genuinely grieving. When I reached the last paragraph of my address he started crying and covered his eyes to hide the tears and Josie had to take his arm. It's hard for a boy to lose his mother no matter what the feelings between them and I'm sure he bitterly regretted what he had said. Speak in haste, repent at leisure as the old saying goes.'

'What was your opinion of Mary Blakiston?'

Osborne didn't answer at once. He continued walking until they had emerged once again in the vicarage garden. 'She was very much part of the village. She'll be missed,' was all he said.

'I would be interested to see the funeral address,' Pünd said. 'Would you by any chance have a copy?'

'Really?' The vicar's eyes brightened. He had put a lot of work into the speech. 'As a matter of fact, I did hang on to it. I've got it inside. Are you coming back in? Never mind. I'll get it for you.'

He hurried in through the French windows. Pünd turned in time to see Fraser emerge from Dingle Dell with the vicar's wife, the light slanting down behind them. It was true, he thought. The wood was a very special place, somewhere worth protecting.

But at what price?

7

That afternoon, there was another death.

Dr Redwing had driven back to Ashton House and this time her husband had accompanied her. The call from the matron had come that afternoon and although she had said nothing specific, there could be no mistaking the tone of her voice. 'It might be best if you were here. I do think you should come.' Dr Redwing had made similar calls herself. Old Edgar Rennard had not, after all, recovered from the slight fall he had taken the week before. On the contrary, it seemed to have jolted or broken something and since then he had begun a rapid slide. He had barely been awake since his daughter's last visit. He had eaten nothing, taken only a few sips of water. The life was visibly draining out of him.

Arthur and Emilia were sitting on the uncomfortable furniture in the overly bright room, watching the rise and fall of the old man's chest beneath the blankets. They both knew what the other was thinking but didn't like to put it into words. How long would they have to sit here? At what time would it be reasonable to call it a day and go back home? Would they blame themselves if they weren't there at the end? In the end, would it make any difference?

'You can go if you like,' Emilia said, eventually.

'No. I'll stay with you.'

'Are you sure?'

'Yes. Of course.' He thought for a moment. 'Would you like a coffee?'

'That would be nice.'

It was impossible to have any sort of conversation in a room with a dying man. Arthur Redwing got to his feet and shuffled off to the kitchenette at the end of the corridor. Emilia was left on her own.

And that was when Edgar Rennard opened his eyes, quite unexpectedly, as if he had merely nodded off in front of the television. He saw her at once and showed not the least surprise. Perhaps, in his mind, she had never gone away for he returned almost at once to the subject he had raised the last time they were together. 'Did you tell him?' he asked.

'Did I tell who, Papa?' She wondered whether she ought to call Arthur back. But she was afraid of raising her voice or doing anything that might disturb the dying man.

'It's not fair. I have to tell them. They have to know.'

'Papa, do you want me to call the nurse?'

'No!' He was suddenly angry, as if he knew that there were only minutes left, that there was no time for delay. At the same moment, a sort of clarity came into his eyes. Later on, Dr Redwing would say that he had been given this one last gift at the end of his life. The dementia had finally retreated, leaving him in control. 'I was there when the children were born,' he said. His voice was younger, stronger. 'I delivered them at Pye Hall. Lady Cynthia Pye. A beautiful woman, daughter of an earl – but she wasn't strong, not built to give birth to twins. I was afraid I might lose her. In the end it all went well. Two children, born twelve minutes apart, a boy and a girl, both healthy.

'But afterwards, before anyone knew what had happened, Sir Merrill Pye came to me. Sir Merrill. He wasn't a good man. Everyone was afraid of him. And he wasn't happy. Because, you see, *the girl had come first*. The estate was entailed on the firstborn child . . . it was unusual but that's how it was. Not the eldest male child. But he wanted it to be the boy. He'd got the house from his father who'd got it from his father before him – it had always been boys. Do you understand? He hated the idea of the whole estate passing to a girl and so he made me . . . he told me . . . the boy came first.'

Emilia looked at her father with his head resting on the pillow, his white hair forming a halo around him, his eyes bright with the effort of explaining. 'Papa, what did you do?' she asked.

'What do you think I did? I told a lie. He was a bit of a bully, Sir Merrill. He could have made my life a misery. And at the time, I told myself, what did it matter? After all, they were just two babies. They didn't know anything. And they would both grow up in the house together. It wasn't as if I was hurting anyone. That was what I thought.' A tear trickled out of the corner of his eye and made its way down the side of his face. 'So I filled in the form the way he wanted it. 3.48 a.m. – a boy and 4.00 a.m. – a girl. That's what I wrote.'

'Oh Papa!'

'It was wrong of me. I see that now. Magnus got everything and Clarissa got nothing and I often thought that I should tell her, tell both of them the truth. But what good would it do? Nobody would believe me. Sir Merrill is long gone. And Lady Cynthia. They're all forgotten! But it's haunted me. It's always haunted me. What I wrote was a lie. A boy! I said it was a boy!'

By the time Arthur Redwing returned with the coffees, Dr Rennard had breathed his last. He found his wife sitting in shock and assumed, obviously, that it was due to the loss. He stayed with her while the matron was called and the necessary arrangements made. Dr Rennard had taken out funeral insurance with the well-known company of Lanner & Crane and they would be informed first thing in the morning – it was too late now. In the meantime, he would be transferred to a small chapel within Ashton House that was reserved for such occasions. He was going to be buried in the cemetery at King's Abbott, close to the house where he had lived. He had made that decision when he retired.

It was only as they were driving home that Emilia Redwing repeated what her father had told her. Arthur, behind the wheel, was shocked. 'Good God!' he exclaimed. 'Are you sure he knew what he was saying?'

'It was extraordinary. He was completely lucid – just for the five minutes you were gone.'

'I'm sorry, dear. You should have called me.'

'It doesn't matter. I just wish you'd been there to hear it.'

'I could have been a witness.'

Dr Redwing hadn't considered that – but now she nodded. 'Yes.'

'What are you going to do?'

Dr Redwing didn't answer. She watched the Bath Valley slipping by, cows dotted here and there, grazing on the other side of the railway line. The summer sun hadn't set but the light was soft, the shadows folding themselves into the sides of the hills. 'I don't know,' she said, at length. 'In a way, I wish he hadn't told me. It was his guilty secret and now it's mine.' She sighed. 'I suppose I'm going to have to tell someone. I'm not sure it'll make any difference. Even if you had been there, there isn't any proof.'

'Maybe you should tell that detective.'

'Mr Pünd?' She was annoyed with herself. It had never occurred to her that there might be a connection, but of course she had to pass on what she knew. Sir Magnus Pye, the beneficiary of a huge estate, had been violently murdered and now it turned out that the estate had never been his in the first place. Could that be the reason why he had been killed? 'Yes,' she said. 'I suppose I had better let him know.'

They drove on in silence. Then her husband said, 'And what about Clarissa Pye? Will you tell her?'

'Do you think I should?'

'I don't know. I really don't.'

They reached the village. And as they drove past the fire station and then the Queen's Arms with the church just behind it, they were unaware that they were both having the same thought.

What if Clarissa had already known?

8

At exactly that moment, inside the Queen's Arms, James Fraser was carrying a tray with five drinks to a quiet table in the far corner. There were three pints of beer – for himself, for Robert Blakiston and for Inspector Chubb, a Dubonnet and bitter lemon for Joy Sanderling, and a small sherry for Atticus Pünd. He would have liked to have added a couple of bags of crisps but something told him that they would be inappropriate. As he sat down, he examined the man who had brought them there. Robert Blakiston, who had lost both a mother and a mentor in the space of two weeks, had come straight from work. He had changed out of his overalls and put on a jacket but his hands were still covered with grease and oil. Fraser wondered if it would ever come off. He was a strange-looking young man, not unattractive but almost like a bad drawing of himself with his badly cut hair, his over-pronounced cheekbones, his pale skin. He was sitting next to Joy, quite possibly holding her hand under the table. His eyes were haunted. It was obvious that he would have preferred to be anywhere but here.

'You don't need to worry, Rob,' Joy was saying. 'Mr Pünd only wants to help.'

'Like he helped you when you went to London?' Robert was having none of it. 'This village won't let us alone. First they said it was me who killed my own mother, not that I would ever have laid a finger on her. You know that. And as if that wasn't enough for them, then they start their whispering about Sir Magnus.' He turned to Atticus. 'Is that why you're here, Mr Pound? Is it because you suspect me?'

'Did you have a reason to wish Sir Magnus harm?' Pünd asked.

'No. He wasn't an easy man, I'll give you that. But he was always very good to me. I wouldn't have a job if it weren't for him.'

'I must ask you many things about your life, Robert,' Pünd went on. 'It is not because you are under suspicion any more than anyone else in this village. But both deaths occurred at Pye Hall and it is true to say that you have a close association with that place.'

'I didn't choose it that way.'

'Of course not. But you can perhaps tell us a great deal about its history and about the people who lived there.'

Robert's one visible hand curled round his beer. He looked up at Pünd defiantly. 'You're not a policeman,' he said. 'Why should I have to tell you anything?'

'*I'm* a policeman,' Chubb cut in. He had been about to light a cigarette and stopped with the match inches away from his face. 'And Mr Pünd is working with me. You should mind your manners, young man. If you don't want to co-operate, we'll see what a night behind bars will do to change your mind. It won't be the first time you've seen the inside of a jail, I understand.' He lit the cigarette and blew out the match.

Joy put a hand on her fiancé's arm. 'Please, Robert...'

He shrugged her off. 'I've got nothing to hide. You can ask me what you want.'

'Then let us begin at the very beginning,' Pünd suggested. 'If it does not distress you, perhaps you can describe for us your childhood at Pye Hall.'

'It doesn't distress me, although I was never very happy there,' Robert answered. 'It's not very nice when your mother cares more about her employer than your own father – but that's how it was almost from the day we moved into the Lodge House. Sir Magnus this, Sir Magnus that! She was all over him, even though she was never more than his skivvy. My dad wasn't happy about it either. It was never easy for him, living in someone else's house in someone else's grounds. But they stuck with it for a time. My dad wasn't getting much work before the war. It was somewhere to live, a regular income. So he put up with it.

'I was twelve years old when we moved in. We'd been living up at Sheppard's Farm, which was my granddad's place. It was pretty rundown but we liked it there, left to our own devices. Me and Tom had been born in Saxby-on-Avon, and we always lived here. As far as I was concerned there was nowhere else in the world. Sir Magnus needed someone to look after the place when the old housekeeper left and my mum was already doing jobs around the village, so it was an obvious choice, really.

'The first year or so was OK. The Lodge House wasn't such a bad place and we had plenty of room after Sheppard's Farm. We all had our own rooms, which was nice – Mum and Dad at the end of the corridor. I used to boast about it at school, having such a grand address, although the other kids just teased me about it.'

'How well did you and your brother get on?'

'We had fights, like all little boys. But we were also very close. We used to chase each other all over the estate. We were pirates, treasure hunters, soldiers, spies. Tom used to make up all the games. He was younger than me but he was a lot smarter too. He used to tap out this code on the wall to me at night. He'd made it up himself. I didn't understand a word of it but I'd hear him tapping it out when we were meant to be asleep.' He half-smiled at the memory and just for a moment some of the tension went out of his face.

'You had a dog, I believe. Its name was Bella.'

At once the frown was back. Fraser remembered the collar that they had found in the bedroom at the Lodge House but he wondered what relevance it could have.

'Bella was Tom's dog,' Robert said. 'My dad got it for

him around the time we left Sheppard's Farm.' He glanced at Joy as if unsure whether to continue. 'But after we moved it – it didn't end well.'

'What happened?'

'We never really found out but I'll tell you this. Sir Magnus didn't want him on his land. That much was clear. He said that Bella chased the sheep. He said right away he wanted us to get rid of it but Tom really loved that dog so Dad said no. Anyway, one day it disappeared. We looked everywhere for it but it was just gone. And then, about two weeks later, we found it in Dingle Dell.' He paused and looked down. 'Someone had cut it's throat. Tom always said it was Brent. But if it was, he was only acting on Sir Magnus's orders.'

There was a long silence. When Pünd spoke again, his voice was low. 'I must ask you now about another death,' he said. 'I am sure it will be painful to you. But you understand...'

'You're talking about Tom.'

'Yes.'

Robert nodded. 'When the war began, my dad went over to Boscombe Down where he worked on the planes and he'd often stay there the whole week so we only saw him now and then. Maybe if he'd been there, maybe if he'd looked out for us more it would never have happened. That's what my mum always said. She blamed him for not being there.'

'Can you tell me what occurred?'

'I'll never forget it, Mr Pound. Not as long as I live. At the time, I thought it was my fault. That was what a lot of people said and maybe it was what my dad believed. He never talked to me about it. He hardly ever spoke to me again and I haven't see him now in years. Well, maybe he's got a point. Tom was two years younger than me and I was meant to be looking after him. But I left him on his own and the next thing I know, they're pulling him out of the lake and he's drowned. He was only twelve years old.'

'It wasn't your fault, Robert,' Joy said. She put her

arm around him, holding him tightly. 'It was an accident. You weren't even there . . .'

'I was the one who led him out into the garden. I left him on his own.' He gazed at Pünd with eyes that were suddenly bright with tears. 'It was the summer, a day like today. We were on a treasure hunt. We were always looking for bits and pieces – silver and gold – we knew how Sir Magnus had found a whole load of the stuff in Dingle Dell. Buried treasure! It was the sort of thing that every boy dreamed about. We'd read stories in the *Magnet* and the *Hotspur* and then we'd try to make them come real. Sir Magnus used to encourage us too. He'd actually set us challenges. So maybe he was partly to blame for what happened. I don't know. It's always about blame, isn't it? These things happen and you have to find some way to make them make sense.

'Tom drowned in the lake. To this day, we don't know how it happened. He was fully dressed so it wasn't as if he'd gone for a swim. Maybe he fell. Maybe he hit his head. Brent was the one who found him and got him out. I heard him shouting and I came running back across the lawn. I helped to get him on dry land and I tried to resuscitate him, the way they showed us at school. But there was nothing I could do. By the time Mum came down and found us, it was too late.'

'Neville Brent was already working there?' Chubb asked. 'He must have been in his teens himself.'

'Yes. He was very young but he used to help his father. In fact he took over the job when his dad died.'

'It must have been a great shock for you, and very upsetting, to see your brother in this way,' Pünd said.

'I threw myself into the water. I grabbed hold of him. I was screaming and I was crying and even now I can't bring myself to look at that damned place. I never wanted to stay in the Lodge House and if I had my way, I'd get out of Saxby-on-Avon altogether and now, what with everything that's happened, maybe I will. Anyway, my dad came back that night. He shouted at my mother. He shouted at me. He never gave us any support. All we got from him was anger.

And a year later, he left us. He said the marriage was over. We never saw him again.'

'How did your mother respond to what had happened?'

'She still stayed working for Sir Magnus. That's the first thing. She would never have thought of leaving him no matter what – that's how much she looked up to him. She'd walk past that lake every day on her way to work. She told me that she never looked, that she kept her head the other way – but I don't know how she did it.'

'She was still caring for you?'

'She was trying to, Mr Pound. I suppose I might as well admit it although I never thanked her for it. Nothing was ever easy after Tom died. Things went wrong at school. The other children could be so bloody cruel. And she was afraid for me. She never let me out of the house! Sometime I felt like a prisoner. She was always watching me. She was terrified something was going to happen to me and she would be left on her own. I think that was the real reason she didn't want me to marry Joy, because I would leave her. She was suffocating me and that was how things went wrong between us. I might as well admit it. I ended up hating her.'

He lifted his glass and took a few sips of his beer.

'You didn't hate her,' Joy said, quietly. 'Things weren't right between you, that's all. You were both living in the shadow of what had happened and you didn't realise how much it was hurting you.'

'You threatened her just before she died,' Inspector Chubb remarked. He had already finished his own beer.

'I never did that, sir. I never did.'

'We will come to that all in good time,' Pünd said. 'You did, in the end, leave Pye Hall. Tell us first about your time in Bristol.'

'It didn't last long.' Now Robert sounded sullen. 'Sir Magnus had arranged it for me. After my dad left, he sort of took over and tried to help as best he could. He wasn't a bad man – not *all* bad, anyways. He got me an apprenticeship with Ford Motorcars but it all went wrong. I'll admit I made a right mess of it. I wasn't happy on my own in a strange city. I drank too much and I got into a fight at the local pub, the Blue Boar. It was all about nothing . . .' He nodded at Chubb. 'But you're right. I did spend a night in jail and there might have been worse trouble for me if Sir Magnus hadn't stepped in once again. He spoke to the police and they agreed to let me off with a caution but that was the end of it for me. I came back to Saxby and he set me up with the job I have now. I've always liked tinkering with cars. I suppose I got that from my dad, although it's all he ever gave me.'

'What was it that made you argue with your mother in the week of her death?' Pünd asked.

'It was nothing. She wanted me to mend a broken light. That's all. You really think I killed her because of that, Mr Pound? I swear to you, I didn't go near her – and I couldn't have. Joy told you. I was with her that evening! All evening and all night. We left the flat together, so if I'm lying, she's lying and why would she do that?'

'You will forgive me, but that is not necessarily the case.' Pünd turned to Joy Sanderling who seemed almost to brace herself for what was to come. 'When you visited me in London, you told me you were together all the time. But are you certain that you were constantly in each other's sight? Did you not take a shower or a bath? Did you not prepare the breakfast?'

Joy flushed. 'I did both, Mr Pünd. Maybe there were ten or fifteen minutes when I didn't see Robert . . .'

'And your motor scooter was parked outside the flat, Miss Sanderling. Although it was too far by foot, it would have taken Robert no more than two or three minutes to reach Pye Hall – by your own admission. It is not impossible that he could have driven there, killed the mother who had caused him so much torment and who stood so resolutely opposed to your marriage and returned, all in the time that you were in the kitchen or in the bath.' He let the proposition hang in the air, then turned again to Robert. 'And what of Sir

Magnus?' he continued. 'Can you tell me where you were at half past eight on the evening of his death?'

Robert slumped, defeated. 'I can't help you there. I was in my flat, having supper on my own. Where else would I have been? But if you think I killed Sir Magnus, maybe you can tell me why. He never did anything to hurt me.'

'Your mother died at Pye Hall. He did not care enough even to attend her funeral!'

'How can you be so cruel?' Joy exclaimed. 'You're spinning fantasies out of thin air, just to accuse Robert. He had no reason to kill either of them. As for the motor scooter, I never heard it leave. I'm sure I would have, even if I was in the bath.'

'Have you finished?' Robert asked. He got to his feet, leaving the rest of his beer untouched.

'I have no further questions,' Pünd said.

'Then if you don't mind, I'm going home.'

'I'm coming with you,' Joy said.

Chubb glanced at Pünd as if to be sure that there was nothing more he wanted to ask. Pünd nodded very slightly and the two young people left together.

'Do you really think he might have killed his mother?' Fraser asked, as soon as they were gone.

'I think it is unlikely, James. To hear him speak of his mother just now . . . he spoke with anger, with vexation and even perhaps with fear. But there was no hatred. Nor do I believe that he drove to Pye Hall on the motor scooter of his fiancée, even though it was interesting to suggest the idea. And why? Because of its colour. Do you not remember? It is something that I remarked to you, when Miss Sanderling first visited us. A man wishing to pass quickly through a village to commit a crime might borrow a motor scooter but not, I think, one that was bright pink. It would be too easily noticed. Could he have had a motive to kill Sir Magnus Pye? It is possible but I will admit that at the moment it is not making itself known.'

'All a bit of a waste of time then,' Chubb concluded. He glanced at his empty glass. 'Still, the Queen's Arms serves a decent pint. And I have something for you, Herr Pünd.' He reached down and produced Mary Blakiston's diary. Briefly, he explained how it had been found. 'It's got something about pretty much everyone in the village,' he said. 'Talk about dishing out the dirt! She's been collecting it by the bucket!'

'You don't suppose she was using the information to blackmail people?' Fraser suggested. 'After all, that might give someone a very good reason to push her down the stairs.'

'You've got a good point there,' Chubb said. 'Some of the entries are a bit vague. She was careful about what she wrote. But if people found out how much she knew about them, she could have had a lot of enemies. Just like Sir Magnus and Dingle Dell. That's the trouble with this case. Too many suspects! But the question is, was it the same person who killed them both?' The detective inspector got to his feet. 'You'll let me have that back in due course, Herr Pünd,' he said. 'I've got to get home. Mrs Chubb is cooking her *Fricassee de Poulet à l'Ancienne*, God help me. I'll see you gentlemen tomorrow.'

He left. Fraser and Pünd were alone.

'The inspector is absolutely correct,' Pünd said.

'You mean there are too many suspects?

'He asks whether the same person killed Sir Magnus Pye and his housekeeper. Everything rests on that. Clearly there is a connection between the two deaths but we are no closer to discovering what it is. And until then, we will remain in the dark. But perhaps the answer now lies in my hands.' He looked at the first page and smiled. 'Already the handwriting is known to me . . .'

'How?'

But Pünd didn't answer. He had begun to read.

FIVE

Silver

1

Detective Inspector Chubb very much liked the police station in Orange Grove, Bath. It was a perfect Georgian construction, solid and serious yet at the same time light and elegant enough to feel welcoming . . . at least, if you were on the right side of the law. He couldn't enter it without a sense that his work mattered and that by the end of the day the world might be a slightly better place. His office was on the first floor, overlooking the main entrance. Sitting at his desk, he could look out of a window that stretched the full height of the room and this too gave him a sense of comfort. He was, after all, the eye of the law. It was only right that he should have a view that was so expansive.

He had brought John Whitehead to this room. It was a deliberate move, to winkle the man out of the false shell that Saxby-on-Avon had provided and to remind him who was in charge. There were to be no lies told here. In fact there were four people facing him: Whitehead, his wife, Atticus Pünd and his young assistant, Fraser. He normally had a photograph of Mrs Chubb on the desk but he had slid it into a drawer just before they came in. He wasn't quite sure why.

'Your name is John Whitehead?' he began.

'That's right.' The antique dealer was sullen and downcast. He knew the game was up. He wasn't trying to disguise it.

'And you came to Saxby-on-Avon how long ago?'

'Three years.'

'We've done nothing wrong,' Gemma Whitehead cut in. She was such a small woman, the seat looked much too big for her. She was cradling a handbag in her lap. Her feet barely touched the floor. 'You know who he is and what he's done. But he's left that all behind him. He served his time and he was let out for good behaviour. We moved out of London, just to be together somewhere quiet – and all this business with Sir Magnus, that had *nothing* to do with us.'

'I think you should let me be the judge of that,' Chubb replied. Mary Blakiston's diary was lying on the desk in front of him and for a moment he was tempted to open it. But there was no need. He already knew the relevant contents well enough. 'On 9 July a certain Arthur Reeve had his home broken into. Mr Reeve used to be the landlord at the Queen's Arms and is now living in retirement with his wife. A window was broken and he was very distressed to find that his medal collection, including a rare George V1 Greek medal, had been stolen from his front room. The entire collection was valued at a hundred pounds or more although of course it had great sentimental value too.'

Whitehead drew himself up but next to him, his wife had paled. She was hearing this for the first time. 'Why are you telling me this?' he demanded. 'I don't know anything about any medal.'

'The thief cut himself on the window,' Chubb said.

'One day later, on 10 July, you were treated by Dr Redwing,' Pünd added. 'You required stitches for an unpleasant cut on your hand.' He smiled briefly to himself. In the landscape of this particular crime, two minor byways had just reached a crossroads.

'I cut my hand in the kitchen,' Johnny said. He glanced at his wife who did not look convinced. 'I never went anywhere near Mr Reeve or his medal. It's a pack of lies.'

'What can you tell us about the visit Mary Blakiston made to you on 11 July, four days before she died?'

'Who told you that? Have you been watching me?'

'Do you deny it?'

'What's there to deny? Yes. She came into the shop. Lots of people come into the shop. She never said a thing about any medals.'

'Then maybe she talked to you about the money that you had paid to Brent.' Pünd had spoken softly, reasonably but there was something in his tone that suggested he knew everything, that there was no point arguing. In fact, Fraser knew this wasn't true. The groundsman had done his best to cover his tracks. He had said the five pounds was owed to him, perhaps for work he had done. Pünd was taking a stab in the dark. However, his words had an immediate effect.

'All right,' Whitehead admitted. 'She did come in, nosing around, asking me questions – just like you. What are you trying to say? That I pushed her down the stairs to shut her up?'

'Johnny!' Gemma Whitehead let out a cry of exasperation.

'It's all right, love.' He reached out to her but she twisted away. 'I've done nothing wrong. Brent came into the shop a couple of days after Mary's funeral. He had something to sell. It was a silver belt buckle, Roman, a nice little piece. I'd say about fourth century BC. He wanted twenty quid for it. I gave him five.'

'When was this?'

'I can't remember. Monday! It was the week after the funeral.'

'Did Brent say where he got it from?' Chubb asked.

'No.'

'Did you ask him?'

'Why should I have?'

'You must have been aware that there'd been a burglary at Pye Hall only a few days before. A collection of silver jewellery and coins was stolen from Sir Magnus. It was the same day as Mrs Blakiston's funeral.'

'I did hear about that. Yes.'

'And you didn't put two and two together?'

Whitehead drew a breath. 'A lot of people come into my shop. I buy a lot of things. I bought a set of Worcester coffee mugs off Mrs Reeve and a brass carriage clock off the Finches – and that was just last week. Do you think I asked them where they got them? If I went round treating everyone in Saxby like criminals, I'd be out of business in a week.'

Chubb drew a breath. 'But *you* are a criminal, Mr Whitehead. You did three years in prison for receiving stolen goods.'

'You promised me!' Gemma muttered. 'You promised you weren't going back to all that.'

'Stay out of it, love. They're just trying to wind me up.' Whitehead glanced balefully at Chubb. 'You've got it all wrong, Mr Chubb. Yes. I bought a silver belt buckle off Brent. Yes. I knew there's been a break in at Pye Hall. But did I put two and two together? No. I didn't. Call me stupid if you like, but there's no crime in stupidity – and for all I know he could have had it in his family for twenty years. If you're saying it was stolen from Sir Magnus, then your argument is with Brent, not with me.'

'Where is the belt buckle now?'

'I sold it to a friend in London.'

'And for rather more than five pounds, I'll be bound.'

'That's my business, Mr Chubb. That's what I do.'

Atticus Pünd had been listening to all this in silence. Now he adjusted his glasses and observed, quietly: 'Mrs Blakiston visited you before the break-in at Pye Hall. It was the theft of the medal that interested her. Did she threaten you?'

'She was a nosey cow – asking questions about things that had nothing to do with her.'

'Did you purchase any other items from Brent?'

'No. That's all he had. If you want to find the rest of Sir Magnus's treasure trove, maybe you should be searching his place instead of wasting your time with me.'

Pünd and Chubb exchanged a glance. There was clearly nothing more to be gained from the interview. Even so, the detective inspector was determined to have the last word. 'There have been a number of petty thefts in Saxby-on-Avon since you arrived,' he said. 'Windows broken, antiques and jewellery gone missing. I can promise you we'll be looking into every one of them. And I'm going to want a record of everything you've bought and sold in the past three years too.'

'I don't keep records.'

'The tax office may take a dim view of that. I hope you're not planning on going anywhere in the next few weeks, Mr Whitehead. We'll be in touch again.'

The antique dealer and his wife got up and left the room, showing themselves out. Ahead of them, there was an upper landing and then a staircase leading down. They continued in silence but the moment they were in the open air, Gemma burst out: 'Oh Johnny! How could you lie to me?'

'I didn't lie to you,' Johnny replied, miserably.

'After everything we talked about. All the plans we had!' It was as if she hadn't heard him. 'Who did you see when you were in London? This silver belt buckle of yours – who did you sell it to?'

'I told you.'

'You mean Derek and Colin. Did you tell them about Mary? Did you tell them she was on to you?'

'What are you talking about?'

'You know what I mean. In the old days, when you were part of the gang, if people stepped out of line, things happened. We never mentioned it and I know you weren't part of it, but we both know what I'm talking about. People disappeared.'

'What? You think I took out a contract on Mary Blakiston to get her off my back?'

'Well, did you?'

Johnny Whitehead didn't answer. They walked to their car in silence.

2

A search of Brent's house had produced nothing that related either to the murder or the stolen treasure trove.

Brent lived on his own in a row of terraced houses in Daphne Road, a simple two-up, two-down that shared a porch with its neighbour, the two front doors meeting at an angle. From the outside, the building had a certain chocolate-box charm. The roof was thatched, the wisteria and the flower beds well cared for. The interior told another story. Everything had a sense of neglect, from the unwashed dishes in the sink to the unmade bed and the clothes thrown carelessly on the floor. A certain smell lingered in the air, one that Chubb had come upon many times before and which always made him frown. It was the smell of a man living alone.

There was nothing in the house that was new or luxurious and everything had a make-do-and-mend quality, years after those words had gone out of fashion. Plates were chipped, chairs held together by string. Brent's parents had once lived here and he had done nothing to the place since they had died. He even slept in the same, single bed with the same blanket and eiderdown that must have been his as a boy. There were comics on the bedroom floor, too. And Scout magazines. It was as if Brent had never fully grown up and if he had stolen the entire hoard of Sir Magnus's Roman silver, he clearly hadn't sold it yet. He had just a hundred pounds in his bank account. There was nothing hidden in the house: not under the floorboards, in the attic, up the chimney. The police had done a thorough search.

'I didn't take it. I didn't do it. It wasn't me.' Brent had been brought home in a police car from Pye Hall and was sitting with a look of shock on his face, surrounded by policemen who had invaded the shabby sanctity of his home. Atticus Pünd and James Fraser were among them.

'Then how did you come upon the silver belt buckle that you sold to John Whitehead?' Chubb asked.

'I found it!' Brent continued hurriedly as the detective inspector's eyes glazed in disbelief. 'It's the truth. It was the day after the funeral. A Sunday. I don't work the weekend, not as a rule. But Sir Magnus and Lady Pye, they'd only just got back from their holiday and I thought they might need me. So I went down the hall just to show willing. And I was in the garden when I saw it, shining, on the lawn.

I didn't have any idea what it was but it looked old and there was a picture of a man carved into it, standing there with no clothes.' He smirked briefly as if sharing a rude joke. 'I popped it into my pocket and then on the Monday I took it into Mr Whitehead and he gave me a fiver for it. It was twice what I was expecting.'

Yes. And half what it was worth, Chubb thought. 'There were police called into Pye Hall that day,' he said. 'Sir Magnus reported a burglary. What do you have to say about that?'

'I left before lunchtime. I didn't see any police.'

'But you must have heard about the break-in.'

'I did. But by then it was too late. I'd already sold what I'd found to Mr Whitehead and maybe he'd sold it too. I looked in the shop window and it wasn't there.' Brent shrugged. 'I'd done nothing wrong.'

That much was questionable. But even Chubb would have been forced to admit that Brent's crime was a very minor one. If, that is, he was telling the truth. 'Where did you find the buckle?' he asked.

'It was in the grass. In front of the house.'

Chubb glanced at Pünd, as if asking for guidance. 'It would be interesting, I think, to see the exact spot,' Pünd said.

Chubb agreed and the four of them left together, Brent complaining all the while as he was carried back to Pye Hall. Once again they drove past the Lodge House with its two stone griffins almost seeming to whisper to each other and for a moment Fraser was reminded of the game that the two boys, Robert and Tom Blakiston, had played together at night, the code words that they had rapped out to each other when they were in bed. It suddenly struck him that the game had a significance he had overlooked but before he could mention it to Pünd, they had arrived. Brent called to them to stop and they pulled in about halfway up the drive, opposite the lake.

'It was over here!' He led them across the lawn. In front of them the lake stretched out, dank and oily with the woodland behind. Perhaps it was the story that Robert had told them earlier but there was something indisputably evil about it. The brighter the sun, the blacker the water appeared. They stopped about fifteen or twenty feet from the edge, Brent pointing down as if he remembered the exact spot. 'It was here.'

'Just lying here?' Chubb sounded unconvinced.

'The sun was glinting off it. That's how I saw it.'

Chubb considered the possibilities. 'Well, I suppose if someone had been carrying a whole pile of the stuff, if they were on foot and in a hurry, they might have dropped a piece without noticing it.'

'It is possible.' Pünd was already working out the angles. He looked back at the driveway, the Lodge House, the front door. 'And yet it is strange, Detective Inspector. Why would the burglar come this way? He broke into the house through the back . . . ?'

'That's right.'

'Then to reach the gate, it would have been faster to continue along the other side of the driveway.'

'Unless they were heading for Dingle Dell . . .' The inspector examined the line of trees with the vicarage somewhere on the other side of the lake. 'No chance of being seen if they go out through the wood.'

'That is true,' Pünd agreed. 'And yet, you will forgive me, Detective Inspector. You are a thief. You are carrying a great many pieces of silver jewellery and coins. Would you wish to make your way through thick woodland in the middle of the night?' His eyes settled on the black surface. 'The lake holds many mysteries,' he said. 'I believe it has further stories to tell and wonder if it would be possible for you to arrange an inspection by police divers, I have a suspicion, an idea . . .' He shook his head as if dismissing the thought.

'Divers?' Chubb shook his head. 'That's going to cost a pretty penny or two. What is it exactly you're hoping to find?'

'The true reason why Pye Hall was burgled on the same evening as Mary Blakiston's funeral.'

Chubb nodded. 'I'll see to it.'

'Do you want anything else?' Brent asked.

'I will keep you only for a few moments more, Mr Brent. I would like you to show us the door that was broken when the burglary took place.'

'Yes, sir.' Brent was relieved that the investigation seemed to be moving away from him. 'We can cut across through the rose garden.'

'There is one other question I wish to put to you,' Pünd said. As they walked, Fraser noticed that the detective was leaning heavily on his stick. 'I understand that Sir Magnus had made it known to you that he wished to dispense with your employment.'

Brent started as if stung. 'Who told you that?'

'Is it true?'

'Yes.' The groundsman was scowling now. His whole body seemed to have become stooped, his curly hair flopping over his forehead.

'Why did you not mention to this to me when we met?'

'You never asked me.'

Pünd nodded. That was fair enough. 'Why did he ask you to leave?'

'I don't know. But he was always on at me. Mrs Blakiston used to complain about me. Them two! They were like – like Bob and Gladys Grove.'

'It's a television programme,' Fraser said, overhearing. '*The Grove Family*.'

This was exactly the sort of thing that Fraser would know. And which Pünd wouldn't.

'When did he tell you?'

'The day Sir Magnus died.'

In other words, just before the first death.

'He must have given you a reason.'

'He gave me no reason. No good reason. I've been coming here ever since I was a boy. My father was here before me. And he come out here and just said that was the end of it.'

They had come to the rose garden. It was surrounded by a wall with an entrance that was an arbour shaped out of dark green leaves. Beyond, there was crazy paving, a statue of a cherub, all the different roses, and a bench.

And on the bench, Frances Pye and Jack Dartford were sitting, holding hands, engaged in a passionate kiss.

3

In fact, nobody was really very surprised. It had been obvious to Pünd – and even to Fraser – that Lady Pye and her ex-tennis partner had been conducting an affair. What else could they possibly have been doing in London on the day of the murder? Chubb had known it too and even the guilty parties only seemed mildly put out that they had been discovered in flagrante. It was going to happen sooner or later so why not now? They were still on the bench, sitting slightly apart, facing the three men who stood over them. A smirking Brent had been sent on his way.

'I think you should explain yourself, Lady Pye,' Chubb said.

'There's nothing really to explain,' she replied, coolly. 'Jack and I have been seeing each other for almost two years. That day in London . . . I was with him the whole time. But there was no shopping, no art galleries. After lunch, we had a room at the Dorchester. Jack stayed with me until about half past five. I left at seven. You can ask them if you don't believe me.'

'You lied to me, Lady Pye.'

'That was wrong of me, Detective Inspector, and I'm sorry. But the fact is, it doesn't make any real difference, does it? The rest of my story was true. Coming home on the train. Arriving at half past eight. Seeing the green car. Those are the salient points.'

'Your husband is dead. You were deceiving him. I'd say those are also salient points, Lady Pye.'

'It wasn't like that,' Jack Dartford cut in. 'She wasn't

deceiving him. That's not how I saw it anyway. You have no idea what Magnus was like. The man was a brute. The way he treated her, his infantile rages, it was disgusting. And she gave up her career for him!'

'What career was that?' Pünd asked.

'In the theatre! Frances was a brilliant actress. I saw her on the stage long before I met her.'

'That's enough, Jack,' Frances cut in.

'Is that where your husband met you? In the theatre?' Chubb asked.

'He sent flowers to my dressing room. He'd seen me as Lady Macbeth.'

Even Chubb knew that one: a play in which a powerful woman persuades a man to commit murder. 'Were you ever happy together?' he asked.

She shook her head. 'I knew very quickly that I'd made a mistake but I was younger then and I suppose I was too proud to admit it. The trouble with Magnus was that it wasn't enough for him to marry me. He had to own me. He made that clear very quickly. It was as if I were part of the package – the house, the grounds, the lake, the woods and the wife. He was very old-fashioned, the way he saw the world.'

'Was he ever violent to you?'

'He never actually struck me, Detective Inspector, but violence can take many forms. He was loud. He could be threatening. And he had a way of throwing himself around that often made me afraid.'

'Tell them about the sword!' Dartford insisted.

'Oh Jack!'

'What happened with the sword, Lady Pye? Chubb asked.

'It was just something that happened a couple of days before I went up to meet Jack. You must understand that, underneath it all, Magnus was a great big child. If you ask me, this whole business with Dingle Dell was more about upsetting people than actually making money. He had temper tantrums. If he didn't get what he wanted, he could become very nasty indeed.' She sighed. 'He had a good idea that I was seeing someone – all those trips to London. And the two of us were sleeping apart, of course. He didn't want me any more, not in the way a husband wants his wife, but it hurt his pride that I might have actually found somebody else.

'We had a row that morning. I can't even remember what started it. But then he started screaming at me – how I was his, how he would never let me go. I'd heard it all before. Only this time, he was crazier than ever. You noticed that there was a painting missing in the great hall. It was a portrait of me, which he'd commissioned as a present for my fortieth birthday. As a matter of fact it was done by Arthur Redwing.' She turned to Pünd. 'Have you met him?'

'He is married to the doctor?'

'Yes.'

'I have seen another work of his but we have not yet met.'

'Well, I think he's very talented. And I loved the painting he did of me. He actually managed to capture a moment of real happiness, standing in the garden near the lake – and that was rare enough, I can tell you. It was a gorgeous summer that year. Arthur did the painting over four or five sessions and although Magnus hardly paid him anything for it – that was typical of him to be so mean – I think it was rather wonderful. We talked about putting it in for the summer exhibition, you know, at the Royal Academy. But Magnus wouldn't put me on show. That would mean sharing me! So it stayed on the wall in the main hall.

'And then we had that argument. I'll admit that I can be quite nasty when I want to be and I certainly let him have a few home truths. Magnus went very red, as if was going to burst. He always did have problems with his blood pressure. He drank too much and he quite easily worked himself up into these rages. I told him I was going up to London. He refused to give me permission. I laughed at him and told him I didn't need his permission or anyone else's. Suddenly he went over to that stupid suit of armour and with a great yell pulled out the sword—'

'The same sword with which he would later be killed?'

'Yes, Mr Pünd. He came over to me, dragging it behind him

and for a moment I thought he was going to attack me with it. But instead he suddenly turned it on the painting and stabbed it again and again in front of my eyes. He knew it would hurt me, losing it. At the same time, he was telling me I was his possession and that he could do the same to me at any time.'

'What happened next, Lady Pye?'

'I just went on laughing. *Is that the best you can do?* I remember shouting those words at him. I think I was a little hysterical. Then I went up to my room and slammed the door.'

'And the painting?'

'I was sad about that. It couldn't be mended. Or maybe it could, but it would have been too expensive. Magnus gave it to Brent to put on the bonfire.'

She fell silent.

'I'm glad he's dead,' Jack Dartford muttered, suddenly. 'He was a total bastard. He was never kind to anyone and he made life a misery for Frances. I'd have done it myself, if I'd had the nerve. But he's gone now and we can start again.' He reached out and took her hand. 'No more hiding. No more lying. We can finally have the life we deserve.'

Pünd nodded at Chubb and the three of them moved away from the rose garden and back across the lawn. There was no sign of Brent. Jack Dartford and Lady Pye had remained where they were. 'I wonder where he was on the night of the murder,' Fraser said.

'You are referring to Mr Dartford?'

'We only have his word for it that he stayed in London. He left the hotel at half past five. That would have given him plenty of time to catch the train ahead of Lady Pye. It's just a thought . . .'

'You think him capable of murder?'

'I think he's a chancer. You can tell just by looking at him. He comes across an attractive woman who's being badly treated by her husband – and it seems to me that if you're going to cut somebody's head off, there has to be a better reason than saving a local wood and those two had a better reason than anyone.'

'There is some truth in what you say,' Pünd agreed.

Their car was parked a short distance away from the front of the house and they moved towards it slowly. Chubb too had noticed that Pünd was resting more heavily on his walking stick. He had once thought that the detective only carried it as a fashion accessory. Today he clearly needed it.

'There's something I forgot to tell you, Mr Pünd,' he muttered. It was the first time the two of them had been alone since the interview with Robert Blakiston, the evening before.

'I will be interested to hear anything you have to say, Detective Inspector.'

'You remember that scrap of paper we found in the fireplace in Sir Magnus's study? You thought there might be part of a fingerprint on it.'

'I remember it very well.'

'There *was* a fingerprint. The bad news is there wasn't enough of it left to be any use to us. It's certainly untraceable and we probably won't even be able to match it to any of our known suspects.'

'That is a pity.'

'There is something though. It turns out that the paper itself was stained with blood. The same blood type as Sir Magnus for what it's worth, although we can't be 100 per cent certain that it was his.'

'That is of great interest.'

'That's a great headache, if you ask me. How does it all add up? We've got a handwritten envelope and a typed up death threat. This scrap of paper clearly didn't belong to either of them and we have no way of knowing how long it had actually been in the grate. The blood would suggest it was thrown in the fire after the murder.'

'But where did it come from in the first place?'

'Exactly. Anyway, where do you want to go next?'

'I was hoping you might tell me, Inspector.'

'As a matter of fact, I was about to make a suggestion. I had a very interesting phone call from Dr Redwing before I left the office last night. Did you know her father's just died? Natural causes, which makes a pleasant change. Well, apparently he had a bit of a story to tell and I rather think we need to talk to Clarissa Pye.'

4

Clarissa Pye came into the living room carrying a tray with three cups of tea and some biscuits, neatly arranged on a plate as if somehow the symmetry would make them more desirable. The room seemed terribly small with so many people in it. Atticus Pünd and his assistant were next to each other on the faux-leather sofa, their knees almost touching. The round-faced detective inspector from Bath had taken the armchair opposite. She could feel the walls hemming them in. But ever since Dr Redwing had told her the news, the house had not been the same. It was not her house. This was not her life. It was as if she had been swapped for someone else in one of those Victorian novels she had always enjoyed.

'I suppose it was understandable that Dr Redwing should tell you what her father said,' she began. Her voice was a little prim. 'Although it might have been considerate to inform me that she was going to make the call.'

'I'm sure she believed she was acting for the best, Miss Pye,' Chubb said.

'Well, I suppose it was only right that the police were informed. After all, whatever you may think of Dr Rennard, he committed a crime.' She set the tray down. 'He lied on the birth certificate. He delivered both of us, but I was the first. He should really be prosecuted.'

'He's gone somewhere far beyond the reach of the law.'

'The reach of human law, certainly.'

'You have had very little time to get used to all this,' Pünd remarked, gently.

'Yes. I only heard yesterday.'

'I imagine it must have come as quite a shock to you.'

'A shock? I'm not quite sure that's the word I would use,

Mr Pünd. It's more like an earthquake. I remember Edgar Rennard very well. He was very much liked in the village and he often came up to the house when Magnus and I were growing up. He never struck me as an evil man and yet it really is a monstrous thing to have done. His lie took away my entire life. And Magnus! I wonder if he knew about it? He was always lording it over me, as if there was some terrific joke and I was the only one who wasn't in the know. He threw me out of my own home, you know. I had to support myself in London and then in America. And all the time there was no need for it.' She sighed. 'I have been very much cheated.'

'What will you do?'

'I will claim what is mine. Why not? I have a right to it.'

Inspector Chubb looked uncomfortable. 'That may not be as easy as you think, Miss Pye,' he said. 'From what I understand, Dr Redwing was alone in the room with her father when he told her what he'd done. There were no witnesses to the conversation. I suppose there's always a chance you may find something in his papers. He may have written something down. But right now it'll just be your word.'

'He may have told someone else.'

'He almost certainly told Sir Magnus,' Pünd cut in. He turned to the detective inspector. 'You remember the notepad that we found on his desk, the day after he was killed. Ashton H. Mw. A girl. Now it is all clear. The call was received from Ashton House. Edgar Rennard knew that he was dying and, out of a sense of guilt, telephoned Sir Magnus to explain that, when he delivered the twins, the first-born had in fact been a girl. The notepad also contained a number of crossings out. Sir Magnus was clearly perturbed by what he heard.'

'Well, that could explain something,' Clarissa said and there was real anger in her voice. 'He came to this very house, sat where you're sitting on the very day of his death. And he offered me a job at Pye Hall! He wanted me to move into the Lodge House and take over from Mary Blakiston. Can you imagine it! Maybe he was afraid that the truth was about to come to light. Maybe he actually wanted to *contain* me. If I'd moved in, I might have been the one with my head lopped off my shoulders.'

'I wish you luck, Miss Pye,' Chubb said. 'It's clearly a great injustice that's been done and if you can find any other witnesses that will certainly help your case. But if it doesn't offend you, I'd offer you this advice. You might be better off just accepting things as they are. You have a nice enough house here. You're well known and respected in the village. It's none of my business, but sometimes you can spend so much time chasing something that you lose everything else while you're about it.'

Clarissa Pye looked puzzled. 'Thank you for your advice, Inspector Chubb. However, I had assumed that the reason for this visit was that you had come to assist me. Dr Rennard committed a crime and we only have his daughter's word that he wasn't actually paid for his trouble. At any event, I assume it is a matter you would wish to investigate.'

'I must be honest. That hadn't really occurred to me.' Chubb was suddenly uncomfortable, looking to Pünd for help.

'You must remember that there have been two unexplained deaths in this village, Miss Pye,' Pünd said. 'I can understand your wish that the police should investigate the events that took place at the time of your birth and yet we are here on another matter. I would not wish to distress you any further in what is clearly a difficult time for you but I am afraid that I must ask you a question in connection with the two deaths – of Sir Magnus and of Mary Blakiston. It concerns a vial of liquid that went missing from Dr Redwing's surgery quite recently. The vial contained a poison, physostigmine. Would you know anything about that?'

Clarissa Pye's face went through a range of emotions, each one drawn so distinctly that they could have hung together like a series of portraits. First she was shocked. The question had been so unexpected – how could they possibly have known? Then there was fear. Were there to be consequences? Then came indignation, perhaps manufactured.

She was outraged that they should suspect her of such a thing! And finally, all within a split second, came acceptance and resignation. Too much had happened already. There was no point denying it. 'Yes. I took it,' she said.

'Why?'

'How did you know it was me? If you don't mind my asking . . .'

'Mrs Blakiston saw you leaving the surgery.'

Clarissa nodded. 'Yes. I saw her watching me. Mary had this extraordinary ability to be in the wrong place at the wrong time. I don't know how she did it.' She paused. 'Who else knows?'

'She kept a diary which Inspector Chubb has in his possession. As far as we are aware, she told nobody else.'

That made things easier. 'I took it on an impulse,' she said. 'I happened to find myself in the surgery on my own and I saw the physostigmine on the shelf. I knew exactly what it was. I'd done some medical training before I went to America.'

'What did you want it for?'

'I'm ashamed to tell you, Mr Pünd. I know it was wrong of me and I may have been just a little bit out of my mind. But in the light of what we've just been saying, you of all people will understand that very little in my life has worked out the way I wanted. It's not just Magnus and the house. I never married. I never had any real love, not even when I was young. Oh yes, I have the church and I have the village, but there have been times when I've found myself looking in the mirror and I've wondered – what's the point? What am I doing here? Why should I even want to go on?

'The Bible is very clear about suicide. It's the moral equivalent of murder. "God is the giver of life. He gives and He takes away." That's from the book of Job. We have no right to take matters into our own hands.' She stopped and suddenly there was a hardness in her eyes. 'But there have been times when I have been very much in the shadows, when I have looked into the valley of death and wished – and wished I could enter. How do you think it's been for me, watching Magnus and Frances and Freddy? I used to live in that house! All that wealth and comfort was once mine! Forget the fact that it was actually stolen from me, I should never have come back to Saxby-on-Avon! It was mad of me to humiliate myself by returning to the emperor's table. So the answer is – yes. I thought about killing myself. I took the physostigmine because I knew it would do the job quickly and painlessly.'

'Where is it now?'

'Upstairs. In the bathroom.'

'I'm afraid I must ask you to give it to me.'

'Well, I certainly don't need it now, Mr Pünd.' She spoke the words lightly, almost with a glint in her eye. 'Are you going to prosecute me for theft?'

'There won't be any need for that, Miss Pye,' Chubb said. 'We'll just make sure it gets back to Dr Redwing.'

They left a few minutes later and Clarissa Pye closed the front door, glad to be alone. She stood quite still, her breasts rising and falling, thinking over what had just been said. The business with the poison didn't matter. That wasn't important now. But it was strange that such a tiny theft should have brought them here when so much had been stolen from her. Would she be able to prove that Pye Hall was hers? Suppose the Detective Inspector was right? All she had were the words of a sick and dying man with no witnesses present in the room, no proof that he was actually sane when he spoke them. A legal case resting on twelve minutes that had ticked by more than fifty years ago.

Where could she possibly begin?

And did she actually want to?

It was very strange, but Clarissa suddenly felt as if a weight had been lifted from her shoulders. The fact that Pünd had taken the poison with him was certainly part of it. The physostigmine had been preying on her conscience for all manner of reasons and she knew that she had regretted taking it from the very start. But it was more than that. She remembered what Chubb had said. *You might be better off just accepting things as they are. You have a nice enough house here. You're well known and respected in the village.*

She *was* respected. It was true. She was still a popular teacher at the village school. She always made the most profitable stall at the village fête. Everyone liked her flower displays at Sunday service: in fact, Robin Osborne had often said that he didn't know how he would manage without her. Could it be, perhaps, that now she knew the truth, Pye Hall no longer had the power to intimidate her? It was hers. It always had been. And at the end of the day, it hadn't been Magnus who had stolen it from her. It hadn't been fate. It had been her own father, a man she had always remembered with fondness but who turned out to be antediluvian – a monster! Did she really want to fight him, to bring him back into her life when he had been so long below the ground?

No.

She could rise above it. She might visit Frances and Freddy at Pye Hall and this time she would be the one in the know. The joke would be on them.

With something close to a smile, she went into the kitchen. There was a tinned salmon rissole and some stewed fruit in the fridge. They would do very nicely for lunch.

5

'I thought she took it extremely well,' Emilia Redwing said. 'We weren't even sure at first if we should tell her. But now I'm glad we did.'

Pünd nodded. He and Fraser had come here alone, Inspector Chubb having returned to Pye Hall to meet the two police divers who had been summoned from Bristol, the nearest metropolis to have such a resource. They would be examining the lake that very day although Pünd already had a very good idea what they would find. He was sitting in the doctor's private office. Arthur Redwing was also present. He looked uncomfortable, as if he would rather be anywhere else.

'Yes. Miss Pye is certainly a formidable person,' Pünd agreed.

'So how is your investigation going?' Arthur Redwing asked.

It was the first time Pünd had met Dr Redwing's husband, the man who had painted the portrait of Frances Pye – and also, quite clearly that of the young boy which hung on the wall behind him now. The boy must be his son. He had the same dark, good looks, the slightly crumpled, very English features. And yet the two of them were at odds. There had been some difficulty between them. Pünd had always been interested in the unique relationship that exists between the portraitist and his subject, how there can never be secrets. It was true here. The way the boy had been painted, his pose, the nonchalance of his shoulders resting against the wall, one knee bent, hands in his pockets . . . all this suggested intimacy, even love. But Arthur Redwing had also captured something dark and suspicious in the boy's eyes. He wanted to be away.

'It is your son?' he asked.

'Yes,' Arthur replied. 'Sebastian. He's in London.' The three words somehow contained a lifetime of disappointment.

'We don't see him very often, I'm afraid,' Emilia Redwing added. 'Arthur painted that when Sebastian was seventeen.'

'It's terribly good,' Fraser said. When it came to art, he was the expert, not Pünd, and he was glad to have his moment in the sun. 'Do you exhibit?'

'I'd like to . . .' Arthur mumbled.

'You were about to tell us about your investigation,' Emilia Redwing cut in.

'Yes, indeed, Dr Redwing.' Pünd smiled. 'It is very nearly complete. I do not to expect to spend more than two more nights in Saxby-on-Avon.'

Fraser's ears pricked up when he heard this. He'd had no idea that Pünd was so close and wondered who had said what, and when, to provide the significant breakthrough. He was keen to hear the solution to the crime – and he wouldn't be sorry to get back to the comfort of Tanner Court either.

'Do you know who killed Sir Magnus?'

'I have, you might say, a theory. There are just two pieces of the jigsaw that are missing and which, once found, will confirm what I believe.'

'And what are those, if you don't mind us asking?' Arthur Redwing had suddenly become very animated.

'I do not mind you asking at all, Mr Redwing. The first is taking place almost as we speak. With the supervision of Inspector Chubb, two police frogmen are searching the lake at Pye Hall.'

'What do you expect them to find? Another body?'

'I hope nothing as sinister as that.'

It was evident he was not going to expand any further. 'What about the other piece of the jigsaw?' Dr Redwing asked.

'There is a person to whom I wish to speak. He may not know it, but I believe that he holds the key to everything that has taken place here in Saxby-on-Avon.'

'And who is that?'

'I am referring to Matthew Blakiston. He was the husband of Mary Blakiston and of course the father of the two boys, Robert and Tom.'

'Are you looking for him now?'

'I have asked Inspector Chubb to make enquiries.'

'But you know he was here!' Dr Redwing seemed almost amused. 'I saw him myself, in the village. He came to his wife's funeral.'

'Robert Blakiston did not tell me that.'

'He may not have seen him. I didn't recognise him at first. He was wearing a hat that he kept very low over his face. He didn't talk to anyone and he stayed right at the back. He also left before the end.'

'Did you tell anyone this?'

'Well, no.' Dr Redwing seemed surprised by the question. 'It seemed perfectly natural for him to be there. He and Mary Blakiston had been married for a long time and it wasn't hatred that drove them apart. It was grief. They lost a child. I was a little sorry that he chose not to speak to Robert. And he could have met Joy while he was there. It's a great shame, really. Mary's death could so easily have brought them all together.'

'He might have been the one who killed her!' Arthur Redwing exclaimed. He turned to Pünd. 'Is that why you want to see him? Is he a suspect?'

'That is impossible to say until I have spoken to him,' Pünd replied, diplomatically. 'So far Inspector Chubb has been unable to locate him.'

'He's in Cardiff,' Dr Redwing said.

For once, Pünd was taken by surprise.

'I don't have his address but I can easily help you find him. I had a letter, a few months ago, from a GP in Cardiff. It was perfectly routine. He wanted some notes about an old injury that one of his patients had incurred. It was Matthew Blakiston. I sent him what he wanted and forgot all about it.'

'You remember the GP's name?'

'Of course. It's on file. I'll get it for you.'

But before she could move, a woman suddenly appeared, letting herself into the surgery through the main door. The door of Dr Redwing's office was open and they all saw her; a woman in her forties, plain, round-faced. Her name was Diana Weaver and she had come to the surgery to clean it as she did every day. Pünd had known exactly when she would be arriving. It was she whom he had actually come to see.

For her part, she was surprised to find anyone here so late in the day. 'Oh – I'm sorry, Dr Redwing!' she called out. 'Would you like me to come back tomorrow?'

'No, please come in, Mrs Weaver.'

The woman came into the private office. Atticus Pünd stood up, offering her his seat, and she sat down, looking around her nervously. 'Mrs Weaver,' he began. 'Allow me to introduce myself—'

'I know who you are,' she cut in.

'Then you will know why it is I wish to speak to you.' He paused. He had no wish to upset this woman and yet it had to be done. 'On the day of his death, Sir Magnus

Pye received a letter relating to the new houses that he proposed to build. This would have caused the destruction of Dingle Dell. I wonder if you can tell me – did you write that letter?' She said nothing, so he went on. 'I have discovered that the letter was typed on the machine that sits in this surgery and that only three people might have had access to it: Joy Sanderling, Dr Redwing and yourself.' He smiled. 'I should add that you have nothing to worry about. It is not a crime to send a letter of protest, even if the language is a little intemperate. Nor do I suspect for a single minute that you followed through the threats that were made in that letter. I simply need to know how it got there and so I ask you again. Did you write it?'

Mrs Weaver nodded. There were tears beading at her eyes. 'Yes, sir.'

'Thank you. I can understand that you were upset, quite justifiably, about the loss of the woodland.'

'We just hated seeing the village being knocked about for no good reason. I was talking about it with my husband and with my father-in-law. They've been in Saxby all their lives. We all have. And it's a very special place. We don't need new houses here. There's no call for them. And the Dell! You start there, where does it end? You look at Tawbury and Market Basing. Roads and traffic lights and the new supermarkets – they've been hollowed out and now people just drive through them and—' She stopped herself. 'I'm sorry, Dr Redwing,' she said. 'I should have asked your permission. I acted in the heat of the moment.'

'It doesn't matter,' Emilia Redwing said. 'I really don't mind. In fact, I agree with you.'

'When did you deliver the letter?' Pünd asked.

'It was Thursday afternoon. I just walked up to the door and popped it through.' Mrs Weaver lowered her head. 'The next day, when I heard what had happened . . . Sir Magnus murdered . . . I didn't know what to think. I wished then that I hadn't sent it. It wasn't like me to be so impulsive. I promise you, sir. I really didn't mean anything ill by it.'

'Again, the letter has no relevance to what occurred,'

Pünd assured her. 'But there is something I must ask you, and you must think very carefully before you answer. It concerns the envelope in which the letter was placed and, in particular, the address . . .'

'Yes, sir?'

But Pünd did not speak. Something very strange had happened. He had been standing in the middle of the room, partly resting on his walking stick, but as he had continued the interview with Mrs Weaver, it had been noticeable that he was relying on it more and more. Now, very slowly, he was toppling to one side. Fraser noticed it first and leapt up to catch him before he hit the floor. He was just in time. As he reached him, the detective's legs buckled and his whole body slid away. Dr Redwing was already out of her seat. Mrs Weaver was staring in alarm.

Atticus Pünd's eyes were closed. His face was white. He didn't seem to be breathing at all.

6

Dr Redwing was with him when he woke up.

Pünd was lying on the raised bed that the doctor used to examine patients. He had been unconscious for less than five minutes. She was standing over him, a stethoscope around her neck. She looked relieved to see that he had awoken.

'Don't move,' she said. 'You were taken ill . . .'

'You have examined me?' Pünd asked.

'I checked your heart and your pulse. It may just have been exhaustion.'

'It was not exhaustion.' There was a shooting pain in his temple but he ignored it. 'You do not need to concern yourself, Dr Redwing. I have a condition that was explained to me by my doctor in London. He also gave me medication. If I might rest here a few more minutes, I would be grateful to you. But there is nothing more you can do for me.'

'Of course you can stay here,' Dr Redwing said. She was

still looking into Pünd's eyes. 'Is it inoperable?' she asked.

'You see what others do not. In the world of medicine, it is you who are the detective.' Pünd smiled a little sadly. 'I am told that nothing can be done.'

'Have you had a second opinion?'

'I do not need one. I know that there is not very much time left to me. I can feel it.'

'I am so sorry to hear it, Mr Pünd.' She thought for a moment. 'Your colleague did not seem to be aware of the problem.'

'I have not informed Fraser and I would prefer it if it remained that way.'

'You need have no concern. I asked him to leave. Mrs Weaver and my husband went with him. I told him I would walk over to the Queen's Arms with you as soon as you were feeling well enough.'

'I am feeling a little better already.'

With Dr Redwing's help, Pünd got himself into a sitting position and fumbled for the pills that he carried in his jacket pocket. Dr Redwing went to get a glass of water. She had noted the name – Dilaudid – on the packet. 'That's a hydromorphone,' she said. 'It's a good choice. Very fast-acting. You have to be careful, though. It can make you tired and you may experience mood changes too.'

'I *am* tired,' Pünd agreed. 'But I have found my mood to be remarkably unchanged. In fact, I will be honest with you, I am quite cheerful.'

'Perhaps it's your investigation. It's probably been very helpful to have something to concentrate on. And you were saying to my husband that it's gone well.'

'That is true.'

'And when it's over? What then?'

'When it is over, Dr Redwing, I will have nothing left to do.' Pünd got unsteadily to his feet and reached for his walking stick. 'I would like to return to my room now, if you would be so kind.'

They left together.

7

On the other side of the village, the police divers were emerging from the lake. Raymond Chubb was standing on the grassy shore, watching as they dumped what they had found in front of him. He was wondering how Pünd had known it would be there.

There were three dishes, decorated with sea-nymphs and tritons; a flanged bowl, this one with a centaur pursuing a naked woman; some long-handled spoons; a piperatorium, or pepper-pot, which might actually have been used to store expensive spices; a scattering of coins; a statuette of a tiger or some similar creature; two bracelets. Chubb knew exactly what he was looking at. This was the treasure trove that had been stolen from Sir Magnus Pye. Every item had been described by him when he had called in the police. But why had someone stolen the treasure simply to discard it? He understood now that they must have dropped one piece – the belt buckle that Brent had found – as they made their way across the lawn. They had then reached the edge of the lake and thrown the rest in. Had they been surprised while they were trying to make their getaway? Could they have planned to have come back and retrieve the loot another time? It made no sense.

'I think that's it,' one of the divers called out.

Chubb looked down at the separate pieces, all of it silver . . . so much silver, glinting in the evening sun.

SIX

Gold

1

The house was close to Caedelyn Park in Cardiff, backing onto the railway line that ran from Whitchurch to Rhiwibina. It was in the middle of a short terrace, three identical houses on either side, all of them tired, in need of cheering up: seven gates, seven square gardens full of dusty plants struggling to survive, seven front doors, seven chimney stacks. They were somehow interchangeable but the green Austin A40, with its registration number, FPJ 247 parked outside the middle one, told Pünd immediately where to go.

A man was waiting for them. From the way he was standing there, he could have been waiting all his life. As they pulled in, he raised a hand not so much in welcome as in acknowledgement that they had arrived. He was in his late fifties but looked much older, worn out by a struggle that he had actually lost a long time ago. He had thinning hair, an untidy moustache and sullen, dark brown eyes. He was wearing clothes that were much too warm for the summer afternoon and which needed a wash. Fraser had never seen anyone who looked more alone.

'Mr Pünd?' he asked as they got out of the car.

'It is a pleasure to meet you, Mr Blakiston.'

'Please. Come in.'

He led them into a dark, narrow hallway with a kitchen at the far end. From here, they could look out over a half-neglected garden that sloped up steeply to the railway line at the end. The house was clean but charmless. There was nothing very personal: no family photographs, no letters on the hall table, no sign that anyone else lived here. Very little sunlight made its way in. It had that in common with the Lodge House in Saxby-on-Avon. Everything was hemmed in by shadow.

'I always knew the police would want to speak to me,' he said. 'Will you have some tea?' He put the kettle on the hob and managed to start a flame with a third click of the switch.

'We are not, strictly speaking, the police,' Pünd told him.

'No. But you're investigating the deaths.'

'Your wife and Sir Magnus Pye. Yes.'

Blakiston nodded, then ran a hand over his chin. He had shaved that morning, but with a razor he had used too many times. Hair was sprouting in the cleft underneath his lip and there was a small cut on his chin. 'I did think about calling someone,' he said. 'I was there, you know, on the night he died. But then I thought – why bother? I didn't see anything. I don't know anything. It's got nothing to do with me.'

'That may not be the case at all, Mr Blakiston. I have been looking forward to meeting you.'

'Well, I hope you won't be disappointed.'

He emptied the teapot, which was still full of old leaves, washed it out with boiling water and added new ones. He took a bottle of milk out of a fridge that had little else inside. At the bottom of the garden, a train rumbled past, billowing steam, and for a moment the air was filled with the smell of cinders. He didn't seem to notice. He finished making the tea and brought it to the table. The three of them sat down.

'Well?'

'You know why we are here, Mr Blakiston,' Pünd said. 'Why don't you tell us your story? Begin from the beginning. Leave nothing out.'

Blakiston nodded. He poured the tea. Then he began to talk.

He was fifty-eight years old. He had been living in

Cardiff ever since he had left Saxby-on-Avon twelve years ago. He'd had family here; an uncle who owned an electrical shop, not far away, on the Eastern Road. The uncle was dead now but he had inherited the shop and it provided a living – at least, for the sort of life he led. He was on his own. Fraser had been right about that.

'I never actually divorced Mary,' he said. 'I don't know why not. After what happened with Tom, there was no way the two of us were going to stay together. But at the same time, neither of us was ever going to get married again, so what was the point? She wasn't interested in lawyers and all that stuff. I suppose that makes me officially her widower.'

'You never saw her again after you left?' Pünd asked.

'We stayed in touch. We wrote to each other and I called her now and then – to ask her about Robert and to see if there was anything she needed. But if she'd needed anything, she would never have asked me.'

Pünd took out his Sobranies. It was unusual for him to smoke when he was working on a case but nothing about the detective had been quite the same recently and Fraser had been desperately worried since he had been taken ill in Dr Redwing's surgery. Pünd had refused to say anything about it. In the car, on the way here, he had barely spoken at all.

'Let us go back to the time when you and Mary met,' Pünd suggested. 'Tell me about your time at Sheppard's Farm.'

'That was my dad's place,' Blakiston said. 'He got it from *his* dad and it had been in the family for as long as anyone can remember. I come from a long line of farmers but I never really took to it. My dad used to say I was the black sheep, which was funny, because that's what we had – a couple of hundred acres and lots of sheep. I feel sorry for him, looking back on it. I was his only child and I just wasn't interested so that was that. I'd always been good at maths and science at school and I had ideas about going to America and becoming a rocket engineer which is a bit of a laugh because I worked for twenty years as a mechanic and I never got any further than Wales. But that's how it is when you're a kid, isn't it. You have all these dreams and, unless you're lucky, they never amount to anything. Still, I can't complain. We all lived there happily enough. Even Mary liked it to begin with.'

'In what circumstances did you meet your wife?' Pünd asked.

'She lived in Tawbury, which was about five miles away. Her mother and my mother were at school together. She came over for lunch one Sunday with her parents and that's how we met. Mary was in her twenties then and as pretty as you can imagine. I fell for her the moment I saw her and we were married within a year.'

'And what, I wonder, did your parents make of her?'

'They liked her well enough. In fact, there was a time when I would say everything was pretty much perfect. We had two sons: Robert first, then Tom. They grew up on the land and I can still see them, racing around, helping my dad when they got back from school. I think we were probably happier there than we ever were anywhere else. But it couldn't last. My dad was up to his eyes in debt. And I wasn't helping him. I'd got a job at Whitchurch Airport, which was an hour and half away, near Bristol. This was the end of the thirties. I was doing routine maintenance on planes for the Civil Air Guard and I met a lot of the young pilots coming in for training. I knew there was a war on the way but in a place like Saxby-on-Avon it was easy to forget it. Mary was doing jobs in and around the village. We were already going our separate ways. That's why she blamed me for what happened – and maybe she was right.'

'Tell me about your children,' Pünd said.

'I loved those boys. Believe me, there isn't a day when I don't think about what happened.' He choked on his words and had to pause for a moment to recover. 'I don't know how it all went so wrong, Mr Pünd. I really don't. When we were up at Sheppard's Farm, I won't say it was perfect but we used to have fun. They could be right little sods, always fighting, always at each other's throats. But that's true of any boys, isn't it?' He gazed at Pünd as if needing affirmation and when none came he went on. 'They could be close too. The best of friends.

'Robert was the quiet one. You always got the impression that he was thinking about something. Even when he was quite young, he used to take himself off for long walks along the Bath valley and there were times we'd get quite worried about him. Tom was more of a livewire. He saw himself as a bit of an inventor. He was always mixing potions and putting things together from the insides of old machines. I suppose he might have got that from me and I'll admit he was the one I used to spoil. Robert was closer to his mother. It was a difficult birth. She nearly lost him, and when he was a baby he had all sorts of illnesses. The village doctor, a chap called Rennard, was always in and out of the house. If you ask me, that's what made her so overprotective. There were times when she wouldn't let me come near him. Tom was the easier boy. I was closer to him. Always, him and me . . .'

He took out a packet of ten cigarettes, tore off the cellophane and lit one.

'Everything went wrong when we left the farm,' he said and suddenly he was bitter. 'The day that man came into our life, that's when it began. Sir Magnus bloody Pye. It's easy enough to see it now and I wonder how I could have been so blind, so stupid. But at the time what he was offering seemed an answer to our prayers. A regular salary for Mary, somewhere to live, nice grounds for the boys to run around in. At least, that's how Mary saw it and that's how she sold it to me.'

'You argued?'

'I tried not to argue with her. All it did was turn her against me. I said I had a couple of misgivings, that's all. I didn't like the idea of her being a housekeeper. I thought she was better than that. And I remember warning her that, once we were there, we'd be trapped. It would be like he owned us. But the thing was, you see, we didn't really have any choice. We didn't have any savings. It was the best offer we were going to get.

'And at first it was fine. Pye Hall was nice enough and I got on well enough with Stanley Brent who was the groundsman there with his son. We weren't paying any rent and in some ways it was better to be on our own as a family, without my mum and dad around all the time. But there was something about the Lodge House that rubbed us up the wrong way. It was dark all the year round and it never really felt like home. We all started getting on each other's nerves, even the boys. Mary and I seemed to be sniping at each other all the time. I hated the way she looked up to Sir Magnus, just because he had a title and so much money. He was no better than me. He'd never done a proper day's work in his life. He only had Pye Hall because he'd inherited it. But she couldn't see that. She thought it made her special in some way. What she didn't understand was that when you're cleaning a toilet, you're still cleaning a toilet and what difference does it make if some aristocratic bum is going to sit on it? I said that to her once and she was furious. But the way she saw herself she wasn't a cleaner or a housekeeper. She was the lady of the manor.

'Magnus had one son of his own – Freddy – but he was still very young and he was quite surly. There was no real love there. So his lordship started interesting himself in my boys instead. He used to encourage them to play on his land and spoil them with little gifts – three pence here, sixpence there. And he'd get them to play practical jokes on Neville Brent. His parents were dead by then. They'd been killed in a car accident and Neville had taken over, working on the estate. If you ask me, there was something queer about him. I don't think he was quite right in the head. But that didn't stop them spying on him, teasing him, throwing snowballs, that sort of thing. It was cruel. I wish they hadn't done it.'

'You couldn't stop them?'

'I couldn't do *anything*, Mr Pünd. How can I make you understand? They never listened to me. I wasn't their father any more. Almost from the day we moved into that place, I found myself being pushed to one side. Magnus, Magnus . . . that was all anyone ever talked about. When the boys got their school reports, nobody cared what I thought. You know what? Mary would get the boys to take them up to the main house and show them to him. As if his opinion mattered more than mine.

'It got worse and worse over time, Mr Pünd. I began to loathe that man. He always had a way of making me feel small, reminding me that I was living in his house, on his land . . . as if I'd ever wanted to be there in the first place. And it was his fault, what happened. I swear to you. He killed my son as if he did it with his own hands and at that same moment he ruined me. Tom was the light of my life and when he went there was nothing left for me.' He fell silent and wiped his eye with the back of his hand. 'Look at me! Look a this place! I often ask myself what I did to deserve it. I never hurt anyone and I end up here. I sometimes think I've been punished for something I didn't do.'

'I am sure you are blameless.'

'I *am* blameless. I did nothing wrong. What happened had nothing to do with me.' He stopped, fixing his eyes on Pünd and Fraser, daring them to disagree. 'It was Magnus Pye. Bloody Magnus Pye.'

He took a breath, then went on.

'The war had started and I'd been sent off to Boscombe Down, working mainly on Hawker Hurricanes. I was away from home and I didn't really know what was going on and when I came back occasional weekends, it was like I was a stranger. Mary had changed so much. She was never pleased to see me. She was secretive . . . like she was hiding something. It was hard to believe she was the same girl I'd met and married and been with at Sheppard's Farm. Robert didn't want to have too much to do with me either. He was his mother's child. If it hadn't been for Tom, it would hardly have been worth showing up.

'Anyway, Sir Magnus was there in my place. I told you about games. There was this game he played with the boys – with *my* boys. They were obsessed with buried treasure. Well, all boys like that sort of thing but I'm sure you know the Pyes had dug up a whole load of stuff – Roman coins and the rest of it in Dingle Dell. He had them on display in his house. And so it was easy for him to turn the two of them into treasure hunters. He'd take chocolate bars wrapped in foil or, sometimes, sixpenny pieces or half crowns and he'd hide them all over the estate. Then he'd give them clues and set them off. They might spend the whole day doing that and you couldn't really complain because it got them out in the open air. It was good for them, wasn't it? It was fun.

'But he wasn't their father. He didn't know what he was doing and one day he took it too far. He had a piece of gold. Not real gold. Iron pyrite – what they call fool's gold. He had a big lump of it and he decided to make that the prize. Of course Tom and Robert didn't know the difference. They thought it was the real thing and they were desperate to get their hands on it. And do you know where he put it, the bloody fool? He hid it in a clump of bulrushes, right on the edge of the lake. He led them to the water's edge. Fourteen years old and twelve years old. He led them there as surely as if he'd put up a sign.

'This is what happened. The two boys had separated. Robert was in Dingle Dell, searching in the trees. Tom went down to the water. Maybe he saw the gold glinting in the sun or maybe he'd worked out one of the clues. He didn't even need to get his feet wet but he was so excited, he decided to wade in. And what then? Maybe he stumbled. There are a lot of weeds and they could have wrapped themselves around his legs. Here's what I know. Just after three o'clock in the afternoon, Brent comes along with the lawnmower and he sees my boy lying face down in the water.' Matthew Blakiston's voice cracked. 'Tom had drowned.

'Brent did what he could. Tom was only a few feet out from the shore and Brent dragged him back to dry land. Then Robert came out of the wood and saw what was happening. He plunged into the water. He was screaming. He waded over to them and shouted at Brent to get help. Brent didn't know what to do but Robert had learned basic first aid at school and tried to save his brother with mouth-to-mouth. It was too late. Tom was dead. I only heard about all this later, from the police. They'd talked to everyone involved: Sir Magnus, Brent, Mary and Robert. Can you imagine how I felt, Mr Pünd? I was their father. But I hadn't been there.'

Matthew Blakiston bowed his head. His fist, with the cigarette, was clenched against his head and smoke curled upwards as he sat there, silent. At that moment, Fraser was utterly aware of the smallness of the room, the hopelessness of a life broken. It occurred to him that Blakiston was an outcast. He was in exile from himself.

'Do you want some more tea?' Blakiston asked suddenly.

'I'll do it,' Fraser said.

Nobody wanted tea but they needed time, a pause before he could go on. Fraser went over to the kettle. He was glad to break away.

'I went back to Boscombe Down,' he began again, once the fresh cups had been brought. 'And the next time I came home, I knew exactly which way the wind was blowing. Mary and Robert had pulled up the drawbridge. She never let go of him after that, not for a minute, and it was like they didn't want to know me. I would have done my bit for my family, Mr Pünd, I swear I would have. But they never let me. Robert always said that I walked out on them but that isn't true. I came home but there was nobody there.'

'When was the last time you saw your son, Mr Blakiston?'

'Saturday, 23 July. At his mother's funeral.'

'Did he see you?'

'No.' Blakiston took a deep breath. He had finished his cigarette and stubbed it out. 'They say that when you lose a child, it brings you closer together or tears you apart. What most hurt me about Mary was that after Tom went, she never let me get close to Robert. She was protecting him from me! Can you believe that? It wasn't enough that I had lost one son. I ended up losing two.

'And part of me never stopped loving her. That's the pathetic thing. I told you, I used to write to her on her birthday, at Christmas. I talked to her on the phone sometimes. At least she'd let me do that. But she didn't want me anywhere near. She made that clear enough.'

'Did you speak to her recently?'

'The last time I spoke to her was a couple of months ago – but here's something you won't believe. I actually called her the day she died. It was the weirdest thing. I was woken up that morning by a bird in a tree and it was making this horrible noise, this cawing. It was a magpie. "One for sorrow." Do you know that old song? Well, I looked at it on the other side of the bedroom window, black and white, an evil little thing with its glinting eye and suddenly I felt sick to the stomach. It was like I'd had a premonition. I knew something bad was going to happen. I went to the shop but I couldn't work and no one came in anyway. I was thinking about Mary. I was convinced something was going to happen to her and, in the end, I couldn't stop myself. I rang her. I tried her at the Lodge and then at the main house – but she didn't answer because I was too late. She was already dead.'

He was playing with the cellophane from the cigarette packet, pulling it apart between his fingers.

'I heard about her death a few days later. There was a piece in the newspaper . . . Would you believe it? Nobody even bothered to ring me. You'd have thought Robert might have got in touch, but he didn't care. Anyway, I knew I had to go to the funeral. It didn't matter what had happened.

There'd been a time when the two of us were young and we'd been together. I wasn't going to let her go without saying goodbye. I'll admit, I was nervous about showing my face. I didn't want to make a big thing of it with everyone crowding around me so I arrived late and I wore a hat pulled down over my face. I'm a lot thinner than I used to be and I'm nearly sixty years old. I thought if I kept well clear of Robert I'd be all right and that was how it turned out.

'I did see him there. He was standing with a girl and I was glad to see that. It's just what he needs. He was always very solitary when he was a boy and she looked a pretty little thing. I hear they're going to get married and maybe if they have children, they'll let me visit them. People change in time, don't they? He says I wasn't there for him but maybe, if you see him, you'll tell him the truth.

'It was so strange to be there, back in the village. I'm not even sure I like the place any more. And seeing them all again – Dr Redwing and Clarissa and Brent and all the others. It gave me a shiver, I can tell you. I noticed Sir Magnus and Lady Pye didn't show up and that made me smile. I'm sure Mary would have been disappointed! I always did tell her he was no good. But perhaps it was just as well that he wasn't there. I'm not sure what I'd have done if I'd seen him that day. I blame him for what happened, Mr Pünd. Mary fell down the stairs while she was skivvying for him so that makes two of them. Mary and Tom. They'd both be alive if it weren't for him.'

'Is that why you went to his house five days later?'

Blakiston bowed his head. 'How did you know I was there?'

'Your car was seen.'

'Well, I'm not going to deny it. Yes. It was stupid of me but at the end of the week I went back. The thing is, I couldn't get it out of my head. First Tom, then Mary, both of them at Pye Hall. Listening to me now, you probably think I'm owning up to it, that I went back to kill him.

But it wasn't like that. I just wanted to talk to him, to ask him about Mary. Everyone else who'd gone to that funeral, they'd had someone to talk to – but not me. No one even recognised me – at my own wife's funeral! Was it so unreasonable to want to see him just for five minutes, just to ask him about Mary?'

He thought for a moment, then came to a decision.

'There was something else. You'll think the worse of me for it but I was thinking about money. Not for me. For my son. When someone dies in the workplace, it's your responsibility. Mary had been working for Sir Magnus for more than twenty years and he owed her a duty of care. I thought he might have come to some arrangement with her – you know, a pension. I knew Robert would never accept any financial help from me, even if I could have afforded it, but if he was about to get married, didn't he deserve some sort of start in life? Sir Magnus had always had a soft spot for him. I had this idea that I could ask him for help on Robert's behalf.' He stopped and looked away.

'Please, go on.'

'It took me a couple of hours to drive back to Saxby-on-Avon. I'd been busy at the shop. I remember that it was exactly half past seven when I arrived. I looked at my watch. But the thing is, Mr Pünd, once I'd got there, I had second thoughts. I wasn't sure I did want to see him after all. I didn't want to be humiliated. I sat in the car for about an hour before I decided that since I'd come all this way I might as well give it a try. It must have been about half past eight when I drove to the house. I parked in my usual spot behind the Lodge – I suppose that was force of habit. Someone else had had the same idea. There was a bicycle leaning against the door. I remembered that later. Maybe I should have read more into it at the time.

'Anyway, I walked up the drive. It was all coming back to me, being there again. The lake was on my left and I couldn't bring myself to look at it. The moon was out that night and everything in the garden was crystal clear, like in a photograph. There didn't seem to be anyone else around. I didn't try to hide myself or anything like that. I just walked straight up to the front door and rang the bell. I could see lights on behind the windows on the ground floor so I guessed Sir Magnus must be in and sure enough, a minute or two later, he opened the door.

'I'll never forget the sight of him, Mr Pünd. The last time I'd seen him had been over ten years ago, when I moved out of the Lodge. He was bigger than I remembered, fatter certainly. He seemed to fill the doorway. He was wearing a suit and a tie . . . bright colours. He was holding a cigar.

'It took him a moment or two to recognise me but then he smiled. "You!" That's all he said. He spat the word at me. He wasn't exactly hostile. But he was surprised, and there was something else. He still had that strange smile on his face, like he was amused. "What do you want?"

'"I'd like to talk to you, if I may, Sir Magnus," I said. "It's about Mary . . ."

'He looked back over his shoulder and that was when I realised he wasn't alone.

'"I can't see you now," he said.

'"I just need a few minutes of your time."

'"It's out of the question. Not now. You should have called before you came here. What time of the night do you think this is?"

'"Please—"

'"No! Come back tomorrow."

'He was about to close the door on me. I could see that. But then, at the last minute, he stopped and he asked me one last question. I'll never forget it.

'"Do you really think I killed your bloody dog?" he asked.'

'The dog?' Pünd looked puzzled.

'I should have told you. When we first moved to Pye Hall, we had a dog.'

'Its name was Bella.'

'Yes. That's right. It was a cross-breed: half Labrador half collie. I got her for Tom, for his tenth birthday, and Sir Magnus was against her from the day she arrived. He didn't want her out of control on his lawn, scaring the chickens. He didn't want her digging up the flower beds. Actually, I'll tell you what he didn't want. He didn't want me buying a present for my own son. It's like what I was saying. He wanted to have complete control over me and my family and because the dog was connected to me, the one thing I'd bought that Tom really loved, he had to get rid of it.'

'He killed it?' Fraser asked. He remembered the sad little collar that Pünd had found in the room at the Lodge House.

'I was never able to prove it was him. Maybe he got Brent to do it for him. I wouldn't put it past that snivelling little bastard. But one day the dog was there and the next day it had vanished – and it wasn't until a week later that we found it in Dingle Dell with its throat cut. Tom was devastated. It was the first thing he'd ever had in his life that was really his. Who could do that to a little boy?'

'It seems very strange,' Pünd muttered. 'Sir Magnus has not seen you for many years. You turn up, unexpectedly, at his house, late in the night. Why do you think he chooses this moment to ask you about the dog?'

'I have no idea.'

'What did you say to him?'

'I didn't know what to say. But it didn't matter anyway, because right then he closed the door. He shut it right in my face – a man who'd lost his wife not two weeks before. He wasn't prepared even to invite me over the threshold. That was the sort of person he was.'

There was a long silence.

'The conversation that you have described,' Pünd muttered. 'How close was it, do you think, to the reality? Were those exactly the words used by Sir Magnus?'

'As best as I can remember, Mr Pünd.'

'He did not, for example, greet you by name?'

'He knew who I was, if that's what you mean. But no. It was just that single word – "You!" – as if I'd crawled out from under some stone.'

'What did you do next?'

'What could I do? I went back to my car and drove off.'

'The bicycle that you had seen. Was it still there?'

'I can't remember, to be honest. I didn't look.'

'So you left . . .'

'I was angry. I'd driven a long way and I hadn't expected to be dismissed out of hand. I got about ten or fifteen miles down the road and then – you know what? – I changed my mind. I was still thinking of Robert. I was still thinking of what was right. And who was bloody Magnus Pye to slam the door in my face? That man had been pushing me around since the day I'd met him and suddenly I'd had enough. I drove back to Pye Hall and this time I didn't stop at the Lodge. I drove right up to the front door, got out and rang the bell again.'

'You had been away for how long?'

'Twenty minutes? Twenty-five? I didn't look at my watch. I didn't care about the time. I was just determined to have it out, only this time, Sir Magnus didn't come to the door. I rang twice more. Nothing. So I opened the letter box and knelt down, meaning to shout at him. I was going to tell him he was a bloody coward and that he should come to the door.' Blakiston broke off. 'That was when I saw him. There was so much blood I couldn't miss him. He was lying in the hallway right in front of my eyes. I didn't realise then that his head had been lopped off. The body was facing away from me, thank God. But I knew at once that he was dead. There could be no doubt of it.

'I was shocked. More than that. I was poleaxed. It was like I'd been punched in the face. I felt myself falling and I thought I was going to faint. Somehow, I managed to get back to my feet. I knew that someone had killed Sir Magnus in the last twenty minutes, in the time that I'd left and come back again. Perhaps they'd been with him when I'd knocked the first time. They could actually have been listening to me, inside the hallway. Maybe they waited until I'd gone and killed him then.'

Blakiston lit another cigarette. His hand was shaking.

'I know what you're going to ask, Mr Pünd. Why didn't I go to the police? Well, it's obvious, isn't it? I was the last person to see him alive and at the same time I had every reason to want him dead. I'd lost my son and I blamed Sir Magnus. I'd lost my wife and she was working for him too. That man has been like the devil at the feast and if the police are looking for a suspect, they won't need to look any further than me. I didn't kill him but I knew straight away what they'd think and all I wanted to do was to get the hell out of there. I picked myself up and got back in the car and I drove away as fast as I could.

'Another car arrived just as I passed through the gate. I didn't see anything, just a pair of headlights. But I was afraid that whoever was driving would have got my number plate and reported me. Was that what happened?'

'It was Lady Pye in the car,' Pünd told him. 'She had just returned from London.'

'Well, I'm sorry I had to leave her to it. It must have been horrible for her. But all I wanted to do was get away. That was my only thought.'

'Mr Blakiston, do you have any idea who may have been in the house with Sir Magnus Pye when you visited?'

'How could I possibly know? I didn't hear anyone. I didn't see anyone.'

'Could it have been a woman?'

'Curiously, that was my thought. If he was having a secret assignation, or whatever you might want to call it, he might have behaved the same way.'

'Are you aware that your son is amongst the suspects who are believed to have killed Sir Magnus?'

'*Robert*? Why? That's madness. He had no reason to kill

him. In fact – I've told you – he always looked up to Sir Magnus. The two of them were thick as thieves.'

'But he has precisely the same motivation as yourself. He could have held Sir Magnus responsible for the death of both his brother and his mother.' Pünd raised a hand before Blakiston could answer. 'I just find it puzzling that you did not come forward with the information that you have given me now. You say that you did not kill him and yet by remaining silent you have allowed the real killer to remain undetected. The matter of the bicycle, for example, is of great importance.'

'Maybe I should have come forward,' Blakiston replied. 'But I knew it would go badly for me, like it always has. The truth of it is, I wish I'd never gone near the place. Sometimes you read books about houses that have a curse. I've always thought that was a lot of nonsense but I'd believe it about Pye Hall. It killed my wife and my child and if you tell the police what I've told you, I'll probably end up being hanged.' He smiled mirthlessly. 'And then it will have killed me.'

2

Pünd barely spoke on the way back and James Fraser knew better than to interrupt his thoughts. He handled the Vauxhall expertly, pushing through the various gear changes and holding the middle of the road as the sun set and the shadows closed in on all sides. It was the only time he ever felt completely in control, when he was behind the wheel. They had taken the Aust ferry across the River Severn, sitting together in silence as the Welsh coast slipped away behind them. Fraser was hungry. He'd had nothing to eat since the morning. They sold sandwiches on the ferry but they were none too appetising and anyway, Pünd didn't like food in the car.

They reached the other side and drove through the

Gloucester countryside, the same route that Blakiston would have taken to see Sir Magnus Pye. Fraser hoped to be in Saxby-on-Avon by seven o'clock, in time for dinner.

Eventually, they reached Bath and began to follow the road that would bring them to Pye Hall, with the valley, now quite dark, stretching out on their left.

'Gold!' Pünd hadn't spoken for so long that Fraser started, hearing his voice.

'I'm sorry?' he asked.

'The fool's gold concealed by Sir Magnus Pye. I am convinced that everything revolves around it.'

'But fool's gold isn't worth anything.'

'Not to you, James. Not to me. That is exactly the point.'

'It killed Tom Blakiston. He tried to get it out of the lake.'

'Ah yes. The lake, you know, has been a dark presence in this tale, as in the stories of King Arthur. The children played beside the lake. One of them died in the lake. And Sir Magnus's silver, that too was concealed in the lake.'

'You know, Pünd. You're not making a lot of sense.'

'I think of King Arthur and dragons and witches. In this story there was a witch and a dragon and a curse that could not be lifted . . .'

'I take it you know who did it.'

'I know everything, James. I had only to make the connections and it all became very clear. Sometimes, you know, it is not the physical clues that lead to the solution of the crime. The words spoken by the vicar at a funeral or a scrap of paper burned in a fire – they suggest one thing but then they lead to quite another. The room that is locked at the Lodge House. Why was it locked? We think we have the answer but a moment's thought will assure us we are wrong. The letter addressed to Sir Magnus. We know who wrote it. We know why. But again, we are misled. We have to think. It is all conjecture but soon we see that there can be no other way.'

'Did Matthew Blakiston help you?'

'Matthew Blakiston told me everything I need to know. It was he who started all this.'

'Really? What did he do?'

'He killed his wife.'

Crouch End, London

Annoying, isn't it?

I got to the end of the manuscript on Sunday afternoon and rang Charles Clover immediately. Charles is my boss, the CEO of Cloverleaf Books, publishers of the Atticus Pünd series. My call went straight to voicemail.

'Charles?' I said. 'What happened to the last chapter? What exactly is the point of giving me a whodunnit to read when it doesn't actually say who did it? Can you call me back?'

I went down to the kitchen. There were two empty bottles of white wine in the bedroom and tortilla crumbs on the duvet. I knew I'd been indoors too long but it was still cold and damp outside and I couldn't be bothered to go out. There was nothing decent to drink in the house so I opened a bottle of raki that Andreas had brought back from his last trip to Crete, poured myself a glass and threw it back. It tasted like all foreign spirits do after they've passed through Heathrow. Wrong. I'd brought the manuscript down with me and I went through it again, trying to work out how much might be missing. The last section would have been called 'A Secret Never to be Told', which was certainly appropriate, given the circumstances. Since Pünd had announced that he'd already worked out the solution, it could only have had two or maybe three sections. Presumably, he would gather the suspects, tell them the truth, make an arrest, then go home and die. I knew that Alan Conway had wanted to end the series for a while but it had still come as an unpleasant surprise to find that he had done exactly that. The brain tumour struck me as a slightly unoriginal way to dispatch his main character but it was also unarguable, which I suppose is why he had chosen it. I have to admit that if I shed a tear, it was more for our future sales figures.

So who killed Sir Magnus Pye?

I had nothing better to do so I drew out a pad of paper and a pen and sat down in the kitchen with the typescript beside me. It even occurred to me that Charles might have done this on purpose, to test me. He'd be in the office when I got there on Monday – he was always the first to arrive – and he'd ask for the solution before he gave me the final pages. Charles does have a strange sense of humour. I've often seen him chuckling at jokes that nobody else in the room is aware that he's made.

1. Neville Brent, the groundsman.

He's the most obvious suspect. First of all, he dislikes Mary Blakiston and has just been fired by Sir Magnus Pye. He has a simple, clear-cut reason to do away with both of them. Also, he's the only character in the book connected to all the deaths. He's there at the house when Mary dies and he's virtually the last person to see Sir Magnus alive. Supposedly, he goes straight to the Ferryman when he finishes work on the night of the death but Conway throws in a strange detail on page 77. Brent reaches the pub *twenty-five minutes later*. Why is he so specific about the time? It may be an extraneous detail and it may even be wrong – let's not forget, we're dealing with a first draft here. But I was under the impression that the Ferryman was only ten minutes away from Pye Hall and the extra fifteen minutes might have given Brent time to double back, to slip in through the back door while Sir Magnus was talking to Matthew Blakiston and to kill him immediately afterwards.

There's something else about Brent. It's almost certain that he's a paedophile. 'He was a solitary man, unmarried, definitely peculiar – a certain smell lingered in the air, the smell of a man living alone.' The police find Boy Scout magazines on his bedroom floor and, quite casually, on page 144, we're told that he was once caught spying on Scouts who were camping in Dingle Dell. These details leapt out at me because, by and large, there's so little sex in the Atticus Pünd novels – although it's worth remembering that the killer in *Gin & Cyanide* turns out to be gay (she poisons her lesbian partner). Did Brent have an unhealthy interest in the two boys, Tom and Robert Blakiston? It's surely no coincidence that he is the one who 'discovers' Tom Blakiston when he has drowned in the lake. I even wonder about the deaths of his mother and father, supposedly in a motor accident. And finally, he was probably the one who killed the dog.

All of which said, it is the first law of whodunnits that the most likely suspect never turns out to be the killer. So I suppose that rules him out.

2. Robert Blakiston, the car mechanic

Robert is also linked to all three deaths. In his own way, he's as weird as Brent. He has pale skin and an awkward haircut. He never got on with the other children at school, he was arrested in Bristol and, most pertinently, he has a difficult relationship with his mother that culminates with a public row in which he more or less threatens to kill her. I'm cheating here but, speaking as an editor, it would also be quite satisfying if Robert were the murderer as Joy Sanderling only goes to Pünd because she's trying to protect him. I can easily imagine a last chapter in which her own hopes are destroyed when her fiancé is unmasked. That's the solution I would have chosen.

However, there are two major problems with this theory. The first is that unless Joy Sanderling was lying, Robert couldn't possibly have killed his mother because the two of them were in bed together at the time it occurred. It's probably true that the pink motor scooter would have been noticed as it whizzed down to Pye Hall at nine o'clock in the morning (although it doesn't seem to have stopped the killer from using the vicar's squeaky bicycle at nine o'clock at night). More significantly though, and Pünd mentions this on at least one occasion, Robert doesn't seem to have any motive for killing Sir Magnus who has only ever been kind to him. Could he have blamed Sir Magnus for the death of his younger brother when they were playing at the lake? He had, after all, supplied the fool's gold that had caused the tragedy and Robert was the second person to arrive on the scene, plunging into the water to help drag his brother out. He must have been traumatised. Could he even have blamed him for the death of his mother?

Maybe Robert is my number one suspect after all and Brent my second. I don't know.

3. Robin Osborne, the vicar

Alan Conway has a habit of playing a minor card at the end of the game. In *No Rest for the Wicked*, for example, Agnes Carmichael, who turns out to be the killer, hasn't spoken a word – hardly surprising, as she's a deaf mute. I don't think Osborne kills Sir Magnus because of Dingle Dell. Nor do I think that he kills Mary Blakiston because of whatever it was that she found on his desk. But it's certainly interesting that his bicycle has been used during the second crime. Could he really have been in the church all that time? And on page 98 Henrietta notices a bloodstain on her husband's sleeve. This isn't mentioned again but I'm sure that Conway would have got to it in the missing pages.

I'm also interested in the holiday that Osborne took with his wife in Devonshire. Certainly he's reluctant to talk about it when Pünd questions him ('the vicar seemed nonplussed') and refuses to give even the name of the hotel. I may be reading too much into it but Brent's parents also died in Devonshire. Is this in some way connected?

4. Matthew Blakiston, the father

Really, he should be at the top of my list as we are told, quite unequivocally, that he murdered his wife. Pünd says so at the end of part six – 'He killed his wife' – and it is inconceivable that he's lying. In all eight books, even when he makes a mistake (the false arrest in *Atticus Pünd's Christmas* which infuriated readers who felt that Conway hadn't played fair), he has never been less than 100 per cent honest. If he announces that Matthew Blakiston killed his wife, then that is what happened, although annoyingly he doesn't say why. Nor, for that matter, does he explain how he came to this conclusion. The explanation, of course, will be contained in the missing chapter.

Did Matthew also kill Sir Magnus? I don't think so. I've managed to work out at least one detail: the handprint in the flower bed was left by Blakiston when he was looking through the letter box. 'I felt myself falling and I thought I was going to faint'. These are his own words. He must have stretched out his hand to steady himself and left the print in the soft earth. He kills his wife and for some reason returns to the scene of the crime. If this is the case then, as unlikely as it sounds, there's a second killer in Saxby-on-Avon who deals with Sir Magnus for a quite different reason.

5. Clarissa Pye, the sister

Sometimes, when I read a whodunnit, I get a feeling about someone for no particularly good reason and that's the case here. Clarissa had every reason to hate her brother and might have intended to kill both Lady Pye and her son, Freddy, in order to inherit Pye Hall. The whole story about stealing the physostigmine to commit suicide could have been a lie – and would also explain the need to do away with Mary Blakiston. And let's not forget that Clarissa had a key to the front door of Pye Hall. It's mentioned once – on page 25 – though not again.

There's also the case of Dr Rennard and the twins-exchanged-at-birth. When did Clarissa discover the truth? Was it really when Dr Redwing told her? I only ask this because there's an odd reference to Ashton House, where Dr Rennard lives – on page 62. In his funeral address, the vicar mentions that Mary Blakiston was a regular visitor there. It could be that Rennard had told her what had happened and she, being the sort of person she was, had then told Clarissa. That would give Clarissa a compelling reason to kill both Mary and Sir Magnus. The physostigmine could have been for Lady Pye and Freddy. It could even be that Dr Rennard's fall hadn't actually been an accident... although perhaps I'm taking this too far?

I dismissed the Whiteheads, Dr Redwing and her artist husband, Frances Pye and the slightly improbable Jack Dartford. They all had motives for the murder of Sir Magnus but I couldn't see any reason why any of them would have wanted to harm Mary Blakiston. That just left Joy Sanderling, the least likely suspect of them all. But why would she have wanted to kill anyone and, more to the point, why would she have gone to Atticus Pünd in the first place?

Anyway, that was how I spent Sunday afternoon, leafing through the manuscript, making notes and really getting nowhere. That evening I met a couple of friends at the BFI for a screening of *The Maltese Falcon* but I wasn't able to focus on the labyrinthine plot. I was thinking about Magnus and Mary and bloody scraps of paper, dead dogs and letters in wrong envelopes. I wondered why the manuscript was incomplete and I was annoyed that Charles hadn't called me back.

Later that night I found out why. I'd treated myself to a taxi and the driver had the radio on. It was the fourth item on the evening news.

Alan Conway was dead.

Cloverleaf Books

My name is Susan Ryeland and I am the Head of Fiction at Cloverleaf Books. The role isn't as grand as it sounds as there are only fifteen of us (and a dog) in the building and we produce no more than twenty books a year. I work on about half of them. For such a small operation, we don't have a bad list. There are a couple of well-respected authors who have won literary awards, a bestselling fantasy writer and a children's author who has just been announced as the new laureate. We can't afford the production costs of cookery books but in the past we've done well with travel guides, self-help and biographies. But the simple truth is that Alan Conway was by far our biggest name and our entire business plan depended on the success of *Magpie Murders*.

The company was set up eleven years ago by Charles Clover, who is well known throughout the industry and I'd been with him from the start. We were together at Orion when he decided to branch out on his own, working out of a building that he'd bought near the British Museum. The look of the place absolutely suited him: three floors, narrow corridors, worn carpets, wooden panels, not much daylight. At a time when everyone else was nervously embracing the twenty-first century – publishers are generally not the first off the line when it comes to social or technological change – he was quite happy in his role as a throwback. Well, he had worked with Graham Green, Anthony Burgess and Muriel Spark. There's even a photograph of him having dinner with a very elderly Noël Coward, although he always says he was so drunk he can't remember the name of the restaurant nor a single word that the great man said.

Charles and I spend so much time together that people assume we must once have been lovers although we never were. He's married with two grown-up children, one of whom – Laura – is about to give birth to his first grandchild. He lives in the rather grand double-fronted house in Parson's Green that he and his wife, Elaine, have owned for thirty years. I've been there for dinner a few times and the evenings have always been marked by interesting company, really good wine and conversation that goes on late into the night. That said, he doesn't tend to socialise much outside the office, at least not with people from the world of publishing. He reads a great deal. He plays the cello. I've heard it said that he took a lot of drugs when he was in his teens and early twenties but you wouldn't believe it looking at him now.

I hadn't actually seen him for a week. I'd been on the road with an author from Tuesday to Friday; we'd had events in Birmingham, Manchester, Edinburgh and Dublin along with radio and newspaper interviews. It had gone surprisingly well. When I'd come in late on Friday afternoon, he'd already left for the weekend. The typescript of *Magpie Murders* had been waiting for me on my desk. It occurred to me as I threw my bag down and flicked on my computer the following Monday that he and I must have read it at the same time and that, after all, he couldn't have known it was incomplete when he left it for me.

He was already in his office, which was on the first floor at the opposite end of the corridor to mine. He looked out onto the main road – New Oxford Street and Bloomsbury Way. My part of the building was quieter. He had an elegant, square room with three windows, bookshelves of course, and a surprising number of trophies on display. Charles doesn't actually like award ceremonies. He thinks of them as a necessary evil but over the years Cloverleaf has managed to win quite a few of them – Nibbies, Gold Daggers, IPG Awards – and somehow they've found their way here. It was all very neat. Charles liked to know where everything was and he had a secretary, Jemima, who looked after him although she didn't seem to be around. He was sitting behind his desk with his own copy of *Magpie Murders* in front of him. I saw that he'd been making notes in the margin, using a fountain pen filled with red ink.

I must describe Charles as he was that day. He was sixty-three years old, dressed as always in a suit and tie, with a narrow gold band on his fourth finger. Elaine had given it to him for his fiftieth birthday. Coming into the slightly darkened room, he always struck me as a godfather figure, as in the famous film. There was no sense of menace but Charles looked Italian with piercing eyes, a very thin nose and quite aristocratic cheekbones. He had white hair, which swept down in a careless sort of way, brushing against his collar. He was quite fit for a man of his age, not that he would have dreamed of going anywhere near a gym, and he was very much in command. He often brought his dog when he came in to work and it was there now, a golden Labrador asleep on a folded blanket under the desk.

The dog's name was Bella.

'Come in, Susan,' he said, waving me in from the door.

I was carrying the typescript with me. I came in and sat down and saw now that he was looking very pale, almost in shock. 'You've heard,' he said.

I nodded. There were articles in all the newspapers and I'd heard the author Ian Rankin talking about him on the *Today* programme. My first thought when I heard the news was that he must have had a heart attack. Wasn't that what most commonly struck down men of his age? But I was wrong. Now they were saying it was an accident. It had happened at his home near Framlingham

'It's terrible news,' Charles said. 'Absolutely terrible.'

'Do you know what happened?' I asked.

'The police rang me last night. I spoke to a Detective Superintendent Locke. He was calling from Ipswich, I think. He said exactly what they're saying on the radio – an accident – but he wouldn't go into any more detail than that. And then, this morning, just a few minutes ago, I received this.' He picked up a letter that had been lying on the desk. There was a roughly torn open envelope beside it. 'It came in the morning post. It's from Alan.'

'Can I see it?'

'Of course.' He handed it to me.

The letter is important so I am including an exact reproduction.

1.

ABBEY GRANGE,
FRAMLINGHAM,
SUFFOLK.

28 August 2015

Dear Charles,

I don't like apologies but I wasn't on my best form at dinner last night I will admit. You know I've been out of sorts recently and I didn't want to tell you but I might as well come straight out with it. I'm not well.

Actually, that's putting it mildly. Dr Sheila Bennett at the London Clinic has all the details but effectively I'm about to be killed by the biggest bloody cliché on the planet. I have cancer. It's inoperable.

Why me? I don't smoke. I hardly drink. Both my parents lived to a ripe old age etc etc. Anyway, I have about six months, maybe more if I go for chemotherapy and all the rest of it.

But I've already decided against it. I'm sorry but I'm not going to spend my last remaining days plugged into an intravenous drip with my head halfway down a toilet and my hair all over the bedroom floor. What's the point of that? And I'm not going to have myself wheeled around London literary functions, stick-thin and coughing my guts out with everyone queuing up to tell me how terribly sorry they all are when actually they can't wait to see me go.

2.

Anyway, I know I was pretty foul to you but in a way our whole relationship has been a profound fuck up and it might as well end the way it all began. When you and I first met, I remember the promises you made me and to be fair to you, they've all come true. The money anyway. So thank you for that.

As to the money, there are bound to be rows when I've gone. James isn't going to be happy for one. I don't know why I'm mentioning this to you as it's none of your business but you might as well know that the two of us had more or less gone our separate ways and I'm afraid I've cut him out altogether.

God! I sound like a character in on of my own books. Anyway, he's just going to have to live with it. I hope he doesn't make too much trouble for you.

On the literary side, things didn't work out quite the way I'd hoped but we've talked about that often enough and I'm not going to waste time rehearsing it here. You don't give a damn what I think about my career. You never have. It's one of those things I liked about you. Sales. Best seller lists. Those fucking Nielsen charts. All the stuff I've always loathed about publishing has always been bread, butter and jam to you. What will you do without me? It's just a shame I won't be around to find out.

By the time that you read this, it will all be finished. You will forgive me for not having spoken to you earlier, for not taking you into my confidence but I am sure that in time you will understand.

There are some notes which I have written and which you will find in my desk. They relate to my condition and to the decision that I have made. I want it to be understood that the doctor's diagnosis is clear and, for me, there can be no possibility of reprieve. I have no fear of death. I would like to think that my name will be remembered.

I have achieved great success in a life that has gone on long enough. You will find that I have left you a small bequest in my will. This is partly to recognise the many years that we have spent together but it is also my hope that you will be able to complete the work of my book and prepare it for publication. You are now its only guardian but I am confident that it will be safe in your hands.

Otherwise, there are few people who will mourn for me. I leave behind me no dependents. As I prepare to take leave of this world, I feel that I have used my time well and hope that I will be remembered for the successes that you and I shared together.

4.

It's been quite an adventure, hasn't it? (Why not take another look at The Slide, just for old time's sake?) Don't be angry with me. Remember all the money you've made. And here they are – my two favourite words.

The End.

As ever,
Alan

'This came this morning?' I asked.

'Yes. You know, the two of us had dinner on Thursday night. I took him to the Club at the Ivy. This is dated 28 August, which is the next day. He must have written it as soon as he got home.'

Alan had a flat in Fitzrovia. He would have stayed overnight and taken the train from Liverpool Street the following morning.

'What's *The Slide*?' I asked.

'It was a book that Alan wrote a while back.'

'You never showed it to me.'

'I didn't think you'd be interested, to be honest. It wasn't a whodunnit. It was something more serious, a sort of satire about twenty-first century Britain, set in a stately home.'

'I'd still have liked to have seen it.'

'Trust me, Susan. You'd have been wasting your time. There was no way I was going to publish it.'

'Did you tell Alan that?'

'Not in so many words. I just said that it wouldn't fit into our list.' An old publishing euphemism. You don't tell your most successful author that his new book is no bloody good.

The two of us sat in silence. Underneath the desk, the dog turned over and groaned. 'This is a suicide letter,' I said.

'Yes.'

'We have to send it to the police.'

'I agree. I was about to call them.'

'You didn't know he was ill?'

'I knew absolutely nothing about it. He'd never told me and he certainly didn't mention it on Thursday night. We had dinner. He gave me the manuscript. He was excited! He said it was his best work.'

I hadn't been there and I'm writing this after the event, but this is what Charles told me had happened. Alan Conway had promised to deliver *Magpie Murders* by the end of the year and, unlike some writers I've worked with, he was always very prompt. The dinner had been planned a few weeks before and it was no coincidence, incidentally, that it had been arranged while I was away. Alan and I didn't get on for reasons I'll come to. He had met Charles at the Ivy, not the restaurant but a private, members only club just off Cambridge Circus. There's a piano bar on the first floor and a restaurant above and all the windows have stained glass so you can't see in – or, for that matter, out. Quite a few celebrities go there and it's exactly the sort of place that Alan would have enjoyed. Charles had booked his usual table on the left of the door with a wall of bookshelves behind him. The scene couldn't have been better staged if it had been in a theatre. In fact, the St Martin's Theatre and the Ambassadors which had, between them, shown *The Mousetrap* for God knows how many years, were both down the road.

The two of them started with large martini cocktails, which The Club does very well. They talked about general stuff: family and friends, London, Suffolk, the book trade, a bit of gossip, what was selling, what wasn't. They chose their food and because Alan liked expensive wine, Charles flattered him by ordering a bottle of Gevrey-Chambertin Grand Cru, most of which Alan drank. I could imagine him becoming louder and more loquacious as the meal went on. He always did have a tendency to drink too much. The first course arrived and it was after they had finished it that Alan produced the manuscript from the leather satchel he always carried.

'I was very surprised,' Charles said. 'I wasn't expecting it for at least another couple of months.'

'You know that my copy is incomplete,' I said. 'It's missing the last chapters.'

'Mine too. I was just working on it when you came in.'

'Did he say anything?' I was wondering if Alan had done this on purpose. Perhaps he wanted Charles to guess the ending before it was actually revealed.

Charles thought back. 'No. He just told me how good he thought it was and handed it over.'

That was interesting. Alan Conway must have believed all the chapters were there. Otherwise, surely, he would have explained what he was doing.

Charles had been delighted to receive the new work and made all the right noises. He told Alan he would read it over the weekend. Unfortunately, after that, the evening had taken a turn for the worse.

'I don't know what happened,' Charles told me. 'We were

talking about the title. I wasn't sure I liked it – and you know how touchy Alan could be. Maybe it was foolish of me to bring it up just then. And while we were talking, there was a rather odd incident. A waiter dropped a handful of plates. I suppose it could happen anywhere but The Club is such a quiet place that it was almost like a bomb going off and Alan actually got up and remonstrated with the waiter. He'd been on edge all evening, I had no idea why. But if he was ill and already thinking of doing away with himself, I suppose it's hardly surprising.'

'How did the meal end?' I asked.

'Alan calmed down a bit and we had coffee but he was still out of sorts. You know how he could be after a few glasses of wine. Remember that ghastly Specsavers event? Anyway, as he was getting into his taxi, he said there was a radio interview he wanted to pull.'

'Simon Mayo,' I said. 'Radio Two.'

'Yes. Next Friday. I tried to talk him out of it. You don't want to let these media people down as you never know if they'll invite you back. But he wasn't having any or it.' Charles turned the letter in his hands. I wondered if he should even be touching it. Wasn't it evidence? 'I suppose I should telephone the police,' he said. 'They'll need to know about this.'

I left him to make the call.

Alan Conway

I was the one who discovered Alan Conway.

He was introduced to me by my sister, Katie, who lives in Suffolk and who sent her children to the local independent school. Alan was an English teacher there and had just finished a novel, a whodunnit called *Atticus Pünd Investigates*. I'm not sure how he found out that she knew me – I suppose she must have told him – but he asked her if she would show it to me. My sister and I have very different lives but we've stayed close and I agreed to take a look as a favour to her. I didn't think it would be any good because books that come in this way, through the back door, seldom are.

I was pleasantly surprised.

Alan had captured something of 'the golden age' of British whodunnits with a country house setting, a complicated murder, a cast of suitably eccentric characters and a detective who arrived as an outsider. The book was set in 1946, just after the war, and although he was light with the period detail, he had still managed to capture something of the feelings of that time. Pünd was a sympathetic character and the fact that he had come out of the concentration camps – we eventually cut back on some of this – gave him a certain depth. I liked his Germanic mannerisms, particularly his obsession with his book, *The Landscape of Criminal Investigation*, which would become a regular feature. Setting the story in the forties also allowed for a gentler pace: no mobile phones, computers, forensics, no instant information.

I had a few issues. Some of the writing was too clever. It often felt as if he was fighting for effect rather than simply telling the story. It was too long. But by the time I had come to the end of the manuscript, I was certain that I was going to publish it, my first commission for Cloverleaf Books.

And then I met the author.

I didn't like him. I'm sorry to say it but he just struck me as a bit of a cold fish. You'll have seen photographs of him on the book jackets; the slim face, the closely cropped silver hair, the round, wire-frame glasses. On television or on the radio he'd always had a sort of eloquence, an easy charm. He was nothing like that then. He was puffy and a little overweight, wearing a suit with chalk marks on the sleeves. His manner was at once aggressive and eager to please. He wasted no time telling me how much he wanted to be a published author but he showed almost no enthusiasm now that the moment had come. I couldn't work him out. When I mentioned some of the changes I wanted him to make to his book, he positively bristled. He struck me as one of the most humourless people I had ever met. Later on, Katie told me that he had never been popular with the children and I could understand why.

To be fair though, I have to say that I can't have made a great first impression either. Some meetings just happen that way. We'd arranged lunch at a smart restaurant – him, Charles and me. It was pouring with rain that day, really chucking it down. I'd been at a meeting on the other side of town and my taxi hadn't arrived so I'd had to run half a mile in high heels. I turned up late with my hair plastered down the side of my face, my shirt sodden and my bra showing through. I knocked over a glass of wine as I sat down. I really wanted a cigarette and that made me ratty. I remember we had an absurd argument about one section in the book – he'd gathered all the suspects in the library and I just thought it was too clichéd – but actually this wasn't the right time to talk about that. Afterwards, Charles was quite angry with me and he was right to be. We could have lost him, and there were plenty of other publishers who would have taken the book, particularly with the promise of a series.

In fact, Charles took over and did most of the talking that day and the result was that he was the one who ended up working with Alan. Which is to say, it was Charles who went to all the festivals: Edinburgh, Hay-on-Wye, Oxford, Cheltenham. Charles had the relationship. I just did the work, editing the books with a nifty software programme that meant we didn't even have to meet face to face. It's funny to think that I worked with him for eleven years and never once visited his house: a little unfair considering I actually paid for it.

Of course, I saw him from time to time, whenever he came into the office and I have to admit, the more successful he got, the more attractive he became. He bought expensive clothes. He went to the gym. He drove a BMW i8 coupe. These days all writers have to be media performers and Alan Conway was soon touring the studios on programmes like *The Book Show*, *The Wright Stuff* and *Question Time*. He went to parties and awards ceremonies. He talked at schools and universities. He had been forty years old when he found fame and it was as if it was only then that he began to live his life. He changed in other ways too. He was married with an eight-year-old son when I met him. The marriage didn't last long.

Reading what I've written I sound disenchanted, as if I resented the success that, to a large extent, I had created for him. But that wasn't how I felt at all. I didn't care what he thought about me and I was perfectly happy to let him and Charles hang out together at literary festivals while I set about the serious business, editing the text and overseeing the production of the books. At the end of the day, that was all that mattered to me. And the truth is that I really did love them. I grew up on Agatha Christie and when I'm on a plane or on a beach there's nothing I'd rather read than a whodunnit. I've watched every episode of *Poirot* and *Midsomer Murders* on TV. I never guess the ending and I can't wait for the moment when the detective gathers all the suspects in the room and, like a magician conjuring silk scarves out of the air, makes the whole thing make sense. So here's the bottom line. I was a fan of Atticus Pünd. I didn't need to be a fan of Alan Conway too.

I had to field quite a few phone calls after I left Charles's office. Somehow, even before we had made the police aware of the letter, the news had got out that Alan had committed suicide and there were journalists chasing the story. Friends in the industry called to commiserate. An antiquarian bookshop in Cecil Court wanted to know if we had any signed copies as they were mounting a window display. I thought about Alan a lot that morning – but I thought more about a whodunnit that was missing its solution and, for that matter, a summer publishing schedule that had a huge hole at its centre.

After lunch, I went back in to see Charles.

'I've spoken to the police,' Charles told me. The letter was still in front of him with the envelope next to it. 'They're sending someone round to collect it. They say I shouldn't have touched it.'

'I don't see how you could have known that before you opened it.'

'Quite.'

'Did they tell you how he did it?' I asked. By 'did it' I meant 'killed himself'.

Charles nodded. 'There's a sort of tower attached to his house. The last time I was there – it must have been March or April – I actually had a conversation with Alan about it. I said to him how dangerous it was. There's only a low wall and no railings or anything. It's funny, because when I heard there'd been an accident, I instantly assumed he must have fallen off the bloody thing. But now it looks as if he jumped.'

There was a long silence. Usually, Charles and I know what the other is thinking but this time we were deliberately avoiding each other's eyes. It was really quite horrible that this had happened. Neither of us wanted to confront it.

'What did you think of the book?' I asked. It was the one question I hadn't asked, the first thing, in normal circumstances, I would have wanted to know.

'Well, I read it over the weekend and I was enjoying it very much. It seemed to me every bit as good as all the others. When I got to the last page, I was as irritated as you must have been. My first thought was that one of the girls must have made a mistake here in the office. I had two copies made – one for you, one for me.'

That reminded me. 'Where's Jemima?' I asked.

'She's left. She handed in her notice while you were on the road.' Suddenly he looked tired. 'She couldn't have chosen a worse time. This business with Alan – and there's Laura to think about too.'

Laura was his pregnant daughter. 'How is she?' I asked.

'She's fine. But the doctors are saying it could happen any time. Apparently, with the first one, it's more likely to be early.' He went back to what he'd been saying before. 'There are no missing pages, Susan. Not here anyway. We've checked the copy room. We printed up exactly what Alan gave us. I was going to call him to ask what had happened. And then, of course, I heard the news.'

'He didn't send you a copy electronically?'

'No. He never did that.'

It was true. Alan was a pen and paper man. He actually handwrote his first draft. Then he typed it into his computer. He always sent us a printed copy before he emailed it to us, as if he somehow mistrusted us reading it on the screen.

'Well, we have to find the missing chapters,' I said. 'And the sooner the better.' Charles looked doubtful so I went on. 'They must be somewhere in the house. Did you manage to work out who did it?'

Charles shook his head. 'I was thinking it might be the sister.'

'Clarissa Pye. Yes. She was on my list too.'

'There's always a chance he didn't actually finish it.'

'I'm sure he'd have told you that when he handed it over – and what would have been the point?' I thought about my diary, all the meetings I had in the week ahead. But this was more important. 'Why don't I drive up to Framlingham?' I said.

'Are you sure that's a good idea? The police will still be at the house. If he committed suicide, there'll have to be an enquiry.'

'Yes, I know. But I'd like to get access to his computer.'

'They'll have removed it, won't they?'

'At least I can take a look around. The original could still be on his desk.'

He thought for a moment. 'Well, I suppose so.'

I was surprised that he wasn't more enthusiastic. Although neither of us had said as much, we both knew how much we needed *Magpie Murders*. We'd had a bad year. In May we'd published the biography of a comedian who'd made a joke in spectacularly poor taste, live on TV. Almost overnight, he'd stopped being funny and his book had more or less vanished from the shops. I'd just been touring with the author of a first novel called *The One-Armed Juggler*, a comedy set in a circus. The tour might have gone well but the reviews had been merciless and we were having difficulty getting copies into the shops. We'd had trouble with the building, a lawsuit, trouble with the staff. We weren't going under but we badly needed a hit.

'I'll go tomorrow,' I said.

'I suppose there's no harm in trying. Would you like me to come with you?'

'No. I'll be fine on my own.' Alan had never invited me to Abbey Grange. I would be interested to see what it was like. 'Give my love to Laura,' I said. 'And if there's any news, let me know.'

I got up and left the room and here's the strange thing. It was only as I walked back to my office that I realised what I had seen, even though it had been in front of my eyes all the time. It was very odd. It made no sense at all.

Alan's suicide note and the envelope it had come in had been on Charles's desk. The letter was handwritten. The envelope was typed.

Abbey Grange, Framlingham

The next morning, bright and early, I was speeding across the top of Alexandra Park with the virtually empty carcass of the famous palace above me, heading for the A12. It was a perfect excuse to take out the MGB Roadster that I'd bought myself six years ago, on my fortieth birthday. It was a ridiculous car but I'd known I had to have it the moment I saw it for sale outside a garage in Highgate: a 1969 model, manual with overdrive, and an in-your-face, pillar-box red with black trim. Katie didn't know what to say when I first showed up in it but her children went crazy for it and whenever I saw them I took them out, tearing around country lanes with the roof down and the two of them yelling in the back seat.

I was going against the traffic that was coming into London and made good time until I got to Earl Soham where a particularly annoying roadwork kept me waiting ten minutes. It was a warm day. The weather had been good throughout the summer and it looked as if September was going to be the same. I thought of putting the roof down but it would be too noisy on the motorway. Perhaps when I got nearer.

I've visited most of the seaside villages of Suffolk – Southwold, Walberswick, Dunwich and Orford – but I'd never been to Framlingham before. Maybe the very fact that Alan lived there had put me off. My first impressions as I drove in were of a pleasant, slightly down-at-heel town centring on a main square that wasn't square at all. Some of the buildings had a certain charm but others, an Indian restaurant for example, looked oddly out of place, and if you were planning to go shopping, there wasn't going to be anything very exciting to buy. A large brick structure had imposed itself in the middle and this turned out to contain a modern supermarket. I'd booked a room at the Crown Hotel, a coaching inn that had looked out onto the square for four hundred years and now found itself rubbing shoulders with a bank and a travel agency. It was actually very charming with the original flagstones, lots of fireplaces, and wooden beams. I was glad to see books on the shelves and board games piled up on a community chest. They gave the place a homely feel. I found the receptionist tucked away behind a tiny window and checked in. I had thought about staying with my sister but Woodbridge was a thirty-minute drive away and I would be happy enough here.

I went up to the room and dumped my case on the bed: a four-poster, no less. I wished Andreas was here to share it with me. He had a particular liking for olde England, especially if the olde was spelled with an e. He found things like croquet, cream teas and cricket both incomprehensible and irresistible and he would have been in his element here. I sent him a text, then washed and ran a comb through my hair. It was lunchtime but I didn't feel like eating. I got back in the car and drove out to Abbey Grange.

Alan Conway's home was a couple of miles outside Framlingham and it would have been almost impossible to find without sat nav. I've lived my whole life in a city where roads actually go somewhere because, frankly, they can't afford not to. The same couldn't be said for the country lane that twiddled its way through far too much country before an even narrower lane brought me to the private track that finally led me to the house itself. When did I realise that I was looking at the inspiration for Pye Hall? Well, the stone griffins beside the entrance gate would have been the first clue. The lodge house was exactly as described. The drive curved round to the front door, cutting through extensive lawns. I didn't see any rose gardens but the lake was there and so was the woodland that might have been Dingle Dell. I could easily imagine Brent standing beside the corpse of Tom Blakiston while his brother desperately gave him mouth-to-mouth. Most of the work had been done for me.

And the house itself? 'What remained was a single, elongated wing with an octagonal tower – constructed much later – at the far end.' As I drew up, that was exactly what I saw: a long, narrow building with about a dozen windows spread out over two floors joined to a tower which might provide great views but which was, in itself, ridiculous. I guessed it had all been built in the nineteenth century, the creation of some Victorian industrialist who'd brought his memories of London's mills and mausoleums to rural Suffolk. It was nowhere near as attractive as Sir Magnus Pye's ancestral home, at least as Alan had described it. Abbey Grange was built out of the dirty red brick that I've always associated with Charles Dickens and William Blake. It didn't belong here and it was saved only by its setting. The garden must have spread out over four or five acres with a huge sky and no other houses in sight. I wouldn't want to live here and frankly I couldn't see why it had appealed to Alan Conway either. Wouldn't he have been too metrosexual for this folly?

This was where he had died. I was reminded of it as I got out of the car. Just four days ago, he had thrown himself off the tower that loomed over me even now. I examined the crenellations at the top. They didn't look very safe. If you leant too far, suicidal or not, you might easily topple over. The tower was surrounded by lawn – the grass knotted and uneven. In Ian McEwan's novel *Enduring Love* there's an extremely good description of what happens to a human body when it falls from a great height and I could easily imagine Conway, all mangled up with his bones broken and his limbs pointing in the wrong direction. Would the fall have been enough to kill him instantly or would he have lain there in agony until someone came along and found him? He lived alone so it might have been a cleaner or a gardener who had raised the alarm. Did that make any sense? He had killed himself to avoid suffering but in fact he might have suffered horribly. It wasn't the way I would have chosen. Get in a warm bath and cut your wrists. Jump in front of a train. Either would have been more certain.

I took out my iPhone and moved away from the front door so that I could get a picture of the whole thing. I didn't know why I did that, but then why does anyone take photographs ever? We never look at them any more. I had driven past a large shrub (it wasn't in the book) and, walking back, I noticed two tyre tracks. Quite recently, when the grass was damp, a car had parked behind it. I took a picture of the tyre tracks too; not because they meant anything but simply because I thought I should. I slipped the phone into my pocket and I was walking back to the front door when it opened and a man came out. I'd never met him but I knew instantly who he was. I've mentioned that Alan was married. Shortly after the third book in the Atticus Pünd series came out, so did Alan. He left his family for a young man called James Taylor – and by young I mean barely twenty at a time when Alan himself was in his mid-forties with a son aged twelve. His private life was no concern of mine but I will admit I was a little uneasy and worried about the effect it might have on sales. The story was reported in quite a lot of newspapers but fortunately this was 2009 and the journalists weren't able to sneer too much. Alan's wife, Melissa, and his son moved to the West Country. They agreed terms very quickly. That was when Alan had bought Abbey Grange.

I had never met James Taylor but knew I was looking at him now. He was wearing a leather jacket and jeans with a low-cut T-shirt that showed a thin gold chain around his neck. Although he was now twenty-eight or twenty-nine, he still looked incredibly young with a baby face that thick stubble did nothing to disguise. He had long, fair hair, which he hadn't brushed. It was slightly greasy, following the curve of his neck. He could have just got out of bed. His eyes were haunted, suspicious. I got the feeling that he had been damaged at some time in his life. Or maybe it was just that he wasn't pleased to see me.

'Yes?' he asked. 'Who are you?'

'I'm Susan Ryeland,' I said. 'I work at Cloverleaf Books. We're Alan's publishers.' I fished in my handbag and gave him my business card.

He glanced at it, then looked past me. 'I like your car.'

'Thank you.'

'It's an MG.'

'An MGB actually.'

He smiled. I could tell it amused him, a woman of my age

driving a car like that. 'I'm afraid that if you're here to see Alan, you're too late.'

'I know. I know what happened. Do you think I could come in?'

'Why?'

'It's difficult to explain. I'm looking for something.'

'Sure.' He shrugged and opened the door as if he owned the place. But I had read Alan's letter. I knew he didn't.

If this had been the world of *Magpie Murders*, the front door would have led into a grand hall with wood panels, a stone fireplace and a staircase leading up to a galleried landing. But all that must have come out of Conway's imagination. In fact the interior was disappointing: a reception room, stripped wooden floor, country furniture, expensive modern art on the walls – all very tasteful, but ordinary. No suits of armour. No animal trophies. No dead bodies. We turned right and went along a corridor that ran the full length of the house, finally bringing us into a serious kitchen with an industrial oven, an American fridge, gleaming surfaces and a table that could seat twelve. James offered me a coffee, which I accepted. He fixed it in one of those machines that uses capsules and froths up the milk on the side.

'So you're his publisher,' he said.

'No. His editor.'

'How well did you know Alan?'

I wasn't sure how to answer that. 'It was a working relationship,' I said. 'He never invited me here.'

'This is my home – or at least it was until about two weeks ago when Alan asked me to move out. I hadn't left yet because I didn't have anywhere to go and now I suppose, I may not have to.' He brought the coffees over and sat down.

'Do you mind if I smoke?' I asked. I'd noticed an ashtray on the table and the smell of cigarette smoke in the air.

'Not at all,' he said. 'Actually, if you've got some cigarettes, I'll have one too.' I held out the packet and suddenly we were friends. That's one of the only good things about being a smoker these days. You're part of a persecuted minority. You bond easily. But actually I'd already decided that I liked James Taylor, this boy alone in a big house.

'Were you here?' I asked. 'When Alan killed himself?'

'No, thank God. We weren't together at that stage. I was in London, hanging out with some people I know.' I watched as he tapped ash. He had very long, slender fingers. His nails were dirty. 'I got a call from Mr Khan – he was Alan's solicitor – and I came back late on Monday. By then, the place was crawling with police officers. It was Mr Khan who found him, you know. He came over to drop off some papers, probably cutting me out of the will or something, and Alan was on the lawn in front of the tower. I have to say, I'm glad it wasn't me. I'm not sure I'd have coped.' He sucked in smoke, holding the cigarette cupped in his hand, like a soldier in an old film. 'What is it you're looking for?'

I told him the truth. I explained that Alan had delivered his last novel just a couple of days before he'd died and that it was missing the last chapter. I asked him if he had read any of *Magpie Murders* and he gave a sniff of laughter. 'I read every one of the Atticus Pünd books,' he said. 'You know I'm in them?'

'I didn't know that,' I said.

'Oh yes. James Fraser, the dumb blond assistant – that's me.' He flicked his own hair. 'When I met Alan, he was just about to start *Night Comes Calling*. That's the fourth book in the series. At that time, Atticus Pünd didn't have an assistant. He just worked by himself. But after Alan and I started going out together, he said he was going to change that and he put me in.'

'He changed your name,' I said.

'He changed lots of things. I mean, I never went to Oxford University for a start, although it's true I'd done some acting when we met. That was one of his little jokes. In every book he always says Fraser was out-of-work or unsuccessful or failed and of course he was completely thick – but Alan said that was true of every sidekick. He used to say that they were there to make the detective look cleverer and to divert the attention away from the truth. Everything my character ever said in the books was wrong. He did it quite deliberately, to make you look the wrong way. In fact, you could ignore whatever Fraser said. That was how it worked.'

'So did you read it?' I asked again.

He shook his head. 'No. I knew Alan was working on it. He

used to spend hours in his office. But he never showed me anything until it was finished. To be honest with you, I didn't even know he *had* finished it. Usually, he'd have given it to me before he showed it to anyone it but because of what had happened he might have decided not to. Even so, I'm surprised I didn't know. I could usually tell when he he'd come to the end.'

'How?'

'He became human again.'

I wanted to know what had happened between them but instead I asked if I could see his study and maybe look for the missing pages. James was quite happy to show me and we left the room together.

Alan's office was next to the kitchen, which made sense. If he ever needed a break – lunch or a drink – he didn't have far to go. It was a large room, at the very end of the house with windows on three sides, and it had been knocked through to incorporate the tower. A spiral staircase dominated the space and presumably led all the way to the top. There were two walls of books, the first of which turned out to be Alan's, the nine Atticus Pünd novels translated into thirty-four languages. The blurb (which I had written) says thirty-five but that includes English and Alan liked round numbers. For the same reason, we upped his sales figures to eighteen million, a figure we more or less plucked out of the air. There was a purpose-built desk with an expensive-looking chair; black leather, ergonomically designed with sections that would move to provide support for his arms, his neck and his back. A writer's chair. He had a computer, an Apple with a twenty-seven inch screen.

I was interested in the room. It seemed to me that it was as close as I would get to walking into Alan Conway's head. And what did it tell me? Well, he wasn't out to hide his light. All his awards were on display. PD James had written a letter congratulating him on *Atticus Pünd Abroad* and he had framed it and hung it on the wall. There were also photographs of him with Prince Charles, with JK Rowling and (odd, this one) with Angela Merkel. He was methodical. Pens and pencils, note-pads, files, newspaper clippings and all the other detritus of a writer's life were laid out carefully, with no sense of clutter. There was a shelf of reference books: the *Shorter Oxford English Dictionary* (two volumes), *Roget's Thesaurus*, the *Oxford Dictionary of Quotations*, *Brewer's Book of Phrase and Fable* and encyclopaedias of chemistry, biology, criminology and law. They were lined up like soldiers. He had a complete set of Agatha Christie, about seventy paperbacks arranged, as far as I could see, in chronological order beginning with *The Mysterious Affair at Styles*. It was significant that they were also in his reference section. He had not read them for pleasure: he had used them. Alan had been entirely businesslike in the way he wrote. There were no diversions anywhere to be seen, nothing irrelevant to his work. The walls were white, the carpet a neutral beige. It was an office, not a study.

A leather diary sat beside the computer and I flicked it open. I had to ask myself what I was doing. It was the same reflex that had made me take a photograph of the tyre tracks in the garden. Was I looking for clues? A page torn out of a magazine had been slotted in beneath the cover. It was a black and white photograph, a still from Steven Spielberg's 1993 film *Schindler's List*. It showed the actor Ben Kingsley sitting at a desk, typing. I turned to James Taylor. 'What's this doing here?' I asked.

He answered as if it was obvious. 'That's Atticus Pünd,' he said.

It made sense. '*His eyes, behind the round, wire-framed glasses, examined the doctor with endless benevolence. It had often been remarked that Atticus Pünd looked like an accountant and in his general demeanour – which was both timid and meticulous – he behaved like one too.*' Alan Conway had borrowed, or perhaps stolen, his detective from a film that had been released ten or so years before he had written the first book. This might be where the link with the concentration camps, which I had thought so clever, had begun. For some reason, I was deflated. It was disappointing to find out that Atticus Pünd was not an entirely original creation; that he was in some way second-hand. Perhaps I was being unfair. After all, every character in fiction has to begin somewhere. Charles Dickens used his neighbours, his friends, even his parents as inspiration. Edward Rochester, my favourite character in *Jane Eyre*, was based on a Frenchman called Constantin Héger, with whom Brontë was in love. But tearing an actor out of a magazine was different somehow. It felt like cheating.

I turned the pages of the diary until I arrived at the week we were in now. It would have been busy if he'd managed to live through it. On Monday he was having lunch with someone called Claire at the Jolly Sailor. He had a hair appointment in the afternoon: that was the obvious assumption from the single word *hair* with a circle round it. On Wednesday he was playing tennis with someone identified only by their initials, SK. On Thursday, he was coming to London. He had another lunch – he'd just written 'lch' – and at five he was seeing Henry at the OV. It took me a worrying amount of time to work out that this was actually *Henry the Fifth* at the Old Vic. Simon Mayo was still in the diary for the following morning. This was the interview that Alan had decided to cancel but he hadn't got round to crossing it out. I flicked back a page. There was the dinner with Charles at the Ivy Club. In the morning, he'd seen SB. His doctor.

'Who's Claire?' I asked.

'His sister.' James was standing beside me, peering at the diary. 'The Jolly Sailor's in Orford. That's where she lives.'

'I don't suppose you know the password for the computer?'

'Yes. I do. It's Att1cus.'

The same name as the detective except with the figure one instead of the letter i. James turned the computer on and tapped it in.

I don't need to go into all the details of Alan's computer. I wasn't interested in his emails, his Google history or the fact that he played electronic Scrabble. All I wanted was the manuscript. He used Word for Mac and we quickly found the last two novels – *Red Roses For Atticus* and *Atticus Pünd Abroad*. There were several drafts of each, including the ones I had sent him with the final amendments. But there wasn't a single word of *Magpie Murders* in any of his files. It was as if the computer had been deliberately wiped clean.

'Is this his only computer?' I asked.

'No. He's got another one in London and he also had a laptop. But this is the one he used for the book. I'm sure of it.'

'Could he have put it on a memory stick?'

'I'm not sure I ever saw him with memory sticks, to be honest with you. But I suppose it's possible.'

We searched the room. We went through every cupboard and every drawer. James was keen to help. We found hard copies of all the Atticus Pünd novels apart from the most recent. There were notepads containing lengthy extracts scratched out in pen and ink but anything relating to *Magpie Murders* was curiously absent, as if it had been deliberately removed. One thing I did find that interested me was an unbound copy of *The Slide*, the novel that Charles had mentioned and which he had rejected. I asked James if I could borrow it and set it aside to take back with me. There were piles of newspapers and old magazines. Alan had kept everything ever written about him: interviews, profiles, reviews (the good ones) – the works. It was all very neat. One cupboard was given over to stationery with envelopes stacked up in their respective sizes, reams of white paper, more writing pads, plastic folders, a full spectrum of Post-it notes. There was no sign of a memory stick though, and if it had been there it was probably too small to find.

In the end, I had to give up. I'd been there an hour. I could have continued all day.

'You could try Mr Khan,' James suggested. 'Alan's solicitor,' he reminded me. 'He's got offices in Framlingham, on the Saxmundham Road. I don't know why he would have it, but Alan gave a lot of stuff to him.' He paused, a fraction too long. 'His will, for example.'

He had already joked about that when I arrived. 'Are you going to continue living here?' I asked him. It was a loaded question. He must know that Alan had been intending to disinherit him.

'God no! I couldn't sit here by myself in the middle of nowhere. I'd go mad. Alan once told me that he'd left the house to me, but if that turns out to be the case, I'll go back to London. That's where I was living when we met.' He curled his lip. 'We'd had a bad patch recently. We'd more or less split up. So maybe he changed things… I don't know.'

'I'm sure Mr Khan will tell you,' I said.

'He hasn't said anything yet.'

'I'll go and see him.'

'I'd talk to his sister if I were you,' James suggested. 'She used to do a lot of work for him. She did all his administration and his fan mail. I think she may even have typed some of the earlier books and he used to show them to her in manuscript. There's always a chance he gave her the latest one.'

'You said she's in Orford.'

'I'll give you the address and number.'

While he took out a sheet of paper and a pen, I wandered over to the one cupboard which I hadn't opened and which was set in the middle of the wall, behind the spiral staircase. I thought it might contain a safe – after all, Sir Magnus Pye had had one in his study. It opened peculiarly, one half sliding up, the other down. There were two buttons set in the wall. I realised it was a dumb waiter.

'Alan had that built,' James explained, without looking up. 'He always ate outside if the weather was warm enough – breakfast and lunch. He'd put the plates and food in and send them up.'

'Could I see the tower?' I asked.

'Sure. I hope you've got a head for heights.'

The staircase was modern, made of metal, and I found myself counting the steps as I tramped up. It seemed to go on too long. Surely the tower hadn't been this high? Finally, a door, locked from inside, led out to a wide, circular terrace with a very low, crenulated wall – Charles had been right about that. From here, I could see across a green sea of treetops and fields, all the way back to Framlingham. In the far distance, Framlingham College, nineteenth-century Gothic, perched on a hill. I noticed something else. Although it was screened by woodland and invisible from the road, there was a second property right next to Abbey Grange. I would have reached it if I had continued up the drive, but there was also what looked like a footpath between the trees. It was large and fairly modern with a very well-kept garden, a conservatory, a swimming pool.

'Who lives there?' I asked.

'That's the neighbour. His name is John White. He's a hedge fund manager.'

Alan had arranged a table and four chairs, a gas barbecue and two sun loungers on the terrace. Quite nervously, I made my way to the edge and looked down. From this angle, the ground looked a long way away and I could easily imagine him plunging down.

I had a sick feeling in my stomach and stepped back only to feel James's hands pressing into my back. For a horrible moment I thought he was about to push me. The surrounding wall was really inadequate. It barely came up to my waist.

He stepped away, embarrassed. 'I'm sorry,' he said. 'I was just worried you might get dizzy. A lot of people do, coming up here for the first time.'

I stood there with the breeze tugging at my hair. 'I've seen enough,' I said. 'Let's go down.'

It would have been so easy to throw Alan Conway over the edge. He wasn't a large man. Anyone could have crept up here and done it. I don't know why I thought that because it was clear that no crime had been committed. He had left a handwritten suicide note. Even so, once I'd got back to my car, I rang the Old Vic in London and they confirmed that he had booked two tickets for Henry V on Thursday. I told them he wouldn't be needing them. What was interesting was that he had only made the booking on the Saturday, one day before he had killed himself. His diary had shown that he had also arranged meetings, lunches, a haircut and a tennis match. And despite everything, I had to ask myself.

Was this really the behaviour of a man who had decided to take his own life?

Wesley & Khan, Framlingham

I drove back to Framlingham, parked the car in the main square and walked the rest of the way. The town really was a bit of a mishmash. At the far end there was a well-preserved castle surrounded by swathes of grass and a moat, a perfect fantasy of England as it might have been at the time of Shakespeare, complete with a pub and a duck pond nearby. But another fifty yards and the charm came to an abrupt end with Saxmundham Road, wide and modern, stretching into the distance, a Gulf garage one side and an assortment of very ordinary houses and bungalows on the other. Wesley & Khan, the firm of solicitors used by Alan Conway, occupied a mustard-coloured building on the edge of the town. It was a house, not an office, despite the signage beside the front door.

I wasn't sure if Mr Khan would see me without an appointment but I walked in anyway. I needn't have worried. The place was quite dead, with a girl reading a magazine behind the reception desk and a young man staring vacantly at a computer screen opposite. The building was old with uneven walls and floorboards that creaked. They'd added grey carpets and strip lighting but it still looked like somebody's home.

The girl rang through. Mr Khan would see me. I was shown upstairs and into what must have been the master bedroom, now converted into a no-nonsense office looking out onto the garage. Sajid Khan – his full name was on the door – rose up from behind a reproduction antique desk with a green leather top and brass handles. It was the sort of desk you chose if you wanted to make a point. He was a large, effusive man in his forties, bullish in his movements and in the way he spoke.

'Come in! Come in! Please take a seat. Have you been offered tea?'

He had very black hair and thick eyebrows that almost met. He was wearing a sports jacket with patches on the elbows and what might well be a club tie. It seemed unlikely that he had been born in Framlingham and I wondered what had brought him to such a backwater and, for that matter, how he fitted in with Mr Wesley. There was a photograph frame beside him, one of those modern, digital ones with the image changing every thirty seconds, either sliding or corkscrewing into itself. Before I'd even sat down, I'd been introduced to his wife, two daughters, his dog, and an elderly woman in a hijab who might have been his mother. I don't know how he lived with it. It would have driven me mad.

I declined the offer of tea and sat down in front of the desk. He took his place and I briefly explained why I was there. His demeanour changed at the mention of Alan's name.

'I found him, you know,' he told me. 'I went round there on Sunday morning. Alan and I were having a meeting. Have you been out to the house? And although you may not believe it, I must tell you that I had a feeling something was wrong, even as I drove up. That was before I saw him – and to start with I had no idea what I was looking at. I thought someone had thrown some old clothes onto the lawn, really I did! Then I realised it was him. I knew at once he was dead. I did not go near! I called the police at once.'

'You were quite close to him, I understand.' Sajid Khan was SK in the diary. The two of them played tennis together, and he had gone over to the house on a Sunday.

'Yes,' he said. 'I'd read many of the Atticus Pünd novels before I met him and you could certainly say I was a great admirer of his work. As things turned out, we did a lot of business with him and I'm very happy to say that I got to know him well. In fact, I would go so far as to say that – yes, we were definitely friends.'

'When did you last see him?'

'About a week ago.'

'Did you have any idea he was planning to kill himself?'

'Absolutely none at all. Alan was in this office, sitting exactly where you are now. We were actually talking about the future and he seemed to be in perfectly good spirits.'

'He was ill.'

'So I understand. But he never mentioned it to me, Miss Rye-land. He called me on Saturday evening. I must have been one of the last people who spoke to him while he was still alive.'

It would have been hard to speak to him if he wasn't, I thought. Always the editor. 'May I ask what you talked about, Mr Khan? And why were you visiting him on a Sunday? I know it's not my business . . .' I smiled sympathetically, inviting him to take me into his confidence.

'Well, I suppose it can't hurt telling you now. There had been certain changes to his domestic arrangements and Alan had decided to rethink his will. I'd actually drawn up a new draft and I took it over to show it to him. He was going to sign it on Monday.'

'He was going to cut out James Taylor.'

He frowned. 'Forgive me if I do not go into the details. I don't think it would be appropriate . . .'

'It's all right, Mr Kahn. He wrote to us at Cloverleaf Books. He actually told us he was going to take his own life. And he mentioned that James was no longer in his will.'

'Again, I don't think it's my place to comment on any communication he may have had with you.' Kahn paused, then let out a sigh. 'I will be honest with you and say that I did find that side of Alan quite hard to fathom.'

'You mean his sexuality?'

'No. Of course not. That's not what I meant at all! But having a partner who was quite so much younger than him.' Kahn was getting himself into difficulties, trying to balance his different prejudices. A picture of him, arm in arm with his wife, slid across the frame. 'I knew Mrs Conway quite well, you know.'

I had met Melissa Conway a few times at publishing events. I remembered her as a quiet, fairly intense woman. She always gave the impression that she knew something terrible was about to happen but didn't want to put it in words. 'How did you know her?' I asked.

'Well, actually, she introduced Alan to us. When they bought their first house in Suffolk – that was in Orford – she came to us for the conveyancing. Of course, very sadly, they parted company a few years later. We weren't involved in the divorce, but we did act for Alan when he bought Abbey Grange – or Ridgeway Hall as it was known then. He actually changed the name.'

'Where is she now?'

'She remarried. I believe she lives near Bath.'

I played back what he had just told me. Sajid Khan had drawn up the new will and taken it round on Sunday morning. But when he had got there . . . 'He never signed it!' I exclaimed. 'Alan died before he could sign the new will.'

'That is correct. Yes.'

The unsigned will is one of those tropes of detective fiction that I've come to dislike, only because it's so overused. In real life, a lot of people don't even bother to make a will but then we've all managed to persuade ourselves that we're going to live for ever. They certainly don't go round the place threatening to change it in order to give someone the perfect excuse to come and kill them.

It looked as if Alan Conway had done exactly that.

'I would be grateful if you did not repeat this conversation, Miss Ryeland,' Khan continued. 'As I said to you, I really should not be discussing the will.'

'It doesn't matter, Mr Khan. It's not the reason I'm here.'

'Then how can I help you?'

'I'm looking for the manuscript of *Magpie Murders*,' I explained. 'Alan had finished it just before he died but it's missing the last chapters. I don't suppose . . . ?'

'Alan never showed me his work before it was published,' Khan replied. He was glad to be back on safer ground. 'He was kind enough to autograph a copy of *Atticus Pünd Abroad* before it was published. But I'm afraid he never really talked about his work with me. You might try his sister.'

'Yes. I'm seeing her tomorrow.'

'It would be better not to mention the will to her, if you'd be so kind. The two of us will be meeting later in the week. And we have the funeral next weekend.'

'I'm just looking for the missing pages.'

'I hope you find them. We're all going to miss Alan. It would be nice to have one last memory.'

He smiled and got to his feet. On the desk, the photograph changed again and I saw that it had completed its circuit. It was showing the same picture I'd seen when I came in.

It was definitely time to go.

Extract from *The Slide* by Alan Conway

The dining room at the Crown was almost empty when I went in for dinner and I might have felt a little self-conscious, eating on my own. But I had company. I had brought *The Slide* with me, the novel which Alan Conway had written and which he had pleaded with Charles to publish, even as he prepared to end his life. Was Charles right? Here's how it opened.

> Lord Quentin Trump comes slumping down the staircase, lording it as he always does over the cooks and maids, the under-butlers and the footmen that exist only in his anfractuous imagination, that have in truth slipped hugger-mugger into the adumbration of family history. They were there when he was a boy and in some ways he is still a boy, or perhaps it is more true to say that the boy he was lurks obstinately in the fleshy folds that fifty years of unhealthy living have deposited on the barren, winter tree that is his skeleton. *Two boiled eggs, cookie. You know how I like them. Soft but not runny. Marmite soldiers like Mummy used to make... all present and correct. The chickens not laying? Damn their eyes, Agnes. What's the point of a chicken that don't lay?* Is this not his inheritance? Is it not his right? He lives in the stately pile where he was brought squealing and mewling into the world, a damp, unlovely ball of poisonous mauve, tearing open the curtain of his mother's vagina with the same violence with which he will rampage through the rest of his life. Here he is now with his cheeks

rampaged by spider veins, as ruby red as the oh-so-fine wines that brought them erupting to the surface, his cheeks jostling for position on a face that barely has the room to contain them. A moustache is smeared across his upper lip as if it has crawled out of his nostril, taken one look back at its own progenitor, lost all hope and died. His eyes are mad. Not 'let's cross and walk on the other side of the road mad' but lizardy and definitely dangerous. He has the Trump eyebrows and they are a little mad too, leaping out of his flesh like the hoary ragwort, *senecio aquaticus*, which he has been unable to eradicate from the croquet lawn. Today, it being a Saturday and the weather a little cold for the time of year, he is dressed in tweed. Tweed jacket, tweed waistcoat, tweed trousers, tweed socks. He likes tweed. He even likes the sound of it when he orders a suit from the place he frequents in Savile Row though not so frequently now, not at two thousand pounds a throw. Still, it's worth it; that moment of pleasant reassurance as the black cab stutters round the bend and spits him out at the front door. *Very good to see you, my lord. And how is Lady Trump? Always a pleasure to see you down. How long in town? A nice Cheviot tweed, perhaps, in brown? Where's the tape measure. Look lively, Miggs! I fancy our waistline may need revisiting since our last appointment, my lord.* His waist no longer has a line. It's all just flesh. He is corpulent now almost to pantomime proportions and knows that he is floundering in the scummy waters of ill health. His ancestors watch him from their curling gold frames as he descends the staircase, not one of them smiling, disappointed perhaps that this fat twerp should now be the master of the family home, that four hundred years of careful in-breeding should amount to nothing more. But does he care? He wants his breakfast, his brekky. He infantilises everything. And when he eats he will dribble his food down his chin and still wonder, in one corner of his mind, why nanny doesn't appear to wipe it away.

He enters the breakfast room and sits down, his adipose buttocks narrowly missing the arms of the eighteenth-century Hepplewhite chair that now strains to support him. There is a white linen serviette which he unfolds and tucks into his collar beneath his chin, or rather chins for he has the double ration that is the standard issue of the well-bred English gentleman. There is a *Times* newspaper waiting for him but he does not pick it up quite yet. Why should he share the world's bad news, the daily communion of depression, disorientation and decay, when he has plenty enough of his own to be getting on with? He is deaf to the whining, stentorian voices that warn of the rise of Islamic fundamentalism and the fall of the pound. His childhood home, the manor, is in danger. It may not last until the end of the month. These are the thoughts, the noisome squatters that occupy his mind.

It went on in this vein for some four hundred and twenty pages. I'm afraid I was skim-reading after the first chapter and picking out only the odd sentence after that. The novel seemed to be an attempt at satire, a grotesque fantasy about the British aristocracy. The plot, in so far as it had one, concerned Lord Trump's bankruptcy and his attempts to turn his crumbling stately home into a tourist attraction by lying about its history, inventing a ghost and transferring the elderly and largely docile animals from a local zoo to wander in his grounds. The slide of the title was intended to be the centrepiece in an adventure playground, which he had constructed, although clearly it also referred – portentously – to the state of the nation. It was revealing that when the first visitors arrive – 'the women in nylon puff jackets, fat, thick, ugly, whining slags with nicotine-stained nails, their brain-dead sons trailing wires from their ears, with branded boxer shorts rising over the belts of their sagging, unfit jeans' – they are treated with the same contempt as the Trumps themselves.

The Slide worried me for all sorts of reasons. How could a man who had written nine hugely popular and entertaining novels – the Atticus Pünd series – have come up with something that was, at the end of the day, quite so hateful? It was almost like discovering that Enid Blyton, in her spare time, had turned to pornography. The style was painfully derivative; it reminded me of another writer but at the moment I wasn't quite sure who. It seemed obvious to me that Conway was labouring for effect with every sentence, with every ugly metaphor. Worse still, this wasn't early work, juvenilia written before he had found his voice. The reference to Islamic fundamentalism proved that. He had been tinkering with it recently and had mentioned it in his final letter, asking Charles to take a second look. It had still mattered to him. Did it represent his world view? Did he really think it was any good?

I didn't sleep well that night. I'm used to bad writing. I've looked at plenty of novels that have no hope of being published. But I'd known Alan Conway for eleven years, or I thought I had, and I found it almost impossible to believe that he could have produced this, all four hundred and twenty pages of it. It was as if he was whispering to me as I lay there in the darkness, telling me something I didn't want to hear.

Orford, Suffolk

Magpie Murders is set in a fictitious village in Somerset. Most of the stories take place in villages that Alan has made up and even the two London-based novels (*No Rest for the Wicked* and *Gin & Cyanide*) use false names for anything that might be recognisable: hotels and restaurants, museums, hospitals and theatres. It's as if the author is afraid of exposing his fantasy characters to the real world, even with the protection of a 1950s setting. Pünd is only comfortable when he's strolling on the village green or drinking in the local pub. Murders take place during cricket and croquet matches. The sun always shines. Given that he had named his house after a Sherlock Holmes short story, it's possible that Alan was inspired by Holmes's famous dictum: 'The lowest and vilest alleys in London do not present a more dreadful record of sin than does the smiling and beautiful countryside.'

Why do English villages lend themselves so well to murder? I used to wonder about this but got the answer when I made the mistake of renting a cottage in a village near Chichester. Charles had advised against it but at the time I'd thought how nice it would be to get away now and then for the weekend. He was right. I couldn't wait to get back. I soon discovered that every time I made one friend I made three enemies and that arguments about such issues as car parking, the church bells, dog waste and hanging flower baskets dominated daily life to such an extent that everyone was permanently at each other's throats. That's the truth of it. Emotions, which are quickly lost in the noise and chaos of the city, fester around the village square, driving people to psychosis and violence. It's a gift to the whodunnit writer. There's also the advantage of connectivity. Cities are anonymous but in a small, rural community everyone knows everyone, making it so much easier to create suspects and, for that matter, people to suspect them.

It was obvious to me that Alan had Orford in mind when he created Saxby-on-Avon. It wasn't in Avon and there were no 'Georgian constructions made of Bath stone with handsome porticos and gardens rising up in terraces' but as soon as I passed the fire station with its bright yellow training tower and entered the village square, I knew exactly where I was. The church was called St Bartholemew's not St Botolph's, but it was in the right place and even had a few broken stone arches attached. There was a pub looking out over the graveyard. The Queen's Arms, where Pünd had stayed, was actually called the King's Head. The village noticeboard where Joy had posted her notice of infidelity was on one side of the square. The village shop and the bakery – it was called the Pump House – was on the other. The castle, which cast a shadow over Dr Redwing's house, and which must have been built around the same time as the one I had seen in Framlingham, was a short distance away. There was even a Daphne Road. In the book it had been Neville Brent's address but in the real world it was Alan's sister who lived there. The house was very much as he had described it. I wondered what this meant.

Claire Jenkins had been unable to see me the day before but had agreed to meet me at lunchtime. I got there early and strolled around the village, following the main road all the way down to the River Alde. The river doesn't exist in Alan's book – it's been replaced by the main road to Bath. Pye Hall is somewhere over to the left, which would in reality place it on land belonging to the Orford Yacht Club. I still had time in hand so I had a coffee at a second pub, the Jolly Sailor. In the book, it's called the Ferryman although both names reference boats. I also walked past a wild meadow which had to have been the inspiration for Dingle Dell, although there was no vicarage that I could see, and only a small patch of woodland.

I was beginning to get an idea of the way Alan's mind worked.

He had taken his own house – Abbey Grange – and placed it, complete with lake and trees – in the village where he had lived until his divorce. Then he had taken the entire construction and transported it to Somerset – which was also, incidentally, where his ex-wife and son now lived. It was evident that he used everyone and everything around him. Charles Clover's golden retriever, Bella, had made it into the narrative. James Taylor had a supporting role. And I had little doubt that Alan's sister, Claire, would turn out to be recast as Clarissa.

Which made Alan Conway the real-life Magnus Pye. It was interesting that he identified with the main character of his book: an obnoxious and arrogant landowner. Did he know something I didn't?

Claire Jenkins was not wearing a hat with three feathers. Her house wasn't unpleasantly modern. In short, it was nothing like the building in Winsley Terrace that Alan had described. It was admittedly quite small, modest compared to some of the other properties in Orford, but it was cosy and tasteful and quite lacking in any religious iconography. She herself was a short, rather pugnacious woman dressed in a turtleneck jersey and jeans that didn't flatter her. Unlike Clarissa Pye, she didn't colour her hair, which was lost in the dead man's land between brown and grey. It swept down in a fringe over eyes that were tired and filled with grief. She looked nothing like her brother – and the first thing I noticed when she showed me into her living room was that she had none of his books on display. Maybe she had turned them face down in mourning. She had invited me at lunchtime but she didn't offer me any lunch. She gave every impression of wanting to get rid of me as soon as possible.

'I was shocked when I heard about Alan,' she said. 'He was three years younger than me and we had been close all our lives. He's the reason I moved to Orford. I had no idea he'd been ill. He never told me about it. I saw James only a week ago, shopping in Ipswich, and he didn't tell me either. I always got on very well with him, by the way, although I was very surprised when he turned up as Alan's partner. We all were. I can't think what my parents would have said if they'd still been alive – my father was a headmaster, you know – but they died a very long time ago.

James never mentioned anything about Alan being ill. I wonder if he even knew?'

When Atticus Pünd interviews people, they usually make sense. Perhaps it's his skill as an interrogator but he manages to make them start at the beginning and answer his questions logically. Claire wasn't like that. She talked in the way that someone with a punctured lung might breathe. The words came out in fits and starts and I had to concentrate to follow what she was saying. She was very upset. She told me that her brother's death had knocked her for six. 'What I can't get over is that he didn't reach out to me. We'd had our difficulties lately, but I'd have been happy to talk to him and if he was worried about something...'

'He killed himself because of his illness,' I said.

'That's what DS Locke told me. But there was no need to do anything quite so drastic. These days, there are so many sorts of palliative care. My husband had lung cancer, you know. The nurses were absolutely wonderful, the way they looked after him. I think he was happier in the last few months of his life than he'd ever been with me. He was the centre of attention. He liked that. I came to Orford after he died. It was Alan who brought me here. He said it would be nice if we were close. This house... I would never have been able to afford it if it hadn't been for him. You really would have thought, after what I'd been through, that he would have confided in me. If he was really thinking of killing himself, why didn't he let me know?'

'Perhaps he was afraid you'd talk him out of it.'

'I couldn't have talked Alan out of anything. Or into it. We weren't like that.'

'You said you were close to him.'

'Oh yes. I knew him better than anyone. There are so many things I could tell you about him. I'm surprised you never published his autobiography.'

'He never wrote one.'

'You could have got someone else to write it.'

I didn't argue. 'I'd be interested to know anything you could tell me,' I said.

'Would you?' She leapt on my words. 'Maybe I should write about him. I could tell you about our time at Chorley Hall when we were children. I'd like to do that, you know. I read the obituaries and they hardly described Alan at all.'

I tried to steer her towards the point. 'James mentioned to me that you helped him with his work. He said that you typed up some of his manuscripts.'

'That's right. Alan always did the first draft by hand. He liked to use a fountain pen. He didn't trust computers. He didn't want to have all that technology between him and his work. He always said he preferred the intimacy of pen and ink. He said he felt closer to the page. I did his fan mail for him. People wrote him such lovely letters but he didn't have time to answer them all. He taught me how to write in his voice. I would write the letters and he would sign them. And I also helped him with research: poisons and things like that. I was the one who introduced him to Richard Locke.'

It had been a Detective Superintendent Locke who had telephoned Charles with the news of Alan's death.

'I work for the Suffolk constabulary,' Claire explained. 'In Ipswich. We're in Museum Street.'

'Are you a police officer?'

'I work in HR.'

'Did you type *Magpie Murders* for him?' I asked.

She shook her head. 'I stopped after *Gin and Cyanide*. The thing is, you see, well, he never gave me anything. He was quite generous to me in some ways. He helped me to buy this house. He would take me out, and things like that. But after I'd done three of the books, I suggested that he might put me on . . . I don't know . . . a salary. It seemed reasonable. I wasn't asking for a great deal of money. I just thought I ought to be paid. Unfortunately I'd got it quite wrong because I saw at once that I'd upset him. He wasn't mean. I'm not saying that. He just didn't think it was right to employ me – because I was his sister. We didn't exactly argue but after that he just typed the manuscripts himself. Or maybe he got James to help him. I don't know.'

I told her about the missing chapters but she was unable to help me.

'I didn't read any of it. He never let me see it. I used to read all the books before they were published but after we argued he didn't show them to me any more. Alan always was like that, you know. He was someone who was very easy to offend.'

'If you do write about him, you should put all this down,' I said. 'The two of you grew up together. Did he always know he was going to be a writer? Why did he write whodunnits?'

'Yes, I will. I'll do exactly that.' And then, in the blink of an eye, she came out with it. 'I don't think he killed himself.'

'I'm sorry?'

'I don't!' She blurted out the words as if she had wanted to from the moment I had arrived and couldn't wait any longer. 'I told DS Locke but he wouldn't listen to me. Alan didn't commit suicide. I don't believe it for a minute.'

'You think it was an accident?'

'I think someone killed him.'

I stared at her. 'Who would want to do that?'

'There were plenty of people. There were people who were jealous of him and there were people who didn't like him. Melissa, for one. She never forgave him for what he did to her and I suppose you can understand it. Leaving her for a young man. She was humiliated. And you should talk to his neighbour, John White. The two of them fell out over money. Alan talked to me about him. He said he was capable of anything. Of course, it may not have been someone who actually knew him. When you're a famous writer, you always have stalkers. There was a time, not that long ago, when Alan got death threats. I know, because he showed them to me.'

'Who were they from?'

'They were anonymous. I could hardly bear to read them. The language in them was horrible. Swear words and obscenities. They were from some writer he'd met down in Devonshire, someone he was trying to help.'

'Do you have any of them?'

'They might have them in the police station. We had to go to the police in the end. I showed them to DS Locke and he said we should take them seriously but Alan had no idea who they'd come from and there was no way we could trace them. Alan loved life. Even if he was ill, he would have wanted to go on until the end.'

'He wrote a letter.' I felt I had to tell her. 'The day before he killed himself he wrote to us and told us what he was going to do.'

She looked at me with a mixture of disbelief and resentment in her eyes. 'He wrote to you?'

'Yes.'

'To you personally?'

'No. The letter was addressed to Charles Clover. His publisher.'

She considered this. 'Why did he write to you? He didn't write to me. I can't understand that at all. We grew up together. Until he was sent away to boarding school, the two of us were inseparable. And even afterwards, when I saw him . . .' Her voice trailed away and I realised that I had been foolish. I had really upset her.

'Would you like me to leave?' I asked.

She nodded. She had taken out a handkerchief but she wasn't using it. She was balling it in her fist.

'I'm very sorry,' I said.

She didn't come with me to the door. I showed myself out and when I looked back through the window, she was still sitting where I had left her. She wasn't crying. She was just staring at the wall, offended, angry.

Woodbridge

Katie, my sister, is two years younger than me although she looks older. It's a running joke between us. She complains that I've had it easy, living on my own in a small, chaotic flat while she's looked after two hyperactive children, a variety of pets and an unreconstructed husband who can be kind and romantic but who still likes his food on the table at the right time. They have a large house and half an acre of garden, which Katie keeps like something out of a magazine. The house is seventies modern with sliding windows, gas-effect fires and a giant TV in the living room. There are almost no books. I'm not making any judgment. It's just the sort of thing I can't help but notice.

The two of us live in different worlds. She's much slimmer than I am and takes more care with her appearance. She dresses in sensible clothes, which she buys from catalogues, and has her hair done once a fortnight, somewhere in Woodbridge where, she tells me, the hairdresser is her friend. I hardly know my hairdresser's name – it's Doz, Daz or Dez or something but I don't know what it's short for. Katie doesn't need to work but she's spent ten years managing a garden centre half a mile down the road. God knows how she's been able to balance that with her full-time job as wife and mother. Of course, there's been a succession of au pairs and nannies as the children have grown up. There was the anorexic one, the born-again Christian one, the lonely Australian one, and the one who disappeared. We talk to each other two or three times a week on FaceTime and it's funny how, although we have so little in common, we've always been such good friends.

I certainly couldn't leave Suffolk without seeing her. Woodbridge was only twelve miles from Orford and, as luck would have it, she had the afternoon off. Gordon was in London. He commuted there every single day: Woodbridge to Ipswich, Ipswich to Liverpool Street, and then back again. He said he didn't mind but I didn't like to think how many hours he'd wasted on trains. He could easily afford a pied-à-terre but he said he hated being apart from his family, even for one or two nights. They always made a big deal about going away together: summer holidays, skiing at Christmas, various expeditions at weekends. The only time I ever felt lonely was when I thought about them.

After I'd left Claire Jenkins, I drove straight over. Katie was in the kitchen. Despite the size of the house, that's where she always seemed to be. We embraced and she brought me tea and a great slab of cake, home-made of course. 'So what are you doing in Suffolk?' she asked. I told her that Alan Conway had died and she grimaced. 'Oh yes. Of course. I heard about it on the news. Is that very bad?'

'It's not good,' I said.

'I thought you didn't like him.'

Had I really said that to her? 'My feelings have got nothing to do with it,' I said. 'He was our biggest author.'

'Hadn't he just finished another book?'

I told her that the manuscript was missing two or three chapters, that there was no trace of it on his computer and that all his handwritten notes had disappeared too. Even as I was explaining all this, I realised that it sounded very odd, like a conspiracy thriller. I remembered what Claire had said to me, that her brother would never have committed suicide.

'That's very awkward,' Katie said. 'What will you do if you can't find them?'

It was something I had been thinking about and which I intended to raise with Charles. We needed *Magpie Murders*. But when you consider all the different types of story out there in the market, the whodunnit is the one that really, absolutely, needs to be complete. *The Mystery of Edwin Drood* was the one example

I could think of that had managed to survive but Alan was no Charles Dickens. So what were we going to do? We could find another writer to step in and finish it. Sophie Hannah had done a great job with Poirot but she would have to solve the murder first, something which I had signally failed to do. We could publish it as a very annoying Christmas present: something to give someone you didn't like. We could have a competition – *Tell us who killed Sir Magnus Pye and win a weekend on the Orient Express*. Or we could keep looking and just hope that the wretched chapters would turn up.

We talked about this for a while. Then I changed the subject, asking about Gordon and the children. He was fine. He was enjoying work. They were going skiing at Christmas: they'd rented a chalet at Courchevel. Daisy and Jack were coming to the end of their time at Woodbridge School. They had been there for almost all their lives; first at Queen's House, the pre-prep school, then at The Abbey, now in the main school. It was a lovely place. I had visited it a couple of times. You didn't expect to find so much land and so many handsome buildings tucked away in a little town like Woodbridge. It struck me that the school suited my sister's personality very well. Nothing changed. Everything was perfect. The outside world was all too easy to ignore.

'The children never really liked Alan Conway,' Katie said, suddenly.

'Yes. You told me.'

'You didn't like him either.'

'Not really.'

'Are you sorry I introduced him to you?'

'Not at all, Katie. We made a fortune out of him.'

'But he gave you a hard time.' She shrugged. 'From what I heard, nobody was sorry when he left Woodbridge School.'

Alan Conway stopped teaching soon after the first book came out. By the time his second book appeared, he was earning way more than he ever had as a teacher.

'What was wrong with him?' I asked.

Katie thought for a moment. 'I'm not sure I know. He just had a reputation – the way some teachers do. I think he was quite strict. He didn't have much of a sense of humour.'

It's true. There are very few jokes in the Atticus Pünd stories.

'I think he was always quite secretive,' she went on. 'I met him a few times at sports day and things like that and I was never sure what he was thinking. I always got the feeling that he was hiding something.'

'His sexuality?' I suggested.

'Perhaps. When he left his wife for that boy, it was completely unexpected. But it wasn't that. It was just, when you met him, it was as if he was angry about something but had no intention of telling you what it was.'

We had been chatting for a while and I didn't want to get caught up in the London traffic. I finished my tea and refused more cake. I'd already had a huge slice and what I really wanted was a cigarette – Katie hated me smoking. I began to make my excuses.

'Will you be back soon?' she asked. 'The kids would love to see you. We could all have dinner.'

'I'll probably be up and down quite a few times,' I said

'That's good. We miss you.' I knew what was coming and sure enough Katie didn't disappoint me. 'Is everything all right, Sue?' she asked, in the sort of voice that said it clearly wasn't.

'I'm fine,' I said.

'You know I worry about you, on your own in that flat.'

'I'm not alone. I've got Andreas.'

'How is Andreas?'

'He's very well.'

'He must be back at school by now.'

'No. They don't start until the end of the week. He's been in Crete for the summer.' As soon as I said that, I wished I hadn't. It meant I was alone after all.

'Why didn't you go with him?'

'He invited me but I was too busy.' That was only half true. I had never been to Crete. Something in me resisted the idea, stepping into his world, putting myself under examination.

'Is there any chance . . . ? I mean, are the two of you . . . ?'

That's what it always came down to. Marriage, for Katie with twenty-seven years of it behind her, was the be-all and end-all, the only reason really to be alive. Marriage was her Woodbridge

School, her grounds, the wall surrounding her – and as far as she was concerned, I was stuck outside, looking in through the gate.

'Oh, we never talk about it,' I said, breezily. 'We like things the way they are. Anyway, I would never marry him.'

'Because he's Greek?'

'Because he's *too* Greek. He'd drive me mad.'

Why did Katie always have to judge me by her standards? Why couldn't she see that I didn't need what she had and that I might be perfectly happy the way things were? If I sound irritated it's only because I worried she was right. Part of me was asking myself the very same thing. I would never have children. I had a man who had been away the whole summer and who, during term time, only came over at weekends – if he wasn't tied up with football, school play rehearsals or a Saturday trip to the Tate. I had devoted my whole life to books; to bookshops; to booksellers; to bookish people like Charles and Alan. And in doing so, I had ended up like a book: on the shelf.

I was glad to get back into the MGB. There are no speed cameras between Woodbridge and the A12 and I kept my foot hard on the accelerator. When I reached the M25, I turned on the radio and listened to Mariella Frostrup. She was talking about books. By then I felt OK.

The letter

You'd have thought that after twenty years editing murder mysteries I'd have noticed when I found myself in the middle of one. Alan Conway had not committed suicide. He had gone up to the tower to have his breakfast and someone had pushed him off. Wasn't it obvious?

Two people who knew him well, his solicitor and his sister, had insisted that he was not the sort to kill himself, and his diary – which showed that he had been cheerfully buying theatre tickets and arranging tennis games and lunches for the week following his demise, seemed to confirm it. The manner of his death, painful and uncertain, felt wrong. And then there were the suspects already queuing up to take a starring role in the last chapter. Claire had mentioned his ex-wife, Melissa, and his neighbour, a hedge fund manager called John White, with whom he'd had some sort of dispute. She herself had argued with him. James Taylor had the most obvious motive. Alan had died just one day before he intended to sign his new will. James also had access to the house and would know that, if the sun were shining, Alan would have his breakfast on the roof. And August had been warm.

I thought about all this as I drove home but it still took me a while to accept it. In a whodunnit, when a detective hears that Sir Somebody Smith has been stabbed thirty-six times on a train or decapitated, they accept it as a quite natural occurrence. They pack their bags and head off to ask questions, collect clues, ultimately to make an arrest. But I wasn't a detective. I was an editor

– and, until a week ago, not a single one of my acquaintances had managed to die in an unusual and a violent manner. Apart from my own parents and Alan, I hardly knew anyone who had died at all. It's strange when you think about it. There are hundreds and hundreds of murders in books and television. It would be hard for narrative fiction to survive without them. And yet there are almost none in real life, unless you happen to live in the wrong area. Why is it that we have such a need for murder mystery and what is it that attracts us – the crime or the solution? Do we have some primal need of bloodshed because our own lives are so safe, so comfortable? I made a mental note to check out Alan's sales figures in San Pedro Sula in the Honduras (the murder capital of the world). It might be that they didn't read him at all.

Everything came down to the letter. Without telling anyone, I had made a copy of it before Charles sent it to the police and as soon as I got home I took it out and examined it again. I remembered the strange anomaly – a handwritten letter in a typewritten envelope – that I had seen in Charles's office. It was an exact reflection, an inverse of what Atticus Pünd had discovered at Pye Hall. Sir Magnus had been sent a typewritten death threat in a handwritten envelope. What, in each instance, did it mean? And, if you put the two of them together, was there some greater significance, a pattern I could not see?

The letter had been sent the day after Alan had handed over the manuscript at the Ivy Club. I wished now that I had looked at the envelope more closely to see if it had been sent from London or from Suffolk although Charles had ripped off some of the postmark when he opened it. Either way, it was certain that Alan had composed it himself. It was his handwriting – and unless he had been forced to write with a gun at his head, it set out his intentions quite clearly. Or did it? Back in my flat in Crouch End, with a glass of wine in my hand and a third cigarette on the go, I wasn't so sure.

The first page is an apology. Alan has behaved badly. But it's part of a general pattern of behaviour. He's ill. He says that he has decided against treatment and this will kill him very soon anyway. There is nothing on this page about suicide – quite the opposite. It's the cancer that's going to kill him because he's not going to have chemotherapy. And look again at the bottom of page one, all that stuff about London literary functions. He's not writing about his life being over. He's writing about how it's going to continue.

Page two does relate to his death, particularly in the paragraph about James Taylor and the will. But again, it's non-specific. 'There are bound to be rows when I've gone.' He could be talking about any time: six weeks from now, six months, a year. It's only on page three that he cuts to the chase. 'By the time you read this, it will all be finished.' When I first read the letter, so soon after hearing what had happened, I automatically assumed that by 'it', Alan was referring to his life. His life would be over. He would have killed himself. Rereading it, though, it occurred to me he could just as easily have been talking about his writing career – which was the subject of the paragraph before. He had delivered the last book. There weren't going to be any more.

And then we come to 'the decision that I have made' a few lines later. Is it really the decision to jump off his tower? Or is it simply the decision, which he has already explained, not to have chemotherapy, to kill himself in that sense only? By the end of the letter he's writing about the people who will mourn him but, again, he has already established that he is going to die. Nowhere does he state outright that he is planning to take matters into his own hands. 'As I prepare to take leave of this world . . .' Isn't that a bit gentle for what he supposedly has in mind, jumping off a tower?

This was what I thought. And although there was something else about the letter, which I missed completely, and which would prove that almost everything I've written here was wrong, by the end of that day, everything had changed. I knew that the letter was not what it seemed; that it was no more than a general valedictory and that someone must have read it and realised that it could be misinterpreted. Claire Jenkins and Sajid Khan were right. The most successful murder writer of his generation had himself been murdered.

The doorbell rang.

Andreas had telephoned me an hour before and there he was on my doorstep with a bunch of flowers and a bulging supermarket bag that would contain Cretan olives, wonderful thyme honey, oil, wine, cheese, and mountain tea. It wasn't just that he was generous. He had a real love of his country and everything it produced. It's very Greek. The endlessly protracted financial crisis of this summer and the year before might have dropped out of the British newspapers – how many times can you predict the total collapse of a country? – but he had told me how much it was still hurting at home. Business was down. The tourists were staying away. It was as if the more he brought me, the more he would convince me that everything was going to be all right. It was sweet and old-fashioned of him to ring the bell, by the way. He had his own key.

I had tidied the flat, showered and changed and I hoped I looked reasonably desirable. I was always quite nervous about seeing him after these long separations. I wanted to be sure that nothing had changed. Andreas was looking very well. After six weeks in the sunshine his skin was darker than ever and he was slimmer too: a combination of swimming and low-carb Cretan food. Not that he was ever fat. He's built like a soldier with square shoulders, a chiselled face and black hair falling in thick curls like a Greek shepherd – or a god. He has mischievous eyes and a slightly crooked smile, and although I wouldn't say he's a conventionally handsome man, he's fun to be with, intelligent, easy-going, always good company.

He's also linked to Woodbridge School because that's where I first met him. He was teaching Latin and ancient Greek and it's funny to think that he knew Alan Conway before I did. Melissa, Alan's wife, also taught there, so the three of them were together long before I came onto the scene. I was introduced to him at the end of a summer term. It was sports day and I was there to support Jack and Daisy. We got talking and I liked him immediately, but it wasn't until a year later that we met again. By then he had moved to Westminster School in London and he rang Katie to get my number. It was nice that he's remembered me after all that time but we didn't begin a romance straight away. We were friends for a long time before we became lovers: in fact we'd only been in our present relationship for a couple of years. We hardly ever talked about Alan, by the way. There was bad blood between them although I didn't ask why. I would never call Andreas the jealous sort but I got the impression that deep down he resented Alan's success.

I knew all about Andreas's past: he didn't want there to be secrets between us. The first time he had got married, he had been far too young, just nineteen, and the marriage had fallen apart while he was doing his national service in the Greek army. His second wife, Aphrodite, lived in Athens. She was a teacher, like him, and she had come with him to England. That was when things had gone wrong. She missed her family. She was homesick. 'I should have seen she was unhappy and gone back with her,' Andreas told me. 'But it was too late. She went on her own.' They were still friends and he saw her from time to time.

We walked down to Crouch End for dinner. There was a Greek restaurant, actually run by Cypriots, and although you would have thought it was the last food he would want after a summer at home, it was a tradition that we always went there. It was another warm evening so we ate outside, sitting close to each other on the narrow balcony with heaters blazing down unnecessarily above our heads. We ordered taramasalata, dolmades, loukaniko, souvlakia... all prepared in the tiniest of kitchens beside the front door, and shared a bottle of rough red wine.

It was Andreas who raised the subject of Alan's death. He had read about it in the newspapers and he was concerned about what it would mean for me. 'Will it hurt the company?' he asked. He spoke perfect English, by the way. His mother was English and he had been brought up bilingual. I told him about the missing chapters and, after that, quite naturally, the rest of it came out too. I didn't see why I should keep anything back from him and it actually felt good having someone I could use as a sounding board. I described my visit to Framlingham and all the people I'd met there.

'I saw Katie,' I added. 'She asked after you.'

'Ah, Katie!' Andreas had always liked her when he had known her as a parent at the school. 'How are the children, Jack and Daisy?'

'They weren't there. And they're hardly children any more. Jack will be going to university next year...'

I told him about the letter and how I'd come to the conclusion that, perhaps, Alan hadn't killed himself after all. He smiled. 'That's the trouble with you, Susan. You're always looking for the story. You read between the lines. Nothing is ever straightforward.'

'You think I'm wrong?'

He took my hand. 'Now I've annoyed you. I don't mean to. It's one of the things I like about you. But don't you think the police would have noticed if someone had pushed him off the tower? The killer must have broken into the house. There would have been a struggle. They'd have left fingerprints.'

'I'm not sure they looked.'

'They didn't look because it's actually pretty obvious. He was ill. He jumped.'

I wondered how he could be so sure. 'You didn't like Alan very much, did you,' I said.

He thought for a moment. 'I didn't like him at all if you want the truth. He got in the way.' I waited for him to explain what he meant but he shrugged it off. 'He wasn't someone it was easy to like.'

'Why not?'

He laughed and went back to his food. '*You* complained about him often enough.'

'I had to work with him.'

'So did I. Come on, Susan, I don't want to talk about him. It'll only spoil the evening. I think you should be careful – that's all.'

'What do you mean by that?' I asked.

'Because it's not your business. Maybe he committed suicide. Maybe someone killed him. Either way, it's not something you should get involved with. I'm only thinking of you. It could be dangerous.'

'Seriously?'

'Why not? You should always think before you dig around in someone else's life. Maybe I say that because I was brought up on an island, in a small community. We always believed in keeping things in the family. What difference does it make to you how Alan died? I'd stay away—'

'I still have to find the missing chapters,' I interrupted.

'Maybe there *are* no missing chapters. Despite what you say, you can't be sure he ever wrote them. They weren't on his computer. They weren't on his desk.'

I didn't try to argue. I was a little disappointed that Andreas had shot down my theories so carelessly. It also seemed to me that there had been a slight awkwardness between us, a disconnection which had been there from the moment he had turned up at the flat. We've always been very companionable. We're comfortable in each other's silences. But that wasn't true tonight. There was something he wasn't telling me. I even wondered if he'd met somebody else.

And then, at the end of the meal, as we sipped the thick, sweet coffee that I knew never to refer to as Turkish, he suddenly said: 'I'm thinking of leaving Westminster.'

'I'm sorry?'

'At the end of term. I'm want to give up teaching.'

'This is very sudden, Andreas. Why?'

He told me. A hotel had come up for sale on the edge of Agios Nikolaos; an intimate, family-run business with twelve rooms right next to the sea. The owners were in their sixties and their children had left the island. Like so many young Greeks, they were in London, but Andreas had a cousin who worked there and they looked on him almost as a son. They had offered him the opportunity to buy it and the cousin had come to him to see if he could help with the finance. Andreas was tired of teaching. Every time he went back to Crete, he felt more at home and he was beginning to ask himself why he had ever left. He was fifty years old. This was a chance to change his life.

'But Andreas,' I protested. 'You don't know anything about running a hotel.'

'Yannis has experience and it's small. How difficult can it be?'

'But you said tourists weren't going to Crete any more.'

'That was this year. Next year will be better.'

'But won't you miss London . . . ?'

All my sentences were beginning with 'but'. Did I genuinely think it was a bad idea or was this the change that I had been fearing, the realisation that I was about to lose him? It was exactly what my sister had warned me about. I was going to end up on my own.

'I hoped you'd be more excited,' he said.

'Why would I be excited?' I asked, miserably.

'Because I want you to come with me.'

'Are you serious?'

He laughed a second time. 'Of course! Why do you think I'm telling you all this?' The waiter had brought raki and he poured two glasses, filling them to the brim. 'You'll love it, Susan, I promise you. Crete is a wonderful island and it's about time you met my family and friends. They're always asking about you.'

'Are you asking me to marry you?'

He raised his glass, the mischief back in his eyes. 'What would you say if I did?'

'I probably wouldn't say anything. I'd be too shocked.' I didn't mean to offend him, so I added: 'I'd say I'd think about it.'

'That's all I'm asking you to do.'

'I have a job, Andreas. I have a life.'

'Crete is three and a half hours away. It's not the other side of the world. And maybe, after everything you've told me, soon you won't have a choice.'

That was certainly true. Without *Magpie Murders*, without Alan, who could say how long we could go on?

'I don't know. It's a lovely idea. But you shouldn't have sprung it on me so suddenly. You're going to have to give me time to think.'

'Of course.'

I picked up my raki and drank it in one gulp. I wanted to ask him what would happen if I decided to stay. Would that be it? Would he leave without me? It was too soon to have that conversation but the truth is that I thought it unlikely that I would swap my life – Cloverleaf, Crouch End – for Crete. I liked my job and I had my relationship with Charles to consider, particularly now when everything was so difficult. I couldn't see myself as some twenty-first century Shirley Valentine, sitting on the rocks, a thousand miles from the nearest Waterstones.

'I'll think about it,' I said. 'You might be right. By the end of the year I could be out of a job. I suppose I can always make the beds.'

Andreas stayed the night and it was good to have him back again. But as I lay there in the darkness, with his arms around me, there were a whole lot of thoughts racing through my mind, refusing to let me sleep. I saw myself getting out of the car at Abbey Grange with the tower looming over me, examining the tyre tracks, searching Alan's office. Once again the photographs in Sajid Khan's office seemed to slide in front of me but this time they showed Alan, Charles, James Taylor, Claire Jenkins and me. At the same time, I replayed snippets of conversation.

'I was just worried you might get dizzy.' James grabbing hold of me at the top of the tower.

'I think someone killed him.' Alan's sister in Orford.

And that same evening, Andreas at dinner: 'It's not your business. It's not something you should get involved with.'

Much later that night, I thought the door opened and a man came into the bedroom. He was leaning on a stick. He didn't say anything but he stood there, looking sadly at Andreas and me, and as a shaft of moonlight came slanting in through the window, I recognised Atticus Pünd. I was asleep, of course, and dreaming, but I remember wondering how he had managed to enter my world before the thought occurred to me that maybe it was I who had entered his.

The Club at the Ivy

'How did you get on?' Charles asked me.

I told him about my visit to Framlingham, my meetings with James Taylor, Sajid Khan and Claire Jenkins. I had not found the missing chapters. They were not on his computer. There were no handwritten pages. I'm not quite sure why, but I didn't raise the subject of how Alan had really died or my belief that his letter might have been used purposefully to mislead us. Nor did I tell him that I had read – or tried to read – *The Slide*.

I had chosen to play the detective – and if there is one thing that unites all the detectives I've ever read about, it's their inherent loneliness. The suspects know each other. They may well be family or friends. But the detective is always the outsider. He asks the necessary questions but he doesn't actually form a relationship with anyone. He doesn't trust them, and they in turn are afraid of him. It's a relationship based entirely on deception and it's one that, ultimately, goes nowhere. Once the killer has been identified, the detective leaves and is never seen again. In fact, everyone is glad to see the back of him. I felt some of this with Charles: there was a distance between us that had never been there before. It struck me that, if Alan really had been murdered, Charles might be a suspect – although I couldn't think of a single reason why he would want to kill his most successful author, ruining himself in the process.

Charles had changed too. He was looking gaunt and tired, his hair less well groomed and his suit perhaps more crumpled than

I'd known. It was hardly surprising. He was involved in a police investigation. He had lost a guaranteed bestseller and seen an entire year's profits potentially wiped out. None of this was very helpful in the run-up to Christmas. Plus he was about to become a grandfather for the first time. It was showing.

But still I waded in. 'I want to know more about the Ivy meeting,' I said. 'The last time you saw Alan.'

'What do you want to know?'

'I'm trying to work out what was going on in his head.' That was only part of the truth. 'Why he deliberately held back some of the pages.'

'Is that what you think he did?'

'It does look that way.'

Charles hung his head. I had never seen him so defeated. 'This whole business is a disaster for us,' he said. 'I've been talking to Angela.' Angela McMahon was our head of Marketing & Publicity. If I knew her, she would already be looking for a new job. 'She says we can expect a spike in sales, especially when the police announce that Alan killed himself. There'll be publicity. She's trying to get a retrospective piece in the *Sunday Times*.'

'Well, that's good, isn't it?'

'Perhaps. But it'll all be over very quickly. It's not even certain that the BBC will continue with the dramatisation.'

'I can't see that his death would make any difference,' I said. 'Why would they pull out now?'

'Alan hadn't signed the contract. They were still arguing about casting and they'll have to wait and find out who owns the rights and that may mean starting negotiations all over again.' Underneath the desk, Bella rolled over and grunted and my thoughts flickered, just for a moment, to the collar that Atticus Pünd had found in the second bedroom at the Lodge. Bella, Tom Blakiston's dog, had had its throat cut. The collar was obviously a clue. How did it fit in?

'Did Alan talk about the TV series – at the Ivy?' I asked.

'He didn't mention it. No.'

'The two of you argued.'

'I wouldn't call it that, Susan. We disagreed about the title of his book.'

'You didn't like it.'

'I thought it sounded too much like *Midsomer Murders*, that's all. I shouldn't have mentioned it – but I hadn't read the book at that stage and there was nothing else to talk about.'

'And this was when the waiter dropped the plates.'

'Yes. Alan was mid-sentence. I can't remember what he was saying. And then there was this almighty crash.'

'You said he was angry.'

'He was. He went over and talked to him.'

'The waiter?'

'Yes.'

'He left the table?' I don't know why I was pressing the point. It just seemed such an odd thing to do.

'Yes,' Charles said.

'You didn't think that was strange?'

Charles considered, 'Not really. The two of them spoke for a minute or two. I assumed Alan was complaining. After that, he went to the toilet. Then he came back to the table and we finished the meal.'

'I don't suppose you can describe the waiter? Do you know his name?'

At this stage, I didn't have a lot to go on but it seemed to me that something must have been going on that evening, when Alan met Charles. All sorts of strands come together and meet at that table. At the very moment when he handed over the manuscript something had upset him, making him argumentative. He had behaved strangely, leaving the table to complain to a waiter about an accident that had nothing to do with him. The manuscript was missing pages and two days later he had died. I said nothing to Charles. I knew he would tell me that I was wasting my time. But later that afternoon I walked down to the private members' club and set about talking my way in.

It wasn't difficult. The receptionist told me that the police had been in the club only the day before, asking questions about Alan's behaviour, his state of mind. I was his editor. I was a friend of Charles Clover. Of course I could come in. I was shown up to the restaurant on the second floor. It was empty, the tables now being laid for dinner. The receptionist had given me the name of the waiter who'd had the accident with the plates on that Friday and he was waiting by the door as I came in.

'That's right. I was meant to be working in the bar that evening but they were short-staffed so I came up and helped in the restaurant. The two gents were starting their main course when I came out the kitchen. They were sitting over in that corner...'

Many of the waiters at the Club are young and Eastern European but Donald Leigh was neither of those things. He was from Scotland, as became obvious the moment he spoke, and in his early thirties. He was from Glasgow, he said, married with a two-year-old son. He had been in London for six years and loved working at the Ivy.

'You should see some of the people we get in here, especially when the theatres come down.' He was a short, stubby man with the weight of life pressing down on his shoulders. 'Not just writers. Actors, politicians – the works.'

I had told him who I was and why I was here. He had already been questioned by the police and he gave me a shorthand version of what he had told them. Charles Clover and his guest had booked a table in the restaurant at half past seven and had left shortly after ten. He hadn't served them. He didn't know what they had eaten, but he remembered that they had ordered an expensive bottle of wine.

'Mr Conway wasn't in a very good mood.'

'How do you know?'

'I'm just telling you. He didn't look happy.'

'He delivered his new novel that evening.'

'Did he? Well, bully for him. I didn't see it, but then I was in and out. It was very busy and as I said, we were short-staffed.'

From the start, I'd had the impression that there was something he wasn't telling me. 'You dropped some plates,' I said.

He looked at me sullenly. 'I'm never going to hear the end of it. What's the big deal?

I sighed. 'Look, Donald – can I call you that?'

'I'm off duty. You can call me what you like.'

'I just want to know what happened. I worked with him. I knew him well and I didn't much like him, if you want the truth. Anything you tell me is just between the two of us but I'm not convinced he killed himself and if you know something, if you heard something, it really might help.'

'If you don't think he killed himself, what *do* you think?'

'I'll tell you if you tell me what I want to know.'

He thought for a moment. 'You mind if I have a cigarette?' he asked.

'I'll join you,' I said.

The good old cigarettes again, breaking down the barriers, putting us on the same side. We left the restaurant. There was a smokers' area outside, a small, square patio walled off from a disapproving world. We both lit up. I told him that my name was Susan and once again promised him that this was just between the two of us. Suddenly he was eager to talk.

'You're a publisher?' he said.

'I'm an editor.'

'But you work for a publisher.'

'Yes.'

'Then maybe we can help each other.' He paused. 'I knew Alan Conway. I knew who he was the moment I set eyes on him and that's why I dropped those bloody plates. I forgot I was holding them and they burned through the serviette.'

'How did you know him?'

He looked at me quite strangely. 'Did you work on one of the Atticus Pünd novels, *Night Comes Calling*?'

That was the fourth in the series, the one set in a prep school. 'I worked on all of them,' I said.

'What did you think of it?'

Night Comes Calling has a headmaster killed during the performance of a play. He is sitting in the darkened auditorium when a figure runs through the audience and the next thing you know, he's been stabbed with surgical precision in the side of the neck. What's clever is that the main suspects are all on stage at the time so couldn't possibly have done it, although it turns out that one of them did. It takes place very shortly after the war and there's a backstory involving cowardice and dereliction of duty. 'I thought it was ingenious,' I said.

'It was *my* story. *My* idea.' Donald Leigh had intense, brown eyes and for a moment they came alive with anger. 'Do you want me to go on?'

'Yes. Please tell me.'

'All right.' He put the cigarette to his lips and sucked hard. The tip glowed a bright red. 'I used to love books when I was a kid,' he said. 'I always wanted to be a writer, even when I was at school. It wasn't the sort of thing you admitted to at the school I went to, Bridgeton, east of Glasgow. Horrible, bloody place where they said you were queer if you used the library. It didn't bother me. I read all the time, as many books as I could get my hands on. Spy stories – Tom Clancy, Robert Ludlum. Adventure stories. Horror stories. I loved Stephen King. But best of all were detective stories. I couldn't get enough of them. I didn't go to university or anything like that. All I've ever wanted to do is to write and I'll get there one day, Susan, I'm telling you. I'm working on a book now. I'm only doing this job to keep me going until I get there.

'But the trouble was, it never worked out the way I wanted. When I started writing I'd have this book in my head. I knew what I wanted to write. I got the ideas and the characters, but when I put it down on the page, it wouldn't come together. I tried and I tried and I just sat there, staring at the page and then I'd rewrite. I could do it fifty times and it still wouldn't work. Anyway, a few years ago I saw this advertisement. There were these people who were offering weekend courses to help new writers and there was one that was available – all the way down in bloody Devonshire. But it was focusing on murder mystery. It wasn't cheap. It was going to cost me seven hundred quid. But I'd saved up enough money and I thought it was worth a shot. So I enrolled.'

I leant forward and tapped ash into one of the neat, silver receptacles the Ivy Club had provided. I knew where this was going.

'We all went to this farmhouse in the middle of nowhere,' Leigh went on. He was standing there with his hands balled into fists, as if he had been rehearsing, as if this was his moment on the stage. 'There were eleven of us in the group. A couple of them were complete tossers and there were these two women who thought they were better than the rest of us. They'd had short stories published in magazines so they were completely full of themselves. You probably meet people like that all the time. The rest of them were OK, though, and I really enjoyed being with them. You know, it made me realise that it wasn't just me, that we all had the same problems and we were there for the same thing. There were three tutors running the course. Alan Conway was one of them.

'I thought he was really good. He drove a beautiful car – a BMW – and they put him up in a little house on his own. We were all sharing. But he still mucked in with the rest of us. He really knew what he was talking about and of course he'd made a ton of money out of the Atticus Pünd books. I read a couple of them before I went down there. I liked them, and they weren't that different from what I was trying to do. We had lectures and tutorials in the day. We ate together – in fact, everyone in the group had to help with the cooking. And there was plenty of booze in the evening so we could just chat and unwind. That was my favourite part of it. We all felt like equals. And one evening there was just the two of us in this little snug area and I told him about the book I was writing.

His fists tightened as he came to the inevitable point of his narrative. 'If I give you my manuscript, will you read it?' he asked.

It's a question I normally dread – but I bowed to the inevitable. 'Are you saying that Alan stole your ideas?' I asked.

'That's exactly what I'm saying, Susan. That's exactly what he did.'

'What's your book called?'

'*Death Treads the Boards*.'

It was a terrible title. But of course I didn't say that. 'I can look at it for you,' I said. 'But I can't promise I can help you.'

'All I want you to do is look at it. That's all I'm asking.' He looked me in the eye as if daring me to refuse. 'I told Alan Conway my story,' he went on. 'I told him all about the murder I'd thought up. It was late and there were just the two of us in the room, no witnesses. He asked me if he could look at the manuscript and I was delighted. Everyone wanted him to read their work. That was the whole point.'

He finished his cigarette and ground it out, then promptly lit a second.

'He read it very quickly. There were only two days of the course left and on the last day he took me aside and gave me some advice. He said I used too many adjectives. He said my dialogue wasn't realistic. What's realistic dialogue meant to sound like for heaven's sake? It's not real! It's fiction! He gave me some quite good ideas about my main character, my detective. I remember one of the things he said was that he should have a bad habit, like he should smoke or drink or something. He said he'd get in touch with me again and I gave him my email address.

'I never heard from him. Not a word. And then, almost exactly a year later, *Night Comes Calling* came out in the shops. It was all about the production of a school play. My book wasn't set in a school. It was set in a theatre. But it was the same idea. And it didn't stop there. He'd nicked my murder. It was *exactly* the same. The same method, the same clues, almost the same characters.' His voice was rising. 'That's what he did, Susan. He took my story and used it for *Night Comes Calling*.'

'Did you tell anyone?' I asked. 'When the book came out, what did you do?'

'What *could* I do? You tell me! Who would have believed me?'

'You could have written to us at Cloverleaf Books.'

'I *did* write to you. I wrote to the managing director, Mr Clover. He didn't write back. I wrote to Alan Conway. I wrote to him quite a few times, as a matter of fact. Let's just say that I didn't hold back. But I got nothing from him either. I wrote to the people who set up the course in the first place. I got a letter from them. They gave me the brush-off. They denied any responsibility, said it had nothing to do with them. I thought about going to the police. I mean, he'd stolen something from me. There's a word for that, isn't there? But when I talked to my wife, Karen, she said to forget it. He was famous. He was protected. I was nobody. She said it would just hurt my writing if I tried to fight it and it was best to move on. So that's what I did. I'm still writing. At least I know I've got good ideas. He wouldn't have done what he did if I hadn't.'

'Have you written any other novels?' I asked.

'I'm working on one now. But it's not a detective story. I've moved on from that now. It's a children's book. Now that I've got a child it felt like the right thing to do.'

'But you've kept *Death Treads the Boards*.'

'Of course I've kept it. I've kept everything I've ever written. I know I've got the talent. Karen loves my work. And one day . . .'

'Send it to me.' I fished in my handbag and took out a card. 'So what happened when you saw him in the restaurant?' I asked.

He was waiting for me to give him my business card. It was a lifeline for him. I was in the ivory tower and he was on the outside. I've seen it in so many new writers, this belief that publishers are any different – smarter, more successful than them – when actually we're just shuffling along, hoping we'll still have a job at the end of the month. 'I came out of the kitchen,' he said. 'I was carrying two main courses and a side for table nine. I saw him sitting there – he was arguing about something – and I was so shocked I just stood there. The plates were hot. They burned through the cloth and I dropped them.'

'And then? I was told that Alan came over. He was angry with you.'

He shook his head. 'That's not how it happened. I cleaned up the mess and put a new order in to the kitchen. I wasn't sure I wanted to go back into the room but I had no choice – and at least I wasn't serving his table. Anyway, the next thing I know, Mr Conway got up to go to the toilet and he walked right past me. I wasn't going to say anything but seeing him so close, inches away, I couldn't stop myself.'

'What did you say?'

'I said good evening. I asked him if he remembered me.'

'And?'

'He didn't. Or he pretended he didn't. I reminded him that we'd met in Devonshire, that he had been kind enough to read my novel. He knew exactly who I was and what I was referring to. So then he got shirty with me. "I don't come here to talk to the waiters." That was what he said, those exact words. He asked me to step out of his way. He was keeping his voice low but I knew exactly what he would do if I wasn't careful. It was the same thing all over again. He's successful, with his fancy car and that big house of his up in Framlingham. I'm no one. He's a member here. I'm waiting tables. I need this job. I've got a two-year-old kid. So I mumbled I was sorry and stepped away. It made me feel sick to my stomach doing that but what choice did I have?'

'You must have been quite pleased to hear he was dead.'

'You want the truth, Susan? I was delighted. I couldn't have been happier if—'

He had said too much but I pressed him anyway. 'If what?'

'It doesn't matter.'

But we both knew what he'd meant. I gave him the business card and he tucked it away in his top pocket. He finished his second cigarette and stubbed that one out too.

'Can I ask you one last thing?' I said as we moved back inside. 'You said that Alan was having an argument. I don't suppose you heard anything of what was being said?'

He shook his head. 'I wasn't near enough.'

'How about the people at the next table?' I had seen for myself the layout of the room. They would have been virtually rubbing shoulders.

'I suppose that's possible. I can tell you who they were, if you like. Their names will still be on the system.'

He left the terrace and went back into the restaurant to do just that. I watched him as he walked into the distance, remembering what he had just said. '*. . . that big house of his up in Framlingham.*' He hadn't had to look up the name of the town. He already knew where Alan lived.

The grandson

The man who had been sitting at the table next to Alan Conway that night and who might or might not have overheard the conversation was called Mathew Prichard. It was very curious. His name may not be familiar to you but I recognised it at once. Mathew Prichard is the grandson of Agatha Christie. He was famously given the rights to *The Mousetrap* when he was nine years old. It feels odd to be writing about him and it may seem unlikely that he should have been there. But he is a member of the Club. The offices of Agatha Christie Ltd are a short walk away, in Drury Lane. And, as I've already mentioned, *The Mousetrap* is still showing at St Martin's theatre, which is just down the road.

I had his number on my mobile. We had met two or three times at literary events and a few years ago I had been in negotiations to buy his memoir, *The Grand Tour*. It was a very entertaining account of a round-the-world trip his grandmother had made in 1922 (I was outbid by HarperCollins). I called him and he remembered me at once.

'Of course, Susan. Lovely to hear from you. How are you?'

I wasn't quite sure how to explain myself. Again, the fact that I was involving him in a real-life mystery that I was investigating struck me as bizarre and I didn't really want to go into all that on the phone. So I simply mentioned the death of Alan Conway – he knew all about that – and said there was something I wanted to ask him about. That was enough. As it happened, he was close by. He gave me the name of a cocktail bar near Seven Dials and we agreed to meet there for a drink that evening.

If there is one word I would use to describe Mathew it is affable. He must be about seventy and looking at him, with his ruffled white hair and slightly ruddy complexion, you get the sense that he has lived life to the full. He has a laugh that you can hear across the room, a raucous, sailor's laugh that sounds as if he has just been told the filthiest joke. He was looking immaculate in a blazer and an open-neck shirt as he wandered into the cocktail bar and although I offered, he insisted on paying for the drinks.

We talked a little about Alan Conway. He expressed his sympathies, said how much he had always enjoyed the books. 'Very, very clever. Always surprising. Full of good ideas.' I remember the words exactly, because there was a nasty part of me that was wondering if it might be possible to slip them onto the back cover: Agatha Christie's grandson endorsing Alan Conway's work could only be a good thing for future sales. He asked me how Alan had died and I told him that the police suspected suicide. He looked pained at that. A man so full of life himself, he would find it hard to understand anyone who could choose to do away with theirs. I added that Alan had been seriously ill and he nodded as if that made some kind of sense. 'You know, I saw him a week or so ago – at the Ivy,' he said.

'That was what I wanted to ask you about,' I replied. 'He was having dinner with his publisher.'

'Yes. That's right. I was at the next table.'

'I'd be interested to know what you saw – or heard.'

'Why don't you ask him?'

'I have. Charles has told me a certain amount but I'm trying to fill in the gaps.'

'Well, I wasn't really listening to the conversation. Of course, the tables are quite close to each other but I can't tell you very much of what was said.'

I found it rather endearing that Mathew hadn't asked me why I was interested in what had happened. He had lived much of his life in the world created by his grandmother and the way he saw it, detectives asked questions, witnesses answered them. It was as simple as that. I reminded him of the moment when Leigh had dropped the plates and he smiled. 'Yes, I do remember that. As a matter of fact, I did hear some of what they were saying just before it happened. Raised voices and all that! They were talking about the title of his new book.'

'Alan delivered it that night.'

'*Magpie Murders*. I'm sure you'll understand, Susan, I can't hear the word "murder" without my ears pricking up.' He chortled at that. 'They were arguing about the title. I think your publisher chap made some comment and Mr Conway wasn't at all happy. Yes. He said he'd planned the title years ago – I heard him say that – and he banged his fist on the table. Made the cutlery jump. That was when I turned round and realised who he was. It hadn't actually dawned on me until then. Anyway, there was a moment's silence. A couple of seconds, perhaps. And then he pointed his finger and he said: "I'm not having the—"'

'The what?' I asked.

Prichard smiled at me. 'I'm afraid I can't help you, because that was when the waiter dropped the plates. It made an absolutely terrible din. The entire room came to a halt. You know how it is. The poor chap went quite red – I'm talking about the waiter now – and started clearing up the mess. I'm afraid I didn't really hear any more after that. I'm sorry.'

'Did you see Alan get up?' I asked.

'Yes. I think he went to the loo.'

'He talked to the waiter.'

'He might have done. But I don't remember anything more. In fact, I'd finished my meal by then and I left shortly afterwards.'

'*I'm not having the—*'

That was what it boiled down to. Four words that could have meant anything. I made a mental note to ask Charles about it the next time I saw him.

Prichard and I talked about his grandmother as we finished our cocktails. It had always amused me how much she had come to hate Hercule Poirot by the time she finished writing about him. What had she famously called him? 'A detestable, bombastic, tiresome, egocentric little creep.' Hadn't she once said that she wanted to exorcise herself of him? He laughed. 'I think that, like all geniuses, she wanted to write all sorts of different books and she got very frustrated when her publishers only wanted, at one stage, for her to write Poirot. She got very impatient when she was told what to do.'

We got up. I had ordered a gin and tonic and it must have been a double because it made my head spin. 'Thank you for your help,' I said.

'I don't think I've been much help at all,' he replied. 'But I'll look forward to seeing the new book when it comes out. As I say, I always liked the Atticus Pünd mysteries – and Mr Conway was obviously a great devotee of my grandmother's work.'

'He had the complete collection in his office,' I said.

'I'm not surprised. He borrowed lots of things from her, you know. Names. Places. It was almost like a game. I'm sure he did it quite deliberately but when I was reading the books, I'd find all sorts of references buried in the text. I'm quite certain he was doing it on purpose and I did sometimes think of writing to him, to ask him what he was up to.' Prichard smiled one last time. He was too good-natured to accuse Alan of plagiarism, although it was a strange echo of my conversation with Donald Leigh.

We shook hands. I went back to the office, closed my door, and took the manuscript out to examine it one more time.

He was right. *Magpie Murders* pays quiet homage to Agatha Christie at least half a dozen times. For example, Sir Magnus Pye and his wife stay at the Hotel Genevieve in Cap Ferrat. There's a villa in *The Murder on the Links* that has the same name. The Blue Boar is the pub in Bristol where Robert Blakiston is involved in a fight. But it also appears in St Mary Mead, home of Miss Marple. Lady Pye and Jack Dartford have lunch at Carlotta's, which seems to have been named after the American actress in *Lord Edgware Dies*. There's a joke, of sorts, on page 124. Fraser fails to notice a dead man on the three-fifty train from Paddington, an obvious reference to the *4.50 From Paddington*. Mary Blakiston lives in Sheppard's Farm. Dr James Sheppard is the narrator of *The Murder of Roger Ackroyd*, which is set in King's Abbott, a village that is also mentioned on page 62, which is where old Dr Rennard is buried.

For that matter, the entire mechanism of *Magpie Murders*, the use of the old nursery rhyme, deliberately imitates a device that

Christie used many times. She liked children's verse. *One Two Buckle my Shoe*, *Five Little Pigs*, *Ten Little Indians* (*And Then There Were None* as it later became), *Hickory Dickory Dock* – all of them appear in her work. You would have thought that any writer whose work has a similarity to an author much better known than himself would do everything he could to disguise the fact. Alan Conway, in his own peculiar way, seems to do the exact opposite. What exactly was going on in his mind when he put these obvious signposts in? Or to put it another way, what exactly were they pointing to?

Not for the first time, I got the sense that he had been trying to tell me something, that he hadn't just written the Atticus Pünd mysteries to entertain people. He had created them for a purpose that was slowly becoming clear.

The road to Framlingham

The following Friday, I drove back to Suffolk for Alan Conway's funeral. Neither me nor Charles had been invited and it was unclear who actually was making the arrangements: James Taylor, Claire Jenkins or Sajid Khan. I'd been tipped off by my sister who had read about it in the local newspaper and emailed me with the time and the place. She told me that the funeral was being conducted by the Reverend Tom Robeson, vicar of Saint Michael's Church, and Charles and I decided to drive up together. We took my car. I was going to stop a little longer.

Andreas had been staying with me all week and he was annoyed that I wasn't going to be around at the weekend. But I needed time alone. The whole question of Crete was hanging over us and, although we hadn't discussed it again, I knew he was waiting for an answer that I wasn't yet ready to give. Anyway, I couldn't stop thinking about Alan's death. I was convinced that another few days in Framlingham would lead me both to the discovery of the missing chapters and, more broadly, the truth of what had happened at Abbey Grange. I was quite sure that the two were related. Alan must have been killed because of something in his book. It might well be that if I could find out who had killed Sir Magnus Pye, I'd know who had killed him. Or vice versa.

The funeral started at three. Charles and I left London just after midday and from the very start I knew it was a mistake. We should have gone by train. The traffic was horrible and Charles looked awkward in the low-slung seat of my MGB. I felt uneasy myself and was wondering why until it dawned on me (just as we hit the M25) that the two of us had always had a face-to-face relationship. That is, I would meet him in his office and he would be on one side of the desk and I would be on the other. We would eat together, facing each other in restaurants. We were often on opposite sides of the conference table. But here we were, unusually, side-by-side and I was simply less familiar with his profile. Being so near to him was also peculiar. Of course, we'd been in taxis together and occasionally on trains, but somehow my little classic car brought us much closer than I would have liked. I had never noticed how unhealthy his skin looked; how years of shaving had scraped the life out of his cheeks and neck. He was dressed in a dark suit with a formal shirt and I was slightly fascinated by his Adam's apple, which seemed to be constrained, bulging over his black tie. He was going back to London on his own and I rather wished I'd been a bit less forward with my invitation and had allowed him to do the same both ways.

Still, we chatted pleasantly enough once we'd left the worst of the traffic behind us. I was more relaxed by the time we hit the A12 and picked up speed. I mentioned that I'd met Mathew Prichard, which amused him, and that allowed me to ask him, once again, about his dinner at the Ivy Club and in particular about the argument concerning the title, *Magpie Murders*. I didn't want him to feel that I was interrogating him and I still wasn't sure why that last conversation meant so much to me.

Charles was also puzzled by my interest. 'I told you I didn't like the title,' he said, simply. 'I thought it was too similar to *Midsomer Murders* on TV.'

'You asked him to change it.'

'Yes.'

'And he refused.'

'That's right. He got quite angry about it.'

I reminded him of what Alan had said, the four words he had spoken just before the waiter had dropped the plates. *I'm not having the—* Did he know what Alan had been about to say?

'No. I can't remember, Susan. I have no idea.'

'Did you know that he thought up the title years ago?'

'I didn't. How do you know?'

In fact Mathew Prichard had overheard Alan telling him exactly that. 'I think he mentioned it to me once,' I lied.

We didn't talk about Alan much more after that. Neither of us was looking forward to the funeral. Well, of course, you never do – but in Alan's case we were only going out of a sense of obligation although I was interested to know who would be there. I'd actually called James Taylor that morning. We were going to have dinner later that evening at the Crown Hotel. I also wondered if Melissa Conway would show up. It had been several years since I had met her and, after what Andreas had said, I was keen to see her again. The three of them together at Woodbridge School – where Atticus Pünd had begun.

We drove in silence for about twenty minutes but then, just after we had entered the county of Suffolk, a sign helpfully informing us that was what we'd done, Charles suddenly announced: 'I'm thinking of stepping aside.'

'I'm sorry?' I would have stared at him except that I was in the process of overtaking a monster four-axle lorry complete with tow-bar trailer, possibly on its way to Felixstowe.

'I've been meaning to talk to you for some time, Susan – before this business with Alan. I suppose that's the last nail in the coffin – if that's not a horribly inappropriate expression, given the circumstances. But I'll be sixty-five soon and Elaine has been on at me to slow down.' Elaine, I may have mentioned, was his wife. I had only ever met her a couple of times and knew she had little interest in the publishing world. 'And then, of course, there's the new baby on its way. Becoming a grandfather certainly makes you think. It just might be the right time.'

'How soon?' I didn't know what to say. The idea of Cloverleaf Books without Charles Clover was unthinkable. He was as much a part of the place as the wooden panelling.

'Maybe next spring.' He paused. 'I was wondering if you might like to take over.'

'What – me? As CEO?'

'Why not? I'll stay on as chairman so I'll still have some involvement, but you'll take over the day-to-day running. You know the business as well as anyone. And let's face it, if I were to parachute someone in, I'm not sure you'd be happy working with them.'

He was right about that. I was hurtling through my forties and I was vaguely aware that the older I got, the more stuck in my ways I became. I suppose it's something that happens in publishing, where people often stay in the same job for a very long time. I wasn't good with new people. Could I do it? I knew about books but I had no real interest in the rest of it: employees, accountants, overheads, long-term strategy, the day-to-day running of a medium-sized business. At the same time, it occurred to me that this was my second job offer in less than a week. I could become CEO of Cloverleaf or I could run a small hotel in Agios Nikolaos. It was quite a choice.

'Would I have complete autonomy?' I asked.

'Yes. We'd come to some sort of financial agreement, but effectively it would be your company.' He smiled. 'It changes your priorities, becoming a grandfather. Tell me you'll consider it.'

'Of course I will, Charles. It's very kind of you to have such confidence in me.'

We stayed silent for the next ten or twenty miles. I'd misjudged the amount of time I needed to get out of London and it looked as if we were going to be late for the funeral. In fact we would have been if Charles hadn't warned me to take a right, cutting round through Brandeston and so missing the roadworks that had held me up at Earl Soham the last time I had come through. That saved us a quarter of an hour and we pulled in to Framlingham comfortably at ten to three. I'd booked the same room at the Crown so I was able to leave the MGB in their car park. They were already setting up the front lounge for drinks after the funeral and we just had time to snatch a coffee, then hurried out the front entrance and across the road.

There was going to be a funeral...

The first words of *Magpie Murders.*

The irony wasn't lost on me as I joined the other mourners who were assembling around the open grave.

The church of St Michael the Archangel, to give it its full name, is really much too large for the town in which it finds itself – but then the whole of Suffolk is studded with monumental buildings, locked in combat with the surrounding landscape as if each parish felt a need to bully its way into peoples' lives. It feels uncomfortable – not just penned in but in the wrong place altogether. As you glance back through the cast-iron gates, it's surprising to find yourself looking across a busy street to Mr Chan's Chinese restaurant. There's something odd about the cemetery too. It's slightly raised up so that the dead bodies are actually buried above street level and the grass is too green, the graves clustered together in irregular lines with so much space around them that there's no economy of scale. The cemetery is both too full and too empty at the same time and yet this was where Alan had chosen to be buried. I guessed that he had selected his plot with some care. It was right in the middle, between two Irish yews. Nobody would be able to miss it as they made their way to the church. His closest neighbours had died almost a century before him and the newly dug earth appeared as a fresh scar; as if it had no right to be there.

The weather had changed during the course of the day. The sun had been shining when we left London but now the sky was grey and there was a thin drizzle sweeping through the air. I understood why Alan had started *Magpie Murders* with a funeral. It had been a useful device, introducing all the main characters in a way that allowed him to consider them at leisure. I was able to do the same now. I was quite surprised how many of them I knew.

First there was James Taylor, wrapped in a black, designer raincoat with his damp hair sticking to his neck and looking for all the world as if he had just stepped out of a spy novel. He was doing his best to look sombre and composed but there was a smile about him that he could not control; not on his lips but in his eyes and the very way he stood. Sajid Khan was standing next to him, holding an umbrella. The two of them had arrived together. So James had inherited. He knew that Alan had failed to sign his most recent will and Abbey Grange and everything else was his. That was interesting. James saw me and nodded and I smiled back at him. I don't know why, but I was really glad for him and it didn't even bother me, the thought that Alan might have died at his hand.

Claire Jenkins was there. She was dressed in black and crying, really sobbing, with the tears coursing down her cheeks, helped on their way by the rain. She was holding a handkerchief but it must have been useless by now. A man stood next to her, awkwardly holding her arm with a gloved hand. I had not met him before but would easily remember him when I saw him again. For a start, he was black, the only black person to come to the funeral. He also had an extraordinary physical presence, very well built with solid arms and shoulders, a thick neck, intense eyes. I thought at first that he might be an ex-wrestler – he had the build – but then it occurred to me that he was more likely to be a policeman. Claire had told me that she worked for the Suffolk constabulary. Was this the elusive Detective Superintendent Locke whose enquiry had been parallel-tracking my own?

My eye settled on another man who was standing on his own with the church tower rising monstrously behind him, too big for a church that was too big for its town. It was his Hunter Wellington boots I noticed first. They were brand new and bright orange – an odd choice for a funeral. I couldn't see much of his face. He was wearing a cloth cap and a Barbour jacket turned up at the collar. As I watched him, his mobile phone rang and instead of putting it on silent, he took the call, turning away for privacy. 'John White . . .' I heard him give his name but nothing else. Still, I knew who he was. This was Alan's neighbour, the hedge fund manager he'd fallen out with just before he died.

Still waiting for the service to begin, I searched through the crowd and found Melissa Conway and her son, standing next to the cemetery's war memorial. She was wearing a raincoat tucked so tightly around her that it appeared to be breaking her in half. Her hands were deep in her pockets, her hair concealed beneath a scarf. I might not have recognised her but for her son who must have been in his late teens now. He was the spitting image of his father – at least in Alan's later incarnation – uncomfortable in a dark suit that was a little too large for him. He was not happy to be here; by which I mean he was angry. He was staring at the grave with something like murder in his eyes.

I hadn't seen Melissa for at least six years. She had come to the launch party of *Atticus Pünd Takes the Case,* which had been held at the German embassy in London, an evening of champagne and miniature Bratwurst. I was seeing Andreas occasionally by then and because we had him in common we were able to strike up a conversation of sorts. I remember her as being polite but disengaged. It can't be much fun being married to a writer and she made it clear that she was only there because it was expected of her. She knew nobody in the room and nobody had anything to say to her. It was a shame that the two of us had never met properly at Woodbridge School: I had no knowledge of her outside her relation to Alan. She had the same blank look on her face now, even though it was a coffin rather than canapés that was being brought in. I wondered why she had come.

The hearse had arrived. The coffin was carried forward. A vicar appeared, walking out of the church. This was the Reverend Tom Robeson whose name had been mentioned in the newspaper. He was about fifty years old and although I had never seen him before I knew him immediately. '*. . . his tombstone face and his long, slightly unkempt hair.*' That was how Alan had described Robin Osborne in *Magpie Murders* and, even as I thought that, something else occurred to me. I had seen it as I entered the cemetery, his name written on a sign. It helped having that visual prompt.

Robeson is an anagram of Osborne.

It was another one of Alan's private jokes. James Taylor had become James Fraser, Claire was Clarissa and, now that I thought about it, John White the hedge fund manager had been turned into Johnny Whitehead the second-hand furniture dealer and petty crook, this the result of an argument about money. As far as I knew, Alan had never been a religious person despite this very conventional funeral and I had to ask myself what his relationship with the vicar has been and why he had chosen to celebrate it in his novel. Osborne had been number three on my list of suspects. Mary Blakiston had discovered some sort of secret, left out on his desk. Could Robeson have had a reason to murder Alan? He certainly looked the part of the vengeful killer with his rather grim, colourless features and his robes hanging forlornly off him in the rain.

He described Alan as a popular writer whose books had given pleasure to many millions of people around the world. It was as if Alan was being introduced on a Radio 4 panel show rather than at his own funeral. 'Alan Conway may have left us all too soon and in tragic circumstances but he will, I am sure, remain in the hearts and the minds of the literary community.' Even ignoring the question of whether the literary community actually had a heart, I thought this was unlikely to be the case. It's my experience that dead authors are forgotten with remarkable speed. Even living authors find it hard to stay on the shelves; there are too many new books and too few shelves. 'Alan was one of our country's most celebrated mystery writers,' he went on. 'He lived much of his life in Suffolk and it was always his wish that he should be buried here.' In *Magpie Murders*, there is something hidden in the funeral address that relates in some way to the murder. On the very last page of the typescript, when Pünd is talking about the clues that will solve the crime, he specifically refers to 'the words spoken by the vicar'. Unfortunately, Robeson's speech was almost deliberately bland and unrevealing. He didn't mention James or Melissa. There was nothing about friendship, generosity, humour, personal mannerisms, small kindnesses, special moments . . . all those things we actually miss when somebody dies. If Alan had been a marble statue stolen from a park, the Reverend Tom Robeson might have cared as much.

There was just one passage that stayed with me. It certainly struck me that it might be worth asking the vicar about it later.

'Very few people are now buried in this cemetery,' he said. 'But Alan insisted. He had given a great deal of money to the church which has allowed us to undertake much needed restoration work to the clerestory windows and the main chancel arch. In return he demanded this resting place and who was I to stand in his way?' He smiled as if trying to make light of what he had just said. 'All his life, Alan had a dominant personality, as I discovered at quite an early age. Certainly I was not going to refuse him this last wish. His contribution assures the future of St Michael's and it is only fitting that he should remain here, within the church grounds.'

This whole section of the speech had an edge to it. On the one hand Alan had been generous. He deserved to be allowed to lie here. But that wasn't quite the case, was it? Alan had 'demanded' it. He had 'a dominant personality'. And 'as I discovered at quite an early age'. Alan and the vicar obviously had some sort of history. Was I really the only person who noticed the discordance in what was being said?

I was going to ask Charles what he thought as soon as the service was over but in fact I never made it to the end. The rain was beginning to ease off and Robeson had reached his closing remarks. Bizarrely, he had forgotten Alan altogether. He was talking about the history of Framlingham and, in particular, Thomas Howard, the third Duke of Norfolk, whose tomb was inside the church. For a moment my attention wondered and that was when I noticed a mourner who must have arrived late. He was lingering over by the gate, watching the service from a distance, anxious to be on his way. Even as I examined him, and with the vicar still speaking, he turned on his heels and walked out onto Church Street.

I had not seen his face. He was wearing a black, Fedora hat.

'Don't leave,' I whispered to Charles. 'I'll meet you at the hotel.'

It had taken Atticus Pünd one hundred and thirty pages to discover the identity of the man who had attended Mary Blakiston's funeral. I couldn't wait that long. Nodding at the vicar and detaching myself from the crowd, I set off in pursuit.

The Atticus Adventures

I caught up with the man in the Fedora hat at the corner of Church Street, just where it met Market Square. Now that he had escaped from the cemetery, he no longer seemed to be in such a hurry to get away. It helped that the drizzle had finally eased off and there were even a few patches of bright sun illuminating the puddles. He was taking his time and I was able to catch my breath before I approached him.

Some instinct made him turn and he saw me. 'Yes?'

'I was at the funeral,' I said.

'So was I.'

'I wondered...' It was only then that it dawned on me that I had no earthly idea what I was going to say. It was all far too difficult to explain. I was investigating a murder which, as far as I knew, nobody else was aware had taken place. I had chased after him only because of his choice of headgear, the relevance of which was tangential, to say the least. I drew a breath. 'My name is Susan Ryeland,' I said. 'I was Alan's editor at Cloverleaf Books.'

'Cloverleaf?' He knew the name. 'Yes. We've spoken a few times.'

'Have we?'

'Not you. There's a woman there... Lucy Butler.' Lucy was our Rights Manager. She had the office next to mine. 'I talked to her about Atticus Pünd.' Suddenly I had a good idea who I was talking to but I didn't need to ask. 'I'm Mark Redmond,' he said.

Charles and I had often talked about Redmond and his company

– Red Herring Productions – during our weekly conferences. He was a TV and film producer and it was he who had optioned the rights to the Atticus Pünd novels, which he was developing with the BBC. Lucy had visited him at his offices in Soho and had reported back favourably: a young, enthusiastic staff, a shelf full of BAFTAs, phones ringing, dispatch riders in and out, a sense that this was a company that made things happen. As the name suggested, Red Herring specialised in murder mystery. Redmond had started his career as a runner on *Bergerac*, presumably running all over Jersey, which was where it was set. From there he'd moved on to another half dozen shows before setting up on his own. Atticus would be his first independent production. From what I understood, the BBC was keen.

He was actually someone I was very glad to meet: his future and mine were intertwined. A television series would give the books a whole new life. There would be new covers, new publicity, a complete relaunch. We needed it more than ever, given our problems with *Magpie Murders*. I still had Charles's offer to consider. If I really was going to take over the running of Cloverleaf Books I would need its star author – and posthumously was good enough for me. Red Herring Productions might make it possible.

He was about to leave for London – he had a car and a driver waiting for him in the square – but I persuaded him to talk to me first and we went into a little café, opposite the hotel. We had less chance of our being disturbed there. He had taken off the Fedora to reveal slicked-back dark hair and narrow eyes. He was a handsome man, slim, expensively dressed. He had built his career in television and there was something of the TV personality about him. I could imagine him presenting a programme. It would be about lifestyle or maybe finance.

I ordered two coffees and we began to talk.

'You left the funeral early,' I said.

'I wasn't sure why I came, if you want the truth. I felt I ought to be there, since I'd been working with him, but once I arrived I decided it was a mistake. I didn't know anyone and it was cold and wet. I just wanted to leave.'

'When did you last see him?'

'Why do you want to know?'

I shrugged as if it wasn't important. 'I just wondered. Alan's suicide has obviously come as a great shock to us and we're trying to work out why he did it.'

'I saw him two weeks ago.'

'In London?'

'No. Actually, I went out to his home. It was a Saturday.'

The day before Alan died.

'Had he invited you?' I asked.

Redmond laughed briefly. 'I wouldn't have driven the whole bloody way if he hadn't. He wanted to talk about the series and he asked me to dinner. Knowing Alan, I thought it best not to refuse. He'd been difficult enough already and I didn't want to have any more rows.'

'What sort of rows?'

He looked at me disdainfully. 'I'm sure I don't need to tell you that Alan was a real piece of work,' he said. 'You say you were his editor. Don't tell me he didn't give you the runaround! I almost wish I'd never heard of Atticus Pünd. He was making life so bloody difficult for me, I could have murdered him myself!'

'I'm so sorry,' I said. 'I had no idea. What exactly was the problem?'

'It was one thing after another.' The coffees arrived and he stirred his, the spoon making endless circles as he went through the process of working with Alan Conway. 'Getting him to sign the option in the first place was hard enough. The amount of money he was asking, you'd think he was JK bloody Rowling. And don't forget, this was risk money as far as I was concerned. At the time, I hadn't completed a deal with the BBC and the whole thing could have gone west. But that was just the start of it. He wouldn't go away. He wanted to be an executive producer. Well, that's not so unusual. But he also insisted on adapting the book himself even though he had no TV writing experience and, I can tell you, the BBC weren't at all happy about that. He wanted casting approval. That was the biggest headache of all. No author *ever* gets casting approval! Consultancy, maybe, but that wasn't good enough. He had ridiculous ideas. Do you know who he wanted to play Atticus Pünd?'

'Ben Kingsley?' I suggested.

He stared at me. 'Did he tell you?'

'No. But I know he was a fan.'

'Well, you're right. Unfortunately, it was out of the question. Kingsley would never take the part and anyway, he's seventy-three – much too old. We argued about that. We argued about everything. I wanted to start with *Night Comes Calling*. It's much the best book, in my view. But he wasn't having that either. He wouldn't explain why not. He just said he didn't want to do it. The option comes to an end quite soon so I had to be careful what I said.'

'Will you still go ahead?' I asked. 'Now that he's gone?'

Redmond visibly brightened. He put down his spoon and drank some of his coffee. 'I'll go ahead with it *because* he's gone. Can I be honest with you, Susan? I shouldn't speak ill of the dead but, frankly, his departure is the best thing that could have happened. I've already spoken to James Taylor. He owns the rights now and he seems pleasant enough. He's already agreed to give us another year and by that time we should have the whole thing set up. We're hoping to make all nine books.'

'He didn't finish the last one.'

'We can deal with that. It doesn't matter. They've made a hundred and four episodes of *Midsomer Murders* but the original author only wrote seven books. And look at *Sherlock*. They're doing things Doyle never dreamed of. With a bit of luck we'll do a dozen seasons of *The Atticus Adventures*. That's what we're going to call it. I never much liked the name Pünd – it sounds a bit too foreign and you may not agree with me but I think the umlaut on the u is really off-putting. But Atticus is good. It reminds me of *To Kill a Mockingbird*. Now we can go ahead and get a decent writer in and that'll make my life a whole lot easier.'

'Haven't the public had enough of murder?' I asked.

'You're joking. *Inspector Morse*, *Taggart*, *Lewis*, *Foyle's War*, *Endeavour*, *A Touch of Frost*, *Luther*, *The Inspector Lynley Mysteries*, *Cracker*, *Broadchurch* and even bloody *Maigret* and *Wallander* – British TV would disappear into a dot on the screen without murder. They're even bumping people off in the soap operas. And it's the same the world over. You know, they say in America that the average child sees eight thousand murders before they leave elementary school. Makes you think, doesn't it.' He finished the rest of his coffee as if he was suddenly anxious to be on his way.

'So what did Alan Conway want?' I asked him. 'When you saw him two weeks ago?'

He shrugged. 'He complained about the lack of progress. He had no idea how the BBC works. It can take them weeks to answer the phone. The fact of the matter is that they didn't like his script. Of course, I hadn't told him that. We were trying to find someone else to take over.'

'Did you talk about the option?'

'Yes.' He hesitated for a moment, the first time I had seen any flaw in the armour of his self-confidence. 'He told me there was another production company he was talking to. It didn't matter that I'd already invested thousands in *The Atticus Adventures*. He was quite ready to start all over again.'

'So what happened?' I asked.

'We had lunch at his house. It didn't get off to a great start. I was late. I got held up at some endless roadworks at Earl Soham – he said it had been like that for weeks – and he was in a bad mood. Anyway, we talked. I made my pitch. He promised to get back to me. I left about three in the afternoon and drove home.' He glanced down at his empty cup. He was keen to be on his way. 'Thank you for the coffee. It's very nice to meet you. As soon as we get a green light for production, I'll let you know.'

Mark Redmond walked out, leaving me to pay for the coffee. *I could have murdered him myself.* I didn't need to be a fan of *Midsomer Murders* to recognise a motive when I heard one and it occurred to me that when it came to suspects, in the league of sheer bloody obviousness, Redmond had just put himself at the top of the list. Even so, there was one thing I wasn't expecting. Later that afternoon, when I signed into the Crown, I flicked back a few pages in the guest registry. I was acting on a whim – but there it was. Mark Redmond's name. He had been booked into the hotel and stayed there two nights. When I asked the receptionist, she remembered him leaving after breakfast on Monday morning. He and his wife. He hadn't mentioned that she'd been there too.

But that wasn't relevant. The fact was that he had actually been in Framlingham at the time Alan died. In other words, he'd been lying. I could think of only one good reason why.

After the funeral

The reception rooms were crowded by the time I got to the Crown. There had only been about forty people at the funeral and it had felt a little sparse but in the confines of the front lounge with two fires blazing, red and white wine circulating, trays of sandwiches and sausage rolls laid out, there was something close enough to a party atmosphere and even a few of the hotel guests had joined in on the grounds that free wine and food were worth having even if they had no idea who had actually died. Sajid Khan was there with his wife – I recognised her from the sliding photograph – and greeted me as I came in. He was in an unusually cheerful mood, as if his former client had been filed away rather than buried and a whole new business opportunity had begun. James Taylor was standing next to him and muttered just three words as I made my way past. 'See you tonight.' He clearly couldn't wait to leave.

I found Charles who was deep in conversation with the Reverend Tom Robeson. The vicar was much larger than he had appeared in the cemetery. He certainly towered over Charles and the other guests. Seeing him more closely, and out of the rain, I was also struck by how unattractive he was. He had the dull eyes and the slightly misplaced features of a boxer who has been in too many fights. He had changed out of his robes. He was wearing a worn-out sports jacket with patches on the sleeves. As I approached, he was making a point, jabbing with a half-eaten sandwich.

'. . . but there are villages that simply won't survive. Families are being split up. It's morally unjustifiable.'

Charles glanced at me a little irritably as I joined them. 'Where did you go?' he asked.

'There was someone I knew.'

'You left very suddenly.'

'I know. I didn't want them to get away.'

He turned back to the vicar. 'This is Tom Robeson. Susan Ryeland. We were just talking about second homes,' he added.

'Southwold, Dunwich, Walberswick, Orford, Shingle Street – all along the coast.' Robeson had to make his point.

I cut in. 'I was interested in the address you made at the funeral,' I said.

'Oh yes?' He looked at me blankly.

'You knew Alan when you were young?'

'Yes. We met a long time ago.'

A waiter went past with a tray and I snatched a glass of white wine. It was warm and sluggish, a Pinot Grigio, I think. 'You suggested that he bullied you.'

Even as I spoke the words, it didn't seem likely. Alan had never had much of a physical presence and Robeson must have been twice his size when they were kids. He didn't deny it though. Instead he became flustered. 'I'm sure I said no such thing, Mrs Ryeland.'

'You said he demanded a place in the cemetery.'

'I'm sure that's not the word I would have used. Alan Conway showed exceptional generosity towards the church. He made no demands whatsoever. When he asked if he might one day be laid to rest in the cemetery, I felt it would be deeply ungrateful of me to refuse even if, I will admit, I had to request a special dispensation.' The vicar was glancing over my shoulder, looking for a way out. If he had squeezed his hand any tighter, his glass of elderflower juice would have exploded. 'It was a great pleasure to meet you,' he said. 'And you, Mr Clover. If you'll excuse me . . .'

He slipped between us and waded into the crowd.

'What was all that about?' Charles asked. 'And who was it you met when you went rushing off?'

The second question was easier to answer. 'Mark Redmond,' I said.

'The producer?'

'Yes. You know he was here the weekend Alan died?'

'Why?'

'Alan wanted to talk to him about the television series, *The Atticus Adventures*. Redmond told me that Alan was giving him a hard time.'

'I don't understand, Susan. Why exactly did you want to talk to him? And why were you so aggressive with the vicar just now? You were almost interrogating him. What exactly is going on?'

I had to tell him. I didn't know why I hadn't told him already. So I took him through the whole thing: my visit to Claire Jenkins, the suicide letter, the Ivy Club – all of it. Charles listened to me in silence and I couldn't help but feel that the more I spoke, the more ridiculous I sounded. He didn't believe what I was saying and listening to myself I wasn't sure I believed it either. Certainly, I had little or no evidence to support it. Mark Redmond had stayed a couple of nights in a hotel. Did that make him a suspect? A waiter had had his idea stolen. Would he have travelled all the way to Suffolk to get revenge? The fact remained that Alan Conway had been terminally ill. At the end of the day, why kill someone who was going to die anyway?

I finished. Charles shook his head. 'A murder writer murdered,' he said. 'Are you really serious about this, Susan?'

'Yes, Charles,' I said. 'I think I am.'

'Have you told anyone else? Have you been to the police?'

'Why do you ask?'

'For two reasons. I don't want to see you make a fool of yourself. And frankly I think you could be stirring up more trouble for the company.'

'Charles . . .' I began but then came the sound of a fork being struck against the side of a glass and the room fell silent. I looked round. James Taylor was standing on the staircase that led up to the bedrooms with Sajid Khan next to him. He was at least ten years younger than anyone else in the room and couldn't have looked more out-of-place.

'Ladies and gentlemen,' he began. 'Sajid has asked me to say a few words … and I'd like to start by thanking him for making all the arrangements today. As most of you know, I was Alan's partner until very recently and I want to say that I was very fond of him and I will miss him very much. Quite a lot of you have been asking what I plan to do next so I might as well tell you that now that he's gone, I won't be staying in Framlingham although I've always been very happy here. In fact, if anyone's interested, Abbey Grange is about to go on the market. Anyway, I want to thank you all for coming. I'm afraid I've never much liked funerals but, as I say, I'm glad to have had this chance to see you all and to say goodbye. And goodbye to Alan especially. I know it meant a lot to him, being buried in the cemetery at St Michael, and I'm sure lots of people will come here and visit him – people who liked his books. Please have some more to eat and drink. And thank you again.'

It wasn't much of a speech and it had been delivered not just awkwardly but a little carelessly too. James had already told me that he couldn't wait to get out of Suffolk and he had made it clear to everyone else too. While I was speaking, I had glanced around the room, trying to gauge the different reactions. The vicar was standing to one side, stony-faced. A woman had joined him, much shorter than him, plump with sprawling, ginger hair. I presumed she was his wife. John White hadn't come to the reception but Detective Superintendent Locke was there – if indeed he was the black man I had identified at the cemetery. Melissa Conway and her son had left the moment James had started speaking. I saw them slip away through the back door and I could understand how they must have felt, listening to Alan's boyfriend. It was still annoying, though, as I'd wanted to talk to them. But I couldn't dash off a second time.

James shook hands with the solicitor and left the room, stopping briefly to mutter a few words to one or two well-wishers. I turned back to Charles, expecting to pick up our conversation, but at that moment his mobile pinged. He took it out and glanced at the screen.

'My car's here,' he said. He had arranged a taxi to take him to Ipswich station.

'You should have let me drive you,' I said.

'No. It's all right.' He reached for his coat and draped it over his arm. 'Susan, we really need to talk about Alan. If you're going to go on with this enquiry of yours, obviously I can't stop you. But you should think what you're doing . . . the implications.'

'I know.'

'Are you any closer to finding the missing chapters? If you want my honest opinion, that's much more important.'

'I'm still looking.'

'Well, good luck. I'll see you on Monday.'

We didn't kiss each other goodbye. I have never kissed Charles, not once in all the years I've known him. He's too formal for that, too strait-laced. I can't actually even imagine him kissing his wife.

He left. I threw back the rest of my wine and went to fetch my key. I planned to have a bath and a rest before my dinner with James Taylor but as I made my way back towards the stairs – the other guests were dispersing now, leaving trays of uneaten sandwiches behind – I found my way blocked by Claire Jenkins. She was holding a brown A4 envelope, which must have contained at least a dozen sheets of paper from the look of it. For a moment, my heart leapt. She had found the missing pages! Could it really be as easy as that?

It wasn't.

'I said I'd write something about Alan,' she reminded me, waving the envelope uncertainly in front of her. 'You asked what he was like as a boy, how we grew up together.' Her eyes were still red and weepy. If there was a website that sold exclusive funeral wear, she must have found it. She was wearing velvet and lace, slightly Victorian and very black.

'That's very kind of you, Mrs Jenkins,' I said.

'It made me think about Alan and I enjoyed writing it. I'm not sure it's any good. I couldn't write the way he did. But it may tell you what you want to know.' She weighed the envelope one last time as if reluctant to part with it, then pushed it towards me. 'I've made a copy so you don't need to worry about sending it back.'

'Thank you.' She was still standing there, as if expecting something more. 'I'm so sorry for your loss.'

Yes. That was it. She nodded. 'I can't believe he's gone,' she said. And then she went herself.

My brother, Alan Conway

I can't believe Alan is dead.

I want to write about him but I don't know where to start. I've read some of Alan's obituaries in the newspapers and they don't even come close. Oh yes, they know when he was born, what books he wrote, what prizes he won. They've said some very nice things about him. But they haven't managed to capture Alan at all and I'm frankly surprised that not one of those journalists telephoned me because I could have given them a much better idea of the sort of man he was, starting with the fact (as I told you) that he would never have killed himself. If Alan was one thing, it was a survivor. We both were. He and I were always close, even if we did disagree from time to time, and if his illness really had driven him to despair, I know he would have called me before he did anything foolish.

He did not jump off that tower. He was pushed. How can I be so sure? You need to understand where we had come from, how far we had both travelled. He would never have left me on my own, not without warning me first.

Let me go back right back to the beginning.

Alan and I were brought up in a place called Chorley Hall, just outside the Hertfordshire town of St Albans. Chorley Hall was a preparatory school for boys and our father, Elias Conway, was the headmaster. Our mother also worked at the school. She had a full-time job as the headmaster's wife, dealing with parents and helping the matron when the children fell sick, although she often complained that she was never actually paid.

It was a horrible place. My father was a horrible man. They were well suited. He had come to the school as a maths teacher and as far as I know he had always worked in the private sector, perhaps because, back then, they weren't too fussy about the sort of people they employed. That may sound a terrible thing to say about your own father, but it's the truth. I'm glad I wasn't taught there. I went to a day school for girls in St Albans – but Alan was stuck with it.

The school looked like one of those haunted houses you get in a Victorian novel, perhaps something by Wilkie Collins. Although it was only thirty minutes from St Albans it was at the end of a long, private drive, surrounded by woodland and felt as if it was in the middle of nowhere. It was a long, institutional sort of building with narrow corridors, stone floors and walls half-covered in dark-coloured tiles. Every room had huge radiators but they were never turned on because it was part of the school's ethos that biting cold, hard beds and disgusting food are character-forming. There were a few modern additions. The science block had been added at the end of the fifties and the school had raised money to build a new gymnasium, which also doubled as a theatre and an assembly hall. Everything was brown or grey. There was hardly any colour at all. Even in the summer, the trees kept out a lot of the sunshine and the water in the school swimming pool – it was a brackish green – never rose above fifty degrees.

It was a boarding school with one hundred and sixty boys aged from eight to thirteen. They were housed in dormitories with between six and twelve beds. I used to walk through them sometimes and I can still remember that strange, musty and slightly acrid smell of so many little boys. Children were allowed to bring a rug and a teddy bear from home but otherwise they had few personal possessions. The school uniform was quite nasty: grey shorts and very dark red V-neck jerseys. Each bed had a cupboard beside it and if they didn't hang their clothes up properly they would be taken out and caned.

Alan wasn't in a dormitory. He and I lived with our parents in a sort of flat that was folded into the school, spread over the second and third floor. Our bedrooms were next to each other and I remember that we used to tap out coded messages to each other on the dividing wall. I always liked hearing the first knocks coming quick and slow just after mother had turned out the lights, even though I didn't ever really know what he meant. Life was very difficult for Alan; perhaps our father wanted it to be. By day he was part of the school, treated exactly the same as the other boys. But he wasn't exactly a boarder because at night he was at home with us. The result of this was that he never fitted into either world and, of course, being the son of the headmaster he was a target from the day he arrived. He had very few friends and as a result he became solitary and introspective. He loved reading. I can still see him, aged nine, in short trousers, sitting with a large volume of something in his lap. He was a very small boy so the books, particularly the old-fashioned ones, often looked curiously oversized. He would read whenever he could, often late into the night, using a torch hidden under the covers.

We were both afraid of our father. He was not what you would call a physically powerful man. He was old before his time with curly hair that had gone white and which had thinned out to allow his skull to show through. He wore glasses. But there was something about his manner that transformed him into something quite monstrous, at least to his children. He had the angry, almost fanatical eyes of someone who knew they were always right and when he was making a point, he had a habit of jabbing a single finger in your face as if daring you to disagree. That was something we never did. He could be viciously sarcastic, putting you in your place with a sneer and a whole tirade of insults that searched out your weaker points and hammered them home. I won't tell you how many times he humiliated me and made me feel bad about myself. But what he did to Alan was worse.

Nothing Alan ever did was right. Alan was stupid. Alan was slow. Alan would never amount to anything. Even his reading was childish. Why didn't he like playing rugby or football or going out camping with the cadets? It's true that Alan was not physically active when he was a child. He was quite plump and perhaps a bit girlish with blue eyes and long, fair hair. During the day he was bullied by some of the other boys. At night he was bullied by his own father. And here's something else that may shock you. Elias beat the boys in the school until they bled. Well, there was nothing unusual about that, not in a British prep school in the seventies. But he beat Alan too, many times. If Alan was late for class or if he hadn't done his homework or if he was rude to another teacher, he would be marched down to the headmaster's study (it never happened in our private flat) and at the end of it he would have to say 'Thank you, sir.' Not 'thank you, Father,' you notice. How could any man do that to his son?

My mother never complained. Maybe she was scared of him herself or maybe she thought he was right. We were a very English family, locked together with our emotions kept firmly out of sight. I wish I could tell you what motivated him, why he was so unpleasant. I once asked Alan why he had never written about his childhood although I have a feeling that the school in *Night Comes Calling* owes a lot to Chorley Hall – it even has a similar name. The headmaster who gets killed is also similar in some ways to our father. Alan told me he had no interest in writing an autobiography, which is a shame because I would have been interested to see what he made of his own life.

What can I tell you about Alan during this time? He was a quiet boy. He had few friends. He read a lot. He didn't enjoy sport. I think he was already living very much in the world of his imagination although he didn't begin writing until later. He loved inventing games. During the school holidays, when the two of us were together, we would become spies, soldiers, explorers, detectives . . . We would scurry through the school grounds, searching for ghosts one day, for buried treasure the next. He was always so full of energy. He never let anything get him down.

I say he wasn't writing yet, but even when he was twelve and thirteen years old, he loved playing with words. He invented codes. He worked out quite complicated anagrams. He made up crosswords. For my eleventh birthday, he made me a crossword that had my name in it, my friends, and everything I did as clues. It was brilliant! Sometimes he would leave out a book for me with little dots underneath some of the letters. If you put them together they would spell out a secret message. Or he would send me acrostics. He would write a note, which would look ordinary if mother or father picked it up, but if you took the first letter of every sentence, once again it would spell out a message that would be known just to the two of us. He liked acronyms too. He often called mother 'MADAM' which actually stood for 'Mum and Dad are mad'. And he'd refer to father as 'CHIEF' which meant 'Chorley Hall is extremely foul'. You may think all this a bit childish but we were only children and anyway, it made me laugh. Because of the way we were brought up, we both got used to being secretive. We were afraid of saying anything, expressing any opinion that might get us into trouble. Alan invented all sorts of ways of expressing things so that only he and I understood. He used language as a place for us to hide.

Chorley Hall came to an end for both of us in different ways. Alan left when he was thirteen and then, a couple of years later, my father suffered a massive stroke that left him semi-paralysed. That was the end of his power over us. Alan had moved to St Albans School and he was much happier there. He had an English teacher he liked, a man called Stephen Pound. I once asked Alan if this was the inspiration for Atticus Pünd but he laughed at me and said that the two weren't connected. Anyway, it was clear that, one way or another, his career was going to be in books. He had started writing short stories and poetry. When he was in sixth form, he wrote the school play.

From this time on, I saw less and less of him and I suppose in many ways we grew apart. When we were together, we were close, but we were beginning to live our own, separate lives. When we got to university age, Alan went to Leeds and I didn't go to university at all. My parents were against it. I got a job in St Albans working in the records department of the police force and that's how I ended up marrying a police officer and eventually coming to live and work in Ipswich. My father died when I was twenty-eight. By the end, he was bedridden and needed round-the-clock support and I'm sure my mother was grateful when he finally conked out. He had taken out a life insurance policy so she was able to support herself. She's still alive, although I haven't seen her for ages. She moved back to Dartmouth, where she was born.

But back to Alan. He studied English literature at Leeds University and after that he moved to London and went into advertising, something a lot of young graduates were doing at the time, particularly if they had a degree in humanities. He worked at an agency called Allen Brady & Marsh and as far as I can tell he had a wonderful time, not working very hard, getting paid quite well and going to a lot of parties. This was the eighties and advertising was still a very self-indulgent industry. Alan worked as a copywriter and actually came up with quite a famous line: WHAT A LOVELY LOOKING SAUSAGE! It's another one of his acrostics. It spells out the name of the brand. He rented a flat in Notting Hill and for what it's worth he had plenty of girlfriends.

Alan stayed in advertising throughout his twenties but in 1995, the year before he turned thirty, he surprised me by announcing that he had left the agency and enrolled in a two-year postgraduate course in creative writing at the University of East Anglia. He had invited me down to London especially to tell me. He took me to Kettner's and ordered champagne and it all came spilling out of him. Kazuo Ishiguro and Ian McEwan had both gone to East Anglia. They had both been published. McEwan had even been shortlisted for the Booker prize! Alan had applied and although he didn't think he would be accepted, that was what had happened. There had been a written application, a portfolio of writing and then a tough interview with two faculty members. I had never seen him happier or more animated. It was as if he had found himself and it was only then that I realised how much being an author mattered to him. He told me he would have two years to write a novel of eighty thousand words under supervision and that the university had strong links with publishers, which might help him get a deal. He already had an idea for a novel. He wanted to write about the space race, seen from the British perspective. 'The world is getting smaller and smaller,' he said. 'And at the same time we're getting smaller within it.' That was what he wanted to explore. The main character would be a British astronaut who never actually left the ground. It was called *Look to the Stars*.

We had a lovely weekend and I was very sad to leave him and go back on the train to Ipswich. There's not much I can say about the next couple of years because I hardly saw him at all, although we talked on the telephone. He loved the course. He wasn't too sure about some of the other students. I'll be honest and say that there was a prickly side to Alan, which I hadn't noticed before, but which seemed to be growing. Maybe it was because he was working so hard. He clashed with one or two of the tutors who criticised his work. The funny thing is that he had gone to UEA for guidance, but now that he was there he had come to believe he didn't need it. 'I'll show them, Claire,' he used to say to me. I heard it all the time. 'I'll show them.'

Well, *Look to the Stars* never got published and I'm not sure what became of it. In the end, it was over a hundred thousand words long. Alan showed me the first two chapters and I'm glad he didn't ask me to read the rest because I didn't like them very much. The writing was very clever. He still had this wonderful ability to use language, to twist words and phrases the way he wanted but I'm afraid I didn't understand what he was going on about. It was like every page was shouting at me. At the same time, I knew I wasn't the audience for the book. What did I know? I liked reading James Herriot and Danielle Steel. Of course I made the right noises. I said it was very interesting and I was sure publishers would like it, but then the rejection letters started coming in and Alan was terribly disheartened. He was just so sure that the book was brilliant and you have to ask yourself, if you're a writer sitting alone in a room, how can you keep going otherwise? It must be awful having that total self-belief, only to find that you've been wrong all the time.

Anyway, that was how it was for him in the autumn of 1997. He'd sent *Look to the Stars* to about a dozen literary agents and a whole lot of publishers and nobody was showing any interest. It was even worse for him because two of the students on the course with him had actually got deals. But the thing is, he didn't give up. That wasn't in his nature. He told me he wasn't going back to advertising. He was afraid that he wouldn't continue with his real work – that was what he called it now – because he'd be too distracted and he wouldn't have the time and the next thing I knew, he'd got a job as a teacher, teaching English literature at Woodbridge School.

He was never particularly happy there and the children must have sensed it because I got the impression that he wasn't very popular either. On the other hand, he had long holidays, weekends, plenty of time to write and that was all that mattered to him. He wrote another four novels. At least, those are the ones that he mentioned to me. None of them were published and I'm not sure Alan would have been able to continue at Woodbridge if he had known that it would be eleven years before he finally got a taste of success. He once said to me that it was like being in one of those Russian prisons where they lock you up without telling you the length of your sentence.

Alan got married while he was at Woodbridge. Melissa Brooke, as she was then, taught foreign languages, French and German, and started the same term as him. I don't need to describe her to you. You've met her often enough. My first impressions were that she was young, attractive and that she was very fond of Alan. I don't know why but I'm afraid the two of us didn't get on very well. She barely even acknowledged me at Alan's funeral but I have to admit that it may have been partly my fault. I felt we were in competition, that she had taken Alan away from me. Writing this now, I can see how stupid that is but I'm trying to give you as honest an account as I can of Alan and me and that's how it was. Melissa had read all his novels. She believed in him 100 per cent. They were married at the register office in Woodbridge in June, 1998 and had their honeymoon in the south of France, in Cap Ferrat. Their son, Freddy, was born two years later.

It was Melissa who advised Alan to write the first Atticus Pünd novel. By this time, they had been married seven years. I know that's a giant leap forward but there's nothing else I can write about in this period of time. I was working for Suffolk constabulary. Alan was teaching. We weren't living far apart geographically but we had completely different lives.

Melissa had her light-bulb moment in the Woodbridge branch of W.H. Smith. Who were the bestselling authors on the shelves? They were Dan Brown, John Grisham, Michael Crichton, James Patterson, Clive Cussler. She knew Alan could write better than any of them. The problem was that he was aiming too high. Why bother writing a book which all the critics rave about but which hardly anyone reads? He could use his talents to write something quite simple, a whodunnit. If it sold, it would launch his career and later on he could try other things. What was important was to get started. That was what she said.

Alan showed me *Atticus Pünd Investigates* not long after he'd written it and I absolutely loved it. It wasn't just the cleverness of the mystery. I thought the main character of the detective was brilliant. The fact that he'd been in a concentration camp and seen so much death and here he was in England solving murders – it just seemed so right. It had only taken him three months to write the book. He had done most of it during the summer holidays. But I could tell that he was pleased with the result. The first question he asked me was if I'd guessed the ending and he was delighted when I told him I'd been completely wrong.

I don't need to add much more because you know the rest as well as me. The manuscript found its way to Cloverleaf Books and you bought it! Alan went down to your offices in London and that night we all had dinner together: Alan, Melissa and me. Melissa cooked; Freddy was asleep upstairs. It was meant to be a celebration but Alan was in a strange mood. He was apprehensive, subdued. There was something between him and Melissa, a tension that I couldn't quite understand. I think Alan was nervous. When you've been pursuing an ambition all your life, it's actually quite frightening to achieve it because where will you go next? And there was something else. Suddenly Alan saw that the world is full of first novels; that every week dozens of new books fall onto the shelves and not many of them make any impact. For every famous writer, there must be fifty who simply disappear and it was quite possible that Atticus Pünd might not just be the realisation of a dream. It might be the end of it.

Of course, that didn't happen. *Atticus Pünd Investigates* was published in September 2007. I loved seeing the first copy when it arrived with Alan's name on the front cover and his photograph on the back. Somehow it made everything feel all right, as if our whole lives had been leading to this one moment. The book got a wonderful review in the *Daily Mail*. 'Watch out Poirot. There's a smart new foreigner in town and he's stepping into your shoes.'

By Christmas, Atticus Pünd was appearing in the bestseller lists. There were more good reviews. They even talked about Atticus on the *Today* programme. When the paperback came out the following spring, it seemed that the whole country wanted to buy a copy. Cloverleaf Books asked Alan to write three more and although he never told me how much he was paid, I know it was a fantastic amount.

He was suddenly a famous writer. His book was translated into lots of different languages and he was invited to all the literary festivals: Edinburgh, Oxford, Cheltenham, Hay-on-Wye, Harrogate. When the second book came out, he did a signing in Woodbridge and the queue stretched all the way round the corner. He left Woodbridge School (although Melissa continued working there) and bought a house in Orford, looking out over the river. It was just at this time that Greg, my husband, died and Alan suggested I move closer to him. He helped me buy the house in Daphne Road that you visited.

The books kept on selling. The money was pouring in. Alan asked me to help him with the third book, *Atticus Pünd Takes the Case*. He'd always been a terrible typist. He always did his first drafts in pen and ink and he asked me to type up the first draft on the computer. Then he would make his revisions by hand and I would type them up again before he sent the manuscript to his publisher. He also asked me to help him with the research. I introduced him to one of the detectives in Ipswich and dug out information about poisons and things like that. I actually worked on four of the books. I loved being involved and I was sorry when that came to an end. It was completely my fault.

Alan changed as a result of his success. It was as if he was overwhelmed by it. If he wasn't writing the books, he was travelling all over the world promoting them. I used to read about him in the newspapers. Sometimes I would hear him on Radio 4. But at this stage, I was seeing him less and less. And then, in 2009, just a few weeks after *Night Comes Calling* was published, Alan shocked me by telling me that he was leaving Melissa and I couldn't believe it when I read that he had moved in with a young man.

It's very difficult to explain how I felt because there was such a whirl of emotions in my head and so much that I didn't know. Living in Orford, I saw Melissa all the time but I had absolutely no idea that the marriage wasn't working. They always seemed so comfortable together. It all happened very quickly. No sooner had Alan told me the news than Melissa and Freddy had moved out and their home was on the market. There were no lawyers involved in the divorce. They agreed to split everything fifty-fifty.

Speaking personally, I found it quite hard to come to terms with this new side of him. I've never had a problem with homosexual men. There was a man I worked with who was openly gay and I got on with him perfectly well. But this was my brother, someone I had been close to all my life, and suddenly I was being asked to look at him in a completely different light. Well, you might say, he had changed in many ways. He was fifty now, a rich and successful author. He was more reclusive, harder-edged, the father of a child, a public figure. And he was gay. Why should this last fact have any special significance? Well, part of the answer was that his partner was so very young. I had nothing against James Taylor. In fact I liked him. I never thought of him as a gold-digger or anything like that although I will admit that I was horrified when Alan mentioned that he had once worked as a rent boy. I was just uneasy seeing the two of them together, sometimes holding hands or whatever. I never said anything. These days, you're not allowed to, are you? I just felt uncomfortable. That's all.

That wasn't the reason we fell out, though. I was doing an awful lot of work for Alan. Somehow it hadn't ended with the books. I was helping him with his fan mail. Some weeks he was getting more than a dozen letters and although he had a standard reply, someone still had to do the administration. I worked on some of his tax returns, in particular the double tax forms that had to be filled in so he didn't pay tax twice. He often sent me out to get stationery or new printer cartridges for him. I looked after Freddy. In short I was working as a secretary, an office manager, an accountant and a nanny as well as holding down a full-time job in Ipswich. I didn't mind doing any of this but one day I suggested he ought to put me on his payroll, partly as a joke. Alan was furious. It was the only time he was ever really angry with me. He reminded me that he had helped me buy my house (although he had made it clear at the time that it was a loan rather than a gift). He said he thought I had been glad to help and that if it was such a chore he would never have asked in the first place. I backed down as fast as I could but the damage had been done. Alan didn't ask me to do anything for him again and a short time later he moved out of Orford altogether when he bought Abbey Grange.

He never told me he was ill. You have no idea how much that upsets me. But I will finish where I began. Alan was a fighter all his life. Sometimes this could make him seem difficult and aggressive but I don't think he was either of those things. He simply knew what he wanted and he never allowed anything to get in his way. Above all, he was a writer. His writing meant everything to him. Do you really believe he would finish a novel and kill himself before he saw it published? It's unthinkable! It's just not the Alan Conway I knew.

St Michael's

It seemed to me that Claire had arrived at her conclusion for all the wrong reasons. She was right to believe Alan had not committed suicide. But the way she had got there was confused. '*I know he would have called me before he did anything foolish.*' That's where she begins. That's her main justification. By the end, though, she's trying another tack. '*Do you really believe he would finish a novel and kill himself before he saw it published?*' They're two quite different arguments and we can deal with them separately.

Alan was never one to forget a grudge. The two of them fell out badly when Claire asked to be paid for the work she was doing and despite what she thought, I don't believe they were ever really that close again. For example, although he told her that he was leaving Melissa it's clear that she knew nothing about his relationship with James Taylor: he left her to read about that in the newspapers. It may be that when Alan came out as a gay man, he had left his old life behind him like a discarded suit and sadly that included Claire. If he wasn't prepared to share his sexuality with her, why should he have shared his suicide?

She also makes the mistake of thinking that the leap from the tower was something he had planned. '*He would never have left me on my own, not without warning me first.*' But that's not necessarily the case. He could have just woken up and decided to do it. He might have completely forgotten that he had a book coming out. He would have been dead before it was published anyway. What did it matter to him?

Her account was interesting in other ways. I hadn't realised, even now, how much of his private life Alan had woven into *Magpie Murders*. Did he know, before he was diagnosed, that this would be his final novel? 'We were pirates, treasure hunters, soldiers, spies,' Robert Blakiston tells Atticus Pünd but he's also talking about Alan's childhood. Alan liked codes – Robert rapped out codes on his bedroom wall. And then there are the anagrams and the acrostics. Robeson becomes Osborne. Clarissa Pye solves an anagram in the *Daily Telegraph* crossword. Could Alan have hidden some sort of secret message inside his book, something that he knew about someone? What message could it be? For that matter, if he knew something horrible enough to get himself killed, why play around? Why not just come straight out with it?

Or could it be that the message was actually concealed in the final chapters? Had someone stolen them for that reason, killing Alan at the same time? That made some sort of sense, although it would beg the question of who, if anyone, had read them.

There were still a couple of hours until dinner and I decided to walk up to the Castle Inn. I needed to clear my head. It was already getting dark and Framlingham had a forlorn quality, the shops closed, the streets empty. As I passed the church, I saw a movement, a shadowy figure moving between the tombstones. It was the vicar. I watched him disappear into the church, the door booming shut behind him, and on an impulse I decided to follow. My steps took me past Alan's grave and it was horrible to think of him lying beneath that freshly dug earth. I had thought him cold and silent when I had met him. He was eternally so in death.

I hurried forward and entered the church. The interior was huge, cluttered, draughty, a collage of different centuries. It was probably unhappy to have arrived at this one: the twelfth century had provided the arches, the sixteenth the lovely wooden ceiling, the eighteenth the altar – and what had the twenty-first bestowed upon St Michael? Atheism and indifference. Robeson was at the back of the pews, quite close to the door. He was on his knees and for a brief moment I assumed he was praying. Then I saw that he was attending to an old radiator, bleeding it. He turned a key and there was a hiss of stale air followed by a rattle as the pipes began to fill. He turned as I approached and half-remembered me, getting unsteadily to his feet. 'Good evening, Mrs . . . ?'

'Susan Ryeland,' I reminded him. 'Miss. I was the one who asked you about Alan.'

'A lot of people have been asking me about Alan today.'

'I asked if he bullied you.'

He remembered that and looked away. 'I think I told you what you wanted to know.'

'Were you aware that he had put you in his latest book?'

That surprised him. He ran a hand over the slab that was his chin. 'What do you mean?'

'There's a vicar in it who looks like you. He even has a similar name.'

'Does he mention the church?'

'St Michael's? No.'

'Well, that's all right then.' I waited for him to continue. 'It would be quite typical of Alan to say something unpleasant about me. He had that sort of sense of humour – if you can call it that.'

'You didn't like him very much.'

'Why are you asking me these questions, Miss Ryeland? What exactly is your interest?'

'Didn't I tell you? I was his editor at Cloverleaf Books.'

'I see. I'm afraid I never read any of his novels. I've never been very interested in whodunnits and mysteries. I prefer non-fiction.'

'When did you meet Alan Conway?'

He didn't want to answer but he could see I wasn't going to stop. 'Actually, we were at school together.'

'You were at Chorley Hall?'

'Yes. I came to Framlingham a few years ago and I was quite surprised to see him in my congregation – not that he came to church very often. The two of us were exactly the same age.'

'And?' There was a silence. 'You said he had a dominant personality. Did he bully you?'

Osborne sighed. 'I'm not sure it's quite appropriate to be discussing these things, today of all days. But if you must know, the circumstances were quite unusual in that his father was the headmaster at the school. That gave him a certain power. He could say things . . . do things . . . and he knew that none of us would dare to say a word against him.'

'What sort of things?'

'Well, I suppose you could say that they were practical jokes. I'm sure that's how he viewed them. But they could also be quite hurtful and malicious. In my case, certainly, he caused me a certain amount of upset although it's all water under the bridge now. It was a very long time ago.'

'What did he do?' Robeson was still reluctant, so I pressed him. 'It is very important, Mr Robeson. I believe Alan's death wasn't quite as straightforward as it seems and anything you can tell me about him, in confidence, would be very helpful.'

'It was a prank, Miss Ryeland. Nothing more.' He waited for me to go away and when I didn't, he added: 'He took photographs . . .'

'Photographs?'

'They were horrible photographs!'

It wasn't the vicar who had spoken. The words had come from nowhere. That's the thing about church acoustics. They lend themselves to surprise appearances. I looked round and there was the ginger-haired woman I had seen at the hotel, presumably his wife, striding towards us, her shoes rapping out a determined rhythm on the stone floor. She stopped next to him, gazing at me with undisguised hostility. 'Tom really doesn't want to talk about it,' she said. 'I don't understand why you're bothering him. We buried Alan Conway today and as far as I'm concerned, that's an end to it. We're not going to engage in any further tittle-tattle. Did you fix the radiators?' She had asked this last question in exactly the same tone, without stopping for breath.

'Yes, dear.'

'Then let's go home.'

She put her arm in his and although her head barely came up to his shoulder, it was she who propelled him out of the church. The door banged shut behind them and I was left wondering exactly what the photographs had shown and, at the same time, whether it had been photographs that Mary Blakiston had found on the kitchen table in the vicarage at Saxby-on-Avon and if, perhaps, they had been responsible for her death.

Dinner at the Crown

I didn't mean to get drunk with James Taylor and I still can't remember how it happened. It's true that he was quite distracted when he arrived and promptly ordered a bottle of the most expensive champagne on the menu followed by a good wine and several whiskies but I'd intended to leave the drinking to him. I'm not sure how much I learned in the next two hours. I was certainly no closer to learning *who* might have killed Alan Conway, or why, and when I woke up the following morning, I was fairly close to death myself.

'God, I hate this fucking place.' Those were his opening words as he slumped down at the table. He had changed into the same black leather jacket he had been wearing when I first met him and a white T-shirt. Very James Dean. 'I'm sorry, Susan,' he went on. 'But I couldn't wait for the funeral to end. That vicar didn't have anything good to say about Alan. And that voice of his! I mean, gravelly is one thing but he could have been digging the grave himself. I didn't even want to be there but Mr Khan insisted and he's been helping me so I felt I owed him. Of course, everyone knows by now.' I looked at him, questioning. 'The money! I get the house, the land, the cash, the book rights, the lot! Well, he left quite a bit to Freddy – that's his son – and he looked after his sister too. There's a bequest to the church. Robeson made him pay that in return for the plot. One or two other things. But I've got more money than I've ever had in my life. Dinner's on me, by the way – or on Alan. Did you find the missing pages of the manuscript?'

I told him that I hadn't.

'That's a shame. I've been rummaging around for you but no luck. It's funny to think that you'll be dealing with me from now on, about the books, I mean. I've already had someone called Mark Redmond on the phone about *The Atticus Adventures*. He's welcome to them as long as I don't have to watch the bloody thing.' He glanced at the menu, made an instant decision and slid it aside. 'They all hate me, you know. Of course, they have to pretend. Everyone's too nervous to come out with it but you can still see the way most of them were looking at me. I'm Alan's bum boy and now I've got the lot. That's what they were thinking.'

The champagne arrived and he waited while the waitress poured two glasses. I couldn't help smiling. He had just become a millionaire and he was complaining about it but he was doing it in a light-hearted, even a humorous way. It was a deliberate self-parody.

He drained his glass in one go. 'I'm putting Abbey Grange on the market first thing tomorrow,' he said. 'They'll probably hold that against me too but I can't wait to go. Mr Khan says it could be worth a couple of million pounds and I've already had interest from John White. Did I mention him to you? He's the hedge fund guy next door. Super-rich. He and Alan had this huge argument a short while ago. Something to do with investments. After that, the two of them weren't even speaking. It's funny, isn't it? You buy a house in the middle of the countryside with about fifty acres and the one person you don't get on with is your neighbour. Anyway, he might buy me out – to get the extra land.'

'Where will you go?' I asked.

'I'll buy a place in London. It's what I always wanted. I'm going to try and kick-start my career. I want to get back into acting. If they make *The Atticus Adventures*, they might even offer me a part. That would be a turn-up for the books, wouldn't it? They could cast me as James Fraser so I'd end up playing a character based on me in the first place. Do you know why he was called Fraser, by the way?'

'No. I don't.'

'Alan named him after Hugh Fraser, the actor who played Poirot's sidekick on TV. And the flat that Atticus Pünd lived in, Tanner Court in Farringdon? That was another of Alan's jokes. There's a real place called Florin Court which they used in the Poirot filming. Do you get it? Tanner? Florin? They're both old coins.'

'How do you know?'

'He told me. And he used to do other things too. He used to hide things.'

'What do you mean?'

'Well . . . names. One of the books is set in London and all the names are actually tube stations or something like that. And there's another one where the characters are called Brooke, Waters, Forster, Wilde . . .'

'They're all writers.'

'They're all *gay* writers. It was a game he played to stop himself getting bored.'

We drank more champagne and ordered fish and chips. The restaurant was on the far side of the hotel, tucked around the corner from where the funeral drinks had taken place. There were a couple of families eating but we'd been given a corner table. The lighting was low. I asked James about the way Alan Conway had worked. He had hidden almost as much as he had revealed in his writing and there was an odd disconnect between the bestselling author and the books he had actually produced. Why all these games, these codes and secret references? Wasn't it enough simply to tell the story?

'He never talked to me about it,' James said. 'He worked incredibly hard, sometimes seven or eight hours a day. There was a notebook he filled up with clues and red herrings – all that stuff. Who was where and when, what they were doing. He said it gave him a headache, sorting everything out and if I came into the room and disturbed him, he would really yell at me. There were times when he talked about Atticus Pünd as if he was a real person and I got the idea that they weren't the best of friends – if that doesn't sound a little bit weird. "Atticus is destroying me! I'm fed up with him. Why do I have to write another book about him?" He said that sort of thing all the time.'

'Is that why he decided to kill him?'

'I don't know. Does he die in the last book? I never saw any of it.'

'He gets ill. He may die at the end.'

'Alan always said there would be nine books. He'd decided that from the very start. There was something about that number that was important to him.'

'What happened to the notebook?' I asked. 'I don't suppose you've found it.'

James shook his head. 'I didn't find it. I'm sorry, but I'm pretty sure it's not there.'

So whoever had taken the last chapters of *Magpie Murders,* erasing every last word from Alan's hard drive, had also made sure that his notes had disappeared. That told me something. They knew how he worked.

We talked more about James's life with Alan. We finished the champagne and drank the bottle of wine. The other families finished and left and by nine o'clock we had the room to ourselves. I got the impression that James was lonely. Why would a man in his end-twenties want to bury himself in a place like Framlingham? The truth was that he'd had little choice. He'd been defined by his relationship with Alan and that, if nothing else, must have been a reason to end it. James was very relaxed as he spoke to me. The two of us had become friends; maybe because of that first cigarette, maybe because of the strange circumstances that had brought us together. He told me about his early life.

'I was brought up in Ventnor,' he said. 'On the Isle of Wight. I hated it there. At first, I thought it was because it was an island, because I was surrounded by the sea. But actually it was because of who I was. My mum and dad were Jehovah's Witnesses, which I know sounds crazy but it's the truth. Mum used to go round the island, distributing copies of *The Watchtower*, door to door.' He paused. 'Do you know what her biggest tragedy was? She ran out of doors.'

The problem for James was not so much the religion or even the patriarchal structure of his family life (he had two older brothers). It was that homosexuality was considered a sin.

'I knew what I was when I was ten years old and I lived in

terror until I was fifteen,' he said. 'The worst of it was not having anyone I could tell. I'd never been close to my brothers – I think they knew I was different – and living on the Isle of Wight I felt like I was growing up in the fifties. The place isn't so bad now – at least, that's what I hear. There are gay bars in Newport and gay cruising areas all over the place, but when I was a kid and with the elders coming to the house and all the rest of it, I felt completely alone. And then I met another boy at my school and we began to mess around with each other and that was when I knew I had to get out because if I stayed I would end up being caught with my pants down, quite literally, and then I'd be shunned, which is what Jehovah's Witnesses do to each other when they're pissed off. By the time I got to my GCSEs, I'd decided I wanted to become an actor. I left school at sixteen and managed to get a job at the Shanklin Theatre, working backstage, but two years later I left the island and came up to London. I think my family was quite glad to see me go. I've never been back.'

James couldn't afford drama school but got his training elsewhere. He met a man in a bar and was introduced to a producer who used him in a number of films that would not enjoy a premiere on mainstream British television. I'm the one being coy. He was frank and filthy about his career in hard-core porn and as the second bottle of wine kicked in, we both found ourselves laughing uproariously. He was also working as a rent boy – in London and Amsterdam. 'I didn't mind doing it,' he said. 'A few of my clients were pervy and disgusting but most of them were fine, middle-aged men who were absolutely terrified of being found out. I had plenty of regulars, I can tell you. I enjoyed the sex and the money and I made sure I looked after myself.' James had managed to rent a small flat in West Kensington and he worked out of there. One of his clients was a casting director and he even managed to get him a few legitimate parts.

And then he met Alan Conway.

'Alan was a typical client. He was married. He had a young son. He had found my picture and contact details on the Internet and for a long time he didn't even tell me his name. He didn't want me to know he was a famous writer because he thought I'd blackmail him or sell my story to the Sunday newspapers or something. But that's just silly. No one does that any more.' James only found out who he was when he saw Alan on breakfast TV, promoting one of his books. Actually, that rang a bell for me. When the Atticus Pünd novels had started selling, Alan had done everything he could *not* to appear on television, the exact opposite, in fact, of all our other authors. At the time, I'd assumed he was shy. But if he was leading this double life, it made complete sense.

We had finished the main course and both bottles and staggered out into the yard for a cigarette. It was a clear night and sitting under the stars, with a very pale, slither of a moon in the black sky, James became thoughtful. 'I really liked Alan, you know,' he said. 'He could be a miserable old bastard, especially when he was writing one of his books. All that money he was making from his detective stories, it never seemed to make him happy. But I did. That's not such a bad thing, is it? Whatever people may think or say, he needed me. At first he just paid me for the night. Then we went on a couple of trips. He took me to Paris and Vienna. He told Melissa he was doing research. He even got me onto a book tour in America. If anyone asked, he said I was his PA and we had separate rooms in every hotel but of course they had adjoining doors. By that time he'd put me on an allowance and I wasn't allowed to see anyone else.'

He blew out smoke, then gazed at the glowing tip of his cigarette.

'Alan liked watching me smoke,' he said. 'After we'd had sex, I'd smoke a cigarette, naked, and he'd watch me. I'm sorry I let him down.'

'How did you do that?' I asked.

'I got itchy feet. He had his books and his writing and I was getting bored, sitting in Framlingham. I was more than twenty years younger than him, you know. There was nothing here for me. So I started going back to London. I said I was visiting friends, but Alan knew what I was doing. It was obvious. We had arguments about it but I wouldn't stop and in the end he threw me out, gave me a month to pack my bags. When you and I met, I was two days away from being homeless. Part of me had hoped we might have a reconciliation, but actually I was quite glad it was all over. I wasn't interested in the money. People looked at the two of us together and they think that's all I cared about but it's not true. I cared about him.'

We went back inside and, over several whiskies, James told me about his plans for the future, forgetting that he had already done so. He was going on holiday for a while – somewhere hot. He was going to try acting again. 'I might even go to drama school. I can afford it now.' Despite what he had said about Alan, he had already started another relationship, this time with a boy closer to his age. I don't know why, but looking at him as he sat at the table with his long hair flowing and his eyes blurred by alcohol, I suddenly got the feeling that it wouldn't end well for him. It was a curious thought but perhaps he had needed Alan Conway in much the same way as James Fraser had needed Atticus Pünd. There was no other place for him in the story.

He had come by car but I wouldn't let him drive himself home, even if it was only a mile up the road. Feeling like an elderly aunt, I confiscated his keys and made the hotel call him a taxi.

'I should stay here,' he said. 'I can afford a room. I can afford the whole hotel.'

They were the last words he spoke to me before he left, weaving uncertainly into the night.

'He used to hide things...'

James was right. In *Gin & Cyanide*, which is set in London, there are characters called Leyton Jones, Victoria Wilson, Michael Latimer, Brent Andrews and Warwick Stevens. All these names are taken partly, or in their entirety, from tube stations. The two killers, Linda Cole and Matilda Orre are both anagrams: of Colindale on the Northern Line and Latimer Road. The gay writers make up the cast of *Red Roses for Atticus*. In *Atticus Pünd Takes the Case*, well – you can work it out for yourself.

John Waterman
Parker Bowles Advertising
Caroline Fisher
Carla Visconti
Professor Otto Schneider
Elizabeth Faber

I woke up the next morning just after seven o'clock with a headache and a nasty taste in my mouth. Bizarrely, James's car keys were still clutched in my hand and for a ghastly moment I half expected to open my eyes and find him lying next to me. I went into the bathroom and had a long, hot shower. Then I dressed and went downstairs to black coffee and grapefruit juice. I had the manuscript of *Magpie Murders* with me and, despite my state, it didn't take me long to find what I was looking for.

All the characters are named after birds.

When I'd read the book for the first time, I'd made a note to tackle Alan about Sir Magnus Pye and Pye Hall. The names had struck me as a little childish – old-fashioned at the very least. They felt like something out of *Tintin*. Going through it again, I realised that almost everyone, even the most minor characters, had been given the same treatment. There are the obvious ones – the vicar is Robin and his wife is Hen. Whitehead (antique dealer), Redwing (doctor) and Weaver (undertaker) are all fairly common species, as are Crane and Lanner (the estate agents in Bath) and Kite (the landlord of the Ferryman). Some are a little more difficult to pin down. Joy Sanderling is named after a small wading bird and Jack Dartford after a warbler. Brent, the groundsman, is a type of goose – and his middle name is Jay. A nineteenth-century naturalist called Thomas Blakiston had an owl named after him and inspires the family at the heart of the story. And so on.

Does it matter? Well, yes, actually. It worried me.

Character names are important. I've known writers who've used their friends while others have turned to reference books: the *Oxford Book of Quotations* and the *Cambridge Biographical Encyclopedia* are two I've heard mentioned. What's the secret of a good name in fiction? Simplicity is often the key. James Bond didn't get to be who he was by having too many syllables. That said, the name is often the first thing you learn about a character and I think it helps if it fits comfortably, if it feels appropriate. Rebus and Morse are both very good examples. Both are types of code and as the role of the detective is effectively to decode the clues and the information, you're already halfway there. Nineteenth-century authors like Charles Dickens took the idea a stage further. Who would want to be taught by Wackford Squeers, cared for by Mr Bumble or married to Jerry Cruncher? But these are comic grotesques. He was more circumspect when it came to the heroes and heroines with whom he wanted you to connect.

Sometimes authors stumble onto iconic names almost by accident. The most famous example is Sherrinford Holmes and Ormond Sacker. You have to wonder if they would have achieved the same worldwide success if Conan Doyle hadn't had second thoughts and plumped for Sherlock Holmes and Dr John Watson. I've actually seen the manuscript where the change is made: one sweep of the pen and literary history was made. By the same token, would Pansy O'Hara have set the world on fire in quite the same way as Scarlett did after Margaret Mitchell changed her mind when she finished *Gone With the Wind*? Names have a way of stamping themselves on our consciousness. Peter Pan, Luke Skywalker, Jack Reacher, Fagin, Shylock, Moriarty... can we imagine them as anything else?

The point of all this is that the name and the character are intertwined. They inform each other. But it's not the case in *Magpie Murders* – or in any other of the books that Alan Conway wrote and which I edited. By turning all his subsidiary characters into birds or tube stations (or makes of fountain pen in *Atticus Pünd Takes the Case*), he had trivialised them and that in turn had demeaned them. Maybe I'm overstating this. After all, his detective stories were never meant to be more than entertainments. It just suggested a sort of carelessness, almost a disdain towards his own work and it depressed me. I was also sorry that I hadn't noticed it before.

After breakfast, I packed, paid for the room, then drove over to Abbey Grange to drop off James Taylor's keys. It was strange seeing the house for what I was fairly sure would be the last time. Maybe it was the grey, Suffolk sky but it seemed to have a mournful quality as if it had somehow sensed not only the death of its old owner but the fact that it was no longer wanted by his successor. I could barely bring myself to look at the tower which now seemed grim and threatening. It occurred to me that if ever a building was destined to be haunted, it was this one. Some day, not far in the future, a new owner would be woken in the middle of the night, first by a cry in the wind and then the soft thud of something hitting the turf. James was absolutely right to leave.

I thought of ringing the doorbell but decided against it. Most likely, James was still in bed and anyway, fuelled by alcohol, he might have been more open with me than he had intended. Better to avoid the morning-after recriminations.

I had an appointment in Ipswich. Claire Jenkins had been true to her word and had arranged for me to meet Detective Superintendent Locke, not at the police station but at a Starbucks near the cinema. I'd received a text with instructions. Eleven o'clock. He could give me fifteen minutes. I had plenty of time to get over there but first I wanted to visit the house next door to Alan's. I had seen John White, in his orange wellington boots, at the funeral but we hadn't yet had a chance to talk. James had mentioned that Alan had fallen out with him and he had turned up as a character in *Magpie Murders*. I wanted to know more. This being a Sunday, there was every chance that I would find him at home so I dropped James's keys through the letter box, then drove round.

Despite the name, there was no sign of any apple trees at Apple Farm and nor for that matter did it look anything like a farm. It was a handsome building, much more conventional than Abbey Grange, built, I would have said, in the forties. It was all very presentable with a neat gravel driveway, perfect hedges and extensive lawns cut into green stripes. There was an open garage opposite the front door with a quite fabulous car parked outside: a two-seater Ferrari 458 Italia. I wouldn't have said no to tearing around a few Suffolk lanes in that – but it wouldn't have left me much change out of £200,000. It certainly made my own MGB look a little sad.

I rang the front door. I guessed the house must have at least eight bedrooms and that, given its size, I might wait quite a time before anyone reached me but in fact the door opened almost at once and I found myself facing an unfriendly-looking woman with black hair parted in the middle, dressed in quite masculine clothes: sports jacket, tight-fitting trousers, ankle-length boots. Was she his wife? She hadn't been at the funeral. Somehow, I doubted it.

'I wonder if I could speak to Mr White?' I said. 'Are you Mrs White?'

'No. I'm Mr White's housekeeper. Who are you?'

'I'm a friend of Alan Conway. Actually, I was his editor. I need to ask Mr White about what happened. It's quite important.'

I think she was about to tell me to get lost but at that moment a man appeared behind her, in the hallway. 'Who is it, Elizabeth?' a voice asked.

'It's someone asking about Alan Conway.'

'My name is Susan Ryeland.' I was addressing him over her

shoulder. 'It'll only take five minutes but I really would appreciate it.'

I sounded so reasonable that it would have been difficult for White to refuse me. 'You'd better come in,' he said.

The housekeeper stepped aside and I went past her into the hall. John White was standing in front of me. I recognised him instantly from the funeral. He was quite small, very slim and rather nondescript in appearance with close-shaven, dark hair that was reflected by the permanent stubble on his chin. He was wearing an office shirt and a V-neck pullover. I found it hard to imagine him behind the wheel of the Ferrari. There was nothing aggressive about him at all.

'Can I get you some coffee?' he asked.

'Thank you. That would be nice.'

He nodded at the housekeeper who had been expecting this and went off to get it. 'Come into the sitting room,' he said.

We went into a large room that looked over the back gardens. There was modern furniture and expensive art on the walls including one of those neons by Tracey Emin. I noticed a photograph of two attractive-looking girls, twins. His daughters? I could tell at once that, apart from the housekeeper, he was alone in the house. So either his family was away or he was divorced. I suspected the latter.

'What do you want to know about Alan?' he asked.

It all seemed so very casual, but I'd been on Google that morning and knew that this was a man who had run not one but two of the most successful hedge funds for a big city firm. He had made a name for himself and a fortune for everyone else by predicting the credit crunch and had retired at the age of forty-five with more money than I would ever dream about, if I had those sorts of dreams. He still worked, though. He invested millions and made millions more – from clocks, car parks, property, whatever. He was the sort of man I could easily dislike – in fact, the Ferrari made it easier – but I didn't. I don't know why not. Maybe it was those orange Hunters. 'I saw you at the funeral.'

'Yes. I thought I ought to pop along. I didn't stay for the drinks though.'

'Were you and Alan close?'

'We were neighbours, if that's what you mean. We saw quite a bit of each other. I read a couple of his books but I didn't much like them. I don't get a lot of time to read and his stuff wasn't my sort of thing.'

'Mr White . . .' I hesitated. This wasn't going to be easy.

'Call me John.'

'. . . I understand that you and Alan had a disagreement, shortly before he died.'

'That's right.' He was unfazed by the question. 'Why are you asking?'

'I'm trying to work out how he died.'

John White had soft, hazel eyes but when I said that I thought I saw something spark in them, a sense of some inner machinery clicking into gear. 'He committed suicide,' he said.

'Yes. Of course. But I'm trying to understand his state of mind when he did it.'

'I hope you're not suggesting—'

I was suggesting all sorts of things but I backtracked as gracefully as I could. 'Not at all. As I explained to your housekeeper, I worked for his publishers and, as it happens, he left us one last book.'

'Am I in it?'

He was. Alan had turned him into Johnny Whitehead, the crooked antique dealer who had been sent to prison in London. That was the final finger raised to his erstwhile friend. 'No,' I lied.

'I'm glad to hear it.'

The housekeeper came in with a tray of coffee and White relaxed. I noticed that after she had poured two cups and offered cream and home-made biscuits, she made no effort to leave and he was happy to have her there. 'Here's what happened, since you want to know,' he said. 'Alan and I had known each other from the day he moved in and, like I say, we got along on fine. But it went wrong about three months ago. We did a bit of business together. I want to make it quite clear to you, Susan, that I didn't twist his arm or anything like that. He liked the sound of it and he wanted to come along for the ride.'

'What was it?' I asked.

'I don't suppose you know much about my sort of work. I've

been dealing a lot with NAMA. It stands for the National Asset Management Agency and it was set up by the Irish government after the crash of '98, basically selling off businesses that had gone bust. There was an office development in Dublin that had caught my eye. It would cost twelve million to buy and it needed another four or five spent but I thought I could turn it around and when I mentioned this to Alan, he asked if he could join the SPV.'

'SPV?'

'Special Purpose Vehicle.' If my complete ignorance annoyed him, he didn't let it show. 'It's just a cost-effective way to bring six or seven people together to make this sort of investment. Anyway, I'll cut a long story short. The whole thing went belly-up. We were buying the development from a man called Jack Dartford and he turned out to be a complete rogue – a liar, a fraud – you name it. I'll tell you, Susan, you couldn't meet a more charming man. He's sat where you're sitting now and he'd have the whole room in stitches. But it turned out he didn't even own the property and the next thing I know is he's gone west with four million quid of our cash. I'm still looking for him now but I don't think he's going to be found.'

'Alan blamed you?'

White smiled. 'You could say that. Actually, he was bloody furious. Look. We'd all lost the same and I warned him, going in, you can never be 100 per cent certain in these things. But he got it into his head that I'd somehow ripped him off which was well out of order. He wanted to sue me. He threatened me! I couldn't make him see sense.'

'When was the last time you saw him?'

He had been about to take a biscuit. I saw his hand hesitate and at the same time he glanced in the direction of the housekeeper. He might have learned how to keep a poker face when he was at business school but she hadn't been to the same class and I saw her nervousness, naked and obvious. It signalled the lie that was to come. 'I hadn't seen him for a few weeks,' he said.

'Were you here on the Sunday when he died?'

'I suppose so. But he didn't contact me. If you want the truth, we were only talking through solicitors. And I wouldn't like you to think that his dealings with me were in any way connected with what happened – his death, I mean. Sure, he lost some money. We all did. But it wasn't anything he couldn't afford. He wasn't going to have to sell up or anything like that. If he couldn't afford it, I wouldn't have let him in.'

I left soon after that. I noticed that Elizabeth, the housekeeper hadn't offered me a second cup of coffee. They waited on the doorstep as I climbed into my MBG and they were still standing there together, watching, as I drove back down the drive.

Starbucks, Ipswich

There's a well-marked one-way system that takes you round the edge of Ipswich, which suits me because it's one city I've never much enjoyed entering. There are too many shops and too little else. People who live there probably like it but I have bad memories. I used to take Jack and Daisy, my nephew and niece, to the Crown Pools and I swear to God I can still smell the chlorine. I could never find a space in the bloody car parks. I'd have to queue up for ages just to get in and out. More recently, they'd opened one of those American-style complexes just opposite the station, with about a dozen fast-food restaurants and a multiplex cinema. It seems to me that it kills the city, separating the entertainment like that – but it was here that I met Richard Locke for the fifteen minutes he'd been kind enough to give me.

I arrived first. At twenty past eleven, I had more or less decided that he wasn't going to come but then the door opened and he strode in, looking pissed off. I raised a hand, recognising him at once. He was indeed the man I'd seen with Claire at the funeral but he had no reason to know me. He was wearing a suit but without a tie. This was his day off. He came over and sat down heavily, all that well-toned flesh and muscle hammering into the plastic chair, and my first thought was this wasn't someone I'd want to arrest me. I felt uncomfortable even offering him a coffee. He asked for tea and I went over and got it for him. I bought him a flapjack too.

'I understand you're interested in Alan Conway,' he said.

'I was his editor.'

'And Claire Jenkins was his sister.' He paused. 'She has this idea that he was killed. Is that what you think?'

There was grim, no-nonsense tone to his voice that was actually on the edge of anger. It was in his eyes, too. They were fixed on me as if he was the one who had ordered this interrogation. I wasn't quite sure how to reply. I wasn't even sure what to call him. Richard was probably too informal. Mr Locke was wrong. Detective Superintendent felt too TV but that was the one I plumped for. 'Did you see the body?' I asked.

'No. I saw the report.' Almost grudgingly, he broke off a piece of his flapjack but he didn't eat it. 'Two officers from Leiston were called to the scene. I only got involved because I happened to know Mr Conway. Also, he was famous and there was obviously going to be interest from the press.'

'Claire had introduced you to him?'

'I think it was the other way round, actually, Ms Ryeland. He needed help with his books and so she introduced him to me. But you didn't answer my question. Do you think he was murdered?'

'I think it's possible. Yes.' He was going to interrupt me so I went on quickly. I told him about the missing chapter which had first brought me to Suffolk. I mentioned Alan's diary, the number of appointments he had made for the week after he died. I didn't talk about the people I'd spoken to – it didn't seem fair to drag them in. But for the first time I explained my feeling about the suicide letter, how it didn't quite add up. 'It's only on page three that he talks about dying,' I explained. 'But he was dying anyway. He had cancer. The letter doesn't actually say anywhere that he's about to kill himself.'

'You don't think it's a bit odd then that he sent it to his publisher one day before he threw himself off that tower?'

'Perhaps he wasn't the one who sent it. Perhaps someone read the letter and realised that it could be misinterpreted. They pushed Alan off the tower and then sent the letter themselves. They knew we'd leap to the wrong conclusion precisely because of the timing.'

'I don't think I've leapt to any wrong conclusions, Ms Ryeland.'

He was not looking at me sympathetically and although I was

a little annoyed, the strange thing is that, right then, he was not wrong to doubt me. There was something about the letter which I, of all people, should have noticed but which I hadn't. I called myself an editor but I was blind to the truth even when it was right there in front of my eyes.

'There were a lot of people who didn't like Alan—' I began.

'There are a lot of people who don't like a lot of people but they don't go around the place murdering them.' He had come here with the intention of telling me this and now that he had started, he wasn't going to stop. 'What people like you don't seem to understand is that you've got more chance of winning the lottery than you have of being murdered. Do you know what the murder rate was last year? Five hundred and ninety-eight people – that's out of a population of around sixty million! In fact, I'll tell you something that may amuse you. There are some parts of the country where the police actually solve more crimes than are committed. You know why that is? The murder rate's falling so fast, they've got time to look into the cold cases that were committed years ago.

'I don't understand it. All these murders on TV – you'd think people would have better things to do with their time. Every night. Every bloody channel. People have some sort of fixation. And what really annoys me is that it's nothing like the truth. I've seen murder victims. I've investigated murder. I was here when Steve Wright was killing prostitutes. The Ipswich Ripper – that's what they called him. People don't plan these things. They don't sneak into their victims' houses and throw them off the roof and then send out letters hoping they're going to be misinterpreted, as you put it. They don't put on wigs and dress up like they do in Agatha Christie. All the murders I've ever been involved in have happened because the perpetrators were mad or angry or drunk. Sometime all three. And they're horrible. Disgusting. It's not like some actor lying on his back with a little red paint on his throat. When you see someone who's had a knife in them, it makes you sick. Literally sick.

'Do you know why people kill each other? They do it because they're out of their heads. There are only three motives. Sex, anger and money. You kill someone in the street. You stick a knife in them and you take their money. You have an argument with them and you smash a bottle and rip open their throat. Or you kill them because you get off on it. All the murderers I've met have been thick as shit. Not clever people. Not posh or upper class. Thick as shit. And you know how we catch them? We don't ask them clever questions and work out that they don't have an alibi, that they weren't actually where they were meant to be. We catch them on CCTV. Half the time, they leave their DNA all over the crime scene. Or they confess. Maybe one day you should publish the truth although I'm telling you, nobody would want to read it.

'I'll tell you what really annoyed me about Alan Conway. I helped him – not that he ever gave me anything by way of a thank you. But that's another story. No. First of all, he wasn't interested in the truth. Why are all the detectives in his books so fucking stupid? You know he even based one on me? Raymond Chubb. That's me. Oh, he's not black. He wouldn't have dared go that far. But Chubb – you know who they are? They manufacture locks. Get it? And all that stuff he wrote about the wife in *No Rest for the Wicked*. That was my wife he was writing about. I'd been stupid enough to tell him and he went ahead and put it in his book without ever asking me.'

So this was the source of his anger. From the way Locke was talking, I knew he wasn't interested in me and he wasn't going to help. I might almost have added him to my list of suspects.

'The public have no idea what the police are really doing in this country and it's thanks to people like Alan Conway and people like you,' he concluded. 'And I hope you don't mind my saying this, Ms Ryeland, but I find it a little bit pathetic that you're trying to make a real-life mystery out of what is actually a textbook-case suicide. He had the motive. He was ill. He wrote a letter. He'd just split up with his boyfriend. He was alone. So he makes a decision and he jumps. If you want my advice, you'll go back to London and forget it. Thanks for the tea.'

He had finished drinking and he walked out. He had left the flapjack, in pieces, on his plate.

Crouch End

Andreas was waiting for me when I got in. I could tell the moment I opened the door because of the smell coming from the kitchen. Andreas is a fantastic cook. He cooks in a very masculine way, rattling pans, throwing in the ingredients without measuring them, everything high speed on roaring flames with a glass of red wine in hand. I've never seen him consult a cookery book. The table was laid for two with candles and flowers that looked like they'd come from a garden, not a shop. He grinned when he saw me and gave me a hug.

'I thought you weren't coming,' he said.

'What's for dinner?'

'Roast lamb.'

'Can you give me five minutes?'

'I can give you fifteen.'

I showered and changed into a loose-fitting jumper and leggings, the sort of clothes that assured me I wouldn't be going out again tonight. I came to the table with damp hair and picked up the giant glass of wine that Andreas had poured for me.

'Cheers.'

'Yamas.'

English and the Greek. That was another of our traditions.

We sat down and ate and I told Andreas everything that had happened in Framlingham: the funeral, all the rest of it. I knew at once that he wasn't very interested. He listened politely but that wasn't what I'd hoped for. I wanted him to question me, to challenge my assumptions. I thought we might work it out like some sort of north London Tommy and Tuppence (Agatha Christie's slightly less successful detective duo). But he didn't really care who had killed Alan. I remembered that he hadn't wanted me to investigate in the first place and I wondered if I had annoyed him – the Greek side of him – going ahead anyway.

In fact, his mind was on other things. 'I've given in my notice,' he suddenly announced as he served up.

'At the school? Already?' I was surprised.

'Yes. I'm leaving at the end of term.' He glanced at me. 'I told you what I was going to do.'

'You said you were thinking about it.'

'Yannis has been pushing me to make a decision. The hotel owners won't wait much longer and the money is in place. We managed to get a loan from the bank and there may be various grants available from the EU. It's all happening, Susan. Polydorus will be open next summer.'

'Polydorus? Is that what it's called?'

'Yes.'

'It's a pretty name.'

I have to admit, I was a little thrown. Andreas had more or less asked me to marry him but I'd assumed he would give me a little time to make up my mind. Now it seemed he was offering me a done deal. Just bring out the air ticket and the apron and we could be on our way. He had his iPad with him and slid it round on the table while we ate, showing me pictures. Polydorus did look a lovely place. There was a long verandah with crazy paving and a straw pergola, brightly coloured wooden tables and a dazzling sea beyond. The building itself was whitewashed with blue shutters and I could just make out a bar with an old-fashioned coffee machine, tucked away inside, in the shade. The bedrooms were basic but they looked clean and welcoming. I could easily imagine the sort of people who would want to stay there: visitors rather than tourists.

'What do you think?' he asked.

'It looks lovely.'

'I'm doing this for both of us, Susan.'

'But what happens to "both of us" if I don't want to come?' I closed the cover of the iPad. I didn't want to look at it any more. 'Couldn't you have waited a little longer before you went ahead?'

'I had to make up my mind – about the hotel – and that's what I've done. I don't want to be a teacher all my life and anyway, you and me... is this the best we can do?' He laid down his knife and fork. I noticed how neatly he arranged them on each side of his plate. 'We don't see each other all the time,' he went on. 'There are weeks when we don't see each other at all. You made it clear you didn't want me to move in with you—'

I bridled at that. 'That isn't true. You're welcome here but most of the time you're at school. I thought you preferred it this way.'

'All I'm saying is that we could be together more. We could make this work. I know I'm asking a lot but you won't know until you try. You've never even been to Crete! Come for a few weeks in the spring. See if you like it.' I said nothing so he added: 'I'm fifty years old. If I don't make a move on this, it's never going to happen.'

'Can't Yannis manage without you?'

'I love you, Susan, and I want you to be with me. I promise you, if you're not happy, we can come back together. I've already made that mistake. I'm not going to do it twice. If it doesn't work, I can get another teaching job.'

I didn't feel like eating any more. I reached out and lit a cigarette. 'There's something I haven't told you,' I said. 'Charles has asked me to take over the company.'

His eyes widened when he heard that. 'Do you want to?'

'I have to consider it, Andreas. It's a fantastic opportunity. I can take Cloverleaf in any direction I want.'

'I thought you said Cloverleaf was finished.'

'I never said that.' He looked disappointed so I added: 'Is that what you were hoping?'

'Can I be honest, Susan? I thought, when Alan died, that it would be the end for you, yes. I thought the company would close and you would move on and that the hotel would be the answer for both of us.'

'It's not like that. It may not be easy for a couple of years but Cloverleaf isn't going to disappear overnight. I'll commission new authors—'

'You want to find another Atticus Pünd?'

He had said it with such scorn that I stopped, surprised. 'I thought you liked the books.'

He reached out and took the cigarette from me, smoked it for a moment, then handed it back. It was something we did unconsciously, even when we were angry with each other. 'I never liked the books,' he said. 'I read them because you worked on them and obviously I cared about you. But I thought they were crap.'

I was shocked. I didn't know what to say. 'They made a lot of money.'

'Cigarettes make a lot of money. Toilet paper makes a lot of money. It doesn't mean they're worth anything.'

'You can't say that!'

'Why not? Alan Conway was laughing at you, Susan. He was laughing at everyone. I know about writing. I teach Homer, for God's sake. I teach Aeschylus. He knew what those books were – and he knew when he was putting them together. They're badly written trash!'

'I don't agree. They're very well written. Millions of people enjoyed them.'

'They're worth nothing! Eighty thousand words to prove that the butler did it?'

'You're just being snobbish.'

'And you're defending something that you always knew had no value at all.'

I wasn't sure when the discussion had turned into such an acrimonious argument. The table looked so beautiful with the candles and the flowers. The food was so good. But the two of us were at each other's throats.

'If I didn't know you better, I'd say you were jealous,' I complained. 'You knew him before I did. You were both teachers. But he broke out . . .'

'You're right about one thing, Susan. I did know him before you and I didn't like him.'

'Why not?'

'I'm not going to tell you. It's all in the past and I don't want to upset you.'

'I'm already upset.'

'I'm sorry. I'm just telling you the truth. As for the money he made, you're right about that too. He didn't deserve any of it, not one penny, and all the time I've known you, I've hated the way you've had to kowtow to him. I'm telling you, Susan. He wasn't worthy of you.'

'I was his editor. That's all. I didn't like him either!' I forced myself to stop. I hated the way this was going. 'Why did you never say any of this before?'

'Because it wasn't relevant. It is now. I'm asking you to be my wife!'

'Well, you've got a funny way of going about it.'

Andreas stayed the night but there was none of the companionship we'd had on the first night he'd got back from Crete. He went straight to sleep and left very early the next morning without breakfast. The candles had burned down. I wrapped the lamb in silver foil and put it in the fridge. Then I went to work.

Cloverleaf Books

I've always been fond of Mondays. Thursdays and Fridays make me edgy but there's something that's quite comforting about coming in to the pile on my desk; the unopened letters, the proofs waiting to be read, the Post-it notes from marketing, publicity and foreign rights. I chose my office because it's at the back of the building. It's quiet and cosy, tucked into the eaves. It's the sort of room that really ought to have a coal fire and probably did once until some turn-of-the-century vandal filled in the fireplace. I used to share Jemima with Charles before she left and there's always Tess on reception, who will do anything for me. When I came in that Monday morning, she made me tea and gave me my phone messages: nothing urgent. The Women's Prize for Fiction had asked me to join their judging panel. My children's author needed comforting. There were production problems with a dust jacket (I'd said it wouldn't work).

Charles wasn't in. His daughter, Laura, had gone into labour early as expected and he was waiting at home with his wife. He'd also sent me an email that morning. *I hope you had time to think about our conversation in the car. It would be great for you and I'm confident it would be great for the company too.* Funnily enough, Andreas telephoned me just as I was reading it. Glancing at my watch I guessed he must have slipped out into the corridor, leaving the kids with their Greek primers. He was speaking in a low voice.

'I'm sorry about last night,' he said. 'It was stupid of me just to throw everything at you like that. The school have asked me to reconsider and I won't make any decision until you tell me what you want to do.'

'Thank you.'

'And I didn't mean what I said about Alan Conway either. Of course his books are worthwhile. It's just that I knew him and . . .' His voice trailed off. I could imagine him glancing up and down the corridor, like a schoolboy, afraid of getting caught.

'We can talk about it later,' I said.

'I've got a parents' meeting tonight. Why don't we have dinner tomorrow night'

'I'd like that.'

'I'll call you.' He rang off.

Quite unexpectedly, and without really wanting it, I had come to a crossroads – or more accurately, a T-junction – in my life. I could take over as CEO of Cloverleaf Books. There were writers I wanted to work with, ideas I'd had but which Charles had always vetoed. As I'd told Andreas the night before, I could develop the business the way I wanted.

Or there was Crete.

The choices were so different, the two directions so contrary, that considering the two of them side by side almost made me want to laugh. I was like the child who doesn't know if he wants to be a brain surgeon or a train driver. It was quite frustrating. Why do these things always have to happen at the same time?

I looked through my post. There was a letter addressed to Susan Ryland, which I was tempted to bin. I hate it when people misspell my name, especially when it's so easy to check. There were a couple of invitations, invoices . . . the usual stuff. And at the bottom of the pile, a brown A4 envelope which clearly contained a manuscript. That was unusual. I never read unsolicited manuscripts. Nobody does any more. But it had my name on the envelope (correctly spelled) so I tore it open and looked at the front page.

DEATH TREADS THE BOARDS

Donald Leigh

It took me a moment to remember that this was the book written by the waiter at the Ivy Club, the man who had dropped the plates when he saw Alan Conway. He claimed that Alan had stolen his ideas and used them for the fourth Atticus Pünd mystery, *Night Comes Calling*. I still didn't like his title very much and the first sentence ('There had been hundreds of murders in the Pavilion Theatre, Brighton but this was the first one that was real.') didn't quite work for me either. A nice idea, but too on-the-nose and expressed a little clumsily, I thought. But I had promised him I would read it and with Charles away and with Alan so much on my mind, I thought I'd get to it straight away. I had my tea. Why not?

I skim-read most of it. It's something I've learned to do. I can usually tell if I'm going to like a book by the end of the second or third chapter but if I'm going to talk about it in conference, I'm obliged to hang in there to the last page. It took me three hours. Then I pulled out a copy of *Night Comes Calling*.

And then I compared the two.

Extract from *Night Comes Calling* by Alan Conway

CHAPTER 26: CURTAIN CALL

It ended where it had begun, in the theatre at Fawley Park. Looking around him, James Fraser had a sense of inevitability. He had abandoned his career as an actor to become the assistant of Atticus Pünd and this was where his first case had brought him. The building was even shabbier than when he had first seen it now that the stage had been stripped and most of the seats piled up against the walls. The red velvet curtains had been pulled aside. With nothing to conceal, no play about to begin, they looked tired and threadbare, hanging limply on their wires. The stage itself was a yawning mouth, an ironic reflection of the many young spectators who had been forced to sit through the headmaster's productions of *Agamemnon* and *Antigone*. Well, Elliot Tweed would not be performing again. He had died in this very room, with a knife driven into the side of his throat. Fraser was not yet used to murder and there was one thought that chilled him in particular. What sort of person kills a man in a room filled with children? On the night of the school play, there had been three hundred people sitting together in the darkness: little boys and their parents. They would remember it for the rest of their lives.

The theatre suited Pünd. He had arranged the seats so that they were facing him in two rows. He stood in front of the stage, leaning on his rosewood cane, but he could just as easily have been *on* it. This was his performance, the climax of a drama that had begun three weeks earlier with a frightened man visiting Tanner Court. The spotlights might not be illuminated but still they bowed their heads towards him. The people he had asked to be here were suspects but they were also his audience. Detective Inspector Ridgeway might be standing next to him but it was clear that he had been given only a supporting role.

Fraser examined the staff members. Leonard Graveney had been the first to arrive, taking his place in the front row, his crutch resting awkwardly against the back of his chair. The stump of his leg jutted out in front of him as if purposefully blocking the way for everyone else. The history teacher, Dennis Cocker, had come and had sat next to him although Fraser noticed that neither of them had spoken. Both men had been involved in the last, fateful performance of *Night Comes Calling* when the murder had happened, Graveney as the author of the play, Cocker as its director. The lead part had been taken by Sebastian Fleet. Aged just twenty-one, he was the youngest teacher at Fawley Park and he had ambled in nonchalantly, winking at the matron who deliberately turned her head away, ignoring him. Lydia Gwendraeth was sitting in the row behind, ramrod straight, her hands folded on her lap, her white starched cap seemingly glued in place. Fraser was still convinced that she had been involved in Elliot Tweed's murder. She certainly had a motive – he had behaved horribly towards her – and with her medical training she would have known exactly where to place the knife. Had she run through the audience that night, taking revenge for the humiliation she had suffered at his hands? As she sat, waiting for Pünd to begin, her eyes gave nothing away.

Three more members of the staff came in – Harold Trent, Elizabeth Colne and Douglas Wye. Finally, the groundsman, Garry, arrived, his hands deep in his pockets and a scowl on his face. It was clear he had no idea why he had been summoned.

'The question we must ask ourselves is not why Elliot Tweed was killed. As the headmaster of Fawley Park, he was a man with more, you might say, than his fair share of enemies. The boys feared him. He beat them mercilessly and on the slightest pretext. He made no attempt to disguise the fact that he took pleasure in their pain. His wife wanted to divorce him. His staff, who disagreed on so many issues, were united only by their dislike of him. No . . .' Pünd's eyes swept over the assembly. 'What we must ask is this. I have said it from the start. Why was he murdered in this way, so publicly? The killer appears as if from nowhere and runs the full length of the building, pausing only to strike out with a scalpel taken from the biology laboratory. It is true that it is dark and that the eyes of the audience are focused on the stage. It is the most dramatic moment of the play. There is a mist, a flickering light, and in the shadow appears the ghost of the wounded soldier as portrayed by Mr Graveney. And yet, it is a huge risk. Surely someone will have seen where he comes from or where he goes. A preparatory school such as Fawley Park provides many simpler opportunities for murder. There is a timetable. It is known, at all times, where everyone will be. How convenient for a killer who can plan his movements in the sure knowledge that his victim will be alone and that he will be unseen.

'Indeed, the darkness, the speed with which the crime is committed, results in catastrophe! Inspector Ridgeway was of the belief that the assistant headmaster, Mr Moriston, who was sitting next to Mr Tweed that night, must have witnessed something and that he was subsequently killed in order to silence him. Perhaps blackmail had been involved. The discovery of a large amount of cash in his locker would certainly seem to suggest this. We now know, however, that the two men had swapped seats just before the performance began. Mr Tweed was several inches shorter than Mr Moriston and had been unable to see over the head of the woman who was sitting in front of him as she was wearing a hat. It was Mr Moriston who was the true target. The death of Mr Tweed was an accident.

'And yet it is strange because Mr Moriston was a very popular man. He had often come to the defence of Miss Gwendraeth. It was he who chose to employ Mr Garry, in the full knowledge of his criminal record. He was also able to prevent the suicide of a child. It is hard to find anyone at the school who spoke anything but well of John Moriston – hard, but not impossible. There was, of course, one exception.' Pünd turned to the maths teacher but he did not need to name him. Everyone in the room knew who he meant.

'You're not saying I killed him!' Leonard Graveney barked out the words. He couldn't stop himself smiling.

'Of course it is impossible that you could have committed the murder, Mr Graveney. You lost a leg in the war—'

'Fighting your lot!'

'And you now have a prosthetic. You could not have run through the auditorium. That much is painfully clear. However, you will agree that there was a great deal of enmity between you.'

'He was a coward and a liar.'

'He was your commanding officer in the Western Desert in 1941. You were both involved in the battle of Sidi Rezegh and it was there that you lost your leg.'

'I lost more than that, Mr Pünd. I was in hospital, in constant pain, for six months. I lost a great many of my friends – all of them better men than Major bloody Moriston could ever hope to be. I've already told you all this. He gave the wrong orders. He sent us into that hellhole and then he abandoned us. We were being ripped apart and he was nowhere near.'

'There was a court martial.'

'There was an *enquiry*, after the war.' Graveney sneered as he spoke the word. 'Major Moriston insisted that we had acted on our own initiative and that he had done everything he could to bring us back to safety. It was my word against his. Useful, that, wasn't it! All the other witnesses being blown apart.'

'It must have been a great shock for you to find him teaching here.'

'It made me sick. And everyone was the same as you. They thought the world of him. He was the war hero, the father figure, everyone's best friend. I was the only one who saw through him – and I would have killed him. I'll give you that much. Don't think I wasn't tempted.'

'Why did you remain here?'

Graveney shrugged. To Fraser, he looked worn out by his experiences, his shoulders slumped, his thick moustache drooping. 'I had nowhere else to go. Tweed only gave me the job because I'd married Gemma. How else do you think a cripple with no qualifications manages to earn a living? I stayed because I had to and I avoided Moriston as best as I could.'

'And when he was awarded his medal, when he was given the CBE?'

'It meant nothing to me. You can stick a piece of metal on a coward and a liar but it won't change what he is.'

Pünd nodded as if this was the answer he had expected to hear. 'And so we arrive at the contradiction that is at the heart of the matter,' he said. 'The only man at Fawley Park with a motive to kill John Moriston was also the one man who could not possibly have committed the deed.' He paused. 'Unless, that is, there was a second person who had also a motive – even the same motive – and who had come to the school with the express purpose of exacting his revenge.'

Sebastian Fleet realised that the detective was staring directly at him. He straightened up, the colour rushing into his cheeks. 'What are you saying, Mr Pünd? I wasn't at Sidi Rezegh or anywhere near it. I was ten years old. Rather too young to fight in the war!'

'That is indeed the case, Mr Fleet. Even so, I remarked when we met that you seemed to be unusually qualified to be working as an English teacher in a preparatory school in the middle of the countryside. You received a first from Oxford University. You have youth and talent. Why have you chosen to bury yourself away here?'

'I told you that, when we first met. I'm working on a novel!'

'The novel is important to you. But you interrupted it to write a play.'

'I was asked to do it. Every year, a member of the staff writes a play, which the staff also performs. It's a tradition here.'

'And who was it who asked you?'

Fleet hesitated as if unwilling to provide the answer. 'It was Mr Graveney,' he said.

Pünd nodded and Fraser knew that he'd had no need to ask the question. He'd known all along. 'You dedicated *Night Comes Calling* to the memory of your father,' he continued. 'You told me that he had died quite recently.'

'A year ago.'

'And yet it seemed strange to me, when I visited your room, that there was no photograph of him taken in the recent past. Your mother accompanied you on the day that you entered Oxford. Your father was not there. Nor was he present at your graduation.'

'He was ill.'

'He was no longer alive, Mr Fleet. Do you think it was not an easy matter for me to discover that a Sergeant Michael Fleet, serving with the 60th Field Regiment of the Royal Artillery, died on 21 November 1941? Will you pretend that he was not related to you and that it was merely a coincidence that brought you to this school? You and Mr Graveney had met at the offices of the Honourable Artillery Company in London. He invited you to Fawley Park. You both had good reason to hate Edward Moriston. It was the same reason.'

Neither Fleet nor Graveney spoke and it was left to the matron to break the silence. 'Are you saying they did it together?' she demanded.

'I am saying that they wrote, created and conceived *Night Comes Calling* with the express purpose of committing murder. They had decided to take their revenge for what had occurred at Sidi Rezegh. It was Mr Graveney who, I believe, came up with the idea and Mr Fleet who put it into action.'

'You're talking nonsense,' Fleet hissed. 'I was actually on stage when that person ran through the audience. I was in clear sight of everyone.'

'No. Everything was constructed to make it *seem* that you were there, but that is not how it works.' Pünd got to his feet, using his cane to lever himself up. 'The ghost makes its appearance at the back of the stage. It is dark. There is smoke. He is wearing the uniform of a First World War soldier. He has a moustache identical to that of Mr Graveney. His face is streaked with blood. He has a bandage around his head. He has very few lines to speak – that is how it has been arranged. It is the power of the writer to make everything work to his own purpose. He calls out one word only: "Agnes!" The voice, distorted by the attack of the mustard gas, is not difficult to fake. But it is not Mr Fleet who is on the stage.

'Mr Graveney, the director of the play, has been waiting in the wings and, as planned, the two of you change places for this one short scene. Mr Graveney puts on the trench coat. He applies the bandage and the blood. Slowly, he walks onto the stage. The fact that he is limping will not be noticed over such a short distance and anyway, he is playing a wounded soldier. At the same time, Mr Fleet has removed the false moustache that he has worn for his performance. He puts on the hat and the jacket – which we will later find abandoned in the well. He runs through the auditorium, pausing only to stab the man sitting in seat E 23. How can he know that, moments before the play began, Mr Tweed and Mr Moriston exchanged seats and that the wrong man will die?

'It happens very quickly. Mr Fleet leaves through the main door of the theatre, discards the hat and the jacket, then runs round the side in time to change places, once again, with Mr Graveney who has just exited from the stage. By now, the audience is in an uproar. All eyes are on the dead man. Nobody notices what occurs in the wings. Of course, the two men are horrified when they discover what has occurred. Their victim has been the completely blameless Mr Tweed. But these killers are cold and cunning. They concoct a story that suggests that Mr Moriston was attempting blackmail and two days later they poison him with hemlock stolen from the same laboratory that provided the scalpel. It is clever, is it not? The finger of blame points at the biology teacher, Miss Colne, and this time, their true motive is completely concealed...'

Extract from *Death Treads the Boards* by Donald Leigh

CHAPTER 21: THE FINAL ACT

It was very dark in the theatre. The light of the day was fading quickly outside and the ominous sky was full of heavy, ugly clouds. In just six hours time, 1920 would come to an end and 1921 would begin. But Detective Superintendent MacKinnon was already celebrating the New Year inside his head. He had worked it all out. He knew who had committed the murder and soon he would confront that person, pinning him to the floor with the ruthlessness of a scientist with a rare butterfly.

Sergeant Browne looked carefully at the suspects, asking himself for the thousandth time, which one of them could have stabbed the history teacher, Ewan Jones, in the throat on that unforgettable night? Which one of them?

They were sitting in the half-abandoned theatre, not looking comfortable, each one of them doing their best to avoid the other's eyes. Henry Baker, the director of the play, was stroking his moustache as he always did when he was nervous. The writer, Charles Hawkins, was smoking a cigarette, which he was holding in those stubby fingers that were always stained with ink. Was it just a coincidence that he had been badly wounded at Ypres at the same time as the second victim, the theatre manager, Alastair Short, who had been mysteriously poisoned with arsenic a few days later? Could there be a connection? Short had two hundred pounds stashed away in his bedside cupboard and it looked very much as if blackmail could have been the name of his game. Where else could he have got the money? It was a shame that he hadn't lived to tell the tale.

Which one of them? Browne still suspected Lila Blaire. His thoughts hurtled back to the moment when she had thrown herself at Short, screaming at him and accusing him of destroying her career. 'I hate you!' she had screamed. 'I wish you were dead!' And seventy minutes later he had indeed been dead, just as she had wanted. And what about Iain Lithgow? The young, handsome, smiling actor had been too young to fight at Ypres. There could be no connection there but he had gambling debts and people who need money desperately will often do desperate things. Browne waited for his boss to collect his thoughts.

And now the moment he had been waiting for arrived. As MacKinnon got to his feet, there was a brief roll of thunder in the heavy, oppressive air. The New Year was going to start with a bad storm. Everyone stopped and looked up as he adjusted his monacle and then began to speak.

'On the night of 20 December,' he began, 'a murder was committed here, in the Roxberry Theatre, during a performance of *Aladdin*. But it was the wrong murder! Alastair Short was the real target but the killer got it wrong because, at the last moment, Mr Short and Mr Jones had swapped seats.'

MacKinnon paused for a moment, examining each one of the suspects as they drank in his words. 'But who was the killer who ran off the stage and plunged the knife into Jones's throat?' he continued. 'There were two people who it couldn't have been. Charles Hawkins couldn't have run through the theatre. He only had one leg. And as for Nigel Smith, he was on stage at the time, in full view of the audience. It couldn't be him either.

'At least, that's what I thought . . .'

There can be no doubt that Alan stole Donald Leigh's idea. He changed the time period from the twenties to the late forties and the setting from an end-of-the-pier theatre to a preparatory school, which he based on Chorley Hall, renaming it Fawley Park. Elliot Tweed is a thinly disguised portrait of his father, Elias Conway. Oh yes – and all the teachers are named after British rivers. The name of the detective, Inspector Ridgway, may have been borrowed from Agatha Christie's *Death on the Nile*. Another river. But the mechanism is the same and so is the motive. An officer abandons his men at a time of war and, years later, the only survivor joins forces with the son of one of the men who died. They swap places during the performance of a play, committing the murder in full view of the audience. Detective Superintendent Locke would have found it a tad unlikely, but in the world of whodunnit fiction, it worked just fine.

After I read the two books, I rang the Arvon Foundation, which, I correctly guessed, had hosted the course that Donald had attended. They were able to confirm that Donald Leigh had indeed been at their manor house at Totleigh Barton, Devonshire. It's a lovely place, by the way. I've been there myself. I would have said that the chances of a visiting tutor stealing the work of one of his students was about a million to one, but looking at the two versions, that's what had happened. I felt sorry for Donald. Frankly, he can't write. His sentences are leaden, lacking any rhythm. He uses too many adjectives and his dialogue is unconvincing. Alan was right on both counts. But he didn't deserve to be treated this way. Could he have done anything about it? He told me he had written to Charles and had received no reply. That wasn't surprising. Publishers get crank letters all the time and this one wouldn't have got past Jemima. She'd simply have binned it. The police wouldn't have been interested. It would have been easy enough for Alan to claim that he had given the idea to Donald rather than the other way round.

What else could he have done? Well, he could have found Alan's address in the records of the Ivy Club, travelled up to Framlingham, pushed him off the roof and ripped up the final chapters of his new novel. I'd have been tempted to do the same in his place.

I'd managed to spend most of the morning reading and I was meant to be having lunch with Lucy, our rights manager. I wanted to talk to her about James Taylor and *The Atticus Adventures*. It was half past twelve and I thought I'd slip out for a quick cigarette on the pavement outside the front door – but then I remembered the letter at the top of the pile, the one that had spelled my name wrong. I opened it.

There was a photograph inside. No note. No name of any sender. I snatched the envelope back and looked at the postmark. It had been sent from Ipswich.

The photograph was a little blurry. I guessed it had been taken with a mobile phone, enlarged and printed at one of those Snappy Snaps shops you find everywhere. You can plug directly into their machines so, assuming they paid cash, the person who had taken the photograph would have been completely anonymous.

It showed John White murdering Alan Conway.

The two men were at the top of the tower. Alan had his back to the edge and he was bent over towards it. He was dressed in the same clothes – the loose jacket and black shirt – that he had been wearing when he was found. White had his hands on Alan's shoulders. One push and it would all be over.

So that was it. The mystery was solved. I rang Lucy and cancelled lunch. Then I began to think.

Detective work

It's one thing reading about detectives, quite another trying to be one.

I've always loved whodunnits. I've not just edited them. I've read them for pleasure throughout my life, gorging on them actually. You must know that feeling when it's raining outside and the heating's on and you lose yourself, utterly, in a book. You read and you read and you feel the pages slipping through your fingers until suddenly there are fewer in your right hand than there are in your left and you want to slow down but you still hurtle on towards a conclusion you can hardly bear to discover. That is the particular power of the whodunnit which has, I think, a special place within the general panoply of literary fiction because, of all characters, the detective enjoys a particular, indeed a unique relationship with the reader.

Whodunnits are all about truth: nothing more, nothing less. In a world full of uncertainties, is it not inherently satisfying to come to the last page with every i dotted and every t crossed? The stories mimic our experience in the world. We are surrounded by tensions and ambiguities, which we spend half our life trying to resolve and we'll probably be on our own deathbed when we reach that moment when everything makes sense. Just about every whodunnit provides that pleasure. It is the reason for their existence. It's why *Magpie Murders* was so bloody irritating.

In just about every other book I can think of, we're chasing on the heels of our heroes – the spies, the soldiers, the romantics, the adventurers. But we stand shoulder to shoulder with the detective. From the very start, we have the same aim – and it's actually a simple one. We want to know what really happened and neither of us are in it for the money. Read the Sherlock Holmes short stories. He's hardly ever paid, and although he's clearly well off, I'm not sure he once presents a bill for his services. Of course the detectives are cleverer than us. We expect them to be. But that doesn't mean they're paragons of virtue. Holmes is depressed. Poirot is vain. Miss Marple is brusque and eccentric. They don't have to be attractive. Look at Nero Wolfe who was so fat that he couldn't even leave his New York home and had to have a custom-made chair to support his weight! Or Father Brown who had '*a face as round and dull as a Norfolk dumpling… eyes as empty as the North Sea.*' Lord Peter Wimsey, ex-Eton, ex-Oxford, is thin and seemingly weedy and sports a monocle. Bulldog Drummond might have been able to kill a man with his bare hands (and may have been the inspiration for James Bond) but he was no male model either. In fact H.C. McNeile hits the nail on the head when he writes that Drummond had '*the fortunate possession of that cheerful type of ugliness which inspires immediate confidence in its owner.*' We don't need to like or admire our detectives. We stick with them because we have confidence in them.

All of this makes me a poor choice of narrator/investigator. Quite apart from the fact that I'm completely unqualified, I may not actually be all that good. I have tried to describe everyone I saw, everything I heard and, most importantly, everything I thought. Sadly, I have no Watson, no Hastings, no Troy, no Bunter, no Lewis. So I have no choice but to put everything onto the page, including the fact that, until I opened the letter and saw the photograph of John White, I was getting absolutely nowhere. In fact, in my darker moments, I was beginning to ask myself if there really had been a murder at all. Part of the trouble was that there was no pattern, no shape to the mystery I was trying to solve. If Alan Conway had lent his hand to the description of his own death, as he had with Sir Magnus Pye, I'm sure he'd have given me a variety of clues, signs and indications to lead me on my way. For example, in *Magpie Murders*, there's the handprint in the earth, the dog's collar in the bedroom, the scrap of paper found in the fireplace, the service revolver in the desk, the typed letter in the handwritten envelope. I might not have any idea what they add up to but at least, as the reader, I know that they must have some significance or why else would they have been mentioned? As the detective, I had to find these things for myself and perhaps I'd been looking in the wrong direction because I seemed to have precious little to work with: no torn buttons, no mysterious fingerprints, no conveniently overheard conversations. Well, of course, I had Alan's handwritten suicide letter, which had been sent to Charles in a typed envelope, the exact reverse of what I had read in the book. But what did that mean? Had he run out of ink? Had he written the letter but asked someone else to write the address? If you read a Sherlock Holmes story, you can be pretty sure that the detective will know exactly what's going on even if he won't necessarily tell you. In this case, that's not true at all.

There was also that dinner at the Ivy. I still couldn't get it out of my mind. Alan had become annoyed when Charles had suggested changing the title of his book. Mathew Prichard, sitting at the next table, had heard what he had said. He had pounded the table, then jabbed with a finger. '*I'm not having the—*' The what? I'm not having the title changed? I'm not having the discussion? I'm not having the dessert, thanks? Even Charles wasn't sure what he had meant.

I might as well come straight out with it. I didn't think John White killed Alan Conway even though I had photographic evidence of him committing that very act. It was like the suicide letter that wasn't actually a suicide letter except that this time I didn't even have the beginning of an explanation. I simply didn't believe it. I had met White and I didn't see him as being a particularly violent or aggressive person. And anyway, he had no reason to kill Alan. If anything, it was the other way round.

There were other questions too. Who had sent me the photograph? Why had they sent it to me, rather than the police? It must have been posted on the same day as the funeral and the postmark showed Ipswich. How many people at the funeral knew that I worked at Cloverleaf Books? My name was misspelled on the envelope. Was that a genuine error or a deliberate attempt to make it appear that they didn't know me well?

Sitting on my own in the office – just about everyone else had gone out to lunch – I drew up a list of suspects. I could think of five people who were far more likely than White to have committed the murder and I set them out in order of likelihood. It was quite confusing. I'd already performed exactly the same exercise when I'd finished Alan's book.

1. James Taylor, the boyfriend

As much as I liked James, he was the one who most directly benefited from Alan's death. In fact, if Alan had lived another twenty-four hours, he would have lost several million pounds. He knew Alan was in the house. He would have guessed that Alan would have breakfast on the tower because the weather was so good on that penultimate day in August. He was still living there and could have let himself in, crept upstairs and pushed him off in the blink of an eye. He had told me he was in London over the weekend but I only had his word for that and he'd seemed completely at home when I met him, as if he knew that Abbey Grange was his. Of course, it's the first rule of whodunnits that you discard the most obvious suspect. Was that what I should do here?

2. Claire Jenkins, the sister

In all those pages she gave me, she went on about how much she adored her brother, how generous he was to her and how close they had always been. I wasn't sure I quite believed her. James thought she was jealous of his success and it's certainly true that in the end the two of them argued about money. That wasn't necessarily a motive for murder but there was another very good reason to put her second on my list and it related to the unfinished book.

Alan Conway took a spiteful pleasure in creating characters based on people he knew. James Taylor turned up as the slightly dim, foppish James Fraser. The vicar appeared as an anagram of himself. Even Alan's own son was in there by name. I had no doubt at all that Clarissa Pye, Sir Magnus's lonely, spinster sister was based on Claire. It was a grotesque portrait, which Alan made more pointed by deliberately including his address in Daphne Road (although in the book, it's Brent who lives there). If Claire had seen the manuscript, she might have a very good reason to push her brother off the roof. It would also have been in her interest to ensure that the book was never published – something she would have achieved by stealing the last chapters.

Why then would she insist that Alan had been murdered? Why draw attention to what she had done? I had no real answer to that, but thinking it through I remembered reading somewhere that killers have an urge to claim ownership. It's why they return to the scene of their crime. Could it be that Claire had asked me to investigate her brother's death for the very same reason that she wrote that long account? A pathological desire to be centre stage.

3. Tom Robeson, the vicar.

It was a pity that Robeson wouldn't tell me exactly what had happened at Chorley Hall when I confronted him at the church. If his wife had arrived a few minutes later it would have made all the difference. But the incident had involved a photograph used to humiliate a boy in an all-boys school and I didn't need to work too hard to get the general idea. It was interesting, incidentally, that Claire saw her brother as one of the victims of the school's various cruelties while Robeson saw him as more of an active participant. The more I learnt about Alan, the more I was inclined to believe the vicar's account.

All this had taken place back in the seventies and it had clearly been on Alan's mind because he had written about it in the first chapter of *Magpie Murders,* when Mary Blakiston turns up in the vicarage. '*And there they were, just lying in the middle of all his papers.*' What had she seen? Were Henrietta and Robin Osborne perverts of some sort? Had they left out incriminating photographs, similar in nature to the ones that had tormented Robeson? From what he had said in his funeral address, the vicar hadn't forgotten any of this and, having met him, I could quite easily see him creeping up to the top of the tower to get his revenge. That said, it's always been my belief that vicars make poor characters in crime novels. They're somehow too obvious, too Little England. If Robeson did turn out to be the killer, I think I'd be disappointed.

4. Donald Leigh, the waiter

'*You must have been quite pleased to hear he was dead.*' I had said. '*I was delighted,*' he'd replied. Two men don't see each other for several years. One hates the other. They meet quite by chance and forty-eight hours later, one of them is dead. When I put it in black and white like that, Robert had to be on my list and it would have been a simple matter for him to get Alan's address from the club records. What else is there to say?

5. Mark Redmond, the producer

He lied to me. He said that he went back to London on the Saturday when the register showed that he had actually stayed the entire weekend at the Crown. He also had every reason to want Alan dead. *The Atticus Adventures* would have been worth a fortune if he could get them off the ground and Redmond had invested a lot of his own money seeding the project. He certainly knew a thing or two about murder having masterminded hundreds of them on British TV. Would it really have been so difficult to move from fiction to reality? After all, the murder had been a bloodless one. No guns, no knives. Just a simple push. Anyone could do that.

Those were the five names on my list, the *Five Little Pigs*, if you like, that I suspected of committing the crime. But there were two other names, which I didn't add but which should perhaps have been there.

6. Melissa Conway, the ex-wife

I hadn't had a chance to speak to her yet, but decided I would travel down to Bradford-on-Avon as soon as I could. I was beginning to obsess about Alan's murder and I wasn't going to get any work done at Cloverleaf until it was solved. According to Claire Jenkins, Melissa had never forgiven Alan for the way he had left her. Had they met recently? Could something have happened that might have prompted her to take revenge? I was annoyed that I'd missed her at the hotel. I would have liked to have asked her why she had travelled all the way up to Framlingham to attend her husband's funeral. Had she made the same journey to push him off the tower?

7. Frederick Conway, the son

It may not be fair to include him – I had only glimpsed him at the funeral and knew almost nothing about him – but I still remembered how he had looked that day, staring at the grave, his face positively distorted by anger. He had been abandoned by his father. Worse than that, his father had come out as a gay man and as a schoolboy that might not have been easy for him either. A motive for murder? Alan must have been thinking about him when he wrote *Magpie Murders*. Freddy turns up as the son of Sir Magnus and Lady Pye, the only character who retains his true name.

These were the notes that I made, sitting in my office that Monday afternoon, and by the time I left I had got precisely nowhere. It's all very well having suspects. When push comes to shove (as, indeed, it had) all seven of them – eight, counting John White – could have killed Alan Conway. For that matter, it could have been the postman, the milkman, someone I've forgotten to mention, or someone I hadn't met. What I didn't have was that interconnectivity you get in a murder mystery, the sense that all the characters are moving in tandem, like pieces on a Cluedo board. Any one of them could have knocked on the door of Abbey Grange on that Sunday morning. Any one of them could have done it.

In the end I shoved my notepad aside and went for a meeting with one of our copy editors. If I had just worked a little harder, I would have realised that the clue I had been seeking was actually there, that somebody had said something to me, quite recently, that had identified them as the killer, and that the motive for Alan's murder had been in front of my eyes the moment I had begun reading *Magpie Murders*.

Just half an hour more might have made all the difference in the world. But I was late for my meeting and I was still thinking about Andreas. It was going to cost me dear.

Bradford-on-Avon

Bradford-on-Avon was the last stopping point of my journey into the fictitious world of *Magpie Murders*. Although Alan had used Orford as a model for Saxby-on-Avon, the very name shows where his thoughts lay. What he had done in effect was to synthesise the two. The church, the square, the two pubs, the castle, the meadowland and the general layout belonged to Orford. But it was Bradford-on-Avon, which lay a few miles outside Bath and which was filled with the '*solid, Georgian constructions made of Bath stone with handsome porticos and gardens rising up in terraces*' that the book describes. I don't think it was a coincidence that it happened to be the place where his ex-wife lived. Something had happened that had made him think of her. Somewhere inside *Magpie Murder*s there was a message intended for her.

I had telephoned ahead and travelled down on Tuesday morning, taking the train from Paddington station and changing at Bath. I would have driven, but I had the manuscript with me and planned to work on the way. Melissa had been pleased to hear from me and had invited me to lunch. I arrived just after twelve.

She had given me an address – Middle Rank – that led me to a row of terraced houses high above the town, unreachable except on foot. It was in the middle of an extraordinary warren of walkways, staircases and gardens, which could have been Spanish or Italian in origin if they hadn't been so determinedly English. The houses stretched out in three rows with perfectly proportioned Georgian windows, porticos above many of the front doors and, yes, that honey-coloured Bath stone. Melissa had three floors and a busy garden that picked its way in steps down the hill to a stone pavilion below. This was where she had moved after Orford, and although I hadn't seen where she had lived when she was there, it struck me that this must be the antithesis. It was peculiar. It was secluded. It was somewhere you would come if you wanted to escape.

I rang the doorbell and Melissa answered it herself. My first impression was that she was much younger than I remembered her, although we must have been both about the same age. I had barely recognised her at the funeral. In her coat and scarf with the rain falling, she had blurred into the crowd. Now that she was standing in front of me, in her own home, she struck me as confident, attractive, relaxed. She was slim, with high cheekbones and an easy smile. I was sure her hair had been brown when she was married to Alan. Now it was a dark chestnut and cut short, down to the neck. She was wearing jeans and a cashmere jersey, a white gold chain and no make-up. It's often occurred to me that divorce suits some women. I'd have said that about her.

She greeted me formally and led me upstairs to the main living room which ran the whole length of the house with lovely views over Bradford-on-Avon and on to the Mendip Hills. The furniture was modern/traditional and looked expensive. She'd laid out lunch – smoked salmon, salad, artisan bread. She offered me wine but I stuck to sparkling water.

'I saw you at the funeral,' she said as she sat down. 'I'm sorry I didn't speak to you but Freddy was in a hurry to be away. I'm afraid he's not here. He's got an open day in London. '

'Oh yes?'

'He's applying to St Martin's School of Art. He wants to do a course in ceramics.' She went on quickly. 'He didn't really want to be there, you know, in Framlingham.'

'I was quite surprised to see you.'

'He was my husband, Susan. And Freddy's father. I knew I had to go as soon as I heard he was dead. I thought it would be good for Freddy. He was quite badly hurt by what happened. More than me, I'd say. I thought it might give him some sort of closure.'

'Did it?'

'Not really. He complained all the way there and he said nothing on the way back. He was plugged into his iPad. Still, I'm glad we went. It felt like the right thing to do.'

'Melissa . . .' This was the difficult bit. 'I wanted to ask you about you and Alan. There are some things I'm struggling to understand.'

'I did wonder why you'd come all this way.'

On the telephone, I'd told her that I was searching for the missing chapters and that I was trying to work out why Alan had killed himself. She hadn't needed any more explanation than that and I certainly wasn't going to mention the fact that he might have been murdered. 'I don't want to embarrass you,' I said.

'You can ask me anything you want, Susan.' She smiled. 'We'd been apart for six years when he died and I don't feel embarrassed about what happened. Why should I? Of course, it was very difficult at the time. I really loved Alan and I didn't want to lose him. But it's odd . . . Are you married?'

'No.'

'When your husband leaves you for another man, it sort of helps. I think I'd have been angrier if it had been a younger woman. When he told me about James, I saw it was his problem – if it was a problem. I couldn't blame myself if that was the way he felt.'

'Did you have any inkling of it, while you were married?'

'If you're talking about his sexuality, no. Not at all. Freddy was born two years after we were married. I'd say we had a normal relationship.'

'You said it was harder for your son.'

'It was. Freddy was thirteen when Alan came out and the worst thing was that the newspapers got hold of the story and the children read about it at school. Of course he was teased. Having a gay dad. I think it would be easier if it happened now. Things have moved on so fast.'

She was completely without rancour. I was surprised and made a mental note to cross her off the list I had drawn up the day before. She explained that the divorce had been amicable; that Alan had given her everything she wanted and had continued to support Freddy even though there had been no contact between the two of them. There was a trust fund to take him through university and beyond and, as James Taylor had mentioned, he had been left money in the will. She herself had a part-time job; she was a supply teacher in nearby Warminster. But there was plenty of money in the bank. She didn't need to work.

We talked a lot about Alan as a writer because that was what I had told her interested me. She had known him at the most interesting time in his career: struggling, getting published for the first time, finding fame.

'Everyone at Woodbridge School knew that he wanted to be a writer,' she told me. 'He wanted it desperately. That was all he ever talked about. I was actually going out with another of the teachers there but that ended when Alan came to teach at the school. Are you still in touch with Andreas?'

She had asked it so casually and I don't think she noticed when I froze. We had talked, long ago, at publishing parties, and I had mentioned to her that I knew Andreas but either I hadn't told her that we were going out together or she had forgotten it. 'Andreas?' I said.

'Andreas Patakis. He taught Latin and Greek. He and I had a huge fling – it lasted about a year. We were crazy about each other. You know what these Mediterraneans are like. I'm afraid I treated him badly in the end but, as I say, there was something about Alan that just suited me more.'

Andreas Patakis. *My* Andreas.

All at once, a whole lot of things fell into place. So this was the reason why Andreas had disliked Alan and why he resented Alan's success! It was also the reason why, on Sunday evening, he had been so reluctant to tell me what it was about Alan that had annoyed him. How could he admit that he had been going out with Melissa before he met me? What should I think about it? Should I be upset? I had inherited him second-hand. No. That was ridiculous. Andreas had been married twice. There had been plenty of other women in his life. I knew that. But Melissa . . . ? I found myself looking at her in a completely different light. She was definitely much less attractive than I had thought: too thin, boyish even, better suited to Alan than to Andreas.

She hadn't stopped talking. She was still telling me about Alan.

‘I absolutely love books and I found him fascinating. I’d never met anyone so driven. He was always talking about stories and ideas, the books he’d read and the books he wanted to write. He’d done a course at East Anglia University and he was certain it was going to help him break through. It wasn’t enough for him to be published. He wanted to be famous – but it took a lot longer than he’d expected. I was with him throughout the whole process: writing the books, finishing them and then the horrible disappointment when nobody was interested. You have no idea what it’s like, Susan, being rejected, those letters that turn up in the post with six or seven lines dismissing the work of a whole year. Well, I suppose you’re the one who writes them. But to spend all that time writing something only to find that nobody wants it. It’s horribly destructive. They’re not just rejecting your work. They’re rejecting who you are.’

And who was Alan?

‘He took writing very seriously. The truth is, he didn’t want to write mysteries. The first book he showed me was called *Look to the Stars*. It was actually very clever and funny and a little sad. The main character was an astronaut but he never actually got into space. In a way, I suppose, that was a bit like Alan. Then there was a book set in the south of France. He said it was inspired by Henry James, *The Turn of the Screw*. It took him three years to finish but again no one was interested. I couldn’t understand it because I loved his writing and I completely believed in it. And what makes me angry is that, in the end, I was the one who spoiled it all.’

I poured myself more sparkling water. I was still thinking about Andreas. ‘What do you mean?’ I asked.

‘Atticus Pünd was my idea. No – really, it was! You’ve got to understand that what Alan wanted more than anything was to be published, to be recognised. It killed him to be stuck in a boring independent school in the middle of nowhere, teaching a bunch of kids he didn’t even like and who would forget him the moment they moved on to university. And one day – we’d just been to a bookshop – I suggested that he should write something simpler and more popular. He was always great at puzzles – crosswords and things like that. He had a fascination with tricks and trompe l'oeils. So I told him he should write a whodunnit. It seemed to me that there were writers out there who were earning thousands, millions of pounds from books that weren't half as good as his. It would only take him a few months. It might be fun. And if it was a success he could leave Woodbridge and become a writer full-time, which is what he really wanted.

'I actually helped him write *Atticus Pünd Investigates*. I was there when he thought up the main character. He told me all his ideas.'

'Where did Atticus come from?'

'They'd just shown *Schindler's List* on TV and Alan took him from that. He may have been based on an old English teacher too. His name was Adrian Pound or something like that. Alan read loads of Agatha Christie books and tried to work out how she wrote her mysteries and only then did he begin writing. I was the first person to read it. I'm still proud of that. I was the first person in the world to read an Atticus Pünd novel. I loved it. Of course, it wasn't as good as his other work. It was lighter and completely pointless, but I thought it was beautifully written – and of course, you published it. The rest you know.'

'You said you spoiled things for him.'

'Everything went wrong after the book came out. You have to understand, Alan was such a complex person. He could be very moody, introvert. For him, writing was something mysterious. It was like he was kneeling at the altar and the words were being sent down to him – or something like that. There were writers that he admired, and more than anything in the world he had always dreamed of being like them.'

'What writers?'

'Well, Salman Rushdie, for one. Martin Amis. David Mitchell. And Will Self.'

I remembered the four hundred and twenty pages of *The Slide* that I had read. I had thought it derivative at the time but now Melissa had told me where it had come from. Alan had been imitating a writer he'd admired but who, personally speaking, I had never been able to read. He had produced something close to a pastiche of Will Self.

'The moment Atticus Pünd came out, he was trapped,' Melissa

went on. 'That was what neither of us had anticipated. It was so successful that of course nobody wanted him to do anything else.'

'It was better than his other books,' I said.

'You may have thought that, but Alan didn't agree and nor do I.' She sounded bitter. 'He only wrote Atticus Pünd to get out of Woodbridge School and all it did was put him somewhere worse.'

'But he was rich.'

'He didn't want the money! It was never about money.' She sighed. Neither of us had eaten very much lunch. 'Even if Alan hadn't found this other side of himself, even if he hadn't gone off with James, I don't think we'd have stayed married much longer. He was never the same with me after he got famous. Do you understand what I'm saying, Susan? I'd betrayed him. Worse than that, I'd persuaded him to betray himself.'

After another half an hour – maybe forty minutes – I left. I had to wait for a train at Bradford-on-Avon station but that suited me. I needed time to think. Andreas and Melissa! Why did it bother me so much? It had been over before the two of us even met. I suppose part of it was natural, a spurt of involuntary jealousy. But at the same time I was remembering what Andreas had said to me, the last time we had spoken. '*Is this the best we can do?*' I had always assumed that we had both liked the casual nature of our relationship and I had been annoyed about the hotel because it was changing all that. What Melissa had just told me made me think again. Suddenly I saw how easy it would be to lose him.

There was something else that occurred to me. Andreas had lost Melissa to Alan and he had made it clear that it still rankled. There was certainly no love lost between them. And this time, all these years later, Alan was the main reason why he might lose me. I was his editor. My career was largely predicated on the success of his books. '*I've hated the way you've had to kowtow to him.*' That was what he had said.

I suddenly saw that Andreas, as much as anyone, must have been very glad to see him dead.

I needed to distract myself, so as soon as I was on the train, I took out *Magpie Murders* – but this time, instead of reading it, I tried to decipher it. I couldn't get away from the idea that Alan

Conway had concealed something inside the text and that it might even be the reason he was killed. I remembered the crossword that Clarissa Pye had solved and the code games the two boys had played at the Lodge. When Alan was at Chorley Hall, he had sent his sister acronyms and he had put dots under certain letters in books to send secret messages. There were no dots in the typescript of *Magpie Murders*. I had already checked. But his books had contained British rivers, tube stations, fountain pens, birds. This was a man who played electronic Scrabble in his spare time. '*He was always great at puzzles – crosswords and things like that.*' It was the very reason why Melissa had persuaded him to try his hand at murder mystery in the first place. I was sure that if I looked hard enough there would be something I would find.

I figured I knew where the characters had originated so I ignored them. If I was looking for secret messages, acronyms seemed the more likely possibility. The first letters of the first word of each chapter, for example, spelled out TTAADA. Nothing there. Then I tried the first ten sentences, which began TTTBHTI and the first letters of the first word of each section: TSDW – I didn't need to continue. That didn't mean anything either. I looked at the title of the book. *Magpie Murders* could be rearranged to make Reared Pig Mums, Reread Smug Imp, Premium Grades and many more. It was a puerile activity. I wasn't expecting to find anything, not really. But it occupied my mind as we trundled back to London. I didn't want to think about what Melissa had told me.

And then, somewhere between Swindon and Didcot, I saw it. It just assembled itself in front of my eyes.

The titles of the books.

The clues had always been there. James had told me that the number of books was important. '*Alan always said there would be nine books. He'd decided that from the very start.*' Why nine? Because *that* was his secret message. That was what he wanted to spell out. Look at the first letters.

Atticus Pünd Investigates
No Rest for the Wicked
Atticus Pünd Takes the Case
Night Comes Calling
Atticus Pünd's Christmas

Gin & Cyanide
Red Roses for Atticus
Atticus Pünd Abroad

If you add the last title, *Magpie Murders*, what do you get?

AN ANAGRAM.

And finally that explained something that had been on my mind for a while. The Ivy Club. Alan had got angry when Charles had suggested changing the title of the last book. What was it that he had said? '*I'm not having the—*' That was the moment when Donald Leigh dropped the plates.

But in fact there was no missing word. He had actually completed the sentence. What he was saying was, the book could not be called *The* Magpie Murders because that would spoil the joke that Alan had built into the series almost from the day it was conceived. He'd come up with an anagram.

But an anagram of what?

An hour later, the train pulled into Paddington and I still hadn't seen it.

Paddington Station

I don't like coincidences in novels, and particularly not in murder mysteries, which work because of logic and calculation. The detective really should be able to reach his conclusion without having providence on his side. But that's just the editor in me speaking and unfortunately this is what happened. Getting off the train at two minutes past five in a city of eight and a half million people, with thousands of them crossing the concourse all around me, I bumped into someone I knew. Her name was Jemima Humphries. Until very recently, she had been Charles Clover's PA at Cloverleaf.

I saw her and recognised her at once. Charles always said she had the sort of smile that could light up a crowd and that was what first caught my eye, the fact that she alone looked cheerful among the grey mass of commuters making their way home. She was slim and pretty with long blonde hair, and although she was in her mid-twenties, she had lost none of her schoolgirl exuberance. I remember her telling me that she had wanted to get into publishing because she loved reading. I'd already missed having her around the office. I had no idea why she'd left.

She saw me at the same moment and waved. We made our way towards each other and I thought we were just going to say hello and I was going to ask her how she was. But that wasn't what happened.

'How are you, Jemima?' I asked.

'I'm fine thanks, Susan. It's really great to see you. I'm sorry I didn't get to say goodbye.'

'It all happened so quickly. I was away on a book tour and when I'd got back, you'd already gone.'

'I know.'

'So where are you now?'

'I'm living with my parents in Chiswick. I was just on my way—'

'Where are you working?'

'I haven't got a job yet.' She giggled nervously. 'I'm still looking.'

That puzzled me. I'd assumed she'd been poached. 'So why did you leave?' I asked.

'I didn't leave, Susan. Charles fired me. Well, he asked me to go. I didn't want to.'

That wasn't what Charles had told me. I was sure he'd said she'd handed in her notice. It was already half past five and I wanted to go to the office and go through my emails before I met Andreas. But something told me I couldn't leave it like this. I had to know more. 'Are you in a hurry?' I asked.

'No. Not really.'

'Can I buy you a drink?'

We made our way to one of those grimy, frankly hellish pubs that edge onto the platforms at Paddington Station. I bought myself a gin and tonic, which arrived with not enough ice. Jemima had a glass of white wine. 'So what happened?' I asked.

Jemima frowned. 'I'm not sure, to be honest with you, Susan. I really liked working at Cloverleaf and Charles was fine most of the time. He could be quite snappy now and then but I didn't mind because in a way that was part of the job. Anyway, we had a big row – it must have been the day you went off on that book tour. He said I'd double-booked him for a lunch and there was an agent sitting in a restaurant waiting for him but it simply wasn't true. I never made any mistakes with his diary. But when I tried to argue with him he got really angry. I'd never seen him like that before. He was completely over-the-top. And then, on the Friday morning, I took him a coffee in his office and, as I handed it to him, he sort of fumbled it and it went all over his desk. It was a terrible mess and I went out and got kitchen towel and cleared it up for him and that was when he said he didn't think it was working, him and me, and that I should start looking for another job.'

'He fired you on the spot?'

'Not exactly. I was very upset. I mean, the thing with the coffee, it really wasn't me. I was going to put it on his desk like I always did but he reached out to take it and knocked it out of my hand. And it wasn't as if I'd made loads of mistakes. I'd been with him for a year and everything had gone all right. We had a long talk and I think it was me who said to him that it would be better if I went straight away and he said he'd pay me a month's salary so that was it. He also said he'd give me a good reference and that if anyone asked, I hadn't been fired, I'd just decided to leave.' Charles had stuck with that. It was what he had told me. 'I suppose that was nice of him,' she went on. 'I just left at the end of the day and that was that.'

'What day was that?' I asked.

'It was Friday morning. You were on your way back from Dublin.' She remembered something. 'Did Andreas ever catch up with you?' she asked.

'I'm sorry?' I could feel my head spinning. It was the second time that Andreas had been mentioned today. Melissa had suddenly dragged him into the conversation and now Jemima had done the same. She knew him, of course. She'd met him a few times and taken messages from him. But why was she mentioning him now?

'He came in the day before,' Jemima continued, cheerfully. 'He wanted to see you. After his meeting with Charles.'

'I'm sorry, Jemima.' I tried to take this slowly. 'You must be making a mistake. Andreas wasn't in England that week. He was in Crete.'

'He did look very tanned but I'm not making a mistake. It was a horrible week for me and I sort of remember everything that happened. He came in on Thursday at about three o'clock.'

'And he saw Charles?'

'That's right.' She looked perplexed. 'I hope I haven't done something wrong. He didn't say not to tell you.'

But he hadn't told me himself. Quite the opposite. We'd had our big reunion dinner. He had said he was in Crete.

I wanted to leave Andreas out of this. I went back to Charles. 'There's no way he'd want to lose you,' I said. I wasn't really talking to her. I was talking to myself, trying to work it out. And it was true. I could easily see Charles losing his temper in the way she'd described – but not with her. Jemima had been his third secretary in as many years and I know he liked her. There had been Olivia who'd got on his nerves. And Cat who was always late. Third time lucky – that was what he'd said. Jemima was efficient and hard-working. She made him laugh. How could he have changed his mind so suddenly?

'I don't know,' she said. 'He'd had a bad couple of weeks. When all the reviews came out for that book, *The One-Armed Juggler*, he was really upset and I know he wasn't too happy about *Magpie Murders* either. He was worried about his daughter. Honestly, Susan, I was doing everything I could to help but he just needed someone to shout at and I was the one who happened to be in the room. Did Laura have her baby?'

'Yes,' I said, although actually I didn't know. 'I haven't heard if it's a boy or a girl.'

'Well, send good wishes from me.'

We talked a little more. Jemima was working part-time, helping her mother who was a solicitor. She was thinking about spending the winter in Verbier. She was a keen snowboarder and thought she could get work as a chalet girl. But I didn't really listen to what she was saying. I wanted to telephone Andreas. I wanted to know why he had lied to me.

It was just as we were separating that another thought struck me. I was replaying something she had said to me. 'You mentioned that Charles wasn't happy with *Magpie Murders*,' I said. 'What was the problem?'

'I don't know. He didn't say. But he was definitely upset about something. I thought maybe it wasn't any good.'

'But he hadn't read it yet.'

'Hadn't he?' She sounded surprised.

She was anxious to be on her way but I stopped her. None of this was making any sense. Alan had delivered the new book after

Jemima had left. He had given it to Charles at the Ivy Club on Thursday, 27 August, the same day – it now turned out – Andreas had visited him at Cloverleaf Books. I had got back on the twenty-eighth and had found a copy of the manuscript waiting for me. We had both read it over the weekend – the same weekend Alan died. So what could Charles have been unhappy about?

'Charles was only given the book after you'd left,' I said.

'No. That's not true. It came in the post.'

'When?'

'On Tuesday.'

'How do you know?'

'I opened it.'

I stared at her. 'Did you see the title?'

'Yes. It was on the front page.'

'Was the book complete?'

That confused her. 'I don't know, Susan. I just gave it to Charles. He was very pleased to have it but he didn't say anything afterwards and anyway a few days later the coffee thing happened and that was that.'

There were people swirling past. A voice boomed out over the tannoys, announcing the departure of a train. I thanked Jemima, gave her a brief hug and hurried off to find a taxi.

Cloverleaf Books

I didn't call Andreas. I wanted to. But there was something else I had to do first.

The offices were closed by the time I got there but I had a key and let myself in, deactivated the alarms and climbed the stairs up to the first floor. I turned on the lights, but without anyone in there, the building still felt dark and oppressive, the shadows refusing to budge. I knew exactly where I was going. Charles's office was never locked and I went straight in. There were the two armchairs in empty conference with Charles's desk in front of me. The shelves with all his books, his awards, his photographs, were on one side. Bella's basket was on the other, tucked next to a cabinet that contained bottles and glasses. How many times had I sat here, late into the evening, sipping Glenmorangie malt whisky, talking over the problems of the day? I was here now as an intruder and I had a sense that I was smashing everything that I had helped to build up over the past eleven years.

I walked over to the desk. I was in such a mood that if the drawers had been locked I wouldn't have hesitated to break them open, antique or not. But Charles hadn't taken even this measure of security. The drawers slid open eagerly in my hands to reveal contracts, cost reports, invoices, proofs, newspaper clippings, unwanted wires from old computers and mobile phones, photographs and, at the very bottom, clumsily concealed, a plastic folder containing about twenty sheets of paper. The first page was almost blank with a heading in capitals.

The missing chapters. They had been here all the time.

And in the end, the title had been absolutely true. The solution to the murder of Sir Magnus Pye had to be kept secret because of the way it related to the murder of Alan Conway. I thought I heard something. Had there been a creak on the stairs outside? I turned the page and began to read.

Atticus Pünd took one last walk around Saxby-on-Avon while James Fraser paid the bill at the Queen's Arms. He had arranged to meet Detective Inspector Chubb – and two others – at the Bath police station in an hour's time. He had not been here long but in a strange way he had come to know the village quite intimately. The church, the castle, the antique shop in the square, the bus shelter, the Queen's Arms and the Ferryman . . . he could no longer see them separately. They had become the chessboard on which this particular game, surely his last, had been played.

It was his last game because he was dying. Atticus Pünd and Alan Conway were going out together. That was what this was all about. A writer and a character he hated, both heading towards their Reichenbach Falls.

It had all come to me at Paddington Station, the extraordinary moment that all of them must have felt – Poirot, Holmes, Wimsey, Marple, Morse – but which their authors had never fully explained. What was it like, for them? A slow process, like constructing a jigsaw? Or did it come in a rush, one last turn in a toy kaleidoscope when all the colours and shapes tumbled and twisted into each other, forming a recognisable image? That was what had happened to me. The truth had been there. But it had taken a final nudge for me to see it, all of it.

Would it have happened if I hadn't met Jemima Humphries? I'll never know for sure, but I think I would have got there in the end. There were little bits of information, red herrings that I'd had to get out of my head. For example, the television producer, Mark Redmond, hadn't told me that he'd stayed at the Crown

Hotel in Framlingham over the weekend. Why not? The answer was quite simple when I thought about it. When he'd talked to me, he'd deliberately made it seem that he was on his own. It was only the receptionist at the hotel who'd mentioned that he was with his wife. But suppose it wasn't his wife? Suppose it was a secretary or a starlet? That would have been a good reason for a longer stay – and a good reason to lie about it. And then there was James Taylor. He really had been in London with friends. The photograph of John White and Alan on the tower? White had gone round to see Alan on that Sunday morning. No wonder he and his housekeeper had looked uncomfortable when I spoke to them. The two of them had argued about the lost investment. But it wasn't White who had attempted to kill Alan. It was the other way round. Wasn't that obvious? Alan had grabbed hold of him at the top of the tower and the two of them had grappled for a moment. That was what the photograph showed. It was actually Alan's killer who had taken it.

I flicked through a few more pages. I'm not sure I particularly cared who had killed Sir Magnus Pye, not at that moment anyway. But I knew what I was looking for and, sure enough, there it was, in part two of the final chapter.

It took him a short time to write the letter.

Dear James,

By the time that you read this, it will all be finished. You will forgive me for not having spoken to you earlier, for not taking you into my confidence but I am sure that in time you will understand.

There are some notes which I have written and which you will find in my desk. They relate to my condition and to the decision that I have made. I want it to be understood that the doctor's diagnosis is clear and, for me, there can be no possibility of reprieve. I have no fear of death. I would like to think that my name will be remembered.

'What are you doing, Susan?

That was as far as I'd got when I heard the voice, coming from the door, and looked up to see Charles Clover standing there. So there had been someone on the stairs. He was wearing corduroy trousers and a baggy jersey with a coat hanging loosely open. He looked tired.

'I've found the missing chapters,' I said.

'Yes. I can see that.'

There was a long silence. It was only half past six but it felt later. There was no sound of any traffic outside.

'Why are you here?' I asked.

'I'm taking a few days off. I came to get some things.'

'How's Laura?'

'She had a little boy. They're going to call him George.'

'That's a nice name.'

'I thought so.' He moved into the room and sat down in one of the armchairs. I was standing behind his desk so it was as if our positions had been reversed. 'I can explain to you why I hid the pages,' Charles said. I knew that he had already started thinking up an explanation and that, whatever he said, it wouldn't be true.

'There's no need to,' I said. 'I already know everything.'

'Really?'

'I know you killed Alan Conway. And I know why.'

'Why don't you sit down?' He waved a hand towards the cabinet where he kept his drinks. 'Would you like a glass of something?'

'Thank you.' I went over and poured two glasses of whisky. I was glad that Charles had made it easier for me. The two of us had known each other for a very long time and I was determined that we were going to be civilised. I still wasn't sure what would happen next. I assumed that Charles would telephone Detective Superintendent Locke and turn himself in.

I gave him the drink and sat down opposite. 'I think the tradition is that you tell me what happened,' Charles said. 'Although we can always do it the other way round – if you prefer.'

'Aren't you going to deny it?'

'I can see it would be completely pointless. You've found the pages.'

'You could have hidden them more carefully, Charles.'

'I didn't think you'd look. I must say, I was very surprised to find you in my office.'

'I'm surprised to see you too.'

He raised his glass in an ironic toast. He was my boss, my mentor. A grandfather. The godfather. I couldn't believe we were having this conversation. Nonetheless, I began . . . not quite at the beginning as I would have liked but I was finally wearing the hat of the detective, not the editor. 'Alan Conway hated Atticus Pünd,' I said. 'He thought of himself as a great writer – a Salman Rushdie, a David Mitchell – someone people would take seriously, when all he was doing was churning out potboilers, murder mysteries which were making him a fortune but which he himself despised. That book that he showed you, *The Slide* – that was what he really wanted to write.'

'It was dreadful.'

'I know.' Charles looked surprised, so I told him. 'I found it in his office and I read it. I agree with you. It was derivative and it was rubbish. But it was *about* something. It was his view of society – how the old values of the literary classes had rotted away and how, without them, the rest of the country was slipping into some sort of moral and cultural abyss. It was his big statement. And he just couldn't see that it would never be published and it would never be read because it was no good. He believed that was what he was born to write and he blamed Atticus Pünd for getting in the way and spoiling everything for him. Did you know that it was Melissa Conway who first suggested he should write a detective novel?'

'No. She never told me that.'

'It's one of the reasons he divorced her.'

'Those books made him a fortune.'

'He didn't care. He had a million pounds. Then he had ten million pounds. He could have had a hundred million pounds. But he didn't have what he wanted which was respect, the imprimatur of the great writer. And as mad as it sounds, he wasn't the only successful writer who felt that way. Look at Ian Fleming and Conan Doyle. Even A.A. Milne! Milne disliked Winnie the Pooh *because* he was so successful. But I think the big difference is that Alan hated Pünd from the very start. He never wanted to write any of the novels and when he became famous he couldn't wait to get rid of him.'

'Are you saying I killed him because he wouldn't write any more?'

'No, Charles.' I dug into my handbag and took out a packet of cigarettes. To hell with office regulations. We were talking murder here. 'We'll get to why you killed him in a minute. But first of all I'm going to tell you what happened and also how you gave yourself away.'

'Why don't we start with that, Susan? I'd be interested to know.'

'How you gave yourself away? The funny thing is I remember the moment exactly. It was like an alarm bell went off in my head but I didn't make the connection. I suppose it was because I simply couldn't imagine you as a killer. I kept thinking you were the last person to want Alan dead.'

'Go on.'

'Well, when I was in your office, the day we heard that Alan had committed suicide, you made a point of telling me that you hadn't been to Framlingham for six months, not since March or April. It was an understandable lie. You were trying to distance yourself from the scene of the crime. But the trouble is, when we drove up to the funeral together, you warned me to take a different route to avoid the roadworks at Earl Soham. They'd only just started – Mark Redmond told me that – and the only way you could have known about them is if you'd been up more recently. You must have driven through Earl Soham on the Sunday morning when you killed Alan.'

Charles considered what I had said and smiled half-ruefully. 'You know that's exactly the sort of thing Alan would have put in one of his books.'

'I thought so too.'

'I'll have a little more whisky if you don't mind.'

I poured some for him and a little more for myself. I needed to keep a clear head but the Glenmorangie went very well with the cigarette. 'Alan didn't give you the manuscript of *Magpie Murders* at the Ivy Club,' I said. 'It actually came here in the post on Tuesday, 25 August. Jemima opened the envelope and saw it. You must have read it the same day.'

'I finished it on Wednesday.'

'You had dinner with Alan on Thursday evening. He was already in London because he had an afternoon appointment with his doctor – Sheila Bennett. Her initials were in his diary. I wonder if that was when she told him the bad news – that his cancer was terminal? I can't imagine what must have been going through his head when he sat down with you, but of course it was a horrible evening for both of you. After dinner, Alan went back to his London flat and the following day he wrote you a letter, apologising for his bad behaviour. It was dated 28 August, which was the Friday, and my guess is that he dropped it in by hand. I'll come back to that letter in a minute, but I want to get all my ducks in a row.'

'Timelines, Susan. They always were your strong suit.'

'You faked that business with the spilled coffee and fired Jemima on Friday morning. She was completely innocent but you were already planning to kill Alan. You were going to make it look like suicide but it would only work if you hadn't read *Magpie Murders*. Jemima had actually handed you the novel a few days earlier. She'd probably seen Alan's letter too. You knew I was coming back from Dublin on Friday afternoon and it was absolutely essential that she and I shouldn't meet. As far as I was concerned, you would be at home over the weekend, reading *Magpie Murders*. The same as me. It was your alibi. But what mattered just as much was that you should have no reason to kill Alan.'

'You still haven't told me the reason.'

'I will.' I unscrewed a bottle of ink on Charles's desk and used the lid as an ashtray. I could feel the whisky warming my stomach, encouraging me to continue. 'Alan drove back to Framlingham on either Friday evening or Saturday morning. You must have known that he'd broken up with James and you guessed that he would be alone in the house. You drove up on Sunday morning but when you arrived you saw that there was someone with him, up on the roof. That was John White, his neighbour. You parked your car behind a bush where it wouldn't be seen – I noticed the tyre tracks when I was there – and watched what happened. The two men had an altercation, which turned into a scuffle, and you took a photograph of the two of them, just in case it might be useful. And it was, wasn't it, Charles? When I told you that I believed Alan had been murdered, you sent it to me, to put me on the wrong track.

'But it wasn't White who killed him. He left and you watched him take the shortcut back to his house, through the trees. That was when you made your move. You went into the house. Presumably Alan thought you had come to continue the conversation that had begun at the Ivy Club. He invited you to join him for breakfast on the tower. Or maybe you talked your way up there. How you got up there doesn't really matter. The point is that when you got the opportunity, when his back was to you, you pushed him off.

'That was only part of it. After you'd killed him, you went into Alan's study – because you'd read *Magpie Murders* and you knew exactly what you were looking for. It was a gift! A suicide letter, written in Alan's own hand! We both know Alan always wrote the first draft by hand. You had the letter that Alan had hand-delivered on Friday morning. But there was a second letter in the book and you realised you could use it. I really have to kick myself because I've been an editor for more than twenty years and this must be the only crime ever committed that an editor was born to solve. I knew there was something strange about Alan's suicide letter, but I didn't see what it was. I know now. Alan wrote pages one and two on the Friday morning. But page three, the actual page that signals his intention to kill himself, has been taken from the book. It's no longer Alan's voice. There's no slang, no swearing. It's formal, slightly stilted, as if it's been written by someone for whom English is a second language. "*. . . for me there can be no possibility of a reprieve.*" "*It is my hope that you will be able to complete the work of my book.*" It's not a letter from Alan to you. It's a letter from Pünd to James Fraser – and the book he refers to is not *Magpie Murders*, it's *The Landscape of Criminal Investigation*.

'You were incredibly lucky. I don't know exactly what Alan wrote to you but the new page – what eventually became page three – fitted in perfectly. You had to cut a little bit off the top, though. There's one line missing – the line that reads "*Dear James*".

I could have worked that out if I'd measured the pages, but I'm afraid that was something I missed. And there was something else. To complete the illusion that all four pages belonged to the same, single letter, you added numbers in the right top corner but if I'd looked more closely, I'd have seen that the numbers are darker than the letters. You used a different pen. Otherwise, it was perfect. For Alan's death to appear like suicide you needed a suicide letter and now you had one.

'It still had to be delivered. The letter that Alan had actually sent you, the one apologising about the dinner which you had received the day before, had been hand-delivered. You needed it to appear as if it had been posted from Ipswich. The answer was simple. You found an old envelope – I suppose it was one that Alan had sent you at some other time – and put your manufactured suicide note in there. You assumed that no one would look too closely at the envelope. It was the letter that mattered. But as it happens I did notice two things. The envelope was torn. I assume you'd deliberately ripped through the postmark to obliterate the date. But there was something much more striking. The letter was handwritten but the envelope was typed. It exactly reflected something that had happened in *Magpie Murders* and of course it stuck in my mind.

'So let's get to the heart of the matter. You'd used part of a letter written by Atticus Pünd and unfortunately, if your plan was going to work, nobody could read it. If anyone put two and two together, the entire suicide theory would collapse. So that was why the chapters had to disappear. I have to say, I was puzzled why you were so unenthusiastic when I suggested travelling up to Framlingham to find them but now I know why you didn't want them to be found. You removed the handwritten pages. You took Alan's notebooks. You cleared the hard drive on his computer. It would mean losing the ninth book in the series – or postponing it until we could get someone else to finish it – but for you it was a price well worth paying.'

Charles sighed a little and set down his glass, which was empty again. There was a strange, relaxed atmosphere in the room. The two of us could have been discussing the proof of a novel as we had done so many times in the past. For some reason, I was sorry that Bella wasn't here. I don't know why. Perhaps it would have made everything that was unfolding feel a little more normal.

'I had a feeling that you'd see through it all, Susan,' he said. 'You're very clever. I've always known that. However, the motive! You still haven't told me *why* I killed Alan.'

'It was because he was going to pull the plug on Atticus Pünd. Isn't that right? It all goes back to that dinner at the Ivy Club. That was when he told you. He had a radio interview with Simon Mayo the following week and it would give him the perfect opportunity to do it, the one thing that would give him a good laugh before he died, something that mattered even more than seeing the final book in print. You lied to me when you said he wanted to cancel the interview. It was still in his diary and the radio station didn't know he was going to drop out. I think he wanted to go ahead. I think he was desperate.'

'He was sick,' Charles said.

'In more ways than one,' I agreed. 'What I find extraordinary is that he had been planning this all along, from the very day that he invented Atticus Pünd. What sort of writer builds a self-destruct mechanism into his own work and watches it tick away for eleven long years? But that's what Alan did. It was the reason why the last book had to be called Magpie Murders and nothing else. He had built an acronym into the nine titles. The first letters spelled out two words.'

'An anagram.'

'You knew?'

'Alan told me.'

'An anagram. But an anagram of what? In the end, it didn't take me too long to work it out. It wasn't the titles. They're perfectly innocent. It wasn't the characters. They were named after birds. It wasn't the policemen. They were nicked out of Agatha Christie or based on people he knew. James Fraser was named after an actor. That just leaves one character.'

'Atticus Pünd.'

'It's an anagram of "a stupid..."'

Forgive me if I don't spell out that last word. You can work it out easily enough for yourself but personally, I hate it. Swear words in books have always struck me as lazy and over-familiar.

But the 'c' word is more than that. It's used by sour, frustrated men, nearly always about women. It's a word full of misogyny – crudely offensive. And that's what it all came down to! That was what Alan Conway thought about the character that his ex-wife had got him to write. It was what summed up his feelings about the whole detective genre.

'He told you, didn't he,' I went on. '*That's* what happened at the Ivy Club. Alan told you he was going to share his little secret with the entire world when he went on the Simon Mayo show the following week.'

'Yes.'

'And that was why you had to kill him.'

'You're absolutely right, Susan. Alan had drunk a fair bit – that very good wine I'd ordered – and he told me as we left the restaurant. He didn't care. He was going to die anyway and he was determined to take Atticus with him. He was a devil. Do you know what would have happened if he had told people that? They would have hated him! There would have been no BBC television series – you can forget about that. We wouldn't have sold another book. Not one. The entire franchise would have become valueless.'

'So you did it for the money.'

'That's putting it very bluntly. But I suppose it's true. Yes. I've spent eleven years building up this business and I wasn't going to see it destroyed overnight by some ungrateful bastard who'd actually done very well out of us. I did it for my family and for my new grandson. You could say I did it in part for you – although I know you won't thank me. I also did it for the millions of readers all over the world who had invested in Atticus, who'd enjoyed his stories and bought the books. I had absolutely no compunction whatsoever. My only regret is that you've managed to find out, which I suppose makes you my partner in crime.'

'What do you mean by that?'

'Well, I suppose it depends on what you intend to do. Have you told anyone else what you've told me?'

'No.'

'Then you might take the view that you don't need to. Alan is dead. He was going to die anyway. You've read the first page of his letter. He had at best six months. I shortened his life by that amount of time and quite possibly saved him a great deal of suffering along the way.' He smiled. 'I won't pretend that was uppermost in my mind. I think I did the world a favour. We need our literary heroes. Life is dark and complicated but they shine out. They're the beacons that we follow. We have to be pragmatic about this, Susan. You're going to be the CEO of this company. My offer was made in good faith and it still stands. Without Atticus Pünd there will *be* no company. If you don't want to think of yourself, think of everyone else in this building. Would you like to see them put out of their jobs?'

'That's a little unfair, Charles.'

'Cause and effect, my dear. That's all I'm saying.'

In a way, I'd been dreading this moment. It was all very well to unmask Charles Clover but all along I'd been wondering what I'd do next. Everything that he had just said had already occurred to me. The world was not exactly going to be a worse-off place without Alan Conway. His sister, his ex-wife, his son, Donald Leigh, the vicar, Detective Superintendent Locke – they had all, to a greater or a lesser extent, been harmed by him, and it was certainly true that he had been about to play a very mean trick on the people who loved his books. He was going to die anyway.

But it was that 'my dear' that decided me. There was something quite repellent about the way he had addressed me. They were exactly the sort of words that Moriarty would have used. Or Flambeau. Or Carl Peterson. Or Arnold Zeck. And if it was true that detectives acted as moral beacons, why shouldn't their light guide me now? 'I'm sorry, Charles,' I said. 'I don't disagree with what you say. I didn't like Alan and what he did was horrible. But the fact is that you killed him and I can't let you get away with it. I'm sorry – but I wouldn't be able to live with myself.'

'You're going to turn me in?'

'No. I don't need to be involved and I'm sure it'll be a lot easier for you if you call the police yourself.'

He smiled, very thinly. 'You realise that they'll send me to prison. I'll get life. I'll never come out.'

'Yes, Charles. That's what happens when you commit murder.'

'You surprise me, Susan. We've known each other a very long time. I never thought you'd be so petty.'

'Is that what you think?' I shrugged. 'Then there's nothing else to say.'

He glanced at his empty glass, then back at me. 'How long can you give me?' he asked. 'Would you allow me a week's grace? I'd like to spend some time with my family and with my new grandson. I'll need to find Bella a home... that sort of thing.'

'I can't give you a week, Charles. That would make me an accomplice. Maybe until the weekend...?'

'All right. That's fair enough.'

Charles got up and walked over to the bookshelf. His whole career was spread out in front of him. He had published many of those books himself. I also stood up. I had been sitting down for so long that I felt my knees creak. 'I really am sorry, Charles,' I said. Part of me was still wondering if I'd made the right decision. I wanted to be out of the room.

'No. It's all right.' Charles had his back to me. 'I completely understand.'

'Good night, Charles.'

'Good night, Susan.'

I turned and took a step towards the door and right then something hit me, incredibly hard, on the back of the head. I saw an electric white flash and it felt as if my whole body had been broken in half. The room tilted violently to one side and I crashed down to the floor.

Endgame

I was so shocked, so taken by surprise that it actually took me a few moments to work out what had happened. It may be that I was also briefly unconscious. When I opened my eyes, Charles was standing over me with a look that I can only describe as apologetic. I was lying on the carpet, my head close to the open door. Something trickled round my neck, coming from under my ear, and with difficulty I reached up and touched it. When I moved my hand away, I saw that it was covered in blood. I had been hit, extremely hard. Charles was holding something in his hand but my eyes didn't seem to be working properly, as if something had been disconnected. In the end I managed to focus and if I hadn't been frightened and in pain I might almost have laughed. He was holding the Golden Dagger Award that Alan had won for *Atticus Pünd Investigates*. If you've never seen one of these before, it's a miniature-sized dagger encased in a fairly substantial block of Perspex, rectangular, with sharp edges. Charles had used it to club me down.

I tried to speak but the words wouldn't come. Perhaps I was still dazed or perhaps I simply didn't know what to say. Charles examined me and I think I actually saw the moment when he came to his decision. The life went out of his eyes and it suddenly occurred to me that murderers are the loneliest people on the planet. It's the curse of Cain – the fugitive and the vagabond driven out from the face of the earth. However he might try to justify it, Charles had parted company with the rest of humanity the moment he had pushed Alan off that tower and the man who was standing over me now was no longer my friend or colleague. He was empty. He was going to kill me, to silence me, because when you have killed one person you have entered a sort of existential realm where to kill two more or to kill twenty will make no difference. I knew this and I accepted it. Charles would never know peace. He would never play happily with his grandchild. He would never be able to shave without seeing the face of a murderer. I found a little solace in that. But I would be dead. There was nothing I could do to prevent it. I was terrified.

He set the award down.

'Why did you have to be so bloody obstinate?' he asked in a voice that wasn't quite his own. 'I didn't want you to go looking for the missing chapters. I didn't care about the bloody book. All I was doing was protecting everything I'd worked for – and my future. I tried to get you to back off. I tried to send you in the wrong direction. But you wouldn't listen. And now what am I going to do? I still have to protect myself, Susan. I'm too old to go to prison. You didn't have to go to the police. You could have just walked away. You're so bloody stupid . . .'

He wasn't exactly talking to me. It was more a stream of consciousness, a conversation that he was having with himself. For my part, I lay where I was, unmoving. There was a searing pain in my head and I was furious with myself. He had asked me if I had told anyone else what I knew. I should have lied. At the very least I could have pretended I was with him, that I was happy to be an accomplice to Alan's death. I could have said that and walked out of the office. Then I could have called the police. I had brought this on myself.

'Charles . . .' I croaked the single word. Something had happened to my eyesight. He was going in and out of focus. The blood was spreading around my neck.

He had been looking around him and picked something up. It was the box of matches that I had used to light my cigarette. I only understood what he was doing when I saw the flare of the phosphorous. It looked huge. He seemed to disappear behind it.

'I'm sorry, Susan,' he said.

He was going to set fire to the office. He was going to leave me to burn alive, getting rid of the only witness and, for that matter, the incriminating pages, which were still sitting on the desk where I had left them. I saw his hand move in an arc and it was as if a fireball had streaked across the room, whumping down beside the book shelves. In a modern office, it would have hit the carpet and gone out but everything about Cloverleaf Books was antique; the building, the wood panelling, the carpets, the furnishings. The flames leapt up instantly and I was so dazzled by the sight of them that I didn't even see him throw a second match, starting a second blaze on the other side of the room, this time the fire rushing up the curtains and licking at the ceiling. The very air seemed to turn orange. I couldn't believe how quickly it had happened. It was as if I was inside a crematorium. Charles moved towards me, a huge, dark figure that filled my vision. I thought he was going to step over me. I was lying in front of the door. But before he went he lashed out one last time and I screamed as his foot slammed into my chest. I tasted blood in my mouth. There were tears flooding out of my eyes, from the pain and the smoke. Then he was gone.

The office burned gloriously. The building dated back to the eighteenth century and it was a fire that was worthy of that time. I could feel it scorching my cheeks and hands and I thought I must be alight myself. I might simply have lain there and died but alarms had gone off throughout the building and they jolted me awake. Somehow I had to find the strength to get up and stagger out of there. There was an explosion of wood and glass as one of the windows disintegrated and that helped me too. I felt a cold wind rush in. It revived me a little and prevented the smoke from asphyxiating me. I reached out and felt the side of the door, used it to pull myself up. I could barely see. The orange and red of the flames were burning themselves into my eyes. It hurt me to breathe. Charles had broken some of my ribs and I wondered, even then, how he could have brought himself to behave so brutally, this man I had known for so long. Anger spurred me on and somehow I found myself on my feet but that didn't help me. I had actually been safer closer to the floor. Standing up, I was surrounded by smoke and toxic fumes. I was seconds away from passing out.

The alarms were pounding at my ears. If there were fire engines on the way, I wouldn't be able to hear them. I could hardly see. I couldn't breathe. And then I screamed as an arm snaked round my chest and grabbed hold of me. I thought Charles had come back to finish me off. But then I heard a single word shouted into my ear. 'Susan!' I recognised the voice, the smell, the feel of his chest as he pressed my head against it. It was Andreas who had, impossibly, come out of nowhere to rescue me. 'Can you walk?' he shouted.

'Yes.' I could now. With Andreas next to me, I could do anything.

'I'm going to get you out of here.'

'Wait! There are some pages on the desk...'

'Susan?'

'We're not bloody leaving them!'

He thought I was mad but he knew not to argue. He left me for a few seconds, then dragged me out of the room and helped me down the stairs. Tendrils of grey smoke followed us but the fire was spreading up not down and although I could barely see or think, with my whole body in pain and blood pouring from the wound in my head, we managed to make it out. Andreas dragged me through the front door and across the road. When I turned round, the second and third floors were already ablaze and although I could now hear approaching sirens, I knew that nothing of the building would be saved.

'Andreas,' I said. 'Did you get the chapters?'

I passed out before he could reply.

Intensive care

I spent three days at the University College Hospital on the Euston Road, which actually didn't feel nearly long enough after what I'd been through. But that's how it is these days: the marvels of modern science and all that. And, of course, they need the beds. Andreas stayed with me all the time and the real intensive care came from him. I had two broken ribs, massive bruising, and a linear fracture to the skull. They gave me a CT scan but fortunately I wouldn't need surgery. The fire had caused some scarring to my lungs and mucous membranes. I couldn't stop coughing and hated it. My eyes still hadn't cleared up. This was fairly common after a head injury but the doctors had warned me that the damage might be more permanent.

It turned out that Andreas had come to the office because he was upset about the argument we'd had on Sunday night and had decided to surprise me with flowers and walk with me to the restaurant. It was a sweet thought and it saved my life. But that wasn't the question I most wanted to ask.

'Andreas?' It was the first morning after the fire. Andreas was my only visitor although I'd had a text from my sister, Katie, who was on the way down. My throat was hurting and my voice was little more than a whisper. 'Why did you see Charles? The week when I was on book tour, you came to the office. Why didn't you tell me?'

It all came out. Andreas had been chasing a loan for his hotel, the Polydorus, and had flown back to England and gone to a meeting at his bank. They had agreed to the idea in principal but they'd needed a guarantor and that was what had brought him to Charles.

'I wanted to surprise you,' he said. 'When I realised you were out of the office, I didn't know what to do. I felt guilty, Susan. I couldn't tell you about seeing Charles because I hadn't told you about the hotel. So I asked him to say nothing. I told you about it the very next time I saw you. But I felt bad all the same.'

I didn't tell Andreas that after I had spoken to Melissa, I had briefly suspected him of killing Alan. He'd had a perfectly good motive. He was in the country. And at the end of the day, wasn't he the least likely suspect? It really should have been him.

Charles had been arrested. Two police officers came to see me on the day I left hospital and they were nothing like Detective Superintendent Locke – or, for that matter, Raymond Chubb. One was a woman, the other a nice Asian man. They spoke to me for about half an hour, taking notes, but I couldn't talk very much because my voice was still hoarse. I was drugged and in shock and coughing all the time. They said they would come back for a full statement when I was feeling better.

The funny thing is, after all that I didn't even want to read the missing chapters of *Magpie Murders*. It wasn't that I'd lost interest in who'd killed Mary Blakiston and her employer, Sir Magnus Pye. It was just that I felt I'd had more than my fair share of clues and murder and anyway there was no way I could manage the manuscript; my eyes weren't up to it. It was only after I'd got back to my flat in Crouch End that my curiosity returned. Andreas was still with me. He'd taken a week off school and I got him to skim through the whole book so that he would know the plot before he read the final chapters out loud. It was appropriate that I should hear them in his voice. They had only been saved thanks to him.

This is how it ended.

SEVEN

A Secret Never to be Told

1

Atticus Pünd took one last walk around Saxby-on-Avon, enjoying the morning sunshine. He had slept well and taken two pills when he woke up. He felt refreshed and his head was clear. He had arranged to meet Detective Inspector Chubb at the Bath police station in an hour's time and had left James Fraser to see to the suitcases and to settle the bill while he stretched his legs. He had not been in the village very long but in a strange way he felt he had come to know it intimately. The church, the castle, the antique shop in the square, the bus shelter, Dingle Dell and, of course, Pye Hall – they had always related to each other in various ways but over the past week they had become fixed points in a landscape of crime. Pünd had chosen the title of his magnum opus carefully. There really was a landscape to every criminal investigation and its consciousness always informed the crime.

Saxby could not have looked lovelier. It was still early and for a moment there was nobody in sight – no cars either – so it was possible to imagine the little community as it might have been a century ago. For a moment the murder seemed almost irrelevant. After all, what did it matter? People had come and gone. They had fallen in love. They had grown up and they had died. But the village itself, the grass verges and the hedgerows, the entire backdrop against which the drama had been played, that remained unchanged. Years from now, someone might point out the house where Sir Magnus had been murdered or the place where his killer had lived and there might be an 'Oh!' of curiosity. But nothing more. Wasn't he that man who had his head cut off? Didn't someone else die too? Snatches of conversation that would scatter like leaves in the wind.

And yet there had been some changes. The deaths of Mary Blakiston and Sir Magnus Pye had caused a myriad of tiny cracks that had reached out from their respective epicentres and which would take time to heal. Pünd noticed the sign in the window of the Whiteheads' antique shop: CLOSED UNTIL FURTHER NOTICE. He did not know if Johnny Whitehead had been arrested for the theft of the stolen medals but he doubted that the shop would open again. He walked up to the garage and thought of Robert Blakiston and Joy Sanderling who wanted only to get married but who had found themselves up against forces well beyond their comprehension. It saddened him to think of the girl on the day she had come to visit him in London. What was it she had said? 'It's not right. It's so unfair.' At the time, she could have had no idea of the truth of those words.

A movement caught his eye and he saw Clarissa Pye walking briskly towards the butcher's shop, wearing a rather jaunty three-feathered hat. She did not see him. There was something about the way she carried herself that made him smile. She had benefited from the death of her brother. There could be no denying it. She might never inherit the house but she had regained control of her own life, which mattered more. Would that have been a reason to kill him? It was curious, really, how one man could make himself the target of so much hostility. He found himself thinking of Arthur Redwing, the artist whose best work had been desecrated, sliced apart and burned. Arthur might consider himself an amateur. He had never achieved greatness as an artist. But Pünd knew all too well the passion that burned in the heart of any creative person and which could all too easily be subverted and turned into something dangerous.

Or what of Dr Redwing herself? The last time she had spoken of Sir Magnus, she had been unable to disguise her hatred not just of him but of all he stood for. She, more than anyone, had known the hurt that he had caused her husband and Pünd knew, from past experience, that there is no more powerful person in an English village than the doctor and, in certain circumstances, the doctor will also be the most dangerous.

He had walked some of the way down the High Street and he could see Dingle Dell stretching out on his left. He could have taken the short cut through to Pye Hall but he decided not to. He had no wish to meet with Lady Pye or her new partner. They, of all people, had had the most to gain from the death of Sir Magnus. It was the oldest story in the world: the wife, the lover, the cruel husband, the sudden death. Well, they might think they were free to be together but Pünd was quite certain that it would never work out. There are some relationships that succeed only because they are impossible, that actually need unhappiness to continue. It would not take Frances Pye long to tire of Jack Dartford, as handsome as he undoubtedly was. To all intents and purposes, she now owned Pye Hall. Or was it that Pye Hall owned her? Matthew Blakiston had said it was cursed and Pünd could not disagree. He made a conscious decision and turned back. He did not want to see the place again.

He would have liked to have spoken to Brent one more time. It was odd that the role of the groundsman in everything that had happened had never been fully explained. Inspector Chubb had dismissed him almost entirely from the investigation. And yet Brent had been the first to discover Mary Blakiston after he had drowned as well as the last to see Sir Magnus before he was decapitated. For that matter, it was Brent who claimed to have discovered the body of Mary Blakiston and it was certainly he who had telephoned Dr Redwing. Why had Sir Magnus so arbitrarily dismissed him just before his own death? Pünd feared that the answer to that question might never be known. He had very little time left to him, in every sense. This morning he would set out his thoughts on what had occurred in Saxby-on-Avon. By the afternoon he would be gone.

And what of Dingle Dell? The stretch of woodland between the vicarage and Pye Hall seemed to have played a large part in the narrative but Pünd had never considered it, in itself, a motive for murder if only because the death of Sir Magnus would not necessarily prevent the development going ahead. Even so, people had behaved very foolishly. They had allowed their emotions to run away with them. Pünd thought of Diana Weaver, the stolid cleaning lady who had taken it upon herself to write a poison pen letter, using her employer's typewriter. As things had turned out, he had been unable to ask her about the envelope – but it didn't matter. He had guessed the answer anyway. He had solved this case, not so much by concrete evidence, as by conjecture. In the end, there could be only one way that it would all make sense.

He retraced his steps, walking up the High Street. He found himself back in the cemetery of St Botolph's, passing beneath the large elm tree that grew beside the gate. He glanced up at the branches. They were empty.

He continued towards the newly dug grave with its temporary, wooden cross and plaque.

Mary Elizabeth Blakiston
5 April 1887 – 15 July 1955

This was where it had all begun. It had been the death of Robert's mother, and the fact that the two of them had argued publicly just a few days before that, which had driven Joy Sanderling to his office in Clerkenwell. Pünd knew now that everything that had happened in Saxby-on-Avon had stemmed from that death. He imagined the woman, lying beneath him in the cold soil. He had never met her but he felt he knew her. He remembered the entries she had made in her diary, the poisoned view she had taken of the world around her.

He thought of poison.

There was a footfall behind him and he turned to see the Reverend Robin Osborne walking towards him, making his way between the graves. He did not have his bicycle with him. It was strange that, on the night of the murder, both he and his wife had been in the vicinity of Pye Hall, the one supposedly looking for the other. The vicar's bicycle had also been heard passing the Ferryman during the course of the evening and Matthew Blakiston had actually seen it parked outside the Lodge. Pünd was glad to have come across the vicar one last time. There was still a certain matter to be accounted for.

'Oh, hello, Mr Pünd,' Osborne said. He glanced down at the grave. Nobody had left any flowers. 'Have you come here for inspiration?'

'No. Not at all,' Pünd replied. 'I am leaving the village today. I was merely passing through on my way back to the hotel.'

'You're leaving? Does that mean you've given up on us?'

'No, Mr Osborne. It means the exact opposite.'

'You know who killed her?'

'Yes. I do.'

'I'm very glad to hear it. I've often thought . . . it must be very hard to rest in peace when your murderer is walking on the ground above you. It offends all the ideas of natural justice. I don't suppose there's anything you can tell me – although I probably shouldn't ask.'

Pünd made no reply. Instead, he changed the subject. 'The words that you spoke at the funeral of Mary Blakiston, they were of great interest,' he said.

'Did you think so? Thank you.'

'You said that she was a great part of the village, that she embraced life here. Would you be surprised to learn that she kept a diary in which she recorded nothing but the darkest and most unkind observations about the people who lived in Saxby-on-Avon?'

'I would be surprised, Mr Pünd. Yes. I mean, she did have a way of insinuating herself, but I never detected any particular malice in anything she did.'

'She made an entry about you and Mrs Osborne. It seems that she visited you on 14 July, exactly one day before she died. Do you have any recollection of that?'

'I can't say . . .' Osborne was a terrible liar. His hands

were writhing and his entire face was drawn and unnatural. Of course he saw her, standing in the kitchen. '*I heard you were having trouble with the wasps*.' And the pictures, lying face up on the kitchen table . . . Why were they there? Why hadn't Henrietta put them away?

'She used the word "shocking" in her diary,' Pünd went on. 'She said also that it was "dreadful" and asked herself what action she should take. Do you know to what she was referring?'

'I have no idea.'

'Then I will tell you. It very much puzzled me, Mr Osborne, why your wife should have needed treatment for belladonna poisoning. Dr Redwood had purchased a vial of physostigmine for that very purpose. She had stepped on a clump of deadly nightshade.'

'That's right.'

'But the question I asked myself was – why was your wife not wearing shoes?'

'Yes. You did mention that at the time. And my wife said—'

'Your wife did not tell me the entire truth. She was not wearing shoes because she was not wearing anything else either. This is the reason why you were both so reluctant to tell me where you had been on holiday. In the end, you were forced to give me the name of your hotel – Shelpegh Court in Devonshire – and it was the matter of one simple telephone call to discover that Sheplegh Court is well known as a resort for naturists. That is the truth of the matter, is it not, Mr Osborne? You and your wife are followers of naturism.'

Osborne swallowed hard. 'Yes.'

'And Mary Blakiston found evidence of this?'

'She found photographs.'

'Do you have any idea what she intended to do?'

'No. She said nothing. And the next day . . .' He cleared his throat. 'My wife and I are completely innocent,' he said, suddenly, the words tumbling out. 'Naturism is a political and a cultural movement which is also related very much to good health. There's nothing unclean about it and nothing, I assure you, that would demean or undermine my calling. I could mention that Adam and Eve were unaware that they were naked. It was their natural state and it was only after they had eaten the apple that they became ashamed. Hen and I travelled in Germany together, before the war, and that was where we had our first experience. It appealed to us. We kept it a secret simply because we felt that there were people here who might not understand, who might be offended.'

'And Dingle Dell?'

'It was perfect for us. It gave us freedom, somewhere we could walk together without being seen. I hasten to add, Mr Pünd, that we did nothing wrong. I mean, there was nothing . . . carnal.' He had chosen the word carefully. 'We simply walked in the moonlight. You were there with us. You know what a lovely place it is.'

'And all was well until your wife stepped onto a poisonous plant.'

'All was well until Mary saw the pictures. But you don't think for a minute – you – you can't think that I harmed her because of it?'

'I know exactly how Mary Blakiston died, Mr Osborne.'

'You said – you said you're about to leave.'

'In a few hours from now. And this one secret I will take with me. You and your wife have nothing to fear. I will tell no one.'

Robin Osborne let out a deep breath. 'Thank you, Mr Pünd. We've been so worried. You have no idea.' His eyes brightened. 'And have you heard? According to the agents in Bath, Lady Pye isn't intending to continue with the development. The Dell is going to be left alone.'

'I am very glad to hear it. You were certainly correct, Mr Osborne. It is a very beautiful place. Indeed, you have given me an idea . . .'

Atticus Pünd left the cemetery on his own. He still had fifty minutes until the meeting with Raymond Chubb.

And there was one thing he had to do.

2

It took him a short time to write the letter, sitting with a cup of tea in a quiet corner of the Queen's Arms.

'Dear James,

By the time that you read this, it will all be finished. You will forgive me for not having spoken to you earlier, for not taking you into my confidence, but I am sure that in time you will understand.

There are some notes which I have written and which you will find in my desk. They relate to my condition and to the decision that I have made. I want it to be understood that the doctor's diagnosis is clear and, for me, there can be no possibility of reprieve. I have no fear of death. I would like to think that my name will be remembered.

I have achieved great success in a life that has gone on long enough. You will find that I have left you a small bequest in my will. This is partly to recognise the many years that we have spent together but it is also my hope that you will be able to complete the work of my book and prepare it for publication. You are now it's only guardian but I am confident that it will be safe in your hands.

Otherwise, there are few people who will mourn for me. I leave behind me no dependents. As I prepare to take leave of this world, I feel that I have used my time well and hope that I will be remembered for the successes that you and I shared together.

I would ask you to apologise to my friend, Detective Inspector Chubb. As will become apparent, I have used the physostigmine which I took from Clarissa Pye and which I should have returned to him. I understand it to be tasteless and believe it will provide me with an easy passage, but even so it was a betrayal of trust, even a small crime, for which I am sorry.

Finally, although it surprises me, I would like my ashes to be scattered in the woodland known as Dingle Dell. I do not know why I ask this. You know that I am not of a romantic disposition. But it is the scene of my last case and seems fitting. It is also a very peaceful place. It seems right.

I take my leave of you, old friend, with respectful good wishes. I thank you for your loyalty and companionship and hope that you will consider returning to acting and that you will enjoy a long and prosperous career.'

He signed the letter and slid it into an envelope that he sealed and marked: PRIVATE – TO MR JAMES FRASER.

He would not need it for a while, but he was glad that it was done. Finally, he drank his tea and went out to the waiting car.

3

There were five of them in the office in Bath, framed by two double-height windows, the atmosphere strangely silent and still. Life continued on the other side of the glass but in here it seemed to be trapped in a moment which had always been inescapable and which had finally arrived. Detective Inspector Raymond Chubb had taken his place behind the desk, even though he had little to say. He was barely more than a witness. But this was his office, his desk, his authority and he hoped he had made that clear. Atticus Pünd was next to him, one hand stretched out on the polished surface as if it somehow afforded him the right to be here, his rosewood cane resting diagonally against the arm of his chair. James Fraser was tucked away in the corner.

Joy Sanderling, who had come to London and who had drawn Pünd into this in the first place, sat opposite them in a chair which had been carefully positioned, as if she had been called here for a job interview. Robert Blakiston, pale and nervous, sat next to her. They had spoken little since they had arrived. It was Pünd who was the focus of attention and who now began.

'Miss Sanderling,' he said. 'I have invited you here today because you are in many respects my client – which is to say, I first heard of Sir Magnus Pye and his affairs through you. You came to me not so much because you wanted me to solve a crime – indeed, we could not be sure that any crime had been committed – but to ask for my assistance in the matter of your marriage to Robert Blakiston which you felt to be under threat. It was perhaps wrong of me to refuse to do what you asked but I hope you will understand that I had personal matters to consider at the time and my attention was elsewhere. The day after your visit, I read of the death of Sir Magnus and it was this that changed my mind. Even so, from the moment that I arrived at Saxby-on-Avon, I felt myself to be working not only on your behalf but also for your fiancé, and that is why it is only right that you should both be invited to hear the fruits of my deliberations. I would like you also to know that I was very saddened that you felt the need to take matters into your own hands and to advertise your private life to the entire village. That cannot have been pleasant for you and it was my responsibility. I must ask you to forgive me.'

'If you've solved the murders and Robert and I can get married, I'll forgive anything,' Joy said.

'Ah yes.' He turned briefly to Chubb. 'We have two young people who are evidently very much in love. It has been clear to me how much this marriage means to both of them.'

'And good luck to them,' Chubb muttered.

'If you know who did it, why don't you tell us?' Robert Blakiston had spoken for the first time and there was a quiet venom in his voice. 'Then Joy and I can leave. I've already decided. We're not going to stay in Saxby-on-Avon. I can't stand the place. We're going to find somewhere far away and start again.'

'We'll be all right if we're together.' Joy reached out and touched his hand.

'Then I will begin,' Pünd said. He drew his hand away

from the desk and rested it on the arm of his chair. 'Even before I arrived in Saxby-on-Avon, when I read of the murder of Sir Magnus in *The Times* newspaper, I was aware that I was dealing with a strange coincidence. A housekeeper falls to her death in what appears to be a straightforward domestic accident and then, not two weeks later, the man who employed her also dies and this time it is unmistakably a murder of the most gruesome sort. I say that it is a coincidence but what I mean is in fact quite the opposite. There must be a reason why these two events have collided, so to speak, but what is it? Could there be a single motive for the death of both Sir Magnus Pye and his housekeeper? What end could be achieved if they were both put out of the way?' Briefly, Pünd's eyes burned into the two young people sitting in front of him. 'It did occur to me that the marriage of which you spoke and which you both desired so fervently might provide a motive. We know that, for reasons that may be distasteful, Mary Blakiston was opposed to the union. But I have dismissed this line of thought. First, she had no power to prevent the marriage, at least so far as we know. So there was no reason to kill her. Also, there is no evidence to suggest that Sir Magnus was concerned one way or another. Indeed, he had always been amicably disposed towards Mary Blakiston's son and would surely wish to see it go ahead.'

'He knew about the marriage,' Robert said. 'He didn't have any objections at all. Why would he have? Joy is a wonderful girl and, you're right, he was always kind to me. He wanted me to be happy.'

'I agree. But if we cannot find a single reason for the two deaths, what are the alternatives? Could there have been two murderers in Saxby-on-Avon, acting independently of each other with two quite different sets of motivation? That sounds a little unlikely, to say the least. Or could it be that one death was in some way the cause of the other? We now know that Mary Blakiston collected many secrets about the lives of the villagers. Did she know something about somebody that put her in danger – and had she perhaps told Sir Magnus? Let us not forget that he was her closest confidante.

'And while I was turning these matters over in my mind, there was a third crime that presented itself to me. For on the evening of Mary Blakiston's funeral, somebody broke into Pye Hall. It seemed to be an ordinary burglary but in a month in which two people die, nothing is ordinary any more. This was soon proven to be case, for although one silver buckle was sold in London, the rest of the proceeds were merely thrown in the lake. Why was that? Was the burglar disturbed or did he have some other aim? Could it be that he simply wished to remove the silver rather than to profit from it?'

'You mean it was some sort of provocation?' Chubb asked.

'Sir Magnus was proud of his Roman silver. It was part of his legacy. It could have been taken simply to spite him. That thought did occur to me, Detective Inspector.'

Pünd leant forward.

'There was one other aspect of the case that I found very difficult to understand,' he said. 'And that was the attitude of Mary Blakiston.'

'I never understood her either,' Robert muttered.

'Let us examine her relationship with you. She loses one son in a tragic accident and this makes her watchful, domineering, over-possessive. You know that I met with your father?'

Robert stared. 'When?'

'Yesterday. My colleague, Fraser, drove me to his home in Cardiff. And he told me a great deal that was of interest. After the death of your brother, Tom, your mother closed in on you. Even he was not to be allowed to come near you. She could not bear having you out of her sight and so, for example, she was angry when you chose to go to Bristol. It was the only time that she argued with Sir Magnus who had, all the time, concerned himself with your well-being. All of this makes sense. A woman who has lost one child will quite naturally become obsessive about the other. I can also understand how that relationship can become uncomfortable and even poisonous. The arguments between you were natural. It is very sad but inevitable.

'But this is what I do not understand. Why was she so opposed to the marriage? It makes no sense. Her son has found, if I may say so, a charming companion in Miss Sanderling. Here is a local girl from a good family. Her father is a fireman. She works in a doctor's surgery. She does not intend to take Robert away from the village. It is a perfect match and yet from the very start, Mary Blakiston responds only with hostility. Why?'

Joy blushed. 'I have no idea, Mr Pünd.'

'Well, we can help you there, Miss Sanderling,' Chubb cut in. 'You have a brother with Down's syndrome.'

'Paul? What's he got to do with it?'

'Mrs Blakiston set down her thoughts in a diary that we found. She had some idea that the condition would be passed on to any grandchildren you might have. That was her problem.'

Pünd shook his head. 'I'm sorry, Detective Inspector,' he said. 'But I do not agree.'

'She made it clear enough from where I'm standing, Mr Pünd. "...this awful sickness infecting her family..." Horrible words. But that's exactly what she wrote.'

'They are words that you may have misinterpreted.'

Pünd sighed. 'In order to understand Mary Blakiston, it is necessary to go back in time, the defining moment in her life.' He glanced at Robert. 'I hope it will not distress you, Mr Blakiston. I am referring to the death of your brother.'

'I've lived with it most of my life,' Robert said. 'There's nothing you can say that will upset me now.'

'There are several aspects of the accident that I find puzzling. Let me begin, for a moment, with your mother's reaction to what happened. I cannot understand a woman who continues to live at the very scene where it took place, where she lost her child. Every day she walks past that lake and I have to ask myself: is she punishing herself for something she has done? Or for something that she knows?

Could it be that she has been driven by a sense of guilt ever since that dreadful day?

'I visited the Lodge and tried to imagine what it might be like for her, and indeed for you, living together in that grim place, surrounded by trees, permanently in shadow. The house did not yield many secrets but there was one mystery, a room on the second floor that your mother kept locked. Why? What had been the purpose of that room and why did she never go in there? There was little that remained in the room: a bed and a table and inside the table, the collar of a dog that had had also died.'

'That was Bella,' Robert said.

'Yes. Bella had been a gift from your father to your brother and Sir Magnus did not like having it on his land. When I spoke to your father yesterday, he suggested that Sir Magnus had killed the dog in the cruelest possible way. I could not be sure of the truth of that, but I will tell you what I thought. Your brother drowns. Your mother falls down the stairs. Sir Magnus is brutally killed. And now we have Bella, a cross-breed, who is poisoned. It is another violent death to add to the veritable catalogue of violent deaths that we find at Pye Hall.

'Why was the collar of the dog kept here? There was something else about the room that I noticed immediately. It was the only one in the house that had a view of the lake. That, in itself, I thought most significant. Next, I asked myself, for what purpose was the room used when Mary Blakiston lived at the Lodge? I had assumed, incorrectly, that it was the bedroom used either by yourself or by your brother.'

'It was my mother's sewing room,' Robert said. 'I'd have told you that if you'd asked me.'

'I did not need to ask you. You mentioned to me that you and your brother had a game in which you knocked on the walls of your bedrooms, sending each other codes. You must therefore have had adjoining rooms and so it followed that the room across the corridor must have had another purpose.

Your mother did a lot of sewing and it seemed very likely to me that this was where she liked to work.'

'That's all very well, Mr Pünd,' Chubb said. 'But I don't see where it gets us.'

'We are almost there, Detective Inspector. But first let me examine the accident as it happened for, as I have already stated, that too presents certain problems.

'According to the testimony of both Robert and his father, Tom was searching for a piece of gold which was in fact in the bulrushes beside the water because that is where Sir Magnus had hidden it. Now, let us remember, he was not a small child. He was eleven years old. He was intelligent. I have to ask you, would he have entered the cold and muddy water in the belief that the gold was there? From what I understand, the games that the two boys played were very formal. They were organised by Sir Magnus who concealed the treasure and provided specific clues. If Tom was beside the lake, he might well have worked out where the gold was to be found. But there was no need to walk right past it *into* the lake. That makes no sense at all.

'And there is another detail, also, that troubles me. Brent, the groundsman, discovered the body—'

'He was always skulking around,' Robert cut in. 'Tom and I were afraid of him.'

'I am willing to believe it. But there is now a question that I wish to put to you. Brent was very precise in his description. He pulled your brother out of the water and laid him on the ground. You arrived moments later – and what reason could there be for you to plunge into the water yourself?'

'I wanted to help.'

'Of course. But your brother was already out of the water. Your father said he was lying on dry land. Why would you want to make yourself cold and wet?'

Robert frowned. 'I don't know what you want me to say, Mr Pound. I was thirteen years old. I don't even remember what happened, really. I was only thinking about Tom, getting him out of the water. There was nothing else in my mind.'

'No, Robert. I think there was. I think you wanted to disguise the fact that you were already wet yourself.'

The entire room seemed to come to a halt, as if it were a piece of film caught in a projector. Even outside, in the street, nothing moved.

'Why would he want to do that?' Joy asked. There was a slight tremor in her voice.

'Because he had been fighting with his brother beside the lake a few moments before. He had killed his brother by drowning him.'

'That's not true!' Robert's eyes blazed. For a moment, Fraser thought he was going to leap out of his chair and he readied himself to go to Pünd's rescue if need be.

'So much of what I say is based upon conjecture,' Pünd said. 'And trust me when I say I do not hold you entirely responsible for a crime that you committed as a child. But let us look at the evidence. A dog is given to your brother, not to you. It dies in terrible circumstances. You and your brother search for a piece of gold. He finds it, not you. And this time it is he who is punished. Your father told me that you and Tom fought often. He worried about you because of your moods, the way you would take yourself off for solitary walks, even at so young an age. He did not see what your mother had seen – that from the time of your birth – a difficult birth – there was something wrong with you, that you were prepared to kill.'

'No, Mr Pünd!' This time it was Joy who protested. 'You're not talking about Robert. Robert's nothing like that.'

'Robert is very much like that, Miss Sanderling. You yourself told me what a difficult time he had at school. He did not make friends easily. The other children mistrusted him. Perhaps they were aware that there was something not quite right. And on the one occasion when he had left home, when he was working in Bristol, he became involved in a violent altercation which led to his arrest and a night in jail.'

'He broke the other chap's jaw and three of his ribs,' Chubb added. He had evidently been checking the files.

'It is my belief that Mary Blakiston knew very well the nature of her older son,' Pünd went on. 'And the simple truth is that she was not protecting him from the outside world. She was protecting the world from him. She had known, or suspected, what had happened to the dog, Bella. Why else had she kept the collar? She had seen what had happened at the lake. Yes. Sitting at her table in the sewing room, she had watched as Robert killed Tom, angry that it was his little brother who had found the gold and not he. And from that day on she built a wall around him. Matthew Blakiston told us that she pulled up the drawbridge. She would not allow him to come close to Robert. But he did not understand why. She did not want him to learn the truth.

'And now we can understand, Miss Sanderling, the reason why she was so hostile to the idea of your marriage. Once again, it was not your suitability as a wife that concerned her. She knew her son for what he was and she was determined that he would not become a husband. As for your brother, who is afflicted with Down's syndrome, you completely understood what she meant. She made a significant entry in her diary. '*All the time I was thinking about this awful sickness infecting her family.*' I fear both James Fraser and Inspector Chubb misconstrued what she had written. The sickness that she referred to was the madness of her son. And she feared that it might one day in the future, infect Miss Sanderling's family should the marriage be allowed to go ahead.'

'I'm leaving!' Robert Blakiston got to his feet. 'I don't have to listen to any more of this nonsense.'

'You're staying right where you are,' Chubb told him. 'There are two men on the other side of that door and you're not going anywhere until Mr Pünd has finished.'

Robert looked around him wildly. 'So what other theories do you have, Mr Pound? Are you going to say I killed my mother to stop her talking? Is that what you think?'

'No, Mr Blakiston. I know perfectly well that you did

not kill your mother. If you will sit down, I will tell you exactly what occurred.'

Robert Blakiston hesitated, then retook his seat. Fraser couldn't help noticing that Joy Sanderling had twisted away from him. She looked utterly miserable and was avoiding his eye.

'Let us put ourselves inside the mind of your mother,' Pünd continued. 'Again, much of this must be conjecture but it is the only way that the events which have presented themselves to us will make any sense. She is living with a son whom she knows to be dangerously disturbed. In her own way, she is trying to protect him. She watches his every move. She never lets him out of her sight. But as their relationship becomes more fractious and unpleasant, as the scenes between them become more violent, she gets worried. What if, in his madness, her son turns on her?

'She has one confidante. She looks up to Sir Magnus Pye as a man of wealth and good breeding. He is far above her, an aristocrat no less. He has on many occasions helped with family matters. He has employed her. He has invented games for her children, keeping them amused while their father is away. He stood by her after the break-up of her marriage and later he has twice found work for her surviving son. He has even used his influence to extricate Robert from jail.

'She cannot tell him about the murder. He would be horrified and might abandon them both. But she has an idea. She gives him a sealed envelope, which contains a letter setting out the truth: the murder of her younger son, the killing of the dog, perhaps other incidents about which we will never know. She describes Robert Blakiston as he really is – but here is the trick of it. The letter is to be opened only in the event of her death. And after it has been delivered, after it has been locked away, she tells Robert exactly what she has done. The letter will act as a safety net. Sir Magnus will be true to his word. He will not open it. He will merely keep it safely. But should anything ever happen to her, should she die in strange or suspicious circumstances, then he will read it and he will know who is responsible. It is a perfect arrangement. Robert dare not attack her. He can do her no harm. Thanks to the letter, he has been neutralised.'

'You don't know this,' Robert said. 'You *can't* know it.'

'I know everything!' Pünd paused. 'Let us now return to the death of Mary Blakiston and see how events unfold.'

'Who *did* kill her?' Chubb demanded.

'Nobody!' Pünd smiled. 'That is what is so extraordinary and unfortunate about this whole affair. She really did die as a result of an accident. Nothing more!'

'Wait a minute!' Fraser spoke from the corner of the room. 'You told me that Matthew Blakiston killed her.'

'He did. But not intentionally and he was not even aware that he was responsible. You will remember, James, that he had a strange premonition that his wife was in danger and telephoned her that morning. You will also recall that the telephones in the top part of the house were not working. Lady Pye told us as much when we were with her. So what happened was very simple. Mary Blakiston was cleaning with the Hoover at the top of the stairs. The telephone rang – and she had to run all the way downstairs to answer it. Her foot caught in the wire and she fell, dragging the Hoover with her and wedging it into the top of the bannisters.

'It seemed obvious to me that an accident was the only sensible explanation. Mary Blakiston was alone in the house. Her keys were in the back door, which was locked, and Brent was working at the front. He would have seen anyone if they had come out. And to push somebody down the stairs . . . it is not a sensible way to attempt murder. How can you be sure that they will do no more than themselves a serious injury?

'The inhabitants of Saxby-on-Avon thought otherwise. They spoke only of murder. And to make matters worse, Mary Blakiston and her son had argued only a few days before. "I wish you would die. I wish you would give me some peace." It may not have occurred to Robert immediately, but the exact conditions of his mother's letter, at least in so far as we can imagine it, had been met. She had died violently. He was the prime suspect.

'It was all brought home to him a week later at the funeral. The vicar has kindly lent me his sermon and I have read his exact words. "Although we are here today to mourn her departure, we should remember what she left behind." He told me that Robert was startled and covered his eyes when he heard that – and with good reason. It was not because he was upset. It was because he remembered what his mother had left behind.

'Fortunately, Sir Magnus and Lady Pye were not in the village. They were on holiday in the south of France. Robert had a little time and he acted immediately. That same night he broke into Pye Hall, using the same door that Brent had damaged when the body was found. His task was simple. He must find and destroy the letter before Sir Magnus returns.' Pünd looked again at Robert. 'You must have been furious at the unfairness of it all. You had done nothing! It was not your fault. But if the letter was read, the secrets of your childhood would be known and the marriage would be stopped.' Now he turned to Joy who had been listening to all this with a look of complete dismay. 'I know that this cannot be easy for you, Miss Sanderling. And if gives me no pleasure to destroy your hopes. But if there is a consolation it is that the man sitting beside you does truly love you and did what he did in the hope that he could still be with you.'

Joy Sanderling said nothing. Pünd went on.

'Robert searched the house but he found nothing. Sir Magnus had placed the letter in a safe in his study, along with his other private papers. The safe was concealed behind a painting and required a lengthy combination – which Robert could not possibly know. He was forced to leave empty-handed.

'But now he had another problem: how to explain the break-in. If nothing had been taken, Sir Magnus – and the police – might suspect another motivation and, when the letter came to light, that might lead them to him. The solution was simple. He opened the display case and removed the Roman silver that had once been found in Dingle Dell. He also took some of Lady Pye's jewellery. It now looked like a straightforward burglary. Of course, he had no interest in any of these items. He would not take the risk of selling them. So what did he do? He threw them into the lake where they would have remained undiscovered but for one piece of bad luck. He dropped a silver belt buckle as he hurried across the lawn and the next day Brent found it and sold it to Johnny Whitehead. That led to the discovery, by police divers, of the rest of the hoard, and so to the true reason for the break-in.

'The letter remained in the safe. Sir Magnus returned from France. For the next few days he must have had other matters to occupy him and it cannot have been easy for you, Robert, waiting for the call that you knew must come. What would Sir Magnus do? Would he go straight to the police or would he give you a chance to explain yourself? In the end, on the Thursday when his wife went to London, he summoned you to Pye Hall. And so, at last, we arrive at the scene of the crime.

'Sir Magnus has read the letter. It is hard to be sure of his reaction. He is shocked, certainly. Does he suspect Robert Blakiston of his mother's murder? It is quite possible. But he is an intelligent – one might say a quite diffident – sort of man. He has known Robert well for many years and he has no fear of him. Has he not always acted as Robert's mentor? However, just to be sure, he searches out his service revolver and places it in the drawer of his desk where Inspector Chubb will find it later. It is an insurance policy, nothing more.

'At seven o'clock, the garage closes. Robert returns home to wash and to change into smarter clothes for a meeting at which he intends to plead his innocence and ask for Sir Magnus's understanding. Meanwhile, other forces are at play. Matthew Blakiston is on his way from Cardiff to interrogate Sir Magnus about the treatment of his wife. Brent, who has recently been fired, works late and then goes to the Ferryman. Robin Osborne has a crisis of conscience and goes to seek solace in the church. Henrietta Osborne becomes concerned and searches for her husband. Many of these paths will cross but in such a way that no true pattern will emerge.

'At about twenty past eight, Robert makes his way to the fateful meeting. He sees the vicar's bicycle outside the church and, on a whim, decides to borrow it. He can have no way of knowing that the vicar is in fact inside the church. He arrives, unseen at Pye Hall, parks the bicycle at the Lodge and walks up the drive. He is admitted by Sir Magnus, and what takes place, the actual murder itself, I will describe in a minute. But first let me complete the larger picture. Matthew Blakiston also arrives and parks his car beside the Lodge, at the same time noticing the bicycle. He walks up the driveway and is seen by Brent who is just finishing work. He knocks at the door, which is opened a few moments later by Sir Magnus. You will remember, Fraser, the exchange which took place and which was described to us, quite accurately, by Matthew Blakiston.

'"You!" Sir Magnus is surprised and with good reason. The father has arrived at the very moment when the son is inside and the two of them are engaged in a discussion of the greatest delicacy. Sir Magnus does not say his name out loud. He does not wish to alert Robert to the fact that his father is here, at the worst possible time. But before he dismisses him, he uses the opportunity to ask Matthew a question. "Do you really think I killed your dog?" Why would he ask such a thing unless he was wishing to confirm something he had been discussing with Robert just moments before? At any event, Sir Magnus closes the door. Matthew leaves.

'The murder takes place. Robert Blakiston hurries from the house, using the bicycle that he has borrowed. It is dark. He does not expect to meet anyone. Inside the Ferryman, Brent hears the bicycle go past during a lull in the music and assumes it is the vicar. Robert replaces the bicycle at the church but there has been a great deal of blood and he has managed to transfer some of it to the handlebars. When the vicar comes out of the church and returns home on the bicycle, some of that blood will surely be found on his clothes. It is why, I believe, Mrs Osborne was so very nervous when she spoke to me. It may well be that she believed him to be guilty of the crime. Well, they will know the truth soon enough.

'There is one last act in the drama of the night. Matthew Blakiston has changed his mind and returns to have his confrontation with Sir Magnus. He misses his son by a matter of minutes but sees the dead body through the letter box and collapses into the flower bed, leaving a print of his hand in the soft earth. Afraid that he will be suspected, he leaves as quickly as he can but he is spotted by Lady Pye, who has just returned from London, and who will now enter the house and find her husband.

'That leaves only the murder itself which I must now describe.

'Robert Blakiston and Sir Magnus Pye meet in the study. Sir Magnus has retrieved the letter that Mary Blakiston wrote all those years ago and you will recall that the picture, which covers the safe, is still ajar. The letter is on his desk and the two men discuss its contents. Robert urges Sir Magnus to believe that he has done nothing wrong, that he was not responsible for his mother's tragic death. As chance would have it, there is a second letter, also on the desk. Sir Magnus has received it that day. It concerns the demolition of Dingle Dell and contains some threatening, even some violent language. As we now know, it was written by a local woman, Diana Weaver, using the typewriter of Dr Redwing.

'Two letters. Two envelopes. Remember this.

'The conversation does not go well. It may be that Sir Magnus threatens to expose his former protégé. Perhaps he says he will consider the matter before he goes to the police. I would imagine that Robert is at his most charming and persuasive as Sir Magnus shows him out. But when he reaches the main hall, he strikes. He has already noted the suit of armour and he draws the sword from its sheath. It comes out silently and easily because, as it happens, Sir Magnus has used it quite recently when he attacked the portrait of his wife. Robert is taking no chances. He will not be exposed. His marriage to Joy Sanderling will go ahead. From behind, he decapitates Sir Magnus, then returns to the study to get rid of the evidence.

'But this is where he makes his two critical mistakes. He crumples up his mother's letter and burns it in the fire. At the same time, he manages to get some of Sir Magnus's blood onto the paper and this is what we will later find. But much worse than that – he burns the wrong envelope! I knew at once that an error had been made and not only because Mrs Weaver's letter had been produced on a typewriter while the surviving envelope was handwritten. No. The envelope was addressed quite formally to Sir Magnus Pye and this was completely out of character with its contents. The correspondent had referred to him as 'you bastard'. She had threatened to kill him. Would she then have written *Sir* Magnus on the envelope? I did not think so, and intended to ask Mrs Weaver this, but unfortunately I was taken ill before I could put the question to her. It does not matter. We have the envelope and we have the diary written by Mary Blakiston. As I remarked to Fraser, the writing on both was the same.'

Pünd had drawn to a halt. There was to be no dramatic conclusion, no final declamation. That had never been his style.

Chubb shook his head. 'Robert Blakiston,' he intoned. 'I am arresting you for murder.' He continued with the formal warning, then added, 'Is there anything you want to say?'

For the last few minutes, Blakiston had been staring at a fixed point on the floor as if he could find his whole future there. But suddenly he looked up and there were tears streaming from his eyes. At that moment, Fraser could very easily imagine him as the thirteen-year-old child who had killed his brother in a rage and who had been hiding from that crime ever since. He turned to Joy. He spoke only to her. 'I did it for you, my darling,' he said. 'Meeting you was the best thing that ever happened to me and I knew I could only be completely happy with you. I wasn't going to let anyone take that away from me and I'd do it again if I had to. I'd do it for you.'

4

From *The Times*, August 1955

> The death of Atticus Pünd has been widely reported in the British press but I wonder if I might add a few words of my own as I knew him perhaps better than anyone, having worked for him for six years in the capacity of personal assistant. I first met Mr Pünd when I replied to an advertisement placed in the *Spectator* magazine. It stated that a businessman, recently arrived from Germany, required the services of a confidential secretary to assist him with typing, administration and associated duties. It is revealing that he did not refer to himself as an investigator or private detective even though he already had a formidable reputation, particularly following the recovery of the Ludendorff Diamond and the spectacular series of arrests that followed. Mr Pünd was always modest. Although he helped the police on numerous occasions, including the recent murder of a wealthy landowner in the Suffolk village of Saxby-on-Avon, he preferred to remain in the shadows, seldom taking the credit for what he had achieved.
>
> There has been some speculation about the manner of his death and I wish to set the record straight. It is true that Mr Pünd had come into possession of a large dose of the poison physostigmine during his last investigation and that he should, of course, have returned it to the police. He did not because he had already decided to take his own life, as he made clear in a letter which he had left behind and which was forwarded to me after his cremation. Although I had not been aware of it, Mr Pünd had been diagnosed with a particularly malignant form of brain tumour which would have ended

his life shortly anyway and he had chosen to prevent himself unnecessary suffering.

He was the kindest and the wisest man I ever knew. His experiences in Germany before and during the war had given him a perspective that must have aided him in his work. He had an innate understanding of evil and was able to root it out with unerring precision. Although we spent much time together, he had few friends and I cannot pretend that I completely understood the workings of his remarkable mind. He made it clear that he wanted no monument left behind but requested that his ashes should be scattered close to Saxby-on-Avon in Dingle Dell, the woodland that he in part helped to save.

That said, I am in possession of all the pages, notes and material relating to the treatise, which occupied much of his later life, a major work entitled *The Landscape of Criminal Investigation*. It is a tragedy that it remains unfinished but I have forwarded everything that I have been able to find to Professor Crena Hutton at the Oxford Centre for Criminology and it is very much my hope that this landmark volume will be made available to the public soon.

James Fraser

Agios Nikolaos, Crete

There's not much more to add.

Cloverleaf Books folded – which is about as apt a description as you can get for a publishing firm going out of business. It was all very messy, with Charles in jail and the insurers refusing to pay out for the building, which had been completely destroyed in the fire. Our successful authors jumped ship as fast as they could, which was a little disappointing but not entirely surprising. You don't want to be published by someone who might murder you.

I no longer had a job, of course. Sitting at home after I had got out of hospital, I was surprised to learn that I was getting some of the blame for what had happened. It's like I said in the beginning. Charles Clover was entrenched in the publishing industry and the general feeling was that I had betrayed him. After all, he had published Graham Greene, Anthony Burgess and Muriel Spark and he had only ever killed one writer – Alan Conway, a well-known pain in the neck. Had it really been necessary to make such a fuss about his death when he was going to die anyway? Nobody actually put this into so many words, but when I finally limped out to a few literary events – a conference, a book launch – that was the feeling I got. The Women's Prize for Fiction decided not to have me as a judge after all. I wished they could have seen Charles as I had finally seen him, preparing to burn me alive and kicking me so hard that he broke my ribs. I wasn't going back to work any time soon. I no longer had a heart for it and anyway, my vision hadn't recovered. That remains the case. I'm not quite as blind as poor Mr Rochester in *Jane Eyre* but my eyes tire if I read too much and the words move around on the page. These days I prefer audiobooks. I've gone back to nineteenth century literature. I avoid whodunnits.

I live in Agios Nikolaos, in Crete.

The decision was more or less made for me in the end. There was nothing to keep me in London. A lot of my friends had turned their backs on me and Andreas was leaving whatever happened. I would have been a fool not to go with him and my sister, Katie, spent at least a week telling me exactly that. At the end of the day, I was in love with him. I'd come to realise that when I was sitting on my own at Bradford-on-Avon station and it had certainly been confirmed when he had appeared as my knight in shining armour, battling his way through the blaze to rescue me. If anything, he should have been the one who had second thoughts. I didn't speak a word of Greek. I wasn't much of a cook. My vision was impaired. What possible use could I be?

I did say some of this to him and his response was to take me out to the Greek restaurant in Crouch End, to produce a diamond ring (which was much more than he could afford) and to go down on one knee in front of all the diners. I was horrified, and couldn't accept fast enough just to get him to behave properly, back on his feet. He didn't need a bank loan in the end. I sold my flat and, although he wasn't entirely happy about it, I insisted on investing some of the money in Hotel Polydorus, making myself an equal partner. It was probably madness but after what I'd been through, I didn't really care. It wasn't just that I'd almost been killed. It was that everything I'd trusted and believed in had been taken away from me. I felt that my life had been unravelled as quickly and as absolutely as Atticus Pünd's name. Does that make sense? It was as if my new life was an anagram of my old one and I would only learn what shape it had taken when I began to live it.

Two years have passed since I left England.

Polydorus hasn't actually made a profit yet, but guests seem to like it and we've been full for most of this season so we must be doing something right. The hotel is on the edge of Agios Nikolaos, which is a bright, shabby, colourful town with too many shops selling trinkets and tourist tat, but it's authentic enough to make you feel it's somewhere you'd want to live. We're right on the seafront and I never tire of gazing at the water, which is a quite dazzling blue and makes the Mediterranean look like a puddle. The kitchen and reception area open onto a stone terrace where we have a dozen tables – we're open for breakfast, lunch and dinner – and we serve simple, fresh local food. Andreas works in the kitchen. His cousin Yannis does almost nothing but he's well connected (they call it '*visma*') and comes into his own with local PR. And then there's Philippos, Alexandros, Giorgios, Nell and all the other family and friends who bundle in to help us during the day and who sit drinking raki with us until late into the night.

I could write about it, and maybe one day I will. A middle-aged woman takes the plunge and moves in with her Greek lover and his eccentric family, various cats, neighbours, suppliers and guests, making a go of it in the Aegean sunshine. There used to be a market for that sort of thing, although of course I won't be able to write the full truth, not if I want it to sell. There's still a part of me that misses Crouch End and I miss publishing. Andreas and I are always worrying about money and that puts a strain on us. Life may imitate art – but it usually falls short of it.

The strange thing is that *Magpie Murders* did get published in the end. After the collapse of Cloverleaf, a few of our titles were picked up by other publishers, including the entire Atticus Pünd series, which, as it happened, went to my old firm, Orion Books. They reissued it with new covers and brought out *Magpie Murders* at the same time. By now, the whole world knew the nasty truth behind the detective's name, but in the short term it didn't matter. All the publicity about the real-life murder and the trial made people more interested in the book and I wasn't surprised to see it in the bestseller lists. Robert Harris gave it a very good review in the *Sunday Times*.

I even saw a copy the other day, as I walked along the beach. A woman was sitting in a deckchair reading it, and there was Alan Conway staring out at me from the back cover. Seeing him I felt a spurt of real anger. I remembered what Charles had said about Alan, how he had selfishly, needlessly, spoiled the pleasure of millions of people who had enjoyed the Atticus Pünd novels. He was right. I had been one of them and just for a moment, I imagined that it was I, not Charles, who had been on the tower at Abbey Grange, shoving out with both hands, pushing Alan to his death. I could actually see myself doing it. It was exactly what he deserved.

I had been the detective and now I was the murderer.

And do you know? I think I liked it more.

Anthony Horowitz interviews Alan Conway
Reprinted from the Spectator magazine

When I met Alan Conway at the Ivy Club in London, it struck me that we actually had a great deal in common. At least, that was what I thought at the start.

He and I both write detective fiction although in different ways. He is the author of the phenomenally successful Atticus Pünd series while I've spent many years writing crime drama for television: *Midsomer Murders*, *Foyle's War* and *Agatha Christie's Poirot*. We're now both published by Orion Books. We also have a Suffolk connection. Alan lives in a Victorian folly just outside Framlingham while I have a small house in Orford, just the other side of the A12. Finally, for what it's worth, we're both members of the Ivy Club although it was he who chose to meet here, not me.

A week before the publication of his seventh novel, *Red Roses for Atticus,* I was asked to interview him by the *Spectator* and I was looking forward to it. I'm a fan of the books. I actually spent a couple of months working on *Atticus Pünd Investigates*, the first in the series, adapting it for the BBC. That didn't end well. The production company – Red Herring Productions – abruptly fired me and the last I heard, Alan was adapting the book himself.

To mention this to him was probably a mistake – but his reaction was, to say the least, surprising. 'Yes. I told them I wanted to take it over. To be honest, I was never a big fan of *Midsomer Murders*. It always struck me as very lightweight and silly. I thought there was an opportunity, with the screenplay of my book, maybe to do something more subtle.'

An unspoken contract usually exists between writers promoting a book and the journalists – or whoever – interviewing them. The writer will be pleasant and cooperative. And even if the journalist hates the book, he or she will be polite. It's why you'll never read bad reviews before a book is published. So I was puzzled why Conway should be so carelessly insulting and I suppose, in return, I should have a sly dig at his work.

But I can't because the truth is that *Red Roses for Atticus* is one of the best in the series. It's the first book that's set outside the UK, mainly in the south of France, and initially that worried me. I've always thought Atticus Pünd works best in the English countryside. *No Rest for the Wicked* and *Gin & Cyanide*, which both have a London setting, were somehow less comfortable reads for me. That said, Conway conjures up a very real image of the Côte d'Azur in the late fifties. You can almost smell the bougainvillea.

Also, it's the first story to include a fully fledged love affair. Atticus falls for Lydia Ford, the sister of a famous artist, and is forced to investigate when she is arrested for the murder of a local dealer called Jon Subaru. As the evidence mounts up, it seems certain that she must be guilty and there's a brilliantly unpleasant French detective, Inspector Renault, who adds to the tension. The ending certainly fooled me and I suspect it will fool you too – although, as usual, Conway plays completely fair.

So I begin by suggesting that it's unusual to have a detective who falls in love. He is quick to disagree. 'That's rubbish. What about Holmes and Irene Adler? And Hercule Poirot fell for a Russian countess, Vera Rossakoff...' Actually, I knew that. She appears in a story called *The Double Clue* which I adapted for ITV. But before I can suggest that these are the briefest of brief encounters, he continues, seemingly contradicting himself. 'The trouble is that most detectives are too single-minded. They have no *cojones*. They don't even have character, really. They just have mannerisms.' He smiles to himself. 'When a woman tells a detective he's only interested in one thing, she's not talking about sex. He probably just wants to arrest her.'

That's not true of Atticus Pünd, I say. A character turns up in the new book; Otto Daimler, who was with Pünd at the Sobibór concentration camp – and this adds a very personal, quite moving dimension to the story. Conway disagrees, his language on the edge of offensive. 'People don't read my books because they're interested in Pünd or what happened to him at the hands of the Nazis. They read them to find out who did it.' But surely you have to believe in the detective as a human being? 'Not really. He has a function and that's what counts. Look at Holmes! Even Doyle admits that he has no interest in literature, philosophy or politics. He doesn't have friends. He has acquaintances.'

And yet Holmes is one of the most loved characters in popular fiction. Pünd himself was supposedly based on an English teacher, Stephen Pound, who taught Conway in St Albans. (Pound, who is still teaching, did not return my calls). Is he really nothing more than a cypher? 'Of course he's a cypher. And the killer in *Red Roses for Atticus* is, in a way, neutral. The two of them are a sort of calculation, an equation. You read the book only for the equals sign.'

Really? To listen to Conway talk, you might think he has a certain disdain for his own work – if not for the wealth it has brought him. He has turned up for the interview – forty-five minutes late, incidentally – in jeans, white shirt and jacket, brand new and expensive. While I drink tea, he orders champagne. He fidgets with a gold ring on his fourth finger, twisting it as I speak as if it's some sort of volume control. The more I speak, the faster the ring turns. If I began the interview thinking how similar we were, it soon strikes me that we are complete opposites.

During our conversation, he has been glancing at his watch and just thirty minutes in, a young man appears and introduces himself as James Taylor, Conway's PA. The car is outside. The interview is over. Conway goes to the bar to pay for the drinks and Taylor – who is actually his partner – confides in me. 'I hope he hasn't been too stroppy with you. He doesn't like doing interviews.' Then why did he agree? 'Well, obviously, the publishers made him. We did Edinburgh a few weeks ago and he absolutely hated it. He always says writers shouldn't talk about their books, they should just write them.'

Here I disagree. Writing is such a solitary business that I've always loved literary festivals and it's a pleasure to talk to people who've read my books. There was a story that Conway once reduced a female interviewer to tears at Hay-on-Wye. After meeting him, I'm inclined to believe it.

Eventually, he returns from the bar. 'I hope you got what you wanted. Did you actually read the book?' I tell him, of course I did and he gives me the thinnest of smiles. 'You know, when we were talking, I slipped in the name of the killer. I hope nobody reads your piece. It might spoil the ending.'

It's his parting shot. I'm left wondering quite what motivates Alan Conway who is without any question one of the most disconcerting authors I have ever come across. What exactly did he mean by those final words? I have recorded our conversation and play it back several times before I write this article but I certainly can't find the name of the killer. Is it really there or was he just taunting me?

Sad though it is to say it, there's one name that has rather killed my pleasure in his books. I'm rather afraid it's his.

September 2014